STOLEN MOMENT

"I'll be asking you to decide," Daniel said, tracing the line of her mouth. "Is it your Wade & Company you want? Or do you want to come home to me? That's what I'll be asking, lass."

"A fair question."

"A hard question for you. You've turned yourself into Miranda, but it's Jenny who'd be coming to me."

"Jenny's dead."

"No." Daniel smiled. "She's in there somewhere. Hiding till you're sure it's Miranda you really want to be. Ah, she's a patient lass, Jenny is."

She wrapped her arms around Daniel. "What am I going to do without you?" she murmured. "I miss you already."

Daniel pulled her into his arms. His hands tangled her hair; he kissed her, a long, fiery kiss that made her gasp. There was a roaring in her ears. Little lights seemed to dance before her eyes. "Daniel," she whispered.

Their bodies were locked together, arching, swaying to the ancient rhythms of love. Their passion blazed, a white-hot fire rushing toward some secret and rapturous place. For them there was only this moment, this blissful moment stolen from the world; there was only this truth.

"Daniel," she called softly as her body trembled and shook, as she was carried off to that secret place.

It was the place where love dwelt, and she was a woman in love.

D0197722

STOLEN DREAMS

ALEXANDRA LYLE

PINNACLE BOOKS
WINDSOR PUBLISHING CORP.

PINNACLE BOOKS

are published by

Windsor Publishing Corp.
475 Park Avenue South
New York, NY 10016

First printing: September, 1990

Printed in the United States of America

*To Leslie Gelbman,
with thanks*

*and to "Richard Jury of Scotland Yard,"
with wonder*

Prologue

Logan Falls, Illinois, 1925

Jenny Porter lifted her gaze to the weepy gray skies above Good Shepperd Methodist Cemetery. Funeral weather, she thought, shivering as she thrust her hands into the pockets of her old coat. After a moment she returned her gaze to her father's plain wood coffin, but the sight was more than she could bear and she had to look away. She stood very still, a distance apart from the other black-clad mourners. Her face, shiny with rain and tears, might have been carved of stone.

"Will Porter is no longer among us," said Reverend Trimble, continuing his eulogy, "but the spirit of this fine man lives on. Will was more than our doctor; he was our friend, never too tired or too busy to give of himself. In his steadfast devotion to those who asked his help, we saw all the good one man can do. We saw the true meaning of the Golden Rule."

At these words the mourners bent their heads, lowering their eyes to the ground. Jenny watched the pious tableau, and two spots of color flared in her cheeks. *Hypocrites*, she thought bitterly. *There isn't one of you here who cared a fig about Papa. You wore him out with your problems, found excuses not to pay him, and then laughed at him behind his back. Hypocrites!*

"Will was part of us," declared Reverend Trimble, "a son of Logan Falls."

Jenny's mouth tensed. A strangled cry escaped her lips, for she knew that Logan Falls had destroyed her father, and had done so without regret. Wearily, her mind traveled ten years into the past, to the time when the trouble had begun. She had been a child of eight then, a happy child living with her parents and older sisters in a large house on elegant, exclusive Glenwood Road. Their neighbors had been the aristocracy of Logan Falls, descendants of the town's founders who had inherited both wealth and position. They had, in a sense, inherited the town itself, for they owned everything worth owning: the two factories, the brickyard, the trolley line, the newspaper, the hospital, the department store, the bank, and most of the land.

The Porters, though of considerably more modest means, had been admitted to this charmed circle. Will Porter, his practice thriving, had been elected to the hospital board and had been made medical consultant to the factories. His wife Louise joined the Garden Club, and his daughters the elite Sunday school at St. Tobias Episcopal Church.

Through mists of memory Jenny saw herself as she had been in those days, a smiling, lighthearted little girl in starched dresses and ruffled petticoats, silky hair ribbons spilling down her back. She could still remember the sound of her laughter. And she could remember when the laughter had stopped, when quite suddenly, or so it had seemed, the Porters had become outcasts, shunned by Glenwood Road. She had been too young to understand what had happened; only with the passage of time had the truth been clear to her. "It was Papa," she murmured, staring blindly past rows of neat white headstones. "Papa and his noble causes."

Will Porter had never explained what drove him to fight battles he could not win. He had gone his own way, stubbornly demanding improved hospital conditions for the poorest people of Logan Falls, demanding improved factory conditions and a decent wage for the town's workingmen. The elders of Glenwood Road had at first

8

been amused by Will's zeal. They had humored him, much as one might an earnest, if misguided child. For a year they had listened and smiled but by year's end they had tired of the game. Recognizing that Will would not be influenced, would not be dissuaded, they had judged him a threat to the "harmony" of Logan Falls. Their punishment had been swift: within a space of three months, Will had lost his seat on the hospital board, lost his factory contracts, lost his patients. When the bank had conveniently discovered a missed mortgage payment, he lost his house as well.

Ruined, Will moved his family and his practice to a cramped, airless house on Maple Street. Once more his practice flourished, but his patients in that shabby part of town had little money for doctor's bills. Again and again they promised to "settle up on payday"; to no one's surprise, such promises were rarely kept. There was the occasional fifty-cent piece, the occasional dollar bill grudgingly handed over, and with these Louise Porter had done the best she could. She had not complained. When farmers settled their bills with produce from their own land, she was grateful. "At least we won't starve," she had often joked, though year by year she grew thinner.

Sorrow hooded Jenny's eyes as she recalled the day her mother died. She had died calling for Will, but he had been off tending the Ferguson boy. By the time he returned home, it was too late.

"Earth to earth, ashes to ashes, dust to dust," intoned Reverend Trimble.

Jenny spun around. A lock of long, straight black hair slipped from the knot at the back of her head and absently she swiped at it. She took a step forward, and then another and another, moving as if in a dream to the place where her father's coffin rested. She reached out her hand, her fingers sliding across the rain-slicked dark wood. She remembered how her father had loved the rain. "Papa," she whispered. "Good-bye, Papa."

Reverend Trimble started to put his arm about Jenny's shoulder, but she drew away. She wanted no empty gestures of consolation, no easy words. She wanted nothing from these people who had treated her father so badly. *I'll never forgive them,* she thought. Anger rose within her like an unquenchable flame.

She strode past the other mourners, stopping only when she came to the graves of her mother and her sisters, Amy and Jean. Her mother had died in the winter of 1918; just a few months later her sisters had died also, victims of the devastating influenza epidemic that had ravaged Logan Falls. During that terrible time schools and businesses were closed, but still the infection spread. Somehow, Jenny had been spared the worst of it. She had remained at home, nursing her sisters, while Will was busy with his patients. He was with old Mr. Dempsey when Jean died; he was en route from the Ebson farm when Amy, his first born, died the following week.

"Jenny?"

She turned to see Ethel Gruber, a thin woman with small, sharp features and tight gray curls squashed beneath a close-fitting black hat. "Hello, Mrs. Gruber," she said.

"I'm sorry about your pa."

"Thank you."

Mrs. Gruber closed her umbrella, shaking raindrops from the folds. Her eyes swept to the slivers of blue sky peeking out between the clouds. "Rain's stopped. Maybe we'll see the sun yet." Jenny did not reply, but, undaunted, Mrs. Gruber shifted her handbag to her other arm, settling in for a chat. "Like I said, I'm sorry about your pa. He was a hard worker and that's a fact. Day or night, it didn't matter to him. If there was sickness, he would come. Many's the time he came to us in the middle of the night to see our boys."

"Yes, I remember." The grubby Grubers, they were called — four interchangeable little boys with runny noses and dirty hands. They we're always sick. "I remember all the nights Papa had to go without sleep."

"Well, that was his job, wasn't it?"

Jenny glanced away, watching a tangle of wet leaves

10

cartwheel across the path. Slowly, she raised her eyes to Ethel Gruber, looking the woman up and down. "I see you're wearing a new coat," she said, her voice icy. "Papa could never afford a new coat. And I've been wearing Mama's hand-me-down coat for three years. It would have been nice if some of you had paid Papa for his *job*."

Mrs. Gruber's smile vanished. Her mouth worked, but all she could say was "Well!"

"You know it's true," Jenny went on, raising her voice to include others in the crowd. "You never gave a thought to Papa. Dragged him out at all hours, in all kinds of weather. And when it came time to pay, there was always an excuse." She caught her breath, scanning the small sea of astonished faces. "Your husband gets his wages every week, Mrs. Gruber. And your husband, too, Mrs. Ferguson. And the Howards and the Blands and a dozen more. But what did Papa get? Tall stories, that's what."

Reverend Trimble had pushed this way to Jenny's side, and now the grip on her shoulder was firm. "You're upset, child," he said in his soothing, Sunday-sermon voice. "I'm sure we all understand that. We know you didn't mean those things."

"I meant every word, Reverend. But it's all right; I've had my say. And it's my last. I'm leaving Logan Falls on the next train and I won't be coming back."

"Surely you don't want to leave this way? Your friends and neighbors—"

Jenny laughed. "Friends and neighbors? Except for John Duncan and a few of the other farmers, we had no friends here. We did have neighbors. Neighbors like Mrs. Gruber," she added with a dark look, "who could afford to buy roller skates for her boys but who couldn't afford to pay Papa what was owed him."

"It's wrong to speak of money at a time like this, Jenny."

"Yes, maybe it is. But ask our friends and neighbors if they ever offered Papa even a cup of coffee when they dragged him out at two o'clock in the morning. Ask them

11

if they offered him thanks, or a kind word."

Reverend Trimble looked into her wide gray eyes. He saw the consuming anger, and behind that, the pain. He frowned. "You must learn to forgive, child. You must, for your own sake."

"Someday. Not now." She held out her hand. "Goodbye, Reverend Trimble."

"I'll pray for you, Jenny."

Again she scanned the faces turned in her direction; some were contrite, some indignant, some merely frozen in surprise. "Pray for *them*," she said. She walked away, her back straight, her eyes fixed on a point in the distance. The sun had broken through the clouds and bands of yellow light dappled the path. All was quiet, save for the sound of birds rustling the branches of ancient elms. Jenny kept walking. She slowed her pace when she saw the tall sandy-haired man standing on the church steps. "Hello, Dr. Logan," she said. "What are you doing here?"

"I came to pay my respects to your father." Gardner Logan was the great-great-grandson of the town's first settlers. Pleasant and without airs, he was a surgeon at Glenwood Hospital. "I admired Will, you know."

"No, I didn't know."

"I've been guarding your suitcase," he said, pointing to a cheap cardboard traveling bag. "I thought you might like a ride to the station. My car's right over there."

"It's kind of you, Dr. Logan, but I'll walk."

"Why walk when you can ride?"

"Why not?"

"A martyr to the end, is that it?" He smiled. "Stop being silly, Jenny. Let me drive you. I want to talk to you before you leave us."

"There's nothing to talk about."

"I think there is." Gardner Logan picked up Jenny's suitcase and descended the steps. "I worry about you," he said, taking her arm as they walked toward the black Pierce-Arrow.

"Since when?"

12

"You ought to get that chip off your shoulder."

"Thank you for the advice, Doctor," replied Jenny, each syllable overlaid with frost.

He shook his head, more saddened than amused. "You're like your father in so many ways. Everything was black or white to Will. Black or white, right or wrong. Unfortunately, life isn't that simple."

Jenny climbed into the car. She slammed the door and stared straight ahead. "You said you admired Papa."

"I did. I admired his dedication. And his skill. God knows, I admired his skill. Sometimes the man seemed to work miracles." Gardner Logan turned the key in the ignition, shifting gears as he steered the car past the town square onto Maple Street. "But for all his skill, this is where he wound up."

Jenny looked out at the rows of narrow wood-frame houses in various stages of disrepair, at the sagging front porches facing small patches of yard. She saw her own house, no better than the rest, and she averted her eyes. She had never had a happy day here, and never, really, a friend. From the beginning, the other neighborhood children had taunted her, calling her fancypants; the harder she had tried to fit in, the nastier the taunts had become. She remembered when the Gosden boy had thrown ink on her best Sunday dress, when the Samish twins had poured glue on the wheels of her doll carriage, locking the spokes forever in place. "When we came here," she said, as if to herself, "we had more than everybody else. Mama and I had nicer clothes; I had more toys. I guess I understood why the kids didn't like me. But after a while we were just as poor as everybody else. We had nothing. And still the kids didn't like me."

"Your father was a doctor. That made you special. Made you different. And of course you'd come from Glenwood."

"Exiled. We'd been exiled from Glenwood." Jenny glanced quickly at Gardner Logan. "You should know. You had a hand in it."

"Yes, I suppose I did. But not until I'd tried to reason

13

with Will. Tried hard, too. He could have accomplished some of his goals. If he'd only had patience . . . if he'd only *listened,* made a few compromises here and there. Compromise! Will didn't know the meaning of the word."

"Because he was right."

"That's not enough, Jenny. Besides, a great many people believed he was *wrong.* He might have won them over. Some of them, anyway. Instead he made them angry. You must remember that no one *asked* him to reform Logan Falls. He was self-appointed." Gardner Logan eased the car onto Main Street. He stopped at the single blinking traffic light and then drove on. "Your father was a crusader. Glenwood didn't want a crusader stirring things up."

"At least you're honest about it. The others weren't." Jenny turned, her gaze taking in the post office, the grocery, the mercantile, the hardware store, the barber shop, and the new diner. At the north end of Main Street were the department store and the bank. "Papa tried to get a loan," she said, her gray eyes flashing. "He wanted to buy oxygen equipment for his patients who couldn't afford the hospital. He went crawling to the bank . . . and when they put him off he went crawling again. No matter how many times he went, the answer was always no."

"Your father was always a very poor risk. Bankers can't just hand out money to anyone who asks."

"You could have fixed it at the bank."

"I would have, if Will hadn't been so stubborn about things, throwing good money after bad. It was business, Jenny."

"Papa's *business* was saving lives."

"Everybody's life but his own. He worked and worried himself into an early grave. He left you nothing, Jenny. Tell me, was that right?"

She did not answer immediately; too often she had asked herself the same question. "You're just trying to clear your conscience," she said after several moments.

14

"Papa was a good man."

"Too good. And you needn't look at me that way. Your father should have been the most beloved man in town. He should have been, but he wasn't. Far from it, in fact. He made people uncomfortable."

"Glenwood people, you mean."

"Was it any better on Maple Street? Will's patients certainly should have loved him. Think about it, Jenny. He went out on calls at all hours. He paid for medicines out of his own pocket. I happen to know he paid for Timmy Dale's leg operation out of his own pocket. My God, he did everything for his patients. In the end, they resented him for it." Gardner Logan paused. He made a right turn, and then a left, slowing as they neared the train station. "Will was the *soul* of goodness. He loved humanity . . . but humanity didn't love him back."

New tears stung Jenny's eyes. She found her handkerchief and brushed them away. She was quiet, Dr. Logan's blunt words echoing in her mind. She had had her own doubts over the years, doubts she had never allowed to linger very long. She had wondered at some of her father's actions, but never once had she allowed herself to believe he was wrong. Not even when the house was freezing cold in winter, she thought now. *Not even when I had to go around with holes in my shoes. Not even when Mama got sick.* "I — I didn't know Papa paid for Timmy's operation," she said, swallowing hard. "It's funny, my not knowing. I kept Papa's books."

Gardner Logan pulled his car alongside the station. He turned off the engine and sat back, looking at Jenny. A sad story, he mused, for he knew the sacrifices she had made, leaving school at fifteen to help bring order to the chaos of Will's practice. He knew she had taught herself bookkeeping and shorthand, honing her skills at night, after the housework was done. He knew she had never had a sweetheart; he wondered if she had ever had a date. "Well, it's all in the past," he said quietly. "Best to put it behind you."

"I plan to put this whole town behind me."

15

"Yes, that's what I wanted to talk to you about." He looked at his watch. "The train isn't due for fifteen minutes. Let's walk a little, shall we?"

Jenny got out of the car just as the noon whistle sounded. She had heard that sound every weekday for eighteen years, but now it seemed to startle her. She stumbled and she had to catch Dr. Logan's arm to right herself. "Sorry," she said, embarrassed by her clumsiness. "Stupid whistle! I'm glad I won't have to listen to it anymore."

"There's a lot more noise in Chicago than there is here. You won't like it, Jenny. You won't like city living. It's different from what you're used to."

"I hope so." She glanced up at the clouds scudding across vast brush strokes of blue. She hurried ahead of Dr. Logan, rushing up the steps to the station platform. Mr. Purdy, the lone ticket agent, sat behind his counter reading a newspaper; no one else was about. She settled herself on a bench, turning when Dr. Logan huffed and puffed his way to her side.

"Are you running a race, Jenny? I'm not as young as I used to be."

"Sorry. It's just that I want to have it over with. I want to get on the train and forget all about Logan Falls." She smiled slightly. "I'd go to New York, if I had the courage. Chicago will have to do."

"What about money? Or do you plan to snare a rich husband?"

Jenny colored. "Don't laugh at me, Dr. Logan. I know I'm nothing to look at. I know I'll have to make my own way. And I will. There are offices in Chicago. I'll find a job. I have a little money to tide me over." She clasped her hands together, studying the plump fingers, the nails bitten to the quick. "I'm used to pinching pennies, after all."

"First, I wasn't laughing at you. You're no great beauty, it's true, but looks aren't everything. You're a nice girl. You have character."

She dropped her hands in her lap, looking off toward the long stretch of empty track. Character. That's what

16

they always say when they can't come up with anything else.

"Second, how much money do you have? Cities are expensive."

"I'd wager you know to the dollar what I have. You hear everything that goes on in town, Dr. Logan. You heard I sold the house, and for how much."

"It wasn't much at all. That's my point."

Jenny nodded. She had not wanted to have this conversation, but she could see no way around it. "After all the bills were paid, and the rest of the mortgage, I had eight hundred dollars. I sent half to the old folks' home. For Granny."

"Half! But why? Your grandfather left her an annuity. More than enough to see to her needs. She hasn't much time, Jenny."

"I know that. The doctors told me. Papa told me, too, before he died. I just thought they could use the money to give her some — some extra treats."

"They won't. And why should they? Your grandmother doesn't even know what day it is, what year. I'm surprised at you. To throw good money after —"

"I made up my mind, Dr. Logan." Jenny sighed, listening to the wind in the trees. She wondered if there were trees in Chicago. "I thought about it and I decided. I'll feel better, knowing the money's there for her. Whether she uses it or not. Papa would have wanted it that way."

Gardner Logan threw up his hands. "No doubt," he said curtly. "Will was given to grand gestures he couldn't afford. Now his daughter is following in his footsteps."

"There's a difference. I'll do it for my family, for my own, but that's all. And there's another difference: I'll be paid for my work, whatever it is. No excuses, no tall stories. I'll be paid what I'm worth and that's that."

He saw the defiant thrust of her chin. He almost smiled, for he knew that look, as did many in Logan Falls; in the past it had meant that she was setting out to collect on long overdue bills. At least she had tried, he

17

thought, relenting. He unbuttoned his coat, reaching around to get his billfold. "I'm going to—"

"No," said Jenny. "It's kind of you, but I don't want your money. Thank you, Dr. Logan, but I can't take it. I have enough to live on, even if I don't find a job right away."

"What if I were to get you a job in Roseville? My father-in-law has his factories there. Roseville is larger than Logan Falls, but more congenial than a big city. More suitable as well. A girl alone in a big city . . . anything might happen."

"Oh, I'll be all right." *I have character,* she silently added. "I appreciate the offer, Dr. Logan. But I've made my plans." She looked at him, a thin, sad smile playing about her mouth. "I think I can do better than a factory job."

"I didn't mean that you'd be on the assembly line. Factories have offices, too, you know."

"And lunch pails and noon whistles and men with dead eyes. I want more out of life. Maybe I won't get what I want. Still, I can try."

"I hope you aren't getting fanciful notions, Jenny."

"How could I? I was raised in Logan Falls. Raised to know my place."

Gardner Logan considered her reply. "It's not a bad thing to know one's place," he said after a while. "Of course you may feel otherwise. I quite understand . . . is there nothing I can do for you, then?"

Once, you could have done a great deal, thought Jenny. But that was long ago. "No," she said. "Nothing." Her head snapped up as she heard the low-pitched blast of a train horn. "It's coming," she cried, jumping to her feet. "See, there it is."

"No need to hurry. The Chicago train always makes a five-minute stop." He got to his feet also, moving Jenny's traveling bag along the platform, "What have you got in here? Rocks?"

"Mostly books. Papa's books." She turned and held out her hand. "I want to thank you, Dr. Logan. For the ride

18

and for seeing me off. It was . . ." Her next words were lost in the noise of the train as it clattered into the station, brakes squealing, sparks showering from the track.

"Do you have your ticket?" he asked when the din had subsided.

"Yes." A shadow crossed Jenny's face. "The day they told me at the hospital that Papa was dying . . . well, that was the day I bought my ticket and put the house up for sale. It was summer then. Papa liked to sit by his window and watch the summer storms." She shook her head, as if trying to clear it of thought and memory. "Good-bye, Dr. Logan."

"Good-bye, Jenny. Take care of yourself."

"I will."

Gardner Logan stood on the platform, watching Jenny take up her suitcase and board the train. *The poor girl has spirit,* he conceded, although he could not help wondering if spirit alone would suffice in a big city like Chicago. It was his habit to examine the advantages and disadvantages of any situation, and this he did now. He deemed Jenny's appearance a disadvantage, for she was plain and badly dressed and thirty pounds too heavy. To her appearance he added her gender, her unfinished education, and her sharp tongue. Of course there was the matter of money, or lack of it. There was the matter of experience, or lack of it; he considered her naive in the same way all young girls were naive.

A whistle shrilled and the train began chugging along the track. He glimpsed Jenny at a window. He waved. Good character is always an advantage, he thought, his mind shifting to the other side of the ledger. And youth. And ambition. And poise, for he granted that she was seldom flustered, seldom at a loss for words. He sensed that somewhere within her lay a sense of humor, certainly another advantage. He groped for something more. At the very last he remembered her pretty, wide gray eyes.

Jenny, settled now in her seat, felt the pounding of her

19

heart. She knew it was not fear but excitement, and she willed the train to go faster. She glanced around at the other passengers: a middle-aged couple, a younger couple with a small child, a dozen or so businessmen traveling singly and in pairs. The conductor roamed the aisle, punching tickets. Another man followed in his wake, and to him she gave three pennies for the Chicago newspaper.

Through the window she watched the train approach a bend of land that marked the outer boundaries of Logan Falls. She craned her neck, watching for the sign to come into view, the sign she knew would be there. A smile crept slowly across her face as she saw it:

LOGAN FALLS
POPULATION: 4922
WELCOME TO THE TOWN WHERE EVERYONE'S YOUR FRIEND

She read the sign twice before it disappeared from view. She laughed.

Part I

Chapter One

It was rush hour when Jenny alighted from the train at Chicago's Union Station. Entering the terminal, she could only gape at the hordes of people scurrying like ants from place to place. There were long lines at the ticket booths and information counters, longer lines at the departure gates. Redcaps whizzed past, feet barely touching the ground. She had never seen so many people before, had never heard such confusion of sounds. She listened to a disembodied voice announcing trains and track numbers over a loudspeaker. She smiled. *I'm here,* she thought, astonishment giving way to relief. *It's true; I'm really here.*

She started walking. Almost at once she was swept up in the crowd. She was elbowed and pushed and stepped on, but she kept to her path, following the bright yellow exit signs posted about the station. She was halfway to the exit when she saw a handbag slip from a woman's shoulder and fall to the floor. She hurried forward, rescuing the purse just before it was trampled by an oncoming luggage cart. "Miss?" She called to the woman. "Miss, you dropped your purse." She quickened her pace, her suitcase banging against her leg as she ran. "Your purse," she tried again.

The woman turned, a young woman with masses of coppery hair framing a beautiful heart-shaped face. She looked anxiously into the wicker basket slung over her arm, then touched her shoulder, feeling around for the missing handbag. "Oh, thank you so much," she said when Jenny came to a breathless halt. "I can't thank you enough. I don't know what I would have done . . . I'm always losing purses and umbrellas. Keys, too . . . I'm Miranda Wade," she added, as if that explained everything.

Jenny silently repeated the name. A pretty name, she thought and a pretty girl. No, not pretty, beautiful. Conscious now of her own ungainly appearance, she tried to smooth the drooping knot of hair at the back of her head. Her gaze shifted to the wicker basket. "You have a baby," she said, surprised. "Is it yours?"

"My son," replied Miranda with a brilliant smile. "He's Andrew McAllister Wade. I call him Drew. He's the only Drew in the neighborhood." The two young women began walking toward the exit. "Do you have a name?"

"It's Jenny. Jenny Porter. This is my first day in Chicago. I'm from Logan Falls."

Miranda shook her head and a coppery curl fell across her brow. "I don't know it."

"Nobody does. You could put the whole town in Union Station and have room left over."

They passed through the door, Miranda shielding the baby's basket with her arm. "Are you visiting, or have you come here to live?"

"To live, if I can find a job." Jenny blinked, accustoming her eyes to the twilight of late afternoon. She looked around and her mouth dropped open. Like the small-town girl she was, she stared at the tall buildings, at the endless ribbons of traffic crisscrossing Adams Street. It was noisy; it was a kind of music, an atonal symphony of horns and whistles and clanging streetcars. "My!" she gasped. "This really is the big city!"

Miranda laughed. "Oh, you'll get used to it. It seems big, but when you get settled in your own neighborhood you'll feel right at home. Are you staying with family?"

A gust of wind skittered along Adams Street. Miranda held onto her little feathered hat. Jenny, hatless, tried again to smooth her hair. "No, I have no family."

"I'm sorry. I know how that is." Miranda's clear blue eyes darkened a shade. She looked into Drew's basket and gently touched his cheek. "He's my only family now. I'm a widow."

"A widow? But you're so young."

"My husband died in an accident." A foolish, unnecessary accident. A ladder propped against the side of the house. Donald standing on the top rung, his hand reaching across the roof for the loose shingle. A misstep and then a crash. An ambulance siren and then the words: "I'm sorry, Mrs. Wade. We did all we could." Miranda took a breath, fighting the panic that always came with memory. On the morning of Donald's funeral she had resolved not to let memories destroy her. She would mourn her husband, she would miss him with all her heart, but she would remember only the good times. "Where are you staying? she asked after some moments.

Jenny put her suitcase down and thrust her hand into her pocket. She removed the two pages torn from the Chicago newspaper. "I marked these boardinghouses. They sound all right. Respectable, the ads say. And not too expensive. Would you know where these addresses are?"

Miranda glanced at the ads. "Oh, it's the South Side," she exclaimed. "That's where I live. We can take the same streetcar. Lucky, isn't it? Maybe it's an omen."

Jenny turned, her expression uncertain. "Do you believe in omens?"

"Omens, elves, lucky charms and crystal balls; I believe it all. I'm Irish!"

Jenny said nothing; she did not know what to make of Miranda Wade. She guessed Miranda to be in her very early twenties, educated, and, judging by her clothes, neither rich nor poor but somewhere in between. She liked her; she thought that probably everyone liked her.

"The streetcar's a couple of blocks from here," said Miranda now. "We have a twenty-minute ride, more or less. It depends on traffic. There are so many cars these days." She led Jenny across the street and around a corner. They walked another block and then stopped, joining others in line for the streetcar. She opened her handbag, fishing in it until she found two nickels. "My treat, Jenny."

"Thank you, but I'll pay my way. I have my nickel ready." She bent over Drew's basket, peeking at him. "He's a good baby, isn't he? You'd think he'd be screaming his head off."

"He's wonderful! We make this trip every week. We go to the cemetery to visit his da. The cemetery's in Oakridge. It's pretty there; lots of trees and shrubbery. I take a bottle for Drew and a sandwich for me and we have a picnic."

"I'm — I'm sorry about your husband. It must be hard, raising Drew all by yourself."

"It's hard sometimes. But he's my own little darling. And all I have left of Donald. We had two years together. Two perfect years."

Even in the dusky light Jenny could see Miranda's anguish. She glanced away, knowing she could offer no solace, no balm. Why is life so unfair, she wondered, not for the first time. Why does everything turn out wrong?

"Here's the streetcar."

Warily, Jenny looked from the high step of the streetcar to Drew's basket. "Can you manage?"

"Oh, yes. I'm an old hand at this by now."

The line surged forward. Jenny waited her turn and then followed Miranda onto the streetcar. She maneuvered her suitcase through the crowded aisle, murmuring apologies at each minor collision. There were two empty seats at the rear of the car, and with a quickness that surprised Jenny, Miranda rushed to claim them. "You really *are* an old hand at this," Jenny said. She looked once more into the basket resting on Miranda's lap. Three-month-old Drew slept peacefully, one tiny fist pressed against his cheek. "Is he all right? I mean, he's so quiet."

"He's fine. He's a champion sleeper, that's all. He doesn't even wake up much during the night." Her eyes twinkled as she brushed a wisp of fair hair off his brow. "He's my angel."

Jenny sat back, her head turned to the window. She saw a bewildering array of stores and office buildings; she saw a bank so large and stately it took her breath away. "Do you think I'll be able to find a job?" she asked suddenly, turning back to Miranda.

"Maybe I can help. What sort of job do you want?"

"Something in an office. I don't know typewriting, but I know shorthand and I'm a good bookkeeper."

26

"Is that what you did in—what was it? Logan Falls?"

"I kept Papa's books. The books, the files. He was a doctor; he didn't have time for office work. I did whatever had to be done."

Miranda's blue gaze was thoughtful. "Hmm. That's interesting . . . I might have an idea. Yes, it might be just the thing . . . Do you like chicken pot pie?"

"Chicken pot pie?"

"I made a whole batch this morning," explained Miranda. "They're all ready to pop into the oven. We could talk about my idea over supper."

Jenny's eyes widened. "Supper? Me?"

"You do eat, don't you?" Miranda laughed. "Well, don't you?"

"You're inviting me to supper?"

"Why not?"

"It's just that . . ." It was just that Jenny had not had an invitation of any kind in ten years; since the move to Maple Street. For ten years she had not been asked anywhere, not to a social or a band concert or a simple potluck meal. Books had been her companions. Novels, poetry, and finally plays; these had been her world. She supposed she had read more Shakespeare than anyone else in Logan Falls.

"Jenny? Is something wrong?"

"What? Oh, I'm sorry. No, nothing's wrong. But I couldn't impose on you. For supper, I mean."

"You're not imposing. I want you to come. Truly I do. There's plenty of food, and I want to tell you my idea."

"But the boardinghouses . . . I have to find a room and get settled."

"They're not far from where I live. You can do that after supper."

Jenny looked at Miranda, looked into eyes sparkling with kindness and good humor. She shrugged. "Well, if you're sure . . ."

"I'm sure. It'll be fun! And you have to celebrate your first day in Chicago. It's the first day of a whole new life."

A new life, thought Jenny. *Dear God, let it be better than the old one*. "Thank you," she said, remembering her manners. "Thank you, Miranda, I'd like that very much."

Miranda's South Side neighborhood was mostly Irish; "Lace-curtain Irish," she pointed out, laughingly explaining the difference. The houses were Victorian, not large but well kept, displaying fresh coats of paint, tidy yards, and spotless windows. Trees shaded the streets, handsome elms all russet and gold with autumn.

Miranda's house was on South Crawford Street. She unlocked the door and led Jenny through a narrow hall into the parlor. Soft lamplight fell upon the cozy, flowered chintz chairs and footstools, upon the loveseat and the small tables crowded with family photographs. A fringed cloth decorated the mantel; a potted fern stood in a corner of the room. "Make yourself comfortable, Jenny. I'll be back as soon as I get Drew tucked in. My little darling's had a long day."

"Can I help you with anything?"

"No, just be comfortable."

Jenny put her suitcase aside. She took off her coat and sank into a chair. She was tired, for she, too, had had a long day, and only snatches of sleep the night before. She closed her eyes, lulled by the warm, homey room. She began to drowse, but images of a rainy cemetery brought her quickly awake. "Papa," she murmured.

Her gaze strayed to the photographs on a nearby table. There was an old-fashioned sepia wedding portrait; Miranda's parents, she decided, studying the bridal couple. There were three more pictures of Miranda's father, though in those he was older and alone. In a double silver frame were pictures of another man, a young man with dark hair and a wonderful smile.

"That's Donald," said Miranda, returning to the room. "Wasn't he lovely? Drew has his eyes, I think."

"I hope you don't mind my looking at your pictures. They're such happy faces."

"Yes, we've had a lot of happy times in this house. And sad times, like everybody else. It's supposed to even out. I

28

wonder if that's true. Do you think it is?"

Jenny smiled. "I don't know. Some people are born lucky, aren't they? The rest of us . . . It's different for the rest of us."

The words had been spoken quietly, yet Miranda sensed the anger rippling beneath the surface. She sensed Jenny's loneliness, and she thought to herself that anger and loneliness often went hand in hand. "I have our supper warming. Would you like a sherry while we wait?"

Jenny had never tasted spirits. She shook her head. "No, thank you, Miranda." She glanced up. "Excuse me if I'm being nosy, but how . . . I mean, there's Prohibition, isn't there?"

"Oh, there certainly is. There's also a closet at the back of the hall filled with liquor." Miranda laughed, tossing her head. "Don't be alarmed. I'm not a drunkard or anything like that. Da was in the saloon business. When Prohibition came in, he made his place an ice cream parlor: McAllister's Sweet Shop. Easier than dealing with bootleggers, he said. I'm afraid it's not very successful. Or maybe I'm just no good at managing things."

"You're the manager?"

"Owner and manager. Da passed away last year. Donald was making a go of it, sort of. But then he . . . he died, too."

Her husband and her father both, thought Jenny with a sudden rush of sympathy. How can she stand it? "I'm sorry for all your troubles, Miranda. You've had more than your share."

"I like to think the worst is over now. Anyway, Drew keeps me from brooding."

"Is he all tucked in?"

"Snug as a bug in a rug. He's so cute when he curls up in his crib . . . Listen to me rambling on and on. You must be starved. Come into the kitchen and I'll see about our supper."

Jenny followed Miranda to the hall. She glanced at her reflection in the beveled mirror hanging above a slim gate-leg table. Impatiently, she slapped errant strands of hair from her forehead. "Could I wash up?"

29

"Oh, of course. That door right there. I'll put the coffee on. Unless you'd rather have tea?"

"Coffee's fine," said Jenny. "Thank you."

"Then I'll get started in the kitchen." The kitchen was Miranda's favorite room. Copper pots gleamed against sunny yellow walls, and yellow-striped curtains fluttered at the windows. Leafy plants were massed on the sills and atop the icebox. Four chairs bracketed a sturdy oak table; opposite, a glass-fronted oak cupboard held dishes and a few pieces of crystal. Off the kitchen was the pantry, half of it crammed with liquors and wines from Sean McAllister's pub, the other half with canned goods, sacks of flour and sugar, jars of homemade pickles, and large bottles of ketchup and mustard. Miranda took a bottle of each and carried them to the table. "I don't know how you like your chicken pie," she said as Jenny appeared at the door. "Donald always liked a bit of mustard. Da was a ketchup man . . . Sit down, Jenny."

"Can't I help?"

"There's nothing to do."

Jenny selected a chair and draped her napkin across her lap. The table had been set with pretty blue plates and matching salt and pepper shakers. A basket of rolls sat next to a small tub of sweet butter. Jenny's mouth began to water, for she had not eaten all day.

"Here we are," said Miranda, placing a steaming chicken pie on Jenny's plate. "My foolproof recipe."

"It looks delicious!"

"It is. I'm a pretty good cook, if I do say so myself. Dig in."

Jenny's fork pierced the flaky crust; soon she was scooping tender chucks of chicken and carrots and onions into her mouth. She knew she was eating too fast, knew it was rude, but she could not stop herself. She broke a roll in two and slathered it with butter. Moments later she took another roll and dipped it into the rich gravy. It was as if she had never seen food before. "I — I have to apologize," she said when her plate had been wiped clean. "Making such a pig of myself . . ." She blushed, hiding her hands under her napkin. "I guess I was hungrier than I thought. And it was the best chicken pie I ever tasted."

"Then I insist you have some more." Miranda left the table, returning in a flash with another steaming dish. "There's plenty. I always make a dozen at a time. Force of habit, you know. Donald used to eat three at one sitting. Sometimes Da ate four. A foolproof recipe! Go ahead, Jenny. No need to be shy."

She looked down at her plate. "I couldn't," she said, though her tongue flicked over her lips. "I really couldn't."

"I'm going to have seconds," said Miranda, trying to put her guest at ease. "Don't make me eat alone. I eat alone every night now. It's boring."

Jenny was not deceived. She smiled. "Well, maybe just a little more . . . Where did you learn to cook so well?" she asked between mouthfuls. "Your mother?"

"My mother died when I was born. No, I learned at convent school. We were taught Latin and ancient history and a lot of other fancy subjects, but the nuns taught us cooking, too. Cooking and sewing." Miranda paused, her eyes bright with recollection. "They told us our husbands wouldn't care that we knew history, only that we knew how to run a household. There were no suffragette nuns; I'm sure of that."

"Do you mean they're not modern thinkers?"

"Modern thinkers! They have only one idea: a woman's place is in the home. They're as bad as the priests, some of them. Well, a woman's place *is* in the home. I understand that. But a woman can have *other* places, too. An office, if that what she wants. Why not? Oh, I used to argue with the nuns all the time."

"Who won the arguments?"

"It was hard to say. The nuns always had the last word."

A smile lighted Jenny's face as she finished her second chicken pot pie. All the rolls were gone now, and most of the butter; she was full. She laughed when Miranda started again toward the stove. "No, no more I couldn't eat another bite. It was delicious and I'm stuffed."

"You look better. Not so pale."

"I feel better." *It's true,* she thought. *I feel better than I have in a long time.* "It's nice being here, Miranda. It's nice having someone to talk to. I want to thank you for inviting me."

"I'm enjoying myself. Of course I'm a champion talker. You practically know the story of my life. But now it's your turn. Tell me about you."

"I haven't done anything worth talking about." Jenny cleared the dishes from the table and took them to the sink. She reached for the soap flakes. "I'll wash."

"I'll get the coffee. Do you like chocolate cake?"

"Don't tempt me."

"A small piece, then." Miranda lifted the cover of the cake plate and cut two modest slices. She poured two cups of coffee, setting out a pitcher of cream. "This is Mrs. Sheen's cake. She's my next-door neighbor and has a real way with chocolate."

Jenny dried her hands on a dish towel. She sat down. "I have a way with it, too. That's why I'm fat."

"Plump, not fat." She could lose weight easily enough, thought Miranda, conjuring up a different vision of Jenny. And if she did something about her hair, and bought a decent dress. If she used a bit of lip rouge . . . "Tell me about Logan Falls."

"It's a terrible place. *Terrible.*" Even Jenny was surprised by the intensity of her response. She looked down at the table and stabbed the chocolate cake with her fork. "Don't mind me. I think I've forgotten how to talk to people, how to have a normal conversation. I didn't have any friends in Logan Falls."

"No friends!" To Miranda, a friendly, generous soul, the idea was inconceivable. "But why not?"

"I don't know. First the town decided I wasn't good enough for Glenwood Road, then they decided I was too good for Maple Street. It was something like that, I guess. We lived in those two places. I was born in the Glenwood part of town." Jenny never had occasion to talk about herself, but now the words came tumbling out. She described Logan Falls, its people, its arcane rules and conventions. She described her own family and its uneasy place in the

32

scheme of things. She described the girl she had once been and the girl she had become — an angry, lonely girl who felt her youth had been stolen from her. "It would have been all right if I'd just had someone to talk to. With Mama gone . . . and Jean and Amy . . . And Papa was always so busy."

"How awful for you, Jenny."

"Well, I had my books. I think I read every book in the Logan Falls library. Some of them twice. And I had food. the farmers used to pay Papa in food."

"Things will be different now," said Miranda, her instinctive optimism casting a glow on Jenny's prospects. "You're in Chicago and you can make your life whatever you want it to be. There are opportunities here. You need a start, that's all."

"I saw a couple of things in the newspaper. Jobs. I don't have any references, though. Do you think they'll want references?"

"I know a way you can get references. You can work for me. Oh, just for a while," added Miranda with an earnest smile. "There's no career in the Sweet Shop; I wouldn't expect you to stay. But the accounts are in an awful mess, and the supply room is worse than a mess. I seem to keep putting in the wrong orders, you see. We end up getting thousands of straws and no napkins, or more ice-cream cones when I wanted chocolate sprinkles. It's not that I don't have a head for business. I wouldn't want you to think that. But I'm usually rushing home to Drew. I don't have *time*."

"Yes, I understand."

"Would you consider it, Jenny? I can pay only twelve dollars a week. I won't lie to you; an office job would pay sixteen to eighteen a week, depending on experience. But now that I know you, I can offer room and board as well."

Jenny's head was swimming; everything was happening too fast. She was tired, still feeling the strain of the funeral, and she knew she needed to sleep before any decisions were made. "I hope you don't want an answer right now," she said. "I can't think straight. I appreciate the offer. It's kind of you. But you really *don't* know me. We just met today. You might want to change your mind and if you do —"

33

"Change my mind?" Miranda laughed. "Why should I? I know you're smart. You're a bookkeeper, and I desperately need a bookkeeper. You're good company. That's enough for me."

"But to invite me to live in your house . . ."

Again, Miranda laughed. "Well, you're not a thief or an ax murderer, are you? You don't poison cats?"

Jenny glanced quickly around the room. "Cats? I haven't seen any cats."

"Oh, they don't live here. They come to the kitchen door every morning for breakfast. I call them Zelda and Scott."

Jenny smiled. Miranda takes in strays, she thought to herself, and I guess I'm one of them. "I have *This Side of Paradise* in my suitcase. Papa gave it to me for my birthday a few years ago."

"Wouldn't it be lovely to live in Paris and drink champagne all the time? Zelda and Scott have such romantic lives."

Tired as Jenny was, she could not be certain whether Miranda was talking about Zelda and Scott the cats, or Zelda and Scott the glamorous expatriates. She yawned.

"Poor thing, you're exhausted. I'll take you to your room."

Jenny struggled to her feet. "The dishes," she said.

"Never mind about them. I have to come back down anyway to warm Drew's bottle . . . He gets one at ten, two, and six. I'm not very alert that early in the morning. Don't be scared if you hear a crash; it's just me."

"I don't think I'll hear anything, Miranda. I can hardly keep my eyes open."

"It's my fault. Talking your ear off like that." She touched Jenny's arm, turning her toward the narrow staircase. "Go on up. Second door on the left. I'll just get your bag."

"Second door?"

"On the left."

Jenny climbed the stairs. She paused for an instant at the top of the landing, trying to remember which was her left side. Idiot, she thought, stumbling through the open door. She found the light switch and collapsed in a chair.

Her eyes were blurred with fatigue, but she had a glimpse of rose-sprigged wallpaper and lacy white curtains and polished brass headboards. "Pretty," she said, yawning again. She leaned her head back and closed her eyes; in the next moment she drifted off to sleep.

Jenny did not stir when Miranda entered the room. Miranda, smiling, deposited Jenny's suitcase in a corner and opened the closet door, taking sheets and blankets from a shelf. She made up the bed, opened the window a few inches, and turned on the bedside lamp. "Jenny," she called softly. "Jenny? You can't sleep in that chair all night; you'll hurt your back . . . Jenny, are you awake? Good. The bed will be much more comfortable."

"Did I fall asleep?" She rubbed her eyes. "I guess I did."

"Are you all right?"

"Yes, fine."

"Then I'll leave you. I brought your bag. If you need anything, I'm across the hall."

"Thank you, Miranda."

"Good night. Sleep well."

"Good night."

Miranda left, and Jenny pulled herself from the chair. She went to the bed and sank like a weight onto the feather mattress. After a moment she kicked off her shoes, stripped away her cotton stockings. She started to unbutton her shirtwaist, but her fingers would not work. "Too tired," she murmured. She pulled the blanket up and turned on her side. Once more she closed her eyes. In the darkness she saw splintered images of a rain-splashed cemetery, of a long black train, of a sign whose words ran together: welcometothetownwhereeverybody'syourfriend. She rolled over, punching the pillow. Now she saw a flash of coppery hair and a little feathered hat: Miranda. She knew there was a phrase that perfectly described Miranda Wade, but it eluded her. What *is* it, she persisted even as she surrendered to sleep.

Blithe spirit, thought Jenny, coming awake in the sunny bedroom. It was some moments before she understood why those words had popped into her head, some moments before her eyes adjusted to her new surroundings. All at once she remembered. She was in Chicago, in a house belonging to Miranda Wade, blithe spirit.

She stretched. She threw the blanket off, frowning when she saw her rumpled clothing. There was no clock in the room, but whatever the hour, she wanted a bath. She went to her suitcase, sorting through it until she found a set of underclothes, a skirt, a shirtwaist, and a toothbrush. She opened the bedroom door and peeked outside. The bathroom was at the end of the hall. She glanced around and then dashed toward it, closing the door behind her.

She turned on the taps. She undressed, and the hairpins that had loosened during the night showered from her discarded clothes. She dared not look in the mirror, for she knew she would see puffy eyes and matted clumps of hair drooping around her face. "But I have character," she muttered. "Lucky me."

She lowered herself into the tub and stretched out her long legs. The hot water soothed her, and slowly she began to review the odd events of the day before: the chance meeting at Union Station, the unexpected supper invitation, the even more unexpected job offer. Omens, she thought, recalling Miranda's words. She could not help smiling.

Miranda was waiting in the bedroom when Jenny returned. "I heard the water pipes banging, so I knew you were up. Did you sleep well?"

"Yes, very well. I can't remember ever being so tired." She put her wrinkled traveling clothes on a chair and bent over her suitcase, digging out a hairbrush. "I wish I had your hair," she blurted. "Mine's hopeless."

"Have you thought about getting it bobbed?"

"I'd look silly. Sillier."

"I brought you these." Miranda placed two tortoiseshell combs atop the dresser. "If you use them on each side, you won't have to worry about the wind." She smiled brightly. "It's windy in Chicago." She watched Jenny drag the brush through tangles of black hair. "Why don't you try a center part?"

36

"A center part? Do you think so?" She fussed with her hair for several minutes then gave up. "That's the best I can do."

"The combs look very pretty, Jenny. Come along now, breakfast is ready."

"You didn't have to bother."

"No bother." They went to the stairs. "After you," said Miranda. "I hope you like oatmeal. I make it with cinnamon. I could have made cinnamon toast instead, but I thought oatmeal would be better. A hot breakfast, you know. It's a chilly morning."

Jenny was entertained by Miranda's constant chatter, for it had all the lightness and gaiety that was missing from her own life. It was, she thought, a nice way to start the day. "Is it still morning? I couldn't be sure."

"It's just past ten."

"Ten! I'm usually up at six." She followed Miranda into the kitchen. There was a pot of coffee on the table, a pot of oatmeal on the stove. Six small pastries, white with powdered sugar, were nestled in a cake tin. "You've been busy, haven't you?"

"Busy? Oh, you mean the cakes. They're Mrs. Sheen's handiwork, not mine. I took Drew to stay with her . . . Just in case you wanted to see the Sweet Shop." Miranda ladled oatmeal into a bowl and set it on the table. "I won't nag you while you're eating your breakfast, but I hope you'll think about my idea. Will you?"

"I thought about it while I was soaking in the tub." Jenny sat down. She saw Miranda's eager look and she smiled. "I won't promise anything," she said. "But if you'll let me see your accounts, I'll have a clearer picture. Maybe you don't really need a bookkeeper."

Miranda laughed. "I *need* a miracle worker; I'll *settle* for a bookkeeper. It could be the solution for both of us, Jenny. I know it's not an exciting job. It's not in a big office building or anything like that. It's just a small family business. But you do need a place to start and I need help."

"I understand, Miranda. I'll look at the accounts and then we'll see. I wasn't expecting an exciting job. I'm not an

37

exciting person."

"How do you know?"

Jenny glanced up from her oatmeal. "What?"

"Well, you've been hidden away in Logan Falls all your life. You might be a *very* exciting person, only you don't know it."

Jenny looked closely at Miranda to see if she was serious; she was. "I think I'd know something like that."

"How?"

"I just would."

"How?"

"Different ways."

"What ways?"

An almost playful gleam came into Jenny's gray eyes. "You win, Miranda. Deep down I'm a very exciting person. Deep down I'm Theda Bara."

"Or maybe not. I mean, you can't be certain either way, can you?"

Jenny felt as if she were caught in a maze, traveling all the wrong paths, following all the wrong clues. "Let's change the subject," she suggested. "I'm having trouble keeping up with you on this one."

"Oh? All right, if you'd like. I only meant . . ." And with that, Miranda was off again, taking both sides of the debate and somehow winning both sides. There were no interruptions. Jenny decided it was best to let Miranda talk until she wound down, like a clock. "So that's all I meant," concluded Miranda a minute or two later. "You see my point, don't you?"

"Yes. I think you're trying to give me confidence."

Miranda shrugged. "It's not easy coming from a small town to a city. Everything's different."

Thank God, thought Jenny. She finished her oatmeal and stood up, carrying her bowl and spoon to the sink. "Have you always lived in Chicago?"

"I was born here. Da was only nineteen when he came from Ireland. He went to Boston first, but he saw those awful signs: No Dogs or Irish. So he got right back on the train and kept going." She smiled. "He was luckier than

38

most of the immigrants; he had a little money. Oh, it wasn't much, just enough for him to open a saloon. A pub, he called it. Then a few years later, he bought a bigger place. He didn't get rich, but we had a nice life. This house," she said, her arm sweeping in a wide arc. "And always plenty of food on the table. Da liked to give me special presents, too. I had a real fur cape! It was the talk of the neighborhood."

Jenny turned. "The saloon business was good to you."

"Oh, McAllisters have always been in the saloon business. Going way back. Da broke the chain with his Sweet Shop, but that was because of Prohibition."

"Maybe it was for the best," said Jenny. "You couldn't run a saloon all by yourself. The Sweet Shop makes more sense." She saw something small and shiny on the floor. She bent down. "You lost an earring, Miranda."

"I've been looking high and low and it was here all the time." She shook her head, her copper hair shimmering with morning sun. Now you see what you're in for. You'll spend half the day picking up after me."

Jenny wondered if that was to be her lot in life; first her father, and now Miranda Wade. A trace of a smile flitted about her mouth. "I haven't promised anything yet."

"You will. I know you will. It's fate!"

"Then I guess I should see the Sweet Shop," replied Jenny, her smile widening as she turned toward the door. "Show me my fate."

Chapter Two

McAllister's Sweet Shop was much larger than Jenny had expected. There were at least twenty marble-topped tables, each supplied with a sugar bowl, a napkin holder, an ashtray, and a glass vase sprouting a bouquet of paper straws. There were stools bordering the counter, a pale oak counter so long and smooth she could have skated on it. Glancing around, she saw seven or eight leather booths hugging the wall of a rear alcove. She smiled, for she thought the shop must be a gold mine. "Miranda, it's wonderful!"

"That used to be the bar," replied Miranda, pointing to the counter. "Da couldn't bring himself to part with it. He had it sanded down, and then kept it for the soda fountain. Da was sentimental."

Jenny's glance skimmed the pressed-tin ceiling and the big ceiling fan, silent on this cool morning. She looked again at the soda fountain with its gleaming malted milk machines, syrup dispensers, and ice-cream scoops. She saw bowls of cherries and chopped nuts and chocolate sprinkles; at the end of the counter she saw a child's delight of penny candies in tall glass jars. Only then did it occur to her that the Sweet Shop was empty. "Where are the customers? Is it too early?"

Miranda plucked at her glove. She was spared a reply when a young woman in a pink uniform and tiny pink cap swung through the door adjoining the fountain. "Veda, you're just in time."

"Morning, Mrs. Wade."

"Jenny, I'd like you to meet Veda Brogan. Veda does all

the work around the shop . . . This is Miss Porter."

"Morning."

"Hello, Veda." Jenny watched the young woman slip behind the counter and pour a cup of coffee. She opened a magazine, turning the pages while she sipped. Jenny glanced back at Miranda. "When do the customers start coming in?"

"It varies. I mean, it depends."

"On what?"

"Let's talk in the office."

Jenny, frowning now, followed Miranda through the door into a hallway. To the left was a storage room filled with neat rows of supplies; to the right, a bathroom and a small office. Jenny looked at the desk and then looked again, her astonished gaze taking in the bills strewn all over, the torn scraps of paper, the scribbled note pads, the account book carelessly propped against the telephone. "Miranda, what happened here?"

"I told you it was a mess."

"It's always like this?"

Miranda laughed. "I'm afraid so. I just don't have enough time to put things in order. I have a system, or I *had* one. It didn't seem to work very well . . . as you can see."

"Do you mind if I have a closer look?"

"Be my guest. Better still, be my bookkeeper."

Jenny unbuttoned her coat and sat down behind the desk. She riffled through a ledger and set it aside. Deftly, she sorted the loose papers into four stacks. "Do you have a list of your suppliers?"

"Well, not a list, no. Donald had a list. It got lost."

Just walked off one day and never came back, thought Jenny. "Then how do you . . ." She shook her head. "Never mind. I'll figure it out. Do you have your bank statements?"

"Last month's statement is in the ledger."

"And the others?"

There was an apologetic little shrug, a smile. There was silence.

"I see," said Jenny. "How about your canceled checks?"

Miranda brightened. "In the right-hand bottom drawer."

41

Very slowly, Jenny pulled out the drawer. She was not surprised to see hundreds of checks all jumbled together in a lopsided heap. "This may take a while."

"It's pretty bad, isn't it?"

"Pretty bad."

"But you'll make sense of it, Jenny. The accounts are only four months behind. Not *behind*, exactly. I've paid some bills. Most of them, I think. The problem is I haven't always made the entries in the books. So I'm not really sure what's paid and what isn't. It's all right, though. Everybody seems to understand."

"I guess everybody knows you have a good business here."

"It was better when it was a saloon." Miranda sat in a chair across from Jenny. She removed her gloves, put them down, then picked them up, tapping them lightly against her hand. "Da used to fill the place every night and some afternoons, too. He used to have people three deep at the bar. Now we're glad to have ten customers a day . . . not counting the kids who come in for candy."

Jenny was disappointed, for ten customers a day was definitely not a gold mine. She rested her elbows atop the desk, her chin in her cupped hand. "How do you manage with so few customers? You must be losing money."

"Oh, of course," said Miranda, as if businesses were supposed to lose money, as if that were the whole point. "But I have Da's life insurance. I've been dipping into it to keep the shop going."

Throwing good money after bad; that's what Dr. Logan would say, thought Miranda, and he might be right. She sighed. "Well, let's see what I find in the accounts. There's no reason for you to stay, Miranda. I'll need a couple of hours just to make a dent in all this . . . Don't forget to come back for me," she added smiling. "I don't know my way around the neighborhood yet."

"I'll be back at noon. I'll bring a nice hot lunch. What would you like?"

"Anything. But one o'clock would be better. I need some time."

Miranda rose. She gathered her purse and gloves and went to the door. "Those little pieces of paper are notes I wrote to myself," she explained. "They're not important."

Just like Papa, thought Jenny as Miranda sailed through the door. She took off her coat and draped it over her chair. She switched on the desk lamp, wondering where to start. In one quick motion she swept all of Miranda's notes across the desk and into the wastebasket. She opened the first of the three ledgers and almost immediately a frown crinkled her brow. She had always been able to add columns of figures in her head; it did not take her long to realize that these figures did not balance. She put the ledger aside.

If the ledgers were bad, the accumulated bills and invoices were worse. She saw bills that had not been paid and bills that had been paid twice, although without corresponding credit. There were half a dozen bills that had no similarity to the invoices attached; there were overcharges so obvious she could only shake her head in wonder. She pulled a long yellow notepad toward her and drew a vertical line down the center. For the next hour she filled the pad with numbers. She had filled eight pages when a knock came at the door. She looked up, rubbing her eyes. "Yes, Veda?"

"It's close on twelve. Thought you could use some coffee."

"Thank you. I certainly can."

Veda cleared a space and set the cup on the desk. "Want a sandwich? We have cheese and pickle, ham, ham and cheese, cream cheese and jelly on datenut—"

"No, thanks. I'm not hungry. But could I talk to you for a minute? Are you busy?"

Veda snapped her chewing gum. She shrugged. "The old ladies will be coming in soon. They take lunch here every day regular at quarter past. That's Miss Partridge from the dress shop, and the Boyle sisters from the telephone office."

"I won't keep you. I just want to know . . . Mrs. Wade asked me to straighten out the accounts and it's a little confusing. I'm not being nosy, you understand . . . but your wages are twenty-five dollars a week? Is that right?"

43

"Sure is."

"Could you tell me what you do here?"

Veda looked surprised. "Everything."

"Yes, but could you tell me what 'everything' is?"

"Well, there's the soda fountain . . ."

Veda offered a lengthy Miranda-like description of her duties at the Sweet Shop. Jenny, captive audience of one, listened. She concluded that Veda was the shop's dogsbody—the maid of all work. Veda was the fountain attendant, the candy clerk, the waitress, the busboy, the sweeper, the emergency babysitter, and every Saturday morning the window washer. A lot of jobs, thought Jenny, thinking that twenty-five dollars a week was still much too much. "Thank you," she interrupted, "I have a better picture now."

But Veda was not finished. "See, my ma used to waitress for Himself when it got busy."

"Himself?"

"That was Sean McAllister, rest his soul. When he had a crowd in, he sent around for Ma. For special occasions. When a crowd was celebrating a birthday or a anniversary. Election night was always busy. Nights like that, he sent around for Ma."

"Mr. McAllister gave you your job here. Yes, I understand."

"I'll be getting back. The old ladies . . ." And with another smart snap of her chewing gum, Veda left.

Jenny exhaled a great breath. "Twenty-five dollars a week. Imagine!"

She took several sips of coffee and then put the cup on a file cabinet, out of harm's way. She sat down, continuing her rapid calculations. When she was done, she sorted through the papers again, dividing them into two stacks. Her gaze moved to the ledger; she flipped it open. There were no entries for the month of July, and only random jottings thereafter. She noticed that the entries from January to June were precise and in balance. Donald Wade's entries, she reasoned, certain that he had died early in July. Her heart wrenched when she realized that he had not lived to see his son. She thought about Miranda raising

44

Drew alone. She thought about the frightening responsibility.

"Well, am I bankrupt?" Miranda stood in the doorway. She was smiling, her coppery head tilted to one side. "Is it the poorhouse for us?"

"It's nothing to joke about," said Jenny. "It's no . . ." She stopped herself, for she knew she was getting a certain tone in her voice, a tone that her father had called pedantic, that he had despised. "I've only made a start with all this. I don't have any answers yet. But you were right; you need a bookkeeper."

"Then you'll take the job?"

Jenny stared at the Coca-Cola poster on the wall. After a moment, her gaze slid back to the ledger. "Yes . . . at least until things are sorted out."

"Saints be praised," exclaimed Miranda with a laugh. "I just knew the omens were good."

"We'll see. I want to do an inventory. I think some of your suppliers have been taking advantage."

"Cheating me?"

"It's possible."

"What an awful thing to do!"

"I may be wrong. I don't think I am. Anyway, we'll know soon enough." Jenny stood. "I'll start fresh in the morning, Miranda. There's a personal errand I'd like to see to now. Is there a bank around here?"

"Oh, yes, two blocks away. I'll show you."

"Thanks. I have four hundred dollars that should be put someplace safe."

"Do you have it with you? But where? You don't have a purse."

"I sewed it into the pocket of my coat. I knew I could lose a suitcase or a purse. I couldn't lose my coat; I'd be wearing it."

"That's very clever, Jenny."

"I was nervous about carrying so much money around. It's all I have in the world."

"We'll go to the bank right after lunch. I brought sausage sandwiches from Stachuk's delicatessen. It's Polish sausage

45

called kielbasa. You'll love it. There's a big Polish neigh-borhood not far from here. They have wonderful food . . . Have you ever tasted stuffed cabbage?"

"No, and you shouldn't have spent your money. A cheese sandwich at the counter would have been fine."

"Oh, you need a better lunch than that. A good, hearty Polish lunch!" They left the office. Miranda led the way to a booth, where their lunch awaited. She waved to the trio of gray-haired women sharing a table across the room. The only other customer was an adolescent girl eating a sundae at the fountain. "Business picks up a little after three," she explained. "Some of the high school kids come in for sodas. Veda is famous for her black-and-white ice-cream sodas."

And her twenty-five dollars a week, thought Jenny. She looked at the thick sausage sandwiches on dark bread, at the small bowls of sauerkraut flecked with caraway seeds and bits of onion. Whatever doubts she had were eased by the tantalizing aromas. She took a bite of her sandwich, following it with a forkful of sauerkraut. "Delicious," she said, surprised. "There's nothing like this in Logan Falls."

"You're in the city now. There are different kinds of food and different kinds of people. That's part of the fun. You're going to enjoy yourself here, Jenny. Everybody has a good time in Chicago."

Jenny finished her sandwich. She scraped the last of the sauerkraut from the bottom of the bowl and washed it down with coffee. She turned her head, watching as the gray-haired women paid their bill and left. An instant later she saw Veda walk around the side of the counter to clear the table. "Veda and I had a talk while you were gone."

"She's sweet, isn't she?"

"You pay her too much, Miranda."

"But she does all the work."

"It's true she has a lot of jobs. Add them all together and they're still not worth twenty-five dollars a week." Jenny smiled at Miranda's sheepish expression. "It's *my* job to tell you where you're spending too much money," she ex-plained. "You don't have to listen to me if you don't want to." *Papa never did,* she thought. *I talked and talked, but it was like talking to the wind.* "It's your shop; you have to run it your way."

"Oh, it's not that. I know you're right. It's Da, you see. Veda's mother was a friend of his." Miranda leaned closer, lowering her voice. "He never said, but maybe she was more than a friend to him. I think he wanted to leave Mrs. Brogan something in his will. He didn't; it would have looked funny. Instead he gave Veda this job. And he decided on her salary. I think it was his way of doing something for the Brogans."

Jenny's face was beet red. She glanced off toward the door, fixing her eyes on the little bell suspended over the arch. She wondered if her own father had had a lady friend; it was hard to keep a secret in Logan Falls.

"So that's why I haven't had the heart to make a change."

"Yes, Miranda, I understand."

"Would you like some ice cream?"

Jenny patted her coat pocket. "I'd like to get to the bank."

The United Trust Bank was properly solemn, a hushed fortress of marble and glass with a dozen tellers' cages and four desks for junior officers. It was one of the largest banks on the sprawling South Side, although to Miranda it was simply the neighborhood savings and loan. She seemed to know everybody; tellers, clerks, and even the guard seemed pleased to see her. "I've brought you a new customer," she happily declared to one and all. "This is Jenny Porter."

Jenny reached into her pocket, tearing at the stitches she had so carefully sewn there. Her hand closed over the small envelope and she relaxed.

Just ten minutes later she had her first bankbook. She could not describe the way it made her feel: confident, secure, special, all those things and yet a great many more.

"Now you're an upstanding member of the community," said Miranda, as if reading her thoughts. "You have a job, a place to live, and a bankbook."

Jenny smiled. "And a friend."

"Come along, friend, it's time you had a look around

47

Chicago." Miranda walked Jenny through the South Side's diverse neighborhoods. She pointed out her favorite shops, her favorite parks. She pointed out a popular speakeasy, one of hundreds, perhaps thousands, scattered all over the city. "Have you heard about our gangsters?" she asked, blue eyes twinkling.

"I've read stories in the newspaper. Are they true?"

"The stories? Oh, yes. Johnny Torrio and Al Capone and all that North Side crowd. But Johnny Torrio got shot. Now it's Al Capone who's running things. They call him Scarface."

Jenny stared at Miranda, bemused by her cheerful tone. Miranda might have been discussing a mischievous neighborhood boy: they call him Skippy. "Can't the police do anything?"

"The police!" Miranda laughed. "Oh, they're hand in glove with the police. That's why Da got out of the saloon business. He didn't want any trouble with bootleggers *or* police. Da wasn't one to be pushed around. He laughed at Prohibition. Everybody does. Silly law."

Jenny was startled by this irreverence, for in Logan Falls no one laughed at the law. She was about to reply when she heard a loud rumbling coming from the opposite direction. She turned. "My!" she said, seeing a train running on a track so high above ground it appeared to touch the sky. "Miranda, what's that? I've never seen anything like it."

"That's the elevated, the el train. It's quicker than the streetcar."

"But . . . but can't it fall off?"

"It hasn't yet. I'll take you for a ride Saturday. It's fun! We don't have a subway, like they do in New York. I'm glad of that. I like riding around with my head in the clouds."

Jenny burst into laughter. "That's you, Miranda," she said, "head-in-the-clouds blithe spirit."

It was evening; supper had been eaten, supper dishes washed and dried and put away. Upstairs, Drew slept soundly in his beribboned crib. Downstairs, Jenny sat with Miranda in the parlor. Jenny's gaze moved across the many photographs on the tables. "Why aren't there any pictures of you?"

"I hid them."

"Why?"

Miranda made a face. "Because they're ugly."

"That's impossible."

"They're school pictures." Miranda settled back on the loveseat, tucking her feet beneath her. "My hair was in braids then, and I had a million freckles. And the uniform . . . Oh, how I *hated* that uniform. I hated being away at school, too. Away from Da." She lowered her head and her long copper lashes cast shadows on her rosy cheeks. "The nuns were so strict; you have no idea. I can laugh about it now, but then it didn't seem very funny. When I graduated, I felt like I was getting out of jail."

Jenny smiled. "That's how I felt when the train pulled out of Logan Falls."

"You had Logan Falls and I had convent school . . . After graduation, I kept house for Da. He wouldn't let me help out at the saloon. He just wanted me to enjoy myself. And I did. I went to lots of dances and musicales. To baseball games at Comiskey Park. I had lots of beaux, but I didn't have a sweetheart until I met Donald."

Jenny snuggled in her chair, content to listen to Miranda's recollections. "How did you meet him?"

"It was kind of funny. And it's why I believe in fate." She smiled. Her eyes were bright, aglow with memory. "I never went to the saloon, but one night Da forgot his glasses. I found them in the kitchen and I knew he'd need them, so off I ran. It was a Saturday. Oh, the place was packed. I started looking around for Da and I bumped right into Donald. He'd been working there on weekends, but that Saturday was his last night. He'd found a better job. Anyway, I looked into Donald's eyes and it was love at first sight. It really was. I didn't know his name or who he was or anything about him, but I knew I was in love. He felt the same way. We just stood there, staring at each other. We just *knew*."

"Then if you hadn't gone to the saloon that night —"

49

"We'd never have met! At first, Da *wished* we'd never met. He wanted me to marry an Irishman. But he came around after a while. He liked Donald, and he wanted me to be happy. He gave us his blessing."

"It was fate," said Jenny, smiling.

"It *was*. It was the happiest time of my life."

"Donald was a waiter?"

"Oh, no, he was taking courses at the University of Chicago. He'd already graduated from Yale, but he'd taken mostly business courses there. What he wanted to be was a teacher. His family wouldn't help. He went back to school on his own and worked at different jobs to pay the bills."

Miranda continued to talk about her late husband. Jenny listened to every word, and with every word she was drawn more deeply into Miranda's life. She felt a vicarious pleasure when Miranda described the heady days of courtship, and then the first heady year of marriage. She felt tears mist her eyes when Miranda described Donald's accident. She could imagine the grief, the aching loneliness. "Are you close to your inlaws?"

"Close! I've never *seen* them. They live in New York. Mr. Wade owns a big department store on Fifth Avenue: Wade & Company. The store's been in the family for generations." Miranda laced her long, slender fingers together. "That was the problem. Donald was expected to take his place at the store, but all he wanted to do was teach. Mr. Wade couldn't understand that. He didn't even try. He told Donald it was the store or nothing. So Donald packed his bags and came west. He used to write to his mother, but Mrs. Wade *never* disagreed with Mr. Wade. She took her husband's side against Donald. Marrying me didn't help any, either. Me, a dirty Papist. And Irish to boot. I guess it was the last straw."

"But you're family now."

Miranda shook her head. "No, I'm nothing to them and they're nothing to me. They didn't even come to our wedding. We sent them a wedding picture, but they sent it back. *Unopened*. We wrote letters. They came back unopened, too."

"It must have been hard for Donald."

"I worried about that in the beginning. But Donald . . ." Miranda smiled, remembering. "Donald made a joke of it. He was like that. Oh, I wish you'd known him, Jenny! He was kind and sweet and funny. There were so many good things in him, but the Wades never saw those things."

"Why not?"

"They never paid any attention to him," replied Miranda, wrinkling her nose. "Not even when he was little. He used to call his father 'Old Stuffy,' because Jonah is such a big stuffed shirt. Donald loved his mother, I think. But the way he talked about Daphne . . . Well, she always sounded sort of odd."

"Odd?"

Miranda shrugged. "I never met her, so I don't know. The Wades were in Europe when Donald died. They didn't get back in time for the funeral. Later I learned they came to visit the grave. But they never came to see me. Never telephoned; never wrote a note. I wouldn't have cared, except I wanted them to know about Drew. I sent them a small picture of him." She laughed. "It was a small picture, but I put it in a huge envelope and wrote 'personal' all over the outside. That finally got Mr. Wade's attention."

Jenny leaned forward. "And then what happened?"

"Oh, *then* the Wades started writing. All of a sudden they were interested. Or *he* was, anyway. I get a letter from him the first of every month. Like clockwork! I won't say they're friendly letters, but they're polite. Mrs. Wade usually writes a few lines, too . . . They want Drew and me to go live with them in New York."

"Maybe you should think about it," suggested Jenny.

"They don't care about us. All they want is another heir for Wade & Company."

"They must be rich."

"Well, they're not the Vanderbilts, but I suppose they're doing better than I am." Miranda laughed suddenly. "That's not hard, is it? Me with my empty Sweet Shop and a pile of bills reaching to the sky . . . I hope you can fix things, Jenny. I don't need a lot of money, just a steady income. Maybe I should invest in the stock market. Everybody's doing it. And raking in money hand over fist."

"The stock market!"

"I have Da's life insurance. There's almost three thousand dollars left."

Jenny gasped at the thought of three thousand dollars. It was a fortune to her, a king's ransom. "Miranda, that's security for you and Drew. You wouldn't risk it?"

"I wouldn't *risk* it, no. But where's the risk in the stock market? The newspapers are full of stories about people getting rich overnight. I'd be happy just to double my money."

"Do you think it's that easy?"

"Well, if we picked the right stocks."

"We?" Jenny was incredulous. "Don't count me in on this. I'd never have a minute's peace if I thought I'd had a part in losing your money. I'd never forgive myself."

"But we might *make* money."

"We might not," said Jenny with a firm shake of her head. "And where would you be then? It's not only you, Miranda. There's Drew to consider. No, I won't have a part in it."

"It's just an idea. A way of getting a bit ahead."

Jenny was more puzzled than ever by Miranda's nonchalant attitudes. If she herself had three thousand dollars, she would put it safely in the bank and watch it grow. She would sit back and relax and thank God. "You have a business, Miranda," she said quietly. "The way to get ahead is to make your business pay. To get it out of the red."

"Umm. Well, it's in your hands now."

"Yes." Jenny matched Miranda's smile with her own. "Yes, I guess so." She looked at the cuckoo clock above the mantel. She untangled her legs and rose from the chair. "I'm off to bed. I plan to start early in the morning."

"I'll walk up with you. It's time to have a peek at my little darling. There are times I almost forget he's here. He's not squawky, like other babies. Mrs. Sheen's youngest girl used to cry day and night. We could hear her from one street to the next. It was terrible! I'm lucky with Drew."

Lucky with a lot of things, thought Jenny. *Miranda's had her share of heartache, but still I'd trade places with her. I'd jump at the chance.* "I hope I won't be in your way," she said as they climbed the stairs. "Living here, I mean. You have to let me help with the cooking and cleaning. All the housework."

"Cooking is my department. I'll gladly give you the ironing, though. I hate ironing. We can divide up the rest of it. Okay?"

"Fine."

Miranda paused at the nursery door. "Come say good night to Drew. You two ought to get used to each other."

"I'm not very good with babies."

"Oh, there's nothing to it. Weren't there any babies in Logan Falls?"

"Lots. Papa delivered most of them, but I didn't go along on those calls. It wasn't something an unmarried girl was supposed to see."

Miranda laughed. "It isn't pretty. Not unless it's your own baby; then it's the most beautiful sight in the world. It was to me."

They entered the nursery. Jenny smiled at the teddy bear wallpaper, at the rocking chair heaped with plush bunnies and horses and one huge frog. Pale-blue curtains covered the windows. Blue satin ribbons were threaded through the white wicker of Drew's crib. She tiptoed across the room, peering at the tiny bundle tucked beneath soft blue blankets. She saw a fluff of platinum hair, and platinum lashes encircling clear blue eyes. "He's awake."

"Hello, little darling," said Miranda, lifting the baby from his crib. "Say hello to Jenny . . . she's your new friend."

Drew's eyes seemed to flicker over Jenny's face. He kicked his little legs, as if in greeting. "Hello, Drew. What a handsome boy you are."

"Would you like to hold him?"

"Is it all right?"

Miranda put the baby in Jenny's arms. "There, that's just fine . . . Look, he's smiling."

Jenny glanced up. "Can he? He's so young."

"He's *very* smart. Like his da."

"And his mama." Jenny gazed at him. She touched his downy cheek, his hand. She was surprised when his hand clasped her finger. "How sweet," she exclaimed, and in that moment she lost her heart to Andrew McAllister Wade. "Oh, he's wonderful. So strong, too."

"I knew you'd like each other."

"He's wonderful, Miranda. He really is."

Gently, Miranda took her son and returned him to the crib. "My little darling's made another conquest . . . haven't you? That's right, another conquest." She straightened up. "Now you can see why I have no time for the Sweet Shop. I'd rather be with Drew."

"Yes, I see."

Miranda lowered the lights. She went to the door, stepping back to let Jenny pass. "He'll sleep until his next bottle at ten . . . Don't forget; if you hear noises later, it's only me crashing around."

"I won't hear a thing. Good night, Miranda."

Jenny walked the few steps to her room. She switched on a lamp and closed the door. She undressed, hanging her clothes neatly in the closet. Her eyes darted away from the mirror as she took the combs and pins from her hair. With a sigh, she pulled her old flannel nightgown over her head.

She sat down, pondering her first full day in Chicago. A good day, she decided, stretching out her hand to her bankbook. Four hundred dollars; soon there would be more. The figures danced before her eyes like tiny black snowflakes. She savored the sight. Money, *her* money, and soon there would be more.

Chapter Three

Early-morning sunlight mottled the pavement as Jenny
set off for work. It was Saturday and children streamed from
the houses that lined the streets. She watched them: pig-
tailed little girls uncoiling lengths of jump rope; small boys
in knickers and wool caps, skates looped over their shoulders. She thought of the grubby Grubers and she hurried
on.

The wind was gusting. Tree branches rustled and
swayed. Leaves skipped along the walk, collecting at the
curb in pillows of bronze and gold. Jenny was blown around
a corner, the wrong corner, she realized, and hastily retraced her steps. She followed the street signs, murmuring
their names like a chant. The sudden blast of a car horn
reminded her that this was the city, that she also had to follow traffic lights. She watched the red light turn to green,
and then resumed her journey. She arrived at the Sweet
Shop just as Veda was opening for the day. "Good morning,"
she said, brushing the hair from her eyes. "I wasn't sure
you'd be here."

"Morning, Miss Porter."

"Jenny. Call me Jenny."

"Come on in. I'll get the coffee started . . . Going to work
on the books? I bet they're in a fine mess."

"The books and the supply room. I want to do an inventory."

Veda removed her coat. She looked into the mirror above
the soda fountain, adjusting her tiny pink cap atop her yellow curls. "An inventory, huh? When you're done, maybe
you can answer a question."

"What question?"

Veda unwrapped a stick of chewing gum and popped it in her mouth. "Well, maybe you could tell me why we got ten thousand straws sitting back there."

"Ten thousand straws!"

"And more on the way. A new delivery comes every Saturday regular at noon. I keep telling Mrs. Wade, but she doesn't do anything about it. 'Course it's none of my business." Veda walked behind the counter and began pouring water into the coffee urn. "Ten thousand straws with more on the way. We could build a house."

Just like Papa and the tongue depressors, thought Jenny. There had been so many she had used them for bookmarks and candy apples. "I'll talk to Mrs. Wade. And if you're not too busy later, you might be able to help me in the supply room."

"Sure. Right after I wash the windows."

Jenny went to the office. She dropped her coat on a chair and sat down at the desk. For an instant she could not think where to start. Bank statements? Checks? Invoices? Ledgers? The files? Start at the beginning, she told herself; start with what's owed.

During the next hour she compiled a list of suppliers and noted their overdue bills. When she finished, she cleared the desk and opened the bottom drawer, dumping out all the checks. "Veda was right," she said to the empty room. "It's a fine mess."

And a mess was what Veda saw when she poked her head into the office an hour later. "Getting anywhere?" she asked with a smile.

"It's slow work."

"I wouldn't have the patience for it myself. Want me to show you the supply room? There's time now."

"No customers?"

Veda shrugged. "The usual bunch of kids came in for candy. It'll be quiet now till noon . . . Don't worry; I left the door open so I can hear the bell. But it'll be quiet. It always is."

Jenny stood. She took her pen and pad and hurried after

Veda. "Isn't it *ever* busy here?"

"Used to be, when it was a pub. Crowded in like sardines, they were then. But the Sweet Shop's never been much. Oh, there's good business in summer. Everybody comes in for ice-cream cones." Veda tugged at a cord and the overhead lights flashed on. "This is it," she said. "Enough supplies for the Chinee Army."

Jenny glanced around. There were tall metal shelves, all filled with cardboard boxes of various sizes. Dozens of un-opened cartons were stacked in opposite corners of the room. "It's very neat, Veda."

"I see to that."

"But you wouldn't have a list of what's in here?"

"A list? No, I never had a list."

Jenny nodded; she had been certain of the answer even before she asked the question. "Well, let's have a look."

"First I'll show you our ten thousand straws!"

It was afternoon when Jenny returned to the office. She had spent an hour with Veda; after a brief lunch, she had spent another two hours making lists. These she stacked on the desk, flinging herself into a chair. Her expression was serious, for she was beginning to see the depth of the shop's problems. She could straighten out the accounts, the files, the suppliers. She could bring order to disorder, but the shop would still be in debt and still without customers. She knew that Sean McAllister's life insurance money would soon be gone. And what then, she wondered. What would happen to Miranda? Worse yet, what would happen to Drew?

Drew nagged at her thoughts all afternoon. She pictured him in his crib, so small and helpless, so utterly dependent, and she felt a sharp stab of worry. What *would* happen to him when the money was gone?

These thoughts persisted during the walk home. Several times she reminded herself that the Wades were not her re-sponsibility. They were not family, after all. And she had her own problems, problems by the score. She would have to be tough, she decided; that was the only way. She would harden her heart. But as she neared the house on South

Crawford Street, her resolve was lost in a new wave of concern. She scowled, thinking that she had escaped one impossible situation just to land in the midst of another.

"Jenny? Jenny, over here."

She glanced up to see Miranda standing on the steps of the house next door. "We're having supper with the Sheens tonight," Miranda called. "Come on. You're in for a treat. Irish stew!"

Jenny tried to smooth her straggling hair. "Miranda, I'm a sight. The wind—"

"Oh, you look fine. Besides, we're not going to a fancy dress ball. It's Saturday potluck."

"Where's Drew?"

"Snoozing in the Sheens' parlor. He's had his supper. Now it's our turn."

"But I don't even know them."

"What difference does it make? You didn't know *me* until a couple of days ago."

Jenny had no answer to that. She followed Miranda into the house. Nimbly, she stepped around the boots and skates and bicycles in the hall; she was not quick enough for the cat, a ginger tom who streaked through her legs. She reeled forward and fell into a basket of laundry.

Two-year-old Angie Sheen, watching from the parlor, clapped her hands in delight. "Fa down," she squealed. "Fa down."

"Jenny, are you all right?" asked Miranda, helping her up. "I should have warned you about Lumpy."

"Lumpy?"

"The cat."

Jenny rubbed her sore wrist. "No harm done," she said. She bent, returning towels and pillowcases to the basket. "Good thing I fell where I did . . . And who's this?"

"Angie. She's the youngest."

"Hello, Angie."

"Uhoh." Miranda laughed again. "Careful, here comes Prince."

From the corner of her eye, Jenny saw a flash of reddish fur. She turned and now she saw the big dog loping toward her. He sniffed around her ankles, tail wagging; a moment later he had her pinned to the wall, his paws on her shoulders, his tongue licking her face. "Easy, Prince," she said, grabbing at his collar. "That's a good boy. Get down, Prince. Get down . . . Good boy." He sat, staring up at her; he seemed to be smiling. "Yes, you're a good boy," she said, smiling herself.

Mrs. Sheen bustled into the room then. She was a round, motherly woman with faded blonde hair worn in an old-fashioned pompadour, and blue-green eyes that saw everything. "Jimmy," she called, wiping her hands on her apron. "Jimmy, Mary Catherine, come in here." Her summons brought two older children, and quickly she assigned them their tasks. "Jimmy, take the laundry upstairs and put it away. Didn't I tell you before? How many times do I have to tell you the same thing? Mary Catherine, take your sister upstairs. See she gets a clean diaper; I can smell her from here. Go on, off with you both." She watched them rushing back and forth. When they had gone, she turned and smiled at her guest. "You'd be Jenny."

"Yes. It's very nice of you to ask me to supper."

"Ah, there's always room at my table. I've been hearing about you from Miranda. I'm glad you've come along to help out. Make yourself at home. Supper's almost ready . . . Is Prince bothering you?"

"No, not at all."

Mrs. Sheen looked at the dog. "You better not," she said to him, shaking her finger. "Mind your manners or you'll hear from me!"

Jenny smiled at the woman's retreating back. "Can't we help you in the kitchen?"

"No need. Go on and make yourself at home. Miranda will show you the comfortable chair."

"It's that one." Miranda pointed to a wide armchair with a tasseled green cover. "It's Mr. Sheen's, except when there's company."

Jenny crossed the parlor, Prince trotting at her side. She saw Drew's basket resting atop a table. Lumpy sat nearby, washing a ginger paw. "Is it safe to leave the baby here? The

59

cat might knock his basket over."

"Oh, he wouldn't do that. You worry too much, Jenny."

"Maybe." She looked into the basket. Prince looked, too, but babies were nothing new to him, and so he moved his eyes back to Jenny.

"You've made a friend," said Miranda.

But Jenny did not hear. She continued to gaze at Drew, wondering again what his future would be. She wanted to protect him, though from what, she was not sure. Nor was she sure why such instincts had been stirred. *There's enough on your plate as it is,* she told herself. *You can't worry about the whole world.*

"Is something wrong?"

"What? Oh no, nothing. I guess I was daydreaming." She did not go on, for she heard Mrs. Sheen's voice calling them to supper. With Miranda leading the way and Prince at her side, she walked into the kitchen. "My!" she exclaimed, staring at the huge table, at all the people gathered around it. She counted seven children, seven blond, freckled steps ranging in age from four to twelve. She remembered that little Angie was upstairs. Eight children, she thought, contemplating what it must cost to feed so many mouths. She saw another, smaller, dog sleeping in a corner. She shook her head. Eight children, two dogs, and a cat. "Isn't there anything I can do, Mrs. Sheen?"

"Just sit yourself down. Is that Prince with you? He'll be after your supper, mark my words. He's a beggar, that one . . . Kate, Regina, come help your old ma."

The girls rose obediently and went to the stove. They formed something of a production line, taking bowls from their mother and passing them to the table. Jenny watched, her eyes growing wider, for she had never seen so much food at one meal before. There were four heaping bowls of stew, more bowls of mashed potatoes and peas and noodles. There were two towers of sliced homemade bread and two large crocks of butter. There were three pitchers of milk, two pots of tea.

"Nobody leaves the table hungry in the Sheen house," said Miranda, amused. "And here's Mr. Sheen, king of the castle."

"That I am," he replied, returning her smile. He sat down and tucked his napkin under his chin. "Are you going to introduce me to your miracle worker here?"

"This is Jenny Porter, from Logan Falls."

"Hello, Jenny Porter. Welcome to our table. Sit down and be comfortable."

Jenny sat, draping her coat over the back of her chair. "Thank you for inviting me. But I'm no miracle worker." She blushed, slowly raising her eyes to Mr. Sheen. She saw a man of forty or so, a burly Irishman with a clear, level gaze. She guessed that he was a stern parent, though a loving one. "I'm just trying to get the accounts sorted out."

"She's very modest," said Miranda.

"A good thing in a woman. A virtue."

Jenny felt she had gone up in Mr. Sheen's estimation. She smiled.

"Here we are, then," said Mrs. Sheen, taking her place across from her husband. "Jack, we'll have the blessing."

Heads were bowed and hands folded as Mr. Sheen said grace. The words were unfamiliar to Jenny and she offered her own silent prayer instead. It was a prayer from her childhood, one of the few she remembered.

"Through Christ our Lord, amen," concluded Mr. Sheen.

"Amen," echoed Jenny. She saw the children spring to life. They had been remarkably quiet, but now they found their voices. They shouted at each other to pass the stew, the potatoes, the bread. One of the boys accused his sister of hogging the butter and a small fight broke out, both children yelping in indignation. Milk was spilled and this brought gales of laughter all around. Jimmy spattered Mary Catherine with gravy; she punched him in the shoulder. There was a rising clamor as the boys yelled at the girls and the girls yelled back. "Is it always like this?" whispered Jenny to Miranda.

"Oh, yes. Well, except on Christmas morning."

"Shut your traps, all of you," said Mr. Sheen, addressing his children. "There'll be no hooligans at my table."

They subsided, but not for long; young Kate stuck her

tongue out at Jimmy and the shouting match began once more. Jenny, accustomed to silent, solitary meals, enjoyed every moment. She basked in the noise, the spirited exchanges, for she knew they were part of family life. They'll always have each other, she thought, envying the Sheens. They'll stand together, despite their squabbles. She felt Prince's chin settle on her knee. She sneaked him a piece of stew.

Mrs. Sheen pushed bowls of stew and noodles in Jenny's direction. "Help yourself, dearie," she said. "Don't wait to be asked or Mike will have all the plates scraped clean . . . That's Mike," she added with a fond look at her son. "No use my telling you all their names; there's too many to remember. But Mike's the reason we never have any leftovers around here. Stuffs his face morning, noon, and night, he does."

"Aw, Ma," the boy protested, though he was obviously proud of his hearty appetite. "I'm gonna be a football player," he explained to Jenny.

"Yeah," said Mrs. Sheen, "and last month it was a fireman. Kids!"

Jenny took another helping of stew and noodles. "It's really very good, Mrs. Sheen."

"It was Mrs. Gabor from down the street who gave me the idea about the noodles. Her husband's Hungarian. Maybe he's a Gypsy and she doesn't want to say. Anyhow, their kind of stew is called goulash and they serve it with noodles. You learn something new everyday."

"It's delicious."

"Ah, I'm glad you like it."

There was no doubt of that. Jenny ate everything on her plate save for one chunk of stew, which she gave to Prince.

Mr. Sheen was talking about President Coolidge. "This Coolidge prosperity is all fake," he was saying. "One of these days the roof'll fall in and then you'll see I'm right."

"Now, now, Jack," said Mrs. Sheen.

"I was thinking of investing in the stock market," said Miranda. "Jenny doesn't think I should."

Mr. Sheen pushed his empty plate away and sat back.

"You shouldn't gamble what you can't afford to lose. The stock market is gambling, plain and simple."

"But people are making so much money."

"Republicans!"

"It doesn't have anything to do with politics, Mr. Sheen."

"It doesn't, eh? Politics is behind everything. And if it's Republican politics, you can bet it's just another fancy scheme to help the rich. It's all for the rich, not for working people like us."

Miranda knew she would not win this argument. She smiled at her host. "If you say so, Mr. Sheen."

"That I do."

Dessert was brought: applesauce cake with whipped cream, and lemon custard pie. After dessert the children cleared the table, forming another production line to wash and dry and stack the dishes. It was almost seven when Miranda and Jenny bid good night to the Sheens. "I had a wonderful time," said Jenny. "Thank you very much."

"It was our pleasure, dearie. Any friend of Miranda's is a friend of ours. Isn't that right, Jack?"

"It is," he quickly agreed.

Miranda glanced into Drew's basket. She saw that he was awake and she smiled. "Home we go, little darling."

"I'll get the door," said Jenny. She did so, looking back to see a parade of Sheen children marching from the kitchen to the stairs. "Tell them good night for me."

"We will."

Prince was sitting at the side of the hall. He stared expectantly at Jenny. "Did you think I'd forgotten you?" she asked, bending to pat his sleek head. "I didn't forget. Good night, Prince." She laughed, remembering her Shakespeare. "Good night, *sweet* Prince," she amended. That seemed to satisfy him; he wagged his tail.

Jenny was still laughing as she walked down the steps with Miranda. "That was fun. They're nice people . . . But how can they afford all those children?"

"Mr. Sheen is foreman at a construction company. And he works two nights a week driving a taxicab. They manage all right." Miranda looked up at the pale circle of moon.

63

"Their dream is to send their boys to college. Their *boys*, mind you; they wouldn't think of sending the girls. So that would be four tuitions. It's a lot, even if Mr. Sheen keeps working both his jobs."

"You want Drew to go to college, don't you?"

"Of course." Miranda unlocked her front door. She reached for the lightswitch. "I don't have to worry about that now, though. It's a long way off."

"But if you started saving now . . ."

Miranda laughed. "Saving what? You've seen the books."

"Your father's insurance money."

"Jenny, that's what we're living on. It pays the bills and keeps the Sweet Shop going. That's all there is. Which is where you come in. You'll fix things; I know you will."

A deep frown etched Jenny's forehead. Fix things, she thought. *As if I had a magic wand. As if I could just wish problems away.* "I can only put things in order, Miranda. I can't—"

"Oh, let's not talk about it any more tonight. Come with me while I give Drew his bath. We can decide what we'll do tomorrow . . . I promised you a ride on the el, didn't I? That's what we'll do, then. We'll go for a ride, and afterward we'll have lunch somewhere. I know a lovely tearoom."

"I think I ought to go to the Sweet Shop tomorrow."

"We're not open on Sundays."

"I'll work in the office. No one will know I'm there. It's best, Miranda. There's so much to do."

"Well, if you think it's best . . . But I wish you'd stop worrying."

"Someone has to," murmured Jenny under her breath.

Jenny took her worries with her to the shop each day. She arrived early and stayed until five, stopping only for lunch and for an afternoon ice-cream soda. She worked hard, although she knew no amount of work would change what was there in black and white: the figures were dismal; the shop was draining Miranda's money and would surely have to be closed.

Jenny felt guilty about accepting her salary, but accept it she did. Each week she deposited ten dollars in the bank, holding back two for her own expenses. Most of this money she spent on small presents for Drew and Miranda. It was a way of easing her conscience, a way of putting off what had to be done. As weeks passed and Thanksgiving approached, she knew she could put it off no longer.

The morning was cold and gray. Gazing through the kitchen window, Jenny saw that the trees were bare, the branches shivering in the wind. She turned, her eyes downcast. She managed a tiny smile when Miranda entered the room. "Coffee's almost ready."

"And the table's set." Miranda belted her robe. She pushed her copper hair from her eyes. "You must have been up at dawn. Couldn't you sleep? Drew didn't wake you, did he? He was a little fussy."

"Is he all right?"

"He's *perfect*."

Jenny smiled again. She pulled out a chair and sat down. Over and over she had rehearsed what she would say, but now she did not know how to begin. "I — I'm not going to the shop this morning. I was hoping we could talk."

"Good. You can use a day off."

"I was hoping we could talk about the shop."

Miranda took the coffeepot from the stove and brought it to the table. She poured out two cups. "A serious talk? How can you stand to be serious so early in the morning?"

"Some things can't wait."

"This can."

Jenny shook her head. "No, Miranda. No, it can't. I wish it could." She looked up, meeting her friend's gaze. "I think you know what I'm going to say, so I'll just go ahead . . . I've spent close to two months going through the books. I've gone through them backward and forward. There's nothing to build on. There isn't a way to make the shop pay. If you want my advice . . . Do you?"

Miranda sipped her coffee. "I suppose you've decided it's hopeless."

"It is."

"There must be things you can do, Jenny."

"The books are in order now. There's a complete inventory. There are checks ready to be signed, and there are re-

65

funds from the supplier who was cheating you." She shrugged. "There's nothing more to do. There's no magic."

"There is if you know where to look."

Jenny lips parted in surprise. "You don't *believe* that, Miranda?"

"I want to."

"The shop is too big," continued Jenny. "It was right for what it used to be — a saloon. But the Sweet Shop doesn't get enough customers to fill it, and that's the only way you'd ever make a profit there. The upkeep is too high. The fuel bills, the electricity. And the property taxes! They're twice, almost three times what you pay on this house. Then there's the loan your father took against the shop. You're paying five percent interest on that. If you sold —"

"I can't sell. I need an income."

"But you're not getting an income from the shop. You're putting money *in* and getting nothing back. It's *costing* you money. Every day you stay open costs you more." Jenny took a breath. She saw the confusion in Miranda's eyes, the childlike disappointment. It was as if a favorite toy had suddenly been taken away. "I'm sorry. I'm sorry it's such bad news. But it's your shop, Miranda. You have to decide what's best."

"We could make it something else. It doesn't have to be McAllister's Sweet Shop. It could be McAllister's something else."

"I thought about that. It's a good size for a restaurant, but there's no kitchen. And it would be too expensive to put a kitchen in. It's a good size for a store, maybe a grocery store, but there isn't enough storage space. I've thought about it a lot and I keep getting the same answer: you should sell while you still have some money left."

Miranda rose. She disappeared into the pantry, returning seconds later with two cans of tuna fish. She opened them, scooping the contents into two shallow bowls. In unsteady hands she carried the bowls to the kitchen door. The cats Zelda and Scott were camped on the steps. Scott sat quietly, his tail curled around his paws; Zelda was beside him, grooming her silky black coat. "Breakfast," announced Miranda, putting the bowls down. She stood there for a while, watching the cats. She thought they were lucky to have simple, uncomplicated lives. She felt a tug at her sleeve. She saw Jenny standing in the doorway. "No one gets exactly the life they want," she said.

"Come inside. You'll catch a chill."

Miranda closed the door. All the light seemed to have fled her eyes. She looked pale, older than her years. "Da would turn over in his grave if I sold the shop. He was a proud man . . . proud that he owned a business. He used to say it was something he could give his grandchildren. A legacy."

"You have to be practical."

"God, I wish Donald were here. He'd know what to do . . . Are you *sure* you can't find a way to save the shop?"

"I'm sorry, Miranda. Maybe you should talk to someone at the bank. Or maybe you should talk to an accountant. I'm no expert. I know bookkeeping, that's all." *And I know you can't keep throwing your money away,* she thought to herself. *Not when you have a child to support.* "If you only had family in Chicago; someone who could help."

"Not a soul. The only family I have is in Ireland. I told you Da had eight brothers, didn't I? Of course they all stayed in the old country. Last I heard, I had sixty-one first and second cousins. Sixty-one! But they're over *there.* I've never even met them. Da used to talk about taking me for a visit. He talked about it every spring. Nothing ever came of it, though. Da couldn't leave the saloon."

Jenny sat down. She turned her cup around and around, then shoved it aside. She felt sorry for Miranda, sorrier for Drew. "I wish I had a solution."

"How much money would the shop bring if I sold it?"

"I don't know. I've been looking in the newspapers, trying to get an idea of asking prices. There are all those ads in the business pages, but it's hard to tell. I mean, it depends on different things: the space, the neighborhood, if the building's in good condition or not. I'd guess maybe three thousand dollars. That's just a guess. You'd have to see a real estate agent. Someone who *really* knows the ins and outs."

Miranda paced the kitchen, her head bent, her hands clenched behind her back. "Three thousand. That wouldn't last long. The upkeep on this house is high, too. It's the house Da wanted, but it's expensive to heat. And with the electricity and the water and the taxes . . . The plumbing." She sighed. "The plumbing always breaks down in winter."

"Well, I was thinking . . ." Jenny paused. She knew Miranda would not easily accept the truth. Papa didn't, she thought, leery of imposing her own views. She remembered the time her father had called her bossy. His smile had softened the accusation, but still it had hurt. "I shouldn't be sticking my nose in. I'm interfering."

"Jenny, we're friends. There isn't anything you don't know about me. There isn't anything you can't say."

"Sometimes I say too much."

"But I *want* your opinion. And your suggestions, if you have any." Miranda sank into a chair. Her arms hugged her slim waist; her hands clenched again at her sides. "I knew we'd have this conversation sooner or later. I knew it that first day on the streetcar. But I kept telling myself you'd find a way to fix things."

"There isn't any way to save the shop."

"And if I sell, the money will be gone in a year."

"Not . . . not if you take in boarders." Jenny's gaze skidded to the table. The words were out, but she could not claim to be relieved. From the corner of her eye she saw Miranda's stunned expression. She took a breath and waited.

"Boarders? Did you say boarders?" Miranda put her head in her hands. "Next I'll be taking in *laundry.*"

"I just thought . . . I mean, you have the extra bedrooms. If you had three boarders, that would pay most of your bills. You'd be earning interest on the money you got from selling the shop. That would help. The important thing is you'd have a nest egg. You'd have something for Drew's future."

"Da would turn over in his grave."

"It's Drew you have to worry about now."

"I worry about him all the time, Jenny. But even if I sold the shop and took in boarders . . . even if I did all that, I'd still be pinching pennies the rest of my life."

There was silence as Jenny weighed her reply. "I don't

know how to say this . . . I don't mean any disrespect to Donald, but you won't always be alone. Someday —"

"Someday I'll marry again. Is that what you're thinking? Oh, it's all right; I've had the same thought myself. It seems impossible to me now. In time that will probably change. I don't like living alone, and Drew shouldn't grow up without a father. If I met a nice man . . . *If* he could be a good father to Drew . . . Well, who knows? It might be possible, after all. Donald would understand."

Jenny saw the tears filming Miranda's eyes. "I'm sure he would," she said quietly. "He'd want you and Drew to be happy."

"What do I do in the meantime?"

"I made a list of real estate offices. You could start there, if you decide to sell."

"Yes." Miranda took a handkerchief from her pocket and dried her eyes. "What will happen to Veda?"

"She'll find another job."

"No other job will pay nearly as much as the Sweet Shop. I suppose I'll have to give her some money."

Count to ten, Jenny warned herself, for she felt a quickening anger. It was the kind of anger she had sometimes felt with her father, the kind of anger she would always feel with well-meaning but irresponsible people. "You don't have to decide that now," she said carefully. "There's time."

"But I have to give her notice."

"There's time for that, too. See a real estate agent first, Miranda. See where you stand."

"I *hate* this. I don't want to sell the shop and I don't want to take in boarders. I don't! That's an awful way to live. Well, maybe it's not awful, but it's not the life *I* want. And how would it be for Drew? His mother running a boarding-house?"

Jenny said nothing. Once again she would let Miranda wind down, like a clock.

"It's not fair, you know. Da put almost everything he had into this house. He *loved* this house, and so do I. I don't want strangers clomping around. I'd never have any privacy." Miranda's small fist pounded the table. "I won't do it, Jenny.

69

I won't and that's that!"

"You mustn't upset yourself this way. We'll . . ." She did not finish, for Miranda had bolted from the room. She listened to the rapid footsteps fading away. She sighed, throwing her coat over her shoulders as she went to the door.

The scent of rain was in the air. The sky was the color of pewter. She heard the wind whispering in hedges and shrubs parched with cold. She turned. "Good morning, Mrs. Sheen," she called across the backyard. "You're an early bird this morning."

"I want to get the wash on the line. Can't tell about the weather this time of year."

"Can I help?"

"You can keep me company."

Jenny walked down the four steps and crossed the narrow brick path. She saw a large basket filled with diapers and scores of children's white socks. "You must spend half your day doing laundry. How do you manage it all?"

"I'm used to it. My girls do some of the ironing. All my kids have their chores."

Jenny gathered a handful of clothespins, giving them to Mrs. Sheen one by one. "I wish I had a big family."

"It's a lot of work, but it's worth it. That's what I keep telling Miranda. How is our girl today?"

"I'm afraid she's pretty upset right now. I — I told her she ought to sell the shop and put the money in the bank. Then I made it worse. I suggested she take in boarders so she'd have some income."

"Boarders, eh? It was smart of you to think of that."

"But she's upset."

"Ah, she has her head in the clouds, that girl. We love her like our own, but there's no denying her da spoiled her. He was a good man, God rest his soul. A heart of gold, just like Miranda. Too many fancy notions, though." Mrs. Sheen moved to the end of the clothesline, filling the remaining space with two pairs of overalls. "Too many dreams," she continued. "The Irish are great ones for dreams."

"You don't think I was wrong?"

"Wrong! Why, just the day before you came my Jack told

her the same thing. Not the part about the boarders; he didn't think of that. He told her to sell the shop or she'd be bankrupt. Very firm about it, he was. But you know Miranda — in one ear and out the other." A frown touched Mrs. Sheen's brow. "She's a funny kind of girl, Miranda is. She's forever going on about how women should be this, that, and the other thing. Women should be President, to hear her tell it. And she believes what she says. But she's a bad example, if you see what I mean. She's a scatterbrain. A heart of gold, but a scatterbrain."

Jenny smiled. "I guess it's the heart of gold that really matters."

"That it does, dearie. That it does. Well, I'll be going inside now. I have my baking to do . . . And don't go worrying your head about Miranda. She'll come around. It's all for the best, isn't it?"

"I hope so."

Jenny went back to the house. She walked through the silent kitchen and climbed the stairs to the second floor. Miranda's door was ajar. She knocked.

"Come in." Miranda sat at a rosewood desk littered with papers. She was still wearing her robe, though she had tied a ribbon in her hair. "Listen to this," she said, fingering a sheet of creamy stationery. " 'We would be pleased to provide a home for you and our grandson. In return, we ask only that you conduct yourself in a respectable manner. As to the question of religion, we would expect you to worship at our church and to have young Andrew confirmed in the Episcopalian faith.' What do you think of that?"

"What is it?"

"One of the early letters from my father-in-law, Jonah Wade. A cold fish, wouldn't you say?"

"It's not a very friendly letter."

"No." Miranda looked up at Jenny. "Not very friendly; not very nice . . . But I've decided to accept his offer. I'm going to New York and so are you."

Chapter Four

The ticking of a clock was the only sound in the room. Jenny's hand flew to her throat and froze there. She stared at Miranda, her face a mask of surprise. "New York!"

"I've made up my mind. I'm going to sell the shop, the house, and most of the furniture. I'll sell everything and start out fresh."

"But just a few minutes ago you were telling me how you loved this house."

"I do. I love it as it is. If I have to share it with strangers, I'd rather sell." There was no anger in Miranda's voice now, no rancor. The light had returned to her eyes and to her smile. "Don't look so grim, Jenny," she teased. "It's not as if I'm going to sell *Drew*."

"But I don't understand. When did you decide all this?"

"Maybe it's been in the back of my mind all along. I don't know. Maybe it was meant to be. For Drew's sake, if not mine. The Wades can give him a better life than I can. Unless I married a millionaire. And there aren't too many millionaires running around the South Side. Drew will have a future. A whole big department store, if he wants it."

"What about the Wades?"

Miranda's smile wavered, but only for an instant. "We probably won't like each other. That's all right. We'll stay out of each other's way. Or maybe I'll win them over. It's possible. Anything's possible."

"You'd have to be an Episcopalian."

"Oh, I don't care about that."

"But you're Catholic."

"I'm lapsed."

Jenny sat at the edge of the bed. She had become accustomed to the lightning changes in Miranda's moods, but she would never become accustomed to Miranda's sudden and quixotic decisions. There was something wrong, she thought, about deciding your whole life in ten minutes. "It's such a big step," she said slowly. "Why don't you wait until you've had time to—"

"Time to think?" Miranda laughed. "No, I make my best decisions on the spur of the moment. I'm going to write to Mr. Wade today. You understand, don't you, Jenny? You should. You left Logan Falls so you could have a better life. That's why I'm going to New York. I don't want to run a boardinghouse. I don't want to pinch pennies. I'm young. I want to start enjoying myself again. There's no fun in life if you always have to worry about money. It would be terrible if Drew had to grow up that way."

"What if you don't like New York?"

"I'll love it. You will, too."

"*I* will?"

Now Miranda was surprised. "Of course! You don't think I'd leave you behind? We're *friends*. When I write to Mr. Wade, I'll ask him to arrange a job for you at Wade & Company. You can get yourself a little flat, some pretty clothes. We'll have a wonderful time in New York. It will be an adventure."

"Miranda, I couldn't do that."

"Why not?"

"It's taken me two months to learn my way around Chicago. I can't start all over again."

"Oh, you're talking like an old lady. What's the good of being young if you can't start all over again? That's what being young *is*. It's having tomorrows. It's having dreams."

"Mrs. Sheen says the Irish are great ones for dreams."

"Pretend you're Irish." Miranda's gaze lighted on Jenny's thick black hair. "Black Irish," she added with a laugh.

"My mother's people came from Scotland."

"That explains your thrifty ways. But I'll bet New York loosens your purse strings. There are lovely stores in New York."

Jenny's head was throbbing. Once again she felt everything was happening too fast. She felt her life was spinning out of control, rushing toward some unknown and ominous place. "I'll have to think about it, Miranda. I'm grateful that you want to take me along, but I'm just not sure. The only thing I'm sure of is that I have to find another job right away. I don't want to start dipping into my bank account."

"You have a job. You're still on the payroll."

"No, I won't take your money. There's no more work for me."

Miranda draped herself over the back of her chair. She was smiling, her head tilted to one side. "No work? There'll be *plenty* of work. It will be up to you to sell the shop and the house, to see I get the best price. There'll be a thousand details, and I'm leaving them all to you. Didn't I mention that?"

Jenny massaged her temples, for the throbbing was worse. "I don't know anything about selling property."

"You sold your house in Logan Falls, didn't you?"

"That was different. Miranda, there was *one* real estate office in Logan Falls. Mr. Hull and his secretary; that was the whole office. I went in, said we'd be selling, and he did the rest. It wasn't hard. We all knew that the foreman at the brickyard was looking for a house nearby. Mr. Hull telephoned him and he bought it. There wasn't any haggling or anything like that. The houses on Maple Street always sell for the same price."

Miranda's forehead wrinkled. "But prices should go up. There should be a profit."

"Not on Maple Street. Not in Logan Falls. If they let prices go up, they'd have to raise wages more often." Jenny smoothed a corner of the bedspread. It was patterned with butterflies, and idly her finger traced the pale-blue wings. "I think you should hire a lawyer."

"Oh, I wouldn't waste my money on lawyers. You know

how they are. If you won't help me, I'll have to see to it myself."

Jenny looked up. "This isn't a game, you know. You're talking about thousands of dollars."

"Then help me."

"You need an *expert*. How can I make you understand that this is serious?"

"I understand. But I have faith in you."

Jenny laughed, disarmed by Miranda's reply. "That's no way to do business."

"It's my way."

"You're a stubborn girl, Miranda."

"Stubborn as Paddy's pig. That's what Da used to say. He'd like you, Jenny. And he'd agree with me that you're the one for the job. Won't you say yes?"

"I'll say maybe. First I have to go to the library and read up on real estate."

Miranda's smile was dazzling. "Thank goodness! Now all our problems are solved!"

For Jenny it was not that simple. She spent long days at the library, learning the unfamiliar language of real estate. She learned about binders and closings, about title deeds and title searches. She learned about estimates and commissions and what to look for in a real estate agent. She made endless notes, reviewing them every night after supper. On weekends, she studied the business pages. She learned that the real estate market was booming, and this buoyed her spirits.

Miranda spent Thanksgiving with the Sheens. Jenny stayed at home with her books and notes. Early in December she selected a real estate agent; that same week, Miranda received a letter from Jonah Wade. "Good news," she cried, dashing into Jenny's room. *"Wonderful* news. It's all set. You have a job waiting at Wade & Company!"

"Miranda, you know I haven't decided yet."

"There's nothing to decide. You'll be paid eighteen dollars a week, and you'll have a ten percent discount at the store." Miranda took the letter from its envelope. "Listen to this: 'There are no openings for bookkeepers at the present time, but we always have openings for polite, well-groomed young women to serve our customers.' "

"A salesclerk?"

"You wouldn't mind too much, would you? It's only a starting place. You could end up president of the store someday. At least until Drew's ready. And he might not want any part of Wade & Company. You could move right to the top!"

Jenny smiled at Miranda's rosy imaginings. "I wouldn't mind being a salesclerk," she said. She glanced at herself in the mirror, then quickly glanced away. "It's just that sales-clerks are usually pretty. No, don't say anything; I'm not fishing for compliments. Don't tell me I'm pretty when I know I'm not."

"You could be." Miranda stepped behind Jenny and turned her back to the mirror. "If you fixed your hair . . . If you cut it a little. And if you used a bit of face powder and lip rouge. You have a pretty mouth, Jenny. You have *lovely* eyes. A touch of mascara would work wonders."

Jenny shook her head. "No, I couldn't wear cosmetics. I'd feel silly . . . Did I ever tell you about Miss Grimble? She was a spinster lady in Logan Falls. She had a small dog named Millie. Well, every Sunday she put Millie in a little ruffled dress and a hat like a baby's bonnet. She carried her around town for people to admire. She didn't under-stand that even with fancy clothes, Millie was still just a dog. And that's what I mean. Even with powder and paint, I'd still just be me."

"You're too hard on yourself. I can . . ." Miranda did not finish her thought, for there was a sudden loud cry from the nursery. She ran out of the room, Jenny at her heels. "Mama's coming," she called, almost slipping as she raced across the hall. A moment later she was bending over Drew's crib. She saw his flushed face; she felt his fore-head. "My God, he's burning up."

Jenny touched his cheek. She opened his shirt, relieved to see there were no spots, no signs of a rash. "It could be a throat infection, or maybe his ears. I'll telephone the doctor."

"He's never been sick before."

"He'll be all right," said Jenny, rushing out.

Miranda lifted Drew into her arms. She rocked him, but his cries continued, shrill and insistent. His tiny face was red, damp with perspiration. His legs thrashed about beneath the blanket. "Poor little darling," she murmured. "My poor little boy." Her eyes were anxious as Jenny returned to the nursery. "Did you get Dr. Ryan?"

"He'll be here in an hour." Jenny set a bowl of water and chipped ice on the dresser. She plunged a cloth into the bowl and wrung it out. "Sit down, Miranda. Let's see if we can make Drew more comfortable."

"You don't think it's anything serious?"

"I'm sure it isn't. Babies always run high fevers; that's what Papa used to say. He didn't worry too much about it." Jenny pressed the cloth to Drew's brow. His cries grew louder, but after a while he seemed to exhaust himself. She wet the cloth again and replaced it on his forehead. She stroked his fiery cheek; she looked into his eyes blazing with fever and her heart began to pound. She felt as if a weight had lodged in the center of her chest. It was fear, the same smothering fear she had felt the day her father had been rushed to the hospital. She remembered the terrible sense of helplessness; she forced the thought from her mind. Once more she wet the cloth and returned it to Drew's brow. She caught his hand, smiling slightly when his fingers curled around her thumb. "You're going to be fine," she whispered to him. "Just fine."

Miranda raised her eyes to Jenny. "He's so hot. Do you think I should give him water?"

"You'd better wait for Dr. Ryan."

"What time is it?"

"A little past nine."

"What's keeping him? Where is he?"

"He'll be here, Miranda. Don't worry."

Dr. Ryan arrived half an hour later. A tall, reedy man of thirty-five or so, he stole a wistful glance at Miranda before bending over Drew. His examination was thorough

77

and unhurried. When he finished, he offered his diagnosis without hesitation. "Drew has a bad ear infection. Common enough in babies. I'll leave you some drops." He took a small vial from his black bag and gave it to Miranda. "Two drops in each ear every four hours. Do you know how to put them in?"

"I do," said Jenny.

"Then you can be the nurse," replied Dr. Ryan, though his gaze remained fastened on Miranda. "Cold compresses will help bring down the fever. You can also swab his chest with alcohol. He may not be hungry today, but try to get him to take fluids."

Jenny nodded. "I will. What about the fever?"

"Check it throughout the day. I'll stop by later, perhaps tonight."

"Then there's nothing to worry about?" asked Miranda.

"The sooner his fever comes down, the better. But no, I wouldn't be worried. These things have to run their course. I swabbed ointment in the ear and that should ease Drew's discomfort. The drops are very important," he added, looking at Jenny for the first time. "We don't want any more inflammation."

"I understand, Doctor."

"Good. I'll leave it in your hands. Miranda," he said, lingering over her name, "I'll show myself out. And you can expect me back tonight."

"Thank you, Dr. Ryan. I'm grateful to you." She turned and tucked the blankets around Drew. Gently, her fingers brushed his wisps of hair. "You scared me, little darling," she murmured. "But everything's all right now." She took a breath, smiling at Jenny. "Thank God you were here. I couldn't have gone through this alone."

"I was scared, too. When they're that little . . ."

"Yes, babies seem so fragile. They're not, you know. But they *look* fragile, so when they're sick we all start having awful thoughts. I wasn't prepared. I mean, it's been so easy until now. Never a moment's worry." Miranda sat down. She rubbed the back of her neck. "Do you suppose it will happen again? I'll have to ask Dr. Ryan when he comes tonight."

"He's sweet on you."

Miranda blinked. "What?"

"Dr. Ryan is sweet on you."

"Oh, I hardly know him. He looks after the Sheen children; that's how we met. He has a nice way with children. I noticed that right off . . . I wonder if he can recommend a doctor in New York."

"There must be lots of them in such a big city."

"We'll soon find out, won't we?"

Jenny went to the crib and stared down at Drew. He was sleeping, though even in sleep his legs kicked at the blankets. She soaked another cloth and laid it across his brow. She watched him, feeling a familiar tug at her heart. She loved this little boy, loved him as if he were her own; she knew that she could not bear to be parted from him. New York, she thought, and now her heart began to thump. She remembered what she had said to Gardner Logan: "I'd go to New York if I had the courage."

Drew's eyes opened, twin pools of clear, innocent blue. He seemed to be smiling. Gently, she moved the cloth aside and gathered the child into her arms. She cuddled him, rocked him. "You're all the courage I need," she murmured against his silky head.

"What did you say?" asked Miranda.

"I said we'd find the best doctor in New York."

"Jenny, you've decided! You're coming with us!"

"Oh, I think I should." She smiled. "Who'd put Drew's eardrops in if I stayed behind?"

Christmas came, a joyous occasion on South Crawford Street. Beribboned holly wreaths decorated doors and windows all along the block. In some front yards there were plaster statues of Mary and Joseph and the infant Jesus; in others, there were statues of Santa Claus and his reindeer. In every house was a gaily trimmed Christmas tree and at least one closet stuffed with presents. Children wore eager, expectant looks, for they knew that most of the presents would be theirs; dull presents like pajamas and underwear and woolen mufflers, but exciting presents, too: dolls and sleds and candy-filled Christmas stockings. It was a time of celebration, of carolers and church bells. With any luck, there would be snow.

"Snow," said Miranda early on Christmas day. "That's what we need. Snow would make everything perfect!"

"Everything's perfect right now," replied Jenny. She was in a happy mood, for Drew had completely recovered and the shop had been sold. She had set a price of four thousand dollars, sticking to it through weeks of difficult negotiations. She had been urged to lower her price, to compromise, but all such pleas had been refused. "It's a fair price," she had insisted again and again; the real estate agent had finally agreed, though only after the sale had been made. Jenny was proud of her first venture into the business world. She began to feel easier about her future, even in a huge city like New York. "I have no complaints," she said now, glancing from Miranda to the stacks of presents arrayed around the tree. "This is the nicest Christmas in years, thanks to you."

"To me! Jenny, you're the one who's fixed things. It was all an awful mess before you came here."

"Maybe, but you *brought* me here. If it weren't for you, I'd be alone in some boardinghouse today. I wouldn't be planning to move to New York, either. I'd never have the nerve, on my own. It took all my courage just to come to Chicago. It's funny; that seems so long ago."

"You're a happier person now."

"I hope it lasts. Papa used to say that life gives with one hand and takes away with the other."

"Oh, that's too gloomy. What's important is that you *are* happy." And not as angry, thought Miranda to herself. "City life suits you."

"I hope New York suits me. I hope *I* suit New York." Jenny bent, retrieving a small ivory clip from the floor. "Yours?" she asked, smiling.

"My hair clip! I turned the house upside down looking for it. Sometimes I think I'd lose my head if it weren't attached to me . . . And *what* is my hair clip doing in here anyway? I haven't worn it since Thanksgiving."

Jenny laughed. She had lost track of all the things Miranda had dropped or forgotten or misplaced: keys, gloves, combs, umbrellas, a favorite pair of sewing scissors. Frantic searches always ensued, to no avail. Days later, weeks later, the missing items mysteriously reappeared.

"Do you suppose it's been here all the time?" asked Miranda.

"I don't think your hair clip just walked in this minute." She turned as the cuckoo clock began its hourly concert. "The Sheens will be here soon. Which are the presents for the kids?"

"Over on the left." Miranda rose from the loveseat. She knelt beside the tree, rummaging through the packages. "All these," she said, pushing them to the side. She counted again. "Yes, that's right; eight kids and eight presents."

They were modest presents — crayons and coloring books, sacks of marbles, yo-yos, a pull toy for little Angie — but still Jenny wondered at the cost. She dared not ask, for she, too, had exceeded her Christmas budget. She had spent almost a whole week's salary on gifts for Miranda and Drew; at the last moment she had spent another two dollars on candy for all the Sheens and a bone for Prince. She had never spent that much money before, nor had she ever had quite that much fun. She remembered the meager Christmases on Maple Street. There would be two or three presents beneath a skimpy tree; there would be a dinner only half eaten because her father had to go off on a call. "I'll always remember this Christmas," she said softly. "With you and Drew and the Sheens — it's like a family. In Logan Falls —"

"You should forget Logan Falls, Jenny. That's over. Put it behind you. That's what I try to do with unhappy memories."

"I keep thinking about Papa."

"He'd be proud of you. Look at all you've done these past few months. And in a strange city, too. He'd be proud as punch!"

Jenny smiled. Yes, she thought, yes, maybe he would. The doorbell rang then and she rushed to answer it. "Merry Christmas," she cried, ushering in a crowd of Sheens. The children were scrubbed and brushed and polished, wearing their holiday best. Mr. Sheen, in his one good suit and a plain blue necktie, brought up the rear. "Where's Angie? And Kevin's not here, either."

"They were sniffling during Mass. They're home with the missus. I wanted to leave 'em all home, but they started yapping about their presents. Up at five this morning, they were. There's a parlor full of presents and my hooligans want more."

"It's only once a year, Mr. Sheen," said Miranda with a laugh.

"That it is, but they're forgetting the meaning of Christmas."

Miranda's eyes twinkled. "Heathens," she said. "Do I have heathens in my house? Well, come on and get your presents anyway. I forgive you."

The children rushed to the tree. Jenny handed out the presents, greeting each child in turn. Her smile widened when seven-year-old Mike approached. With his jaunty manner and infectious gap-toothed smile, he was her favorite Sheen.

Miranda watched as wrapping paper and ribbons went flying through the air. The children were squealing, showing off their presents to one another. She turned to Mr. Sheen. "Can I offer you some Christmas cheer?"

"From your da's closet?"

"Of course. I know it's early, but maybe a bit of Irish?"

"I won't refuse your hospitality," replied a smiling Mr. Sheen. "A bit of Old Bushmills to take the chill off."

"Old Bushmills it is."

Miranda left and Mr. Sheen went over to Jenny. "Your first and last Christmas in Chicago, eh?"

"I'll be sorry to leave. Everybody's been so kind."

"Have you found a buyer for the house?"

"There are two families interested in it. Both with lots of kids, playmates for your little ones. It should all be settled right after New Year's."

"And you're keeping to your price, are you?"

Jenny nodded. "It's a fair price. The real estate agent says I drive a hard bargain, but fair is fair. Besides, I want Miranda to have a nice nest egg for Drew. You never know when it'll come in handy."

"You're a smart girl, Jenny Porter. There's not many girls who have such a head for business. I'm thinking God gave you a special gift. Something to tide you over till you find a husband."

"A husband?" asked Miranda, joining them. "What's this about a husband?"

"I was telling our Jenny that her gift for business would see her through till she found herself a husband."

Miranda rolled her eyes. She laughed. "And what happens *after* Jenny finds a husband? Is she supposed to throw her gift in the trash bin?"

"The man's the head of the house, Miranda. Remember that." Mr. Sheen finished his whiskey in two gulps. "The man rules the roost."

"In Ireland maybe."

"It's the same the world over."

Jenny listened as they debated the point, a moot point, for she did not envision a husband in her future. She had noticed the way Dr. Ryan looked at Miranda and she was certain no man would ever look at her that way. At eighteen she was resigned to spinsterhood; she could almost see herself growing a little stranger each year, like Miss Grimble. She was pondering this sad fate when a loud crash pulled her from her thoughts. She whirled around. A table had been overturned; photographs, frames, and shattered glass lay scattered on the floor.

"Jimmy!" roared Mr. Sheen. He was across the room in one great stride, lifting the child by the scruff of his neck. "Look what you've done, lad! Haven't I told you to watch out?"

"But the marbles rolled under — "

"I'll have no backtalk from you," said Mr. Sheen, slapping his son's face.

The other children were silent as statues. Miranda rushed past them, thrusting herself between Jimmy and Mr. Sheen. "It's all right she insisted. "There's no harm done; a little broken glass that's all. I'm sure Jimmy is sorry."

"He's always sorry. Always getting into things, he is."

"It's Christmas, Mr. Sheen. Let's not spoil the day. Accidents happen."

"I'll pay for the damages, Miranda."

She shook her head. "Don't be silly. It's just a little broken glass. I wasn't going to take those heavy frames to New York anyway. Now let's see a smile, Mr. Sheen. Boys will be boys, you know."

"That's what the missus says." He looked down at Jimmy. His expression softened, as it usually did when his anger was spent. "Have a care next time," he mumbled, his big hand tousling the boy's fair hair. "Mind what you're doing."

"I will, Da."

Peace had been restored and the children quickly lost interest. They went back to their games, munching on candy canes while they played. Mr. Sheen had another whiskey; Jenny was persuaded to try a small glass of sherry. She liked the taste, the warmth that spread through her body. For no reason at all, she wondered what Dr. Logan would think if he could see her now.

"Time to be going," said Mr. Sheen when the cuckoo clock announced the hour. He rounded up his children, waiting quietly as they offered their good-byes. Satisfied, he marched them off to the door. "We'll be seeing you at two," he called over his shoulder. "Christmas dinner's at two sharp, so don't be late."

"We won't," chorused Jenny and Miranda.

"The missus told me to remind you. If you come late, the kids'll beat you to the turkey."

"We'll be there, Mr. Sheen." Miranda saw him to the door. She smiled. "But tell Mrs. Sheen I still don't eat turnips. Not even on Christmas!" She watched the solid mass of Sheens crowding the path. She closed the door. When she returned to the parlor, she found Jenny on hands and knees picking up the shattered glass. "Don't worry about that now."

"It won't take a minute."

Miranda knelt again beside the tree. She reached around, sliding several boxes to the front. "Now it's our turn for presents. You first. Start with this big one."

"I hope you didn't spend too much money. We agreed."

"I was very practical."

Jenny put the box on her lap. She tore away the wrapping, folded back the tissue paper. "Miranda," she cried, "is this for *me?*"

"Do you like it?"

It was a coat, a beautiful black wool coat with a shawl collar. Jenny was speechless. She stroked the soft fabric, touched each shiny button. It was the nicest present she had ever gotten. "I love it, Miranda. I really do. But I can't keep it. The money—"

"Oh, never mind the money. That's the least of it, after all you've done for me. And I hate that ratty old coat of yours."

"It was Mama's."

"Yes, it looks it . . . I had another reason, Jenny. You can't go New York looking like a ragamuffin. You can't meet Mr. *Wade* looking like a ragamuffin. You want to make a good impression, don't you?"

"Certainly I do, but—"

"Then it's settled. Now open this one."

Jenny laughed. "I'm afraid to. It's probably an evening gown." Slowly, she opened the box, removing a gray wool dress with a stylishly loose, low waist and wide black velvet cuffs. Tears sprang to her eyes, for it was the first new dress she had had in eight years. "I don't know what to say," she sniffled. "It's too much."

"Jonah Wade will expect you to have a pretty dress."

"With all these fancy clothes, he'll think I don't need the job . . . No, no more," protested Jenny as Miranda held out a tiny round box. "I can't."

"Will you stop worrying about money? This present

isn't from a store; I didn't buy it. It's just something I wanted you to have."

Jenny turned the box around in her hand. After a moment she undid the wrapping and raised the lid. Nestling on a bed of tissue paper was an exquisite antique ring of latticed silver inlaid with opals. She stared at it, shaking her head from side to side. "Miranda, I can't take this. It's beautiful, but I can't."

"It's my way of saying thank you. It's kind of a special ring, Jenny. It belonged to Donald's grandmother. A gift from her parents on her sixteenth birthday. Donald said it was her favorite piece of jewlery. Not because it was worth very much, but because it had sentimental value."

"Then you mustn't give it away. It's a keepsake, a family heirloom."

"It's a ring, and I always lose rings." Miranda looked down at her hand. Her pretty shoulders rose and fell in a sigh. "I even lost my wedding ring," she said quietly. "I was heartbroken. Donald wanted to buy me another one, but I wouldn't let him. I didn't want to go through *that* again. Rings just aren't for me. And his grandmother's ring doesn't even fit . . . So it's yours now, Jenny."

She slipped it on her finger. The opals shone in the morning light and it was as if each small stone had suddenly come to life. "Thank you, Miranda. I'll take good care of it."

"At least you won't lose it!"

The jingling of the telephone silenced Jenny's reply. "I'll see who that is," she said, walking into the hall. She lifted the receiver. "Hello . . . Yes, it is . . . Really?" She smiled. *"Really?* At the price we discussed?" Her smile seemed to stretch from ear to ear. "That's wonderful news, just wonderful . . . Yes, I am, too . . . Yes, all set . . . Two weeks would be fine . . . Very happy, yes. Thank you for calling . . . And merry Christmas to you." She replaced the receiver. She took a deep breath and went back to the parlor. "There are presents for you under the tree," she said. "But this may be the best present of all: Mr. Flannagan has decided to buy the house. It's definite."

"Was that Mr. Flannagan? On *Christmas?*"

"He said his decision was a Christmas present to his family."

"And you got the price you wanted?"

"To the dollar."

Miranda leapt from her chair and threw her arms around Jenny. "I can't believe it," she cried. "No more worries. All that *lovely* money. Oh, Jenny, you did it! You did it!" She danced about the room, her eyes glowing with excitement. "We'll sell most of the furniture. Of course you'll want some of it for your flat, but we'll sell the rest. Except for Da's old desk. I wouldn't sell that for a million dollars!" She flung herself onto the loveseat, almost, but not quite, out of breath. "Da would be glad about this, I know he would. *I* am."

"I couldn't tell," said Jenny with a wry smile.

Miranda picked up their sherry glasses, giving one to Jenny. "We have to have a toast."

"If you say so."

"What shall we drink to? Let's see . . . To New York. To our tomorrows."

"To dreams," added Jenny, raising her glass.

Chapter Five

But Jenny had little time for dreams during the next two weeks. While Miranda was off bidding farewell to the neighbors, to the South Side, to the entire city of Chicago, Jenny remained at home to do the sorting and packing. She inventoried the contents of the house down to the last teaspoon and then proceded from there, deciding what would be sent to New York, what would be sold. She sought out a used-furniture dealer and argued with him over prices, again winning the argument. She tagged the scores of items. She supervised their removal, putting tiny check marks on the lists she carried everywhere. When all this was done, she rolled up her sleeves and cleaned the house from top to bottom.

Now, walking through the empty rooms, she felt a sense of loss. In this house she had found friendship and laughter and the first wary stirrings of hope. She wondered if she would find these things in New York. *New York;* all at once the idea was terrifying. Her mouth was dry as dust, her heart thumping so hard she thought it would surely burst.

"Jenny, what's the matter?"

"I don't know. I — I'm scared."

Miranda frowned "Scared of what?"

"I don't know. I guess it's just dawned on me that I'm really going to New York." Jenny held her hands out, palms down. "Look, I'm shaking."

"But you weren't scared when you came to Chicago."

"No." *I just wanted to get out of Logan Falls,* she thought to herself.

"Well, New York isn't very different from Chicago. It's

88

bigger. There are more people. But there are more opportunities, too. That's the exciting part. Think of the challenge. Think," said Miranda, marshaling her strongest argument, "of all the *money* you can earn in New York."

Jenny leaned against the wall. She wiped her moist brow, fixing her eyes on the floor. Money; yes, there was money to be made in New York, lots of it.

"Besides," continued Miranda, "you won't be alone. You'll have me and Drew. And maybe the Wades won't be *too* awful."

"Don't you mind leaving here?"

"Oh, maybe I do. A little, anyway. But it's the best thing. And it's *done*. I don't like looking back, Jenny. People who look back always see the bogeyman." Miranda tossed her head, and a swirl of coppery hair fell across her cheek. "When I was a child," she said, lowering her voice as if to confide a secret, "I was very scared of the bogeyman. I thought he lived under my bed."

Laughter broke through Jenny's panic. "Did you really?"

"It wasn't funny. Da would have to sit with me until I fell asleep. He'd read me fairy tales. Jack and the Beanstalk was his favorite, especially the part about 'Fe, fi, fo, fum, I smell the blood of an Englishmun.' He loved that. Years later, when Donald was coming to call, Da would stomp around the house *roaring* 'Fe, fi, fo, fum, I smell the blood of her Englishmun.' It was Da's joke. Donald got used to it after a while."

Jenny's panic was gone now. She smiled, and a hint of color to her face. "What would I do without your funny stories?"

"And they're all true! Mr. Sheen has the taxicab waiting outside. Are you ready, then?"

Jenny had a last look around. "Ready."

The two young women walked down the stairs. Mrs. Sheen, Drew in her arms, stood by the front door. "I hope he'll be warm enough," she said. "Trains can be drafty."

"I packed an extra sweater for him." Miranda's glance roamed the length of the hall. She frowned again. "I could swear I left the bags here. I *couldn't* have lost our luggage."

"Jack put your bags in the trunk," replied Mrs. Sheen. "And you'd best be off, or you'll miss the train."

"Do we have everything?" asked Jenny. "Miranda, do you have your check?" It was a teller's check for almost eleven thousand dollars, monies from the sweet Shop, the house, the furniture, and the last of Sean McAllister's life insurance. "Look in your purse," she urged. "Let's be sure."

"Yes, I have it."

Jenny looked in her own purse. Pinned to the lining was a teller's check for $552.64, the proceeds of her bank account. "I guess we're all set."

Miranda took Drew from Mrs. Sheen. "Such a big boy," she said, for he had outgrown his basket and many of his romper suits. "My big boy is going for a train ride!"

"With all this dawdling, you'll miss the train," warned Mrs. Sheen.

Jenny opened the door. She looked over her shoulder at Miranda. "You finally got your wish: snow." Lacy little flakes danced in the air, powdering rooftops and light poles and tree limbs. She glanced down at her new coat, at her brand new shoes. "If only it had waited another day."

Miranda pulled the blanket around Drew's neck. Beneath the blanket he wore woolen booties, a zippered sweater suit, and a knitted cap with a yellow pom-pom. "See the snow? Isn't it pretty?"

"No time for that," said Mrs. Sheen, hurrying them along.

All the Sheen children were lined up at the curb. As Jenny and Miranda neared, the children unfurled a homemade banner, the bright red letters spelling "Good Luck." They waved the banner back and forth; not to be outdone, Prince wagged his tail.

Tears splashed Miranda's cheeks . . . "I'll miss you, Mrs. Sheen, you and all your brood . . . You'll remember to feed Zelda and Scott? They like tuna fish, but they'll eat anything."

"I'll see to it, dearie. Don't worry your head. And I'll be praying for you. You, too, Jenny. I'll say the rosary every night."

90

Jenny wiped her eyes. She said good-bye to the children and to Mrs. Sheen. She took a rubber ball from her pocket and tossed it to Prince. Blinded by tears now, she turned and got into the taxicab. "I'll sit next to you, if you don't mind, Mr. Sheen."

He grinned. "Just don't go drowning me with the waterworks."

Miranda climbed into the backseat and settled Drew on her lap. The car drove off; true to her word, she did not look back. "Wait," she cried as they reached the corner, "here comes Veda. Isn't that sweet? She's come to—"

"Come to make us late," grumbled Mr. Sheen, braking the car to a halt.

Miranda rolled down the window. "Veda, you're just in time."

"I ran all the way." She pushed a package into Miranda's hands. "Sandwiches for your trip. There's some chicken and some meatloaf and it's better than you'll get on the train. I know you're in a rush, so I won't keep you. But I wanted to say good luck in New York. And I wanted to say thank you. That year's salary is going straight into a hamburger stand. I'll have my own business!"

"I'm happy for you, Veda."

"The *train*," said Mr. Sheen.

"Bye, Mrs. Wade. Bye, Jenny."

"Take care of yourself, Veda."

The cab shot away from the curb. Drew, jolted suddenly awake, began to cry. "It's all right, little darling," whispered Miranda. "Soon we'll be on a nice big train."

They arrived at the station with scarcely five minutes to spare. Mr. Sheen unloaded their luggage, passing it to a waiting redcap. After the briefest of good-byes, the race was on.

They boarded the train at one minute to twelve; at twelve, the train pulled out. Jenny fell into a seat, piling Veda's sandwiches, Mrs. Sheen's sandwiches, Miranda's purse and her own, in her lap. "It's really true," she murmured. "I'm going to New York."

It was a Saturday, the twenty-second of January; it was

91

her nineteenth birthday.

"Jenny, why didn't you *tell* me it was your birthday?"

"You know why. You would have gone out and bought me more presents."

"Well, what's wrong with that?"

Jenny smiled. She settled back in her seat and turned her head to the window. The snow was heavier now, the wind stronger. She saw small beads of ice clinging to the window frame. She looked around at the other passengers in the car. There were perhaps two dozen people, some of them reading, some of them trying to sleep. She looked again at the snow. "I hope we're not in for a blizzard."

"Stop worrying, Jenny. We're not *walking* to New York. We're safe and warm on this nice train."

"Don't you want to go to your compartment? Drew might be more comfortable."

"Oh, he's fine. Anyway, I don't want to sit by myself in that crackerbox compartment. If only we had adjoining compartments—"

"I don't *need* a compartment. A berth is good enough for me."

"And cheaper."

Laughter spilled from Jenny. "And cheaper," she agreed. "Are you hungry? Between Veda and Mrs. Sheen, we have enough sandwiches for lunch and supper. We won't have to go to the dining car."

"I'm too excited to eat. You go ahead."

Jenny did so, for she was ravenous. She ate one of Veda's meatloaf sandwiches and one of Mrs. Sheen's ham and cheese. Her eyes lit up when she discovered a box of cupcakes at the bottom of the package. She had a weakness for chocolate cupcakes.

"I saw a man selling coffee in the next car," said Miranda. "I'll get us some." Carefully, she laid Drew on the seat beside Jenny. He was deep in sleep, soothed by the gentle rhythms of the train. "I'll be right back."

Jenny finished a second cupcake. She brushed crumbs from her chin and wiped her sticky fingers on her handkerchief. She heard the wind rattling at the window. She scowled, alarmed by the thick white curtains of snow clouding the glass.

"Coffee," said Miranda, returning to her seat. "Nice and hot."

Jenny took the container. "Look at the way the snow's coming down. It's getting worse. I wonder if they'll have to stop the train."

"For a little snow? They wouldn't do that. They better not. Mr. Wade's meeting us at the station. I'd hate to keep him waiting. I want to get off on the right foot. If he's as difficult as Donald said he was . . . Well, maybe not difficult, exactly. But Donald made him sound very . . . precise."

"He can't blame you for the weather, Miranda."

She lifted Drew back on her lap. "No, I suppose not. Still, to drag him to the station at such an awful hour." She made a face. "Seven o'clock in the morning; he'll have to be up at *dawn*. And on a Sunday."

"I'm sure he won't mind. He offered to meet the train, didn't he?"

Miranda brightened. "Yes, that's true. It was his idea." She smiled down at Drew. "And he's going to meet his wonderful grandson, so that makes it worth the trouble."

They drank their coffee. After a while, Miranda put her head back and dozed. Jenny bought a New York newspaper, turning to the ads for boardinghouses. She thought of the house on South Crawford Street and her spirits sank; no matter how "clean" and "respectable" the boardinghouse, it would not have the warmth of the house she had come to love. She would be living among strangers, New York strangers at that. Once again she would be an outsider.

The train lurched and instinctively she reached her hand across to Drew. Miranda's eyes snapped open. "What was that?"

"I don't know. I wish we weren't traveling today. This terrible weather . . . I wish we could get off the train."

But Miranda was not concerned. She closed her eyes

again and drifted off to sleep.

Jenny finished reading the newspaper and put it on the seat. She tried to stretch out her legs but there was not enough room. She opened her purse and removed a slim volume of sonnets. The wind knocked at the window. The train lights flickered. The snow gathered in ever-deepening drifts. Jenny read her book.

Drew crawled around the floor of the small compartment, smiling and gurgling at each new sound. He had been fed and changed and sponged and buttoned into his pajamas, but he was not yet ready for sleep.

"Let him enjoy himself," said Miranda, looking on. "After all this exercise, he'll sleep through the night. I will, too. Trains are very soothing, don't you think?"

Jenny's glance moved to the window. The wind was a roar, the snow so dense she could see nothing beyond. "Oh yes, very soothing."

"Well, the weather could be better."

Jenny smiled, for it was a reluctant admission. "You're the one who wanted snow."

"Maybe not so much of it. The train's been going too slow." She looked at her watch. "Nine o'clock. We should be almost halfway there by now. I bet we're not. I bet we'll be late getting into New York."

Jenny finished the last cupcake, her fourth since boarding the train. She collected the crumpled boxes and bags and dropped them in the trash basket. "You could ask the conductor," she suggested.

"No, I don't want to know. I'll have nightmares about Jonah Wade waiting at the station. Mad at me even before I get off the train. I do want him to like me. At least a little bit. It would be easier all around."

"Of course he'll like you. You have a way with people." Jenny gazed down at Drew. She bent and swooped him into her arms. "You also have an irresistible son. Where is he going to sleep tonight? Should I ask the porter to make up the berth?"

"I'll make up his bed in the chair. The berth's too high.

94

But first let me give you my watch."

"Your watch?"

Miranda nodded. "I want to be up very early in the morning. You're always up with the birds anyway, so could you wake me at five?"

"Five? Are you sure?"

"Well, by the time I get Drew fed and dressed . . . By the time I get *myself* dressed . . . I want to look just right."

"Why are you so worried about Jonah Wade? You never worry about anything."

Miranda colored. "I want him to know that Donald made the right choice. Does that sound silly? Or vain? I don't mean it that way."

"I know you don't. I understand how you feel. It's natural." Drew was banging his little hand on Jenny's shoulder. She looked at him and smiled. "Are you sleepy yet? I think you are. You just won't admit it."

Miranda put the final touches to his improvised bed. "Let's see if this works." She lifted her son out of Jenny's arms and laid him amidst the pillows cushioning the sides of the chair. She turned the open side to the wall and tucked a blanket around him. "There," she said, stepping back to survey the arrangement. "He can't fall. It's a perfect fit."

"It's time I was going to bed, too."

"It's early."

"I'll read a while." Jenny fastened Miranda's watch on her wrist. "Do you really want me to wake you at five?"

"I'm afraid I'll oversleep. I could ask the porter, but he might forget. You're so reliable."

"I have character," replied Jenny, the corners of her mouth edging upward. "Good night, then. I'll see you at five."

"Sleep well."

Jenny walked through three cars to get to her berth. She drew the heavy curtain aside and climbed in. There was a single small wall lamp with a frosted glass globe, and a window with a plain green shade. In these Spartan surroundings she removed her shoes, her stockings, and her dress. She rested her head against the pillow and watched the

95

snow. She shivered, though it was not cold in the berth. After several moments she pulled the blanket to her chin and tried to sleep.

It was a few minutes before five when Jenny awakened. It was still dark outside, but even in the darkness she could see the blustering snow, the ice glinting on the window. The train seemed to be going faster. *Making up for the time we lost,* she thought, and again she felt uneasy. She struggled into her dress. Her hair was hopelessly tangled; she bunched it into a straggly, lopsided coil at the back of her head. She pulled on her stockings and grabbed her shoes. An instant later she scrambled out of the berth, half walking, half running through the hushed cars to Miranda's compartment.

She knocked at the door; to her surprise, it was opened immediately. "You're up! And dressed!"

"Yes, but I'll keel over if I don't get some coffee. Will you stay with Drew?"

"I'm sure the dining car isn't serving yet."

"That's all right. The porter told me there's a little pantry four cars down. He said I could help myself to coffee. I'll bring some back for you." Miranda glanced toward her sleeping son. "And I'll fix Drew's cereal while I'm at it. Now where did I put . . . Oh, yes, there it is." She snatched his bowl and a small box of oatmeal from the windowsill. "See, I didn't forget!"

"You're very organized this morning."

"I'm very nervous this morning. I hope Mr. Wade is worth all the fuss. I don't care that he's a stuffed shirt, but I hope he's not an ogre."

"Ten minutes with you and he'll be a lamb."

Miranda laughed, tossing her head as she went to the door.

Jenny was tired, for her sleep had been fitful. She remembered that something in a dream had frightened her, but she could not remember what that something was. She yawned. She looked at Drew, wondering if babies had dreams. She was about to straighten his blanket when she heard a tremendous gust of wind slam into the train. The

96

window burst, showering glass across the compartment. The shade, spinning crazily on the roller, slapped at the gaping hole. *"Drew,"* she cried, shielding the startled child with her body.

Roused so abruptly from sleep, he was furious. His outraged cries filled the air, but Jenny knew there was nothing to be done about it. She felt the train pick up speed. She pushed another pillow beneath Drew's head. "Dear God," she gasped, for now the train was hurtling along the icy track, out of control.

She heard screams from the other cars. She heard the piercing blast of the train's whistle. She heard the sputter and screech of brakes that would not hold. "Dear God, we're going to crash." She braced herself, tightening her grip on Drew. She had one last thought as the train jumped the track and blackness engulfed her. "Miranda," she murmured, turning her head toward the door. "Dear God, Miranda."

Chapter Six

"It was the worst thing I ever saw," said a stunned resident of tiny Cornith, New York. "There was terrible noise like bombs exploding. And then there was all the smoke, clouds of black smoke rising up from the snow. There were people screaming. Oh, you could hear them for miles. I started saying my prayers . . . I thought it was the end of the world."

If not quite the end of the world, it was nonetheless one of the worst train wrecks in history. And it had happened in the worst possible place, for Cornith had been devastated by the storm. Power lines had been downed; water mains, frozen solid, had burst. Mountainous snow drifts had blocked off long stretches of unplowed road, blocking access to the highway as well.

It had taken the two-man sheriff's department more than an hour to reach the scene of the accident. The volunteer fire department, detouring their balky fire truck across fields and pastures, had arrived even later. They had done what they could, freeing survivers from prisons of twisted, smoldering metal, using their own clothing for blankets and bandages. But despite these heroic efforts, it had been clear that the situation was beyond their slim resources. The sheriff had gone on foot to the nearest farm, where he had telephoned the state police, the Red Cross, and the forty-six-bed Mercy Hospital. "You better start setting up cots," he had warned the hospital director. "There's maybe a hundred injured here. Maybe two hundred, for all I can see in the dark. It's real bad. There's I don't know how many dead."

Rescue efforts proceeded slowly, continuing throughout the morning and into late afternoon. They were aided by townspeople who fought their way through the storm, some arriving in horse-drawn wagons, some in cars, some on skis. With them came blankets, sweaters, bed sheets, shovels, rope, anything they thought might help. By noon the entire town had arrived, young and old working side by side in the brutal cold.

The bodies of the dead were removed to several huge Red Cross tents serving as temporary morgues. Injured survivors, many suffering also from exposure, were removed to Mercy Hospital. In all the confusion, all the horror, it was the next day before the final toll was known. On Monday, an ashen railroad official announced that eighty-four people had died and two hundred people had been injured.

Some of the injuries were minor — scratches and bruises and wrenched ankles — but most were far more serious. At Mercy Hospital every room, every corridor overflowed with patients too ill to be transferred to facilities in neighboring towns. There were not enough beds, not enough linens, not enough sedatives for pain. Blood supplies were dangerously low. The staff, although supplemented with volunteers, was exhausted.

"We're doing the best we can under the circumstances," said one harried doctor. He looked down at his patient. He frowned. "I'm not worried about the broken wrist. And the leg isn't actually broken; it's more like a chip. But the pneumonia is a different matter. The medicines we have aren't very effective. We're watching her closely. We're bringing down the fever. Believe me, we're doing everything that *can* be done."

Standing with the doctor beside the bed was a portly middle-aged man. His hair was dark, silvered at the temples. His narrow face was devoid of expression. "I'll take your word for that, Dr. Cooper," he replied. "Perhaps you could tell me when there will be some change?"

"I'm sorry, I can't. Pneumonia is a tricky thing."

"I overheard a nurse say something about concussion."

Dr. Cooper nodded. "At first we thought there might be

99

concussion. Fortunately, the head injury wasn't nearly so serious. A bad bump, nothing more. All this sleeping is because of the pain medication and because of shock. The body needs time to adjust. Sleep often helps the process along."

"That's all very well, but my business is in New York City. I should be there right now. I certainly can't remain in Cornith indefinitely."

Dr. Cooper said nothing. He did not trust himself to speak.

"You see my problem, don't you Doctor?"

"I see a great many sick people, Mr. Wade. If you will forgive me, I'm inclined to rank their problems above yours."

There was a weary, disinterested shrug. "I'm simply asking for information. Can you give me any reason to remain here?"

Dr. Cooper looked again at his patient. "Your daughter-in-law," he said. "Isn't she reason enough?"

"I've already explained that she's a stranger to me. I'd never even seen her until yesterday. My wife and I were concerned about the boy, of course. But as for Miranda—"

"I'm sorry," interrupted Dr. Cooper, "I haven't time to listen to family histories. You may go or stay as you wish. I can only tell you that after such a dreadful ordeal, there should be someone here when she wakes."

"I'm willing to engage a private nurse."

"Impossible! Every nurse within two hundred miles is working around the clock as it is. I'm afraid it's either you or no one. And now I must get back to work myself."

There was no chair, no room for a chair. Jonah Wade shifted his weight slightly, staring down at the inert figure in the bed. As much as he disliked the Irish, he had always considered them a handsome people. But not this girl, he thought to himself. He saw thick black hair lying in clumps on the pillow. He saw a face too pale and too plain. Beneath the hospital blanket, he saw a heavy, shapeless body. "I don't understand," he murmured. "How could my son have married such a great lump of a girl?"

"Miranda! Miranda Wade! Wake up, Miranda Wade!"

The words came from some vast and empty distance. The voice was not familiar.

"Miranda! You must wake up now!"

A man's voice, but why is he shouting? Please stop; it hurts too much.

"Miranda!"

Why is he shouting for Miranda? Where is she?

"Miranda!"

The figure in the bed stirred. Dr. Cooper leaned closer and took his stethoscope from his pocket. "Not bad," he said, listening to the steady heartbeat. "Not bad at all . . . Now open your eyes, Miranda . . . Open your eyes . . . Come on, open your eyes . . . That's it . . . Good girl! And what pretty gray eyes," he added, flashing a light in the pupils. "A little out of focus, eh? That's all right. It's to be expected. I want you to try to follow my finger with your eyes. Good, very good. Again . . . Excellent!" He perched at the edge of the bed. He smiled. "I know you're confused. Let me help. You're in a hospital, Miranda. There was a train wreck. You have a broken wrist and a chip in the leg bone. Not a fracture, from what we can tell, but we're not taking any chances . . . You had a touch of pneumonia; that's all gone now . . . Am I talking too fast for you? Let's start at the beginning: There was a train wreck. Do you remember?"

A train. Something about a train, but what?

"You left Chicago on the noon train," continued Dr. Cooper. "It started to snow."

Snow. Union Station. We were late. We? Yes, Miranda and I and . . . "Drew?" cried Jenny as memory came rushing back.

"Your son is fine. You saved his life, shielding him the way you did. That's how you got your broken bones. But you're not to worry; you're healing very well, and your son is safe in New York City with your inlaws."

"My inlaws?"

"The Wades." Dr. Cooper laughed. "I see your memory is

101

still sketchy. That's also to be expected . . . No, Miranda, don't try to talk. I want you to save your strength. We've made a start today. That's quite enough for now."

"Jenny Por—"

"Don't upset yourself, Miranda. You and your son are fine."

"No, it's Jenny. I'm—"

"Easy now. Take it easy. I didn't want to tell you just yet . . ." Dr. Cooper paused, studying his patient. He sighed. "Perhaps it's best to have it over with. I'm sorry, Miranda. Your friend Jenny Porter died in the accident. She died instantly, if that's any consolation . . . There was some trouble with identification, but it's all been straightened out. There's no longer any question about it."

"Died?"

"I'm terribly sorry, Miranda."

He thinks I'm Miranda. But he wouldn't think that unless . . . Oh, dear God, Miranda's dead.

Dr. Cooper reached for his handkerchief and dried her tears. "It's a tragedy, I know. Still, it's best to face these things. Your whole life is ahead of you; be grateful for that. Be grateful for your son."

Jenny remembered everything now. She remembered that Miranda had gone to get coffee. She remembered the wind crashing into the side of the train like a giant fist. She remembered shattered glass flying through the air, and then the train speeding faster and faster until . . . *"No,"* she screamed, blackness engulfing her once more.

Jenny slipped in and out of consciousness during the next twelve hours. In this netherworld, she relived every moment of the train wreck. She saw twisted and grotesque images of death. She heard horrifying screams, desperate calls for help. She felt something pressing on her, a brutal, crushing weight that took all the breath from her body.

There were tears in her eyes when she awoke; her face was chalky. For the first time she noticed the plaster casts on her leg and arm. She noticed something else: the opal ring that Miranda had given her, the ring that was a Wade family heirloom. She began to understand what had happened. *They found me in Miranda's compartment,* she reflected. *They must have found Miranda's purse, too, with all Mr. Wade's letters. The Wades . . . the Wades must have seen my ring and thought I was Miranda . . . But Miranda's dead.*

She died instantly, if that's any consolation. It was not. Jenny turned her face to the wall, mourning the kind, generous young woman who had been her friend. All her anger came back, anger at life, at the random cruelty of life. A veil seemed to drop over her eyes. The line of her mouth seemed to harden, as if suddenly cast in stone.

"Oh, Mrs. Wade, you're up." A nurse in starched and immaculate white leaned across the bed, smoothing the blanket. "Dr. Cooper will be glad," she went on. "He's been worried about you, you know. Would you like a cup of broth?"

Jenny shook her head.

"Maybe later, then. Doctor will be in to see you soon. He's just having a little nap. The poor man's hardly had any sleep at all this past week. Swamped with patients, we were. But Dr. Cooper wouldn't give up. He's been working like a demon. Ever since the accident last Sunday—"

"Last Sunday?"

"Exactly a week ago today."

"I've been here a week?"

"That's right, Mrs. Wade."

"I'm not Mrs. . . ." Jenny fell silent. She knew she had to correct this terrible mistake, but she did not have the strength. Again she turned her face to the wall, watching streaks of morning sun creep toward the ceiling. "Has it stopped snowing?"

"Oh yes, days ago. Of course there'll likely be more. Winter's not done yet."

Slowly, Jenny lifted her eyes to the nurse. "How long do I have to stay here?"

"Dr. Cooper's the one to ask. We want you to be good as new when you go home."

Home. The word was like a knife pressing on Jenny's heart. I have no home, she thought, no place to go. There

103

was a sharp intake of breath as she remembered her check for $552.64, all the money she had in the world. "My purse," she cried, remembering that she had left it in the berth.

"Your father-in-law has your things, Mrs. Wade. You're lucky. A lot of people lost their belongings in the accident. I was out there that first morning to help. There was luggage and purses and clothes scattered all over. Some of it was burned; some of it was crushed. Some was found, 'cause we were looking through it for next of kin. That's how we found your father-in-law. It was just plain luck."

Luck, thought Jenny. She closed her eyes and Miranda's lovely face swam into view. "Dear God," she murmured, her voice filled with despair.

"Don't you worry," said the nurse, patting Jenny's hand. "Everything will be all right. It's not easy being in a hospital, but soon you'll be going home to your son. He's a cute little fella. Drew? Is that his name?"

"Yes." She wondered if she would ever see Drew again. The Wades wouldn't want her around. And why should they? Why should they care about a stranger?

"Well, you just keep thinking about your boy. I'll tell Dr. Cooper you're awake and he'll be in to see you. He'll have you up on crutches in no time. After a while, all you'll need is a cane."

"It doesn't matter."

"What a thing to say! Don't you want to get better?"

"I don't care anymore. Please, leave me alone."

"I'll send Dr. Cooper in to have a word with you, young lady. You need a good talking to."

But Jenny sank into a black depression, and for days she refused to talk to anyone. She refused the food that was brought, the broths and soft-boiled eggs and custards. She ignored the chatter of the other two patients in her room, ignored their visitors. When a letter came from Jonah Wade, she threw it unopened into the wastebasket.

Day after day her mind wandered back to the past. She counted not her blessings but her losses, beginning with the loss of her childhood. From there, her mind moved on to the neat white headstones in Good Shepherd Methodist Cemetery, and from there, to a train speeding along an icy track. She had lost Miranda, her only friend. Now she would lose Drew. *No,* her heart cried, *not Drew; please not Drew.*

But an idea had been drifting through her mind, an idea as fragile and elusive as a cloud. Something in it frightened her, though each day she pulled it a little closer, giving it focus, making it real. The boldness of the idea nearly took her breath away, yet she knew that in one respect it was simple, for the groundwork had already been laid. *Everybody thinks I'm Miranda,* she told herself, mustering her courage. *Well then, I'll be Miranda. No one has to know the truth. I'll be Miranda and let Jenny Porter rest in peace.*

Could she? Could she so easily cast off her identity and become someone else? Lying in her hospital bed in the small blue-black hours of night, she pondered this question. The answer was always the same: she had no family, no friends, no money, no job, no prospects. She had nothing; her identity meant nothing. A new identity would mean a new life.

Her nagging, scolding conscience merely stiffened her resolve, for she believed she was owed some happiness; it was a debt, a debt that would be paid. *I'll probably never have a husband,* she thought, *but I'll have a son: Andrew McAllister Wade.* And that, finally, settled the matter.

She knew she would have to be very careful; nothing must go wrong. She knew she could not look back. *People who look back always see the bogeyman.*

Jenny Porter ceased to exist. There was still a young woman with straggly black hair and beautiful gray eyes and bitten fingernails, but now she answered to the name Miranda Wade. The doctors were pleased with her progress, the nurses with her cooperation. She did her exercises, ate all the food that was placed before her, drank the daily eggnogs that were supposed to build up her strength. She was cheerful, almost sunny. Despite the cast on her wrist, she managed to scribble a letter to Jonah Wade. "I

105

can't wait to hold my son in my arms again," her letter read in part. "I'm counting the days till I leave here. Don't let Drew forget me. Tell him Mama sends a big kiss!"

"Well, Miranda," said Dr. Cooper on a cold morning at the end of February, "today's the day. Are you excited?"

"I can hardly believe it. I was beginning to think I'd never get out of here."

"I had my doubts, too. You were a difficult patient at first. But then you seemed to make up your mind to let us help you."

"Yes, that's it exactly," replied the new Miranda with a smile. "I made up my mind."

"And when you did, we were home free." Dr. Cooper looked at his watch. "Time to go. Are you ready?" He helped her to her feet. She was wearing a plain dark-blue dress that had been sent from Wade & Company. A smaller cast had been fitted to her wrist, and a smaller walking cast to her leg. The nurse had brushed her hair into a tight coil at the back of her neck. "Here's your cane, Miranda. Remember: slow, short steps."

"My coat." The plain navy wool coat had also been sent from Wade & Company. "Could you—"

"I'll bring it along. Just watch where you're going. This is no time to be careless."

Miranda said good-bye to her two roommates and then turned toward the door. She hobbled into the corridor, her shoulders slightly stooped.

"Excellent," declared Dr. Cooper, observing her steady advance to the elevator. "Don't be afraid to put your weight on the cane. That's what it's for."

"I'm only afraid it will break. I must have gained ten pounds since I've been here. All those eggnogs . . ."

"The cane won't break, I assure you. Lean down on it, Miranda. That's right. That's fine. I don't want too much pressure on the leg. You'll have to take it easy when you get home. Don't overdo. In a few weeks your doctor will remove the cast, and in a few months you won't be able to tell you had a broken leg . . . There's the great advantage of youth," added Dr. Cooper, laughing. "Everything heals so

106

quickly."

No, not everything, thought Miranda. Cautiously, she stepped into the elevator, Dr. Cooper following behind. "I don't know how to thank you," she said. "You've been very kind to me. And very patient. I'm sorry for the trouble I caused."

"All in a day's work. No one likes being in the hospital. It's not pleasant. If you'll take my advice, you'll put all of this out of your mind. Think of it as a bad dream and start your life afresh."

"Oh, yes, Dr. Cooper, that's just what I plan to do."

He did not notice the defiant thrust of her chin, the sudden tightening of her mouth. He kept his eyes on the door, and when it opened, he moved aside to let her pass. "You're really managing quite well. You can be proud of yourself."

"Thank you, Doctor." She glanced around the lobby, small and clean and deserted at this early hour. Through the glass doors of the entrance she saw a long gray Pierce-Arrow parked in front "That must be for me. Mr. Wade's letter mentioned something about a Pierce-Arrow."

"It will be far more comfortable than the train."

"Oh, I never want to see another train. Never."

"I'll walk out with you," said Dr. Cooper, holding the door open. "Slow, short steps," he warned.

The sun was bright, the sky a deep, cloudless blue. A cool breeze was blowing; Miranda resisted the urge to smooth wisps of hair from her brow. She held on to the cane and kept walking, her eyes measuring each step. When she looked up, she saw the car door open. She saw a young woman emerge, a tall, striking young woman with a delicately chiseled profile and exquisite platinum hair worn in a long, thick braid. Miranda was startled by this glorious apparition. She looked quickly at Dr. Cooper, as if for reassurance. "That couldn't be Mrs. Wade? Not *Daphne* Wade?"

"I think it's Miss Olsen, your traveling companion. She telephoned yesterday to confirm the details. Don't worry, Miranda. I'm sure she's very nice." They reached the car. Dr. Cooper held out his hand. "Miss Olsen?"

"Lily." She turned; only then did they see the large purple

birthmark that disfigured the otherwise perfect face. It covered her cheek like some strange and hideous mask. "Everybody calls me Lily."

Miranda blushed, ashamed at herself for staring. Another one of life's cruel jokes, she thought.

"Well, Lily," said Dr. Cooper, finding his voice, "here's the patient. I leave her in your hands."

"Glad to meet you, Mrs. Wade."

"Oh, it's Miranda."

"It's Mrs Wade to me," replied Lily with a brief smile. "I'm just the housemaid. The other Mrs. Wade wouldn't like me taking liberties." She pointed to the man sitting behind the wheel of the car. "That's Malcolm Gill. He works at the store, but he does special errands for Mr. Wade, too." She paused, studying Miranda: "If there's anything you don't want repeated," she said finally, "you'd best keep it to yourself when Malcom Gill's around."

Miranda was grateful for the warning. She smiled. "Thank you, Lily. It's kind of you to tell me."

"I have no use for people who carry tales. Now let me help you into the car before you catch your death. Take your time getting in; there's no rush."

"Good-bye, Dr. Cooper. Thank you again."

"Good-bye, Miranda. And good luck to you."

"I'll need it," she murmured. She bent, inching her way into the car. She settled her good leg firmly on the floor and rested her other leg on the pillow that Lily provided. She arranged her coat over her lap and leaned back. "There, that wasn't so bad."

Lily climbed in beside her. She reached across to the front seat and withdrew a fluffy wool shawl. "For your shoulders," she explained. "So you don't get a chill."

"It's nice and warm in here."

"Malcolm Gill keeps his window down while he's driving."

"No law against it," came a surly voice from the front seat.

Lily stuck out her tongue, an unexpected and childish gesture that made Miranda laugh.

"I saw what you did, Lily Olsen. Saw it right in my mirror. You're a nasty girl. I always said that; a nasty girl."

She shrugged. "No law against it."

Muttering to himself, Malcolm Gill started the car.

Lily smiled at Miranda. "The doctor said you wanted to go somewhere before we headed to New York."

"Yes." She took a slip of paper from the pocket of her dress. "It's — it's a cemetery. Dr. Cooper wrote out the directions. It's not far . . . I hope you don't mind."

"It's all the same to me. Here, Malcolm, here's the directions to where Mrs. Wade wants to go."

He tore the paper from her hand. He was about to speak, but glancing again in the mirror, he clamped his mouth shut. There was silence in the car as they drove to the cemetery. Miranda gazed out the window, thinking that Cornith was a pretty town, much prettier than Logan Falls. *But you have to forget Logan Falls,* she chided herself an instant later. *That's in the past; Jenny's past, not yours.*

Handsome wrought-iron gates enclosed All Saints' Cemetery. The grounds were spacious and well-kept; the flat grave markers were aligned in neat rows. There were narrow white benches spaced along the graveled paths. There was a graceful marble fountain, water spilling from the folded hands of an angel.

Miranda and Lily were directed to a path at the left of the fountain. It was a short walk, but a difficult one for Miranda. Several times her cane skidded on the gravel; each time Lily caught her arm, steadying her. "There's no rush, Mrs. Wade. Just take it nice and easy."

"I hate cemeteries."

"We can leave."

"No. No, I have to do this." Miranda's somber gaze moved over the grave markers. Her heart began to pound. She drew a breath, dreading this final good-bye.

"Here it is," said Lily.

Miranda turned her head. She read the inscription:

Jenny Porter
1907–1926
In God's Care

Tears burned her eyes, her throat. Her hand tightened on the cane, for she felt faint. She wanted to pray but the words would not come. In some far corner of her mind she saw a blur of copper hair, heard a rustle of silk. "Good-bye," she whispered as tears streaked her cheeks. "Good-bye, my friend." She stared at the grave a moment longer. *Forgive me,* she silently added.

Part II

Chapter Seven

Miranda leaned as close to the car window as her cast would allow. "So this is New York," she said for the third time. "I'm really here." It was early afternoon and the streets were crowded with people. She noticed how quickly they walked, how confident they seemed. When the traffic light changed, they surged across the avenue in a wave, strangers united only by destination. She noticed the women, for they were well dressed, all of them wearing hats and gloves, some of them wearing fur coats atop their stylish dresses. "Is everyone in New York rich?"

"There's rich and poor," replied Lily. "If we'd come the other way, you'd be looking at slums. But there's no slums around here. Look at the houses; you can always tell by the houses."

Miranda looked. She saw tall apartment buildings, uniformed doormen standing guard outside. As the car turned a corner, she saw rows of lovely brownstones, their windows draped with silk. The car turned again and she saw a long avenue of stores and restaurants; farther south were huge office buildings thronged with people rushing in and out. It was as if the whole city changed from street to street, as if a hundred different cities existed side by side. The shifting sights and sounds mesmerized her. She watched taxicabs swerve around lumbering buses and delivery trucks. She watched newsboys hawking their papers on street corners. She watched a man walking a scaffold ten stories off the ground. She watched a woman parading a dog on a rhinestone-studded leash. *So this is New York.* Her hands were shaking; she was not surprised, for there was a

113

feeling of excitement here, a swagger that quickened the blood. "It's a wonderful city," she exclaimed. "I'm dizzy just looking at it all . . . Is it true that most New Yorkers were born someplace else?"

"Probably. People are always coming here to make their fortune. My father came from Sweden. He thought he'd find gold in the streets." Lily shrugged. "All he found were horse droppings. That was his first job — cleaning up after the horses. Now he has a tobacco shop in Yorkville. That's uptown. You'll get to know the different neighborhoods. 'Course the only neighborhood you really have to know is Murray Hill."

"Is that where we're going?"

Lily's pale-blue gaze strayed to the window. "We're almost there."

I'm not ready, thought Miranda. Her smile faded. Her eyes darted about the car, as if seeking escape. But there was no escape. She had made her decision and now she was in a car on her way to Murray Hill. *God help me,* she murmured to herself.

Murray Hill was one of the city's loveliest residential areas. There were a few large apartment buildings on the avenues, but the tree-shaded side streets were lined with gracious old brownstones and town houses. It was a quiet area, for there were less than a dozen small shops scattered about; there was only one restaurant: Miss Rose's Tearoom, which closed promptly at six o'clock each night. Murray Hill was said to be clannish, and there was some truth to that; most of the houses had been in the same families for fifty years or more.

The Wade town house, a four-story graystone residence of Georgian design, dated to the Civil War. Electricity had been added around the turn of the century, and modern plumbing ten years later. The house was otherwise unchanged, a fact in which Jonah Wade took great pride. Jonah Wade disliked change.

"Mr. Wade's probably at the store now," said Lily as she helped Miranda out of the car. "I'm sure Mrs. Wade is here. She knew we'd be coming about this time."

114

"Drew — it's Drew I want to see."

"Well, he's probably here. His nurse takes him for an outing every afternoon, but she probably kept him home today."

Miranda turned. She looked at the house and all at once she felt safe, as if she had found a haven. "It's beautiful, Lily. I — I never thought I'd live in a house like this."

But Lily had switched her attention to Malcolm Gill. "You locked Mrs. Wade's coat in the car," she said. "Would you mind unlocking the door? Or is it too much trouble?"

He spun around and then took a step back. Lily was at least a head taller than he, and broader in the shoulders. "Mind your tone with me," he warned, although not very convincingly. He unlocked the door.

She reached into the car and grabbed the coat. "Thanks," she said, brushing past him. "Let's get you inside, Mrs. Wade. It's cold out here."

"Thank you for driving me, Malcolm."

"Don't bother about him, Mrs. Wade. The less you have to do with him, the better . . . Here, just let me get the door." They entered into a long foyer. To the right was a cloakroom containing a brass umbrella stand, several umbrellas, a few pairs of overshoes, and a man's raincoat. Directly ahead was a curved, narrow staircase, the newel posts inlaid with mother-of-pearl. To the left of the staircase were two closed doors. "That's where the Wades used to have their Sunday musicales," explained Lily. "And that's what they call the powder room. It's a bathroom without the tub." She looked at Miranda, looked at the cane, looked at the stairs. "We'll go very slow," she said. "I'll be behind you, in case you slip."

"I'm sorry to be such—"

"Don't worry about me, Mrs. Wade; keep your eyes on the steps. There's no rush."

One hand gripping her cane, the other hand gripping the banister, Miranda carefully ascended the stairs. "This is harder than I thought," she said, halfway to the landing.

"You're doing fine."

She was out of breath when they reached the landing.

She felt the perspiration beading her forehead, her upper lip. "I must be a sight. It's no way to meet Mrs. . . . to meet my mother-in-law."

"You better sit down and rest. Here's the living room. No, this door here. Take your time."

Miranda hobbled along. She came to an abrupt stop when she entered the living room, for she thought it the most beautiful room she had ever seen. She gazed around at the creamy walls, the pale silk draperies that seemed to drift like clouds about the windows. She stared at the couch and chairs covered in soft shades of rose and bottle-green. She stared at the tiny velvet footstools, at the slender tables shining as brightly as mirrors. After a moment her gaze settled upon a trio of small rosewood tables laden with delicate porcelain owls and sparrows and swans. "Oh, how lovely."

"Mrs. Wade calls that her aviary," said Lily. "Mrs. Wade likes birds. All kinds of birds . . . Sit down and I'll see if she's home. Take the green chair; it's the softest one."

Miranda lowered herself into the chair. "Could you see about Drew? It's been such a long time. I just want to hold him again."

"I'll ask Mrs. Wade." Lily slipped out of her coat and folded it over her arm. She went to the door. "It's going to be confusing around here with two Mrs. Wades."

Miranda plucked her handkerchief from her pocket and wiped her face. She dropped her cane, bent to pick it up, and bumped her elbow. She pulled her arm back and nearly toppled a fragile glass canary. When she steadied the canary, she dropped her handkerchief.

"What a nervous girl you are."

Miranda's head swiveled around. She blinked, for standing in the doorway was a woman of breathtaking beauty. "I . . . I . . ."

"You're Miranda," said the woman, her voice silky. She glided across the room and sat at the edge of a small gilt chair. "I'm Daphne Wade. Don't try to stand; it's quite all right. I've never had a broken leg, you know. Of course my brother *did* once have a broken nose. A fight, I think. But

116

that was long ago." She smiled, gathering her hands in her lap.

Miranda did not know what to say. She had pictured Daphne Wade as a matronly woman, a wealthy New York version of Mrs. Sheen. But there was nothing matronly about Daphne Wade. Her hair was fashionably short, gleaming chestnut curls dancing around her oval face. Her eyes were topaz, fringed with thick, dark lashes. She had a small, perfect nose and a sensuous mouth enhanced by the faintest touch of rose-colored lip rouge. Her figure was lithe, clad in a short, expensive dress of pale silk charmeuse. Her superb legs were clad in sheer silk stockings. Pearls shimmered at her ears, at her lovely throat. She was in her forties; she looked years younger. "You're Daphne Wade?"

The question seemed to bewilder her. "Why, yes," she said after a pause. "Yes, I am. I was Daphne Frazier before I married," she added, as if this bit of information removed all doubt.

"It's — I'm very happy to meet you, Mrs. Wade."

"Daphne. My husband feels you should call us by our Christian names."

"Thank you."

"I suppose you're tired after your trip."

"I'd like to see Drew. He's all I've been able to think about."

"I'm afraid Nurse has taken him for his afternoon outing. Fresh air is so good for children. So bracing."

Impatience mingled with disappointment in Miranda's eyes. "When will he be back?"

"At three. Nurse *was* going to keep him in today, but my husband feels strongly about schedules . . . Like the postman," continued Daphne. "The postman always keeps to an exact schedule."

Miranda frowned. "The postman? I don't think I understand."

"Well, it's a matter of routine, isn't it? When routines are upset . . ." She shrugged.

"Yes? When routines are upset?"

117

"It makes life so terribly complicated," replied Daphne. "We do try to avoid complications. Every day is the same, you see. There isn't any fuss about anything."

"It sounds very — very comfortable."

"Comfortable. Yes, that's exactly the right word."

"I wanted to thank you for inviting Drew and me to live here. I promise we won't bother you. Drew is such a good little boy."

"Is he?" Daphne tilted her head to one side. "Of course I wouldn't know. All babies seem very much alike to me. Our neighbors, the Selkirks, have a baby."

Miranda was not sure what to say to this. She was not sure about anything, for she was confused by Daphne's manner. It was polite and yet uninterested, friendly and yet remote. It was utterly without emotion.

Miranda tried to shift around in the chair but her casts weighed her down. She was aware of Daphne's eyes on her, aware of the deepening silence. She cleared her throat. "This is a beautiful house."

"My husband will be pleased."

"Pleased?"

"That you think so." Daphne rose and glided serenely to the door. "Lily will show you your room. It's quite pleasant . . . People have different tastes in wallpaper," she added, disappearing into the hall.

Wallpaper? Miranda frowned. A strange conversation, she thought. Daphne had not mentioned her late son; there had been no questions, no curiosity. Certainly there had been no words of welcome. Miranda had wanted to make a good impression; now she wondered if she had made any impression at all.

Lily returned to the living room. Like many tall people, she ducked her head as she passed through the door. "Sorry your son isn't here," she said. "But it's only another hour to wait. Meanwhile I'll take you to your room."

Miranda struggled out of the chair. "Is Mrs. Wade a little . . . vague?"

"You could say that."

"And Mr. Wade?"

"He's pretty definite about things. Wants everything done in a certain way . . . Let me help you. There's more stairs. The bedrooms are one flight up."

Miranda noticed that Lily never smiled. She glanced again at the ugly birthmark and her heart went out to the girl. "I must be keeping you from your chores."

"It's okay, Mrs. Wade. I'm going to be looking after you for a while. Mr. Wade is paying me extra. I saw to that."

Miranda laughed. "You're very blunt, aren't you?"

"I have no use for people who talk out of both sides of their mouth."

"No, of course not. I only meant—"

"Let me take you upstairs, Mrs. Wade. You'll be more comfortable in your own room."

My own room, thought Miranda, looking around. There was a charming old spool bed covered with a silk spread, a chair covered with pale-yellow chintz. There was a double dresser, and opposite, a vanity table with a dainty silk skirt. On the nightstand was a porcelain lamp with a tulip shade. A fluffy white rug stretched out before the hearth. "It's wonderful," she said. She hobbled over to the chair and sat down. "It's wonderful, but it makes me feel clumsy. What if I break something? What if I spill something?"

"Mrs. Wade wouldn't care. Mr. Wade's fussy about his things, especially if they're old. Mr. Wade's grandfather bought a lot of the stuff in this house. In this room," added Lily, pointing to the bed and the lamp. "I guess they're antiques."

"That's what worries me."

"I'll be sleeping in here till you can get around by yourself. Malcom Gill's bringing a cot down from the attic."

"Lily, you can't sleep on a cot. You're too tall; you'll be hanging over the sides."

"I'll manage."

"But—"

"It's part of the arrangement, Mrs. Wade. And now I'd better bring you a tray. Dinner isn't till seven."

"I'm too nervous to eat. I wish Drew were here. Miss Dent? Is that the nurse's name?"

119

Lily nodded. "She's nice, not like some of them who go around with their noses in the air. She knows her job, too. I'll get your tray now, Mrs. Wade. Do you take coffee or tea?"

"Coffee, thank you."

Lily hung Miranda's coat in the closet. "Mr. Wade had some things sent from the store, by the way. Some dresses. There's underwear and nightgowns in the chest of drawers." She went to the door. "I won't be long, but watch yourself getting up. The floors were waxed yesterday."

"I'll be careful." Miranda glanced down at the parquet floor; like everything else in the house, it sparkled. She wondered how many servants there were, how many servants it took to keep all these treasures shined and polished and swept. She smiled, certain that Daphne Wade had never touched a dustpan. After a while, her glance moved to the wallpaper. She laughed, for she saw more birds: tiny yellow doves on a field of white. "Are there any real birds in the house?" she asked when Lily came back.

"No, Mr. Wade wouldn't allow it." She put the tray on the dresser. She turned. "No birds or dogs or cats. Too messy for the furniture. I heard Cook say that Mr. Donald had a turtle once."

"Mr. Donald?"

Lily stood very still. "Your late husband, Mrs. Wade."

Miranda blushed bright red. *Idiot,* she said to herself. *Remember where you are, and* who *you are.* "Sorry, I wasn't thinking."

"It may not be true, about the turtle. Cook's getting old. Sometimes she confuses things."

"It doesn't matter."

"No, I guess not . . . There's a ham sandwich on the tray. And some fruit cup. That should hold you till dinner."

"Maybe I'll be hungry after I see Drew. What time is it?"

Lily pulled out the drawer of the night stand. "Mr. Wade brought this back from the hospital. Your wristwatch; it has your initials on it."

"Yes, my watch. I'd forgotten about it. I mean, I thought it was smashed in the accident." She held it to her ear. She

120

smiled. "Still ticking. Have you been keeping it wound?"

Lily nodded again. "That's the way it is around here. Mr. Wade wants everything done right, even the small things."

"That must be hard on you."

"I'm used to it. Would you like some coffee before it gets cold?"

"Yes, I think I would. Have some with me."

"I take my meals and my coffee in the kitchen, Mrs. Wade."

"Another of Mr. Wade's rules?" There was no reply. Miranda leaned her head against the chair, wondering how she would fare with the difficult Jonah Wade. She had imagined that he would resemble the men pictured in the business pages of newspapers: solid, prosperous, a little smug. She had not imagined a tyrant ruling over every detail of his household.

"Cream and sugar?"

"What? Oh, yes, thank you . . . Thank you," said Miranda, taking the cup from Lily. She sipped her coffee. "It's good."

"Cook makes good coffee."

"How long have you been here?"

"Four years. I tried working in my father's shop, but I didn't like it. I'm better off on my own. I have my own room upstairs. I have my privacy. And I'm saving my money."

"A nest egg?"

"You could say that."

"Tell me if I'm being nosy. I don't mean to pry."

"We're going to be spending some time together, Mrs. Wade, but we can't be friends. I'm just the housemaid."

"What difference does that make?"

"A big difference," replied Lily. She took Miranda's cup and returned it to the tray. "Anyhow, I don't need any friends."

"Everybody needs—"

"I think I hear Miss Dent." Lily poked her head out the door. "They're coming upstairs," she called over her shoul-

121

der. "Miss Dent and Drew . . . Miss Dent? Miranda Wade is here. Would you bring the baby in?"

"Is Drew coming?"

"Miss Dent is bringing him now."

Miranda turned, her eyes fastened on the door. "Drew," she cried as his nurse carried him into the room. "*Drew.*"

"Shall I put him in your lap, Mrs. Wade?"

"Please . . . Oh, what a big boy you are. You've grown so much." Miranda kissed his golden head; she hugged him so tightly he started to cry. "It's all right, my little darling. Mama's here now. Mama's here."

"What did you think of her?" asked Jonah Wade, sitting down behind the desk in his study. "That great lump of a girl."

"She seemed quite anxious to please," replied Daphne. "She seemed very willing."

"I don't doubt she's *willing*. That's how she trapped Donald." Jonah's dark eyes went to the portrait above the mantel, a portrait of Daphne cradling her infant son. "I had such hopes for him. I had so many plans."

"Yes," murmured Daphne sympathetically.

"Why did he throw it all away? And for her. For that great lump. I'll never understand. Never in a million years."

"Well, at least there's Drew."

"*An*drew, my pet." Jonah gazed at his wife and his face softened. "You look far too young to be a grandmother."

"Because you take such wonderful care of me." Daphne had spoken those words, or a variation of those words, every day for the past twenty-six years. She had long since stopped wondering if they were true; she knew only that Jonah expected to hear them. "You spoil me."

"Of course I do," he heartily concurred. "I have good reason; you're my most cherished possession."

Daphne's hands fluttered prettily in her lap. An enigmatic smile shadowed her mouth. "You always say the sweetest things, Jonah. I do hope you'll be sweet to Miranda. I don't know if she likes the wallpaper."

He ignored this last remark, for over the years he had inured himself to his wife's odd turns of mind. "I'll be civil to the girl. She is, after all, a guest in my home. I won't promise more than that. I don't see how I can. The Irish are so . . . Irish. Impossible people."

"Andrew is partly Irish."

"Bah! I'll soon cure him of that! He'll be raised the proper way. A proper, respectable upbringing will overcome any McAllister traits he may have. The important thing is that he will be prepared to take his place at Wade and Company."

"The reverend Smithers says we must all be prepared. Death is such an unpleasant subject. His sermons . . ."

"Andrew won't make Donald's mistakes. No foolish notions for him."

"No," murmured Daphne.

Jonah turned to the mail stacked neatly on his desk. He put letters and invitations to one side; there were several bills, and these he scrutinized, his brows knitting together as he read. "I see the Water Department has raised its rates again. Thievery, that's what it is. They must think I'm a millionaire!"

"I'm sure they don't mean any harm."

"They mean to steal my money, that's what they mean. Well, it can't be helped. We can hardly do without water." Jonah took a heavy gold watch from his pocket. He opened the case and then snapped it shut. "I suppose I had better see Miranda now."

"She's waiting outside. I asked Lily to have her ready at six. It's twenty past."

Jonah nodded. "Yes. Yes, I suppose there's no avoiding it. Miranda will have to know what's expected of her. It's best to have everything clear from the start."

"You won't be too *grim*, Jonah?"

He stared into his wife's beautiful topaz eyes. He smiled. "Do you actually like this girl, my pet?"

"I think it must be very hard for her. She's been through such a terrible experience. And now she's in a strange city. She's so alone. A waif."

"Hardly that," laughed Jonah, "but I will keep your concern in mind'

Daphne rose from her chair. "You're a wonderful husband," she said, turning toward the door.

Jonah's eyes followed her out. He watched the sway of her hips beneath the pale silk, the stride of her shapely legs. *Yes,* he thought to himself, *my most cherished possession.* His smile disappeared when Miranda limped into the room. He saw what he had seen in the hospital — lifeless black hair straggling around a plain face, a heavy, awkward body, plump hands without the slightest grace. He sighed. "I'm Jonah Wade."

"It's very nice to meet you."

"Sit down, Miranda."

She limped to a chair and stumbled into it. "I'm still clumsy with this cane," she explained, coloring. "I—I wanted to thank you for taking care of Drew."

"*An*drew."

"But he's always been called Drew."

"In my house, he will be called *An*drew. That was my grandfather's name. Surely you know the family history."

"I don't know as much as I should," replied Miranda. She sensed it was the right answer, for some of the fierceness left Jonah's face. "I want Drew — Andrew — to know all about his people."

"A sensible attitude."

"Thank you."

"I hope you're sensible about other things as well."

Miranda said nothing, although her eyes remained on Jonah. He looked like the prosperous businessman he was; unlike Daphne, he looked his age and perhaps a few years more. The stern line of his mouth made her uneasy.

"We can't change the past," he continued. "We can, however, reach a sensible arrangement for the future. An understanding, if you will. I've already had Andrew christened in our Episcopal church; he will of course be raised in our faith. You will also be expected to attend services with us. I won't have any Papist trappings in my house — no mumbling over beads, no religious statues hid-

124

den in your room. Is that clear?"

Miranda nodded. "You don't have to worry, Mr. Wade; I'm not a Catholic. I mean, not anymore. I'm lapsed." Once again she sensed that was the right answer. She took a breath and sat back.

"You may call me Jonah."

"Thank you, Jonah."

He removed several papers from a drawer and laid them on his desk. "We come now to the matter of finances. Whatever you may think, I'm not a wealthy man. It's true we live comfortably, but I do not squander money. A penny saved is a penny earned. You will be expected to follow that advice."

"I'm very thrifty." Miranda could not help smiling, for it was a truthful answer. "I hate to waste money."

Jonah was pleasantly surprised. He studied Miranda, thinking that there might be something to this young woman after all. She had not disagreed with his views, had not tried to put herself forward; in the circumstances, he thought he might be able to forgive her unfortunate appearance. "It seems we have a meeting of minds," he conceded. "That's all to the good. It saves tedious explanations." He glanced at the papers on his desk. "I assume you know that most of your belongings were lost in the accident."

"Yes. They told me the whole luggage compartment was smashed to pieces."

"The whole rear section of the train was smashed to pieces. Damages were less severe in other sections." Jonah frowned. "It was rather haphazard. Your wrist was broken, but your wristwatch was unharmed. When they found your handbag, the lining was in shreds, but your papers were in perfect condition. Fortunately, because your check was recovered. Almost eleven thousand dollars, Miranda. That is a considerable sum of money."

"It's not mine. I mean, I . . . I planned to set it aside for Drew. For his future. I planned to put it in the bank for him."

"An excellent plan, but what about your own expenses? I

125

won't ask you to contribute to your room and board here; I feel that would be wrong. But you will have other expenses. You've already *had* large sums spent in your behalf. The hospital bills were shocking. They charged for every little thing, even aspirin tablets. Of course I insisted upon a complete accounting."

"Yes. Of course." Miranda was beginning to understand Jonah Wade. He reminded her of all the pompous penny-pinching men on Glenwood Road, men whose opinions were inflexible and absolute. She thought about the check. The money was rightfully Drew's, but she knew she could not argue the point. "And of course it wouldn't be fair for you to pay my hospital bills. You can take whatever it cost from the check."

Jonah smiled. He was starting to like this girl, this great lump Miranda.

"There's one thing, though."

"Yes?"

"Well, I was thinking . . . That money was from the sale of the house and the shop. It's sort of an inheritance — Andrew's inheritance from his grandfather."

Jonah's eyes narrowed suspiciously. "Yes? Yes, go on."

"Well, I was thinking that when the time was right, I could get a job and pay the money back to Drew's account. He'd still have his inheritance, and I'd be paying my own way . . . if you wouldn't mind."

"Mind? On the contrary, I admire your attitude. It's a sign of a good character. Some young women in your situation might come looking for charity. For a life of leisure on *my* hard-earned money. Far better to work, Miranda. Far better."

She smiled. "I'm glad you agree."

"Indeed I do. You may depend on me to do my part. When the time is right, I promise to find you a suitable position at Wade & Company. I can't offer any special treatment, but you will be given an opportunity. A foot in the door, so to speak."

"It's kind of you, Jonah. Thank you."

"Not at all. I believe we understand each other,

Miranda."

"Oh, yes, I'm sure we do." She watched him basking in the warm glow of his own benevolence; he had done his good deed and now he was puffed up like a pigeon. She thought of her father fighting losing battles against men such as Jonah Wade. Silently, she vowed that she would not make the same mistake. She would choose her battles carefully, and she would win. "I'm relieved it's turned out this way, Jonah."

"We've made a fine start."

"I wanted to ask you about—about my friend Jenny Porter. There were . . . arrangements. The cemetery, the gravestone. Did you pay for that?"

Jonah shook his dark head. "Certainly not! The railroad saw to those expenses. I provided information to the hospital; they dealt with the railroad people. I told them Jenny Porter had no one. That's what you wrote in your letters and that's what I told them." He frowned again. "There wasn't any mistake about that? There wasn't a relative somewhere?"

"No, no relatives. Jenny was alone in the world."

"Lucky for the railroad. They were spared a lawsuit."

"Not so lucky for Jenny."

"The world is filled with unfortunate creatures," replied Jonah. He shrugged. "One can hardly worry about them all. It's nearly dinnertime, Miranda. Shall we go in?"

The dining room was a palette of rich blues and greens. Silver twinkled on the long sideboard. The table was dressed with an ivory cloth, set with ivory china banded in blue. A bowl of winter roses sat at the center of the table, directly below a small crystal chandelier. It was an elegant room, timeless. Miranda thought it had probably looked this way fifty years ago, would probably look this way fifty years in the future. She smiled at Daphne, who fit the room as she herself did not; gingerly, she took a seat. "I love your house," she blurted.

Daphne blinked. "Do you? How nice." She picked up a tiny silver bell and rang it once. Almost immediately, Lily entered. "We're ready now, Lily."

"Yes, Mrs. Wade."

Dinner was brought: a clear soup slivered with mush-rooms, a green salad, a roast of beef with glazed potatoes and pearl onions. Jonah carved the roast, arranging paper-thin slices at one end of the platter, and thick slabs at the other. Daphne took the thinnest slice; she took a single potato, a single onion, a single roll.

Miranda's spirits sank, for she knew she would have to be polite and follow Daphne's example. She stared at the roast, at the velvety gravy, at the crusty rolls still hot from the oven. Her mouth watering, she stared at the butter; Daphne had not taken any butter.

Jonah's dark brows drew together. "Are you window shopping, Miranda?"

"I'm sorry," she said, color rushing to her cheeks. "It's just that everything looks so good."

"It *is* good. I'll match our cook against anybody's. Fine meals and no waste in the kitchen."

Miranda's eyes shifted to his plate. She smiled, for it was heaped with food. Encouraged, she took a hearty cut of meat, a hearty portion of vegetables, and two rolls. "It's delicious," she exclaimed. *"Delicious."*

"Of course it is," replied Jonah. He glanced sidelong at this new daughter-in-law, observing her eager attack on her food. It's no wonder she's fat, he thought, stuffing a potato into his mouth.

Dessert was a chocolate soufflé, the first soufflé Miranda had ever tasted. She savored each bite, rolling the choco-late around on her tongue. She had taken only a few bites when she wondered if Lily would bring seconds. *Don't be a pig,* she scolded herself, though she scraped every last bit of chocolate from her bowl.

Coffee was served with a tray of mint wafers. Daphne took neither sugar nor cream in her coffee; she accepted a mint, nibbling like a mouse around the edges.

Miranda watched. "Now I see how you stay so slim, Daphne."

Her lovely hand seemed to freeze in midair. "How?" she

128

asked, as if she had been puzzling over this mystery.

"Well," replied Miranda, smiling, "you don't eat very much, do you?"

"Food? No, I suppose I don't. I don't think about it. Of course when I was younger . . . There were so many picnics when I was a girl. Picnic food is rather nice. Or perhaps it's being in the outdoors that's nice. I spent my childhood in Connecticut. Until I was twelve, and then we moved to New York. It was quite an exciting time. Four years later I met Jonah." Daphne dropped her napkin on the table. "Now you know all about us."

Not all, thought Miranda. She could not imagine two more different people than Daphne and Jonah. She wondered what had brought them together. She was about to ask how they had met when Daphne rose from the table. She rose also, hobbling after the Wades into the hall. They went to the living room. A fire had been laid in the hearth, the leaping flames casting golden shadows on the parquet floor. The lamps had been lighted; Jonah's humidor had been placed on a table beside a crystal brandy decanter. Here, she thought to herself, was complete serenity, an ordered and untroubled way of life. She envied the Wades their life; with a start, she realized she was part of it now. She was no longer a penniless girl fighting for acceptance in Logan Falls. She was Miranda Wade and she had no regrets.

Jonah took his usual seat on the couch. He reached for a cigar and snipped off the tip. Daphne was ready with a lighter. "Thank you, my pet," he said, blowing a great cloud of smoke. Daphne poured his brandy, unfolded his newspaper. She sat down next to him and opened a fashion magazine.

Miranda eased herself into a chair. Several minutes passed in silence, but she did not mind. Her gaze moved slowly from one end of the room to the other, coming to rest on two miniature oils sitting atop the mantel. Even at a distance she recognized the portrait of Daphne. She stared at the second portrait. She studied the youthful face, the wonderful smile, and she knew it was Donald. The Wades

129

had not mentioned their late son. They had asked no questions, expressed no curiosity about the last years of his life. Strange, she thought. But then they were a strange couple, unlikely at best. She drummed her fingers on her cane. Now the silence was becoming oppressive. "Would it be all right if I went upstairs?"

Jonah glanced in her direction. "Lily will take you up as soon as she's finished helping Cook."

"Would you care to look at a magazine?" asked Daphne.

"No, thank you . . . I wish I had my books. I guess they were lost in the accident too."

"Books? Why, Jonah has books."

"Yes," he agreed, "I have an excellent library. The classics. You may borrow whatever you want. Provided you're careful," he added, wagging his cigar at her. "The bindings are quite valuable."

"I'll be very careful. I promise."

Jonah nodded. "There's a whole wall of books in my study. Lily will show you tomorrow. Write out a receipt for anything you remove and leave it on my desk . . . And keep my books out of Andrew's reach. Children are destructive. Always tearing things apart and making messes."

A sharp reply came to Miranda's lips. It died there, for she knew it would be a mistake to disagree with Jonah Wade. In time she would find her voice, but not now. She had only one goal now: to win Jonah to her side.

Lily entered the room. "Will there be anything else, Mrs. Wade? Mr. Wade?"

"Miranda would like to go upstairs," replied Daphne. "If Cook doesn't need you . . ."

"We're all finished in the kitchen, Mrs. Wade."

"Then it's all right."

Miranda struggled to her feet. "Would you mind if I picked out a book tonight, Jonah? I'm used to reading for a while before bedtime. It's relaxing."

"Tonight? If you wish. Lily, show Miranda to the study." Jonah puffed on his cigar. He put the newspaper down and leaned forward. "Don't forget to write a receipt. There are receipt pads in the walnut cabinet to the left of the door.

130

You know the one, Lily, I'm sure."

"Yes, Mr. Wade."

"I won't forget," said Miranda. "Good night. Good night, Daphne."

"Sweet dreams."

Jonah sat back. He finished off his brandy and reached for the decanter. "We're running low," he said, looking at the half inch of amber liquid. "I must tell Lily to bring another bottle from the cellar."

"Yes." Daphne turned a page of her magazine. "Do you like this dress, Jonah?"

He studied the sketch. "I don't like the price. All those foreign designers charge outrageous prices. I don't know how they get away with it. I certainly wouldn't ask *our* customers to pay such prices."

"No."

"That reminds me, my pet. We're unveiling our new spring fashions next month. I do wish you'd inspect them before you shop elsewhere."

"I never seem to find anything quite right at the store. I try . . . Perhaps it's the weather. It always seems to rain when I go to Wade's." Daphne's long black lashes fluttered. "Have you noticed that?"

Jonah clasped his wife's hand. He smiled. "I really should be very firm about this. How do you suppose it looks for my wife to buy her clothes from my competitors? That's a poor advertisement for Wade & Company."

"But I get *lots* of things at your store. All those things for Miranda . . . She looks well in navy blue, don't you think?"

Jonah sighed. "She could be wearing burlap for all the difference it makes. Although I will admit she isn't the total disaster I had expected. If first impressions can be trusted, I'd judge her to be a sensible girl. A good head on her shoulders. At least that is what I've observed so far. Time will tell." He sipped his drink, his free hand clasping Daphne's silken knee. "Shall we have an early night, my pet?"

She knew what that meant. Obediently, she put her magazine aside and stood up. No one would have guessed how much she dreaded these "early nights," for her face was composed, her smile as enigmatic as ever. She linked her arm in Jonah's, walking with him into the hall. He murmured something to her. She laughed, and it was a silvery sound like the tinkling of bells. But to herself she wondered what she had wondered many times before: Why are men so vile?

Daphne Wade, née Frazier, had been raised to be a good and dutiful wife. The daughter of a minister, she had had a sheltered childhood; almost from the cradle she had been taught the virtues of home and family, the dangers of worldly temptations. Her playmates had been carefully chosen, her activities carefully supervised. In winter there had been skating parties, taffy pulls, and parlor games; in summer there had been picnics, croquet, and the pleasures of homemade ice cream. Solitary pursuits had been discouraged. Apart from *Ivanhoe* and *Little Women*, books had been discouraged, too. Daphne had not rebelled against her father's strictness. Always passive, she had smiled her little half-smiles and followed all the rules.

She had been raised in genteel poverty. The Fraziers had old family silver and china, old family portraits, but they had very little money. Mrs. Frazier had practiced the economies known to generations of ministers' wives. Early in her marriage she had learned to make everything last longer—clothing, coal, food. She had learned to make the most of gifts brought by members of the congregation—cakes and covered dishes and baskets of fruit. Thrift had become her habit, but somehow, money had always been found for Daphne. Even in the worst of times, young Daphne had pretty dresses and shirtwaists trimmed with lace. There had been pretty bonnets and parasols to shield her exquisite skin from the sun, dainty gloves to shield her hands. There had been hair bows made of watered silk. To the Fraziers, these expenses had been an investment; they had wanted their daughter to marry well.

Reverend Frazier had kept a watchful eye on her suitors, sending most of them away. But Jonah Wade had not been sent away. He had been a serious young man, God-fearing, sober, the heir to a prosperous department store. And after a single waltz with Daphne at a summer cotillion, he had fallen desperately in love. The Fraziers had never doubted that Jonah and Daphne would marry. It had been judged a brilliant match.

Daphne had offered no objections. In a way, she had looked upon the smitten Jonah as a refuge from her parents' narrow, unadorned life. She had always been drawn to beauty. She had always wanted to live in a beautiful house, surrounded by beautiful things, wearing beautiful clothes. Jonah Wade had promised all this and more; she had accepted his proposal.

Sex had not been mentioned during the months of Daphne's engagement. Mrs. Frazier had delicately alluded to the physical side of marriage, to men's physical needs. She had suggested that these needs might be distasteful but that they were nonetheless part of a wife's duties. To her young and impressionable daughter she had given one piece of advice: "Close your eyes and think of something pleasant."

Now, entering their bedroom suite, Daphne's mind had already begun to drift away from Jonah. She would play her role, for like an actress she always played her role, but her mind, her thoughts would be in another place, a gentler place. "I won't be a moment," she said, gliding into her dressing room.

She stood before the triple mirror and removed her clothes. She dabbed scent on her throat, on the rise of her breasts. She ran a brush through her hair, and then stepped into a nightgown of shimmering ivory satin. With a resigned toss of her head, she turned and walked into the bedroom. She was smiling.

Jonah sat naked at the edge of the bed. His eyes glinted as they moved from Daphne's exquisite face to the curves of her body. She stood very still; he went to her, pulling the nightgown down about her waist. His fleshy hands squeezed her breasts. "Daphne," he murmured, crushing his mouth on hers. He pulled at the gown until it fell to the floor. He dimmed the light, hurried her to the bed. He was on top of her now, his moans growing louder as he moved inside her body. Blood suffused his face; his breath was quick. Incoherent murmurings poured from his wet mouth. The bed shook with his exertions, with the sheer force of his thrusts. There was a long, shuddering moan, and finally an explosive cry, quick and sharp and very loud.

"Dear God, what was that?" Miranda stopped so suddenly she almost dropped her cane. "Did you hear that?"

"It's nothing," replied Lily. "Come along, Mrs. Wade. We can't be listening at doors."

"But maybe something's wrong."

"Nothing's wrong. That's Mr. and Mrs. Wade's bedroom."

"But—"

"They're married," said Lily, taking Miranda's arm.

"I know they're married. What does that have to do . . ." She reddened. "Oh, I see." And she did, for her father had told her about the "marriage bed." "I'm sorry. I—I wasn't thinking. I mean, I—"

"It's all right, Mrs. Wade. Come along now. Let's get you and your book tucked in for the night."

Miranda's face was burning as she limped toward her room. She felt foolish and she wondered what Lily must think of her. All at once Lily's opinion seemed very important, for all at once she realized how alone she was. She needed an ally in this house; first an ally and then perhaps a friend.

Chapter Eight

But Lily offered few signs of friendship in the weeks that followed. There was nothing servile about her and yet she kept a servant's distance, deflecting personal questions, asking none of her own. Her feelings, her emotions, were hidden behind a mask of competence. Only in the presence of Malcolm Gill did she display flashes of impatience, though even these brief lapses were unexplained. She was correct, if not exactly polite. She was always helpful. Miranda came to depend upon her.

For weeks, Lily was Miranda's sole respite from the numbing isolation of her recovery. Hindered by cast and cane, she could not climb the steep stairs to the nursery, could not accompany Drew on his daily outings with Miss Dent. The child was brought to her room every morning and afternoon, but the visits were awkward, for she could do little more than hold him in her lap — a pastime that quickly bored the eight-month-old.

The days seemed to drag on forever. Between seven A.M. and seven P.M., Lily was busy with chores. Daphne, getting a later start, was busy with shopping, luncheons, and bridge, which she played surprisingly well. Miranda was on her own. She ate her morning and noon meals in bed, afterward losing herself in books. Each night she ate dinner with the Wades, sat with them for a while, and then returned again to her bed. It was Lily who helped her in and out of her clothes, who gave her sponge baths, who coerced her thick hair into a firmly anchored knot at the back of her head. Miranda appreciated all these things, but most of all she appreciated Lily's company. She felt less alone, less cut off from the world; Lily was not the friendly confidante she had hoped for, but still she felt she could count Lily on her side. It was a comforting thought.

Miranda's casts were removed early in April. The skin beneath was shriveled and sickly white, but she considered this a small price to pay for her freedom. "I feel as if I've been let out of a cage," she exulted, swinging her leg back and forth. "It's wonderful."

"You mustn't try to do too much at first," cautioned Dr. Wentworth. "I wouldn't enter any Charleston contests," he added, smiling in his fatherly way. "But moderate exercise will strengthen your leg. Do you like to walk?"

"Yes. I used to walk a lot."

"A good brisk walk twice a day; that's my prescription." Dr. Wentworth helped Miranda step down from the examination table. "You're young and in excellent health. You shouldn't have any problems."

"Thank you, Doctor. Can I start today? I mean, can I go for a walk right now? I've been hearing about New York, but I haven't seen much of it yet."

"Well, don't try to see *all* of it today. Your leg will tire easily at first. Ten blocks or so should be quite enough for a start."

Miranda smiled. "That's perfect! Lily is going to take me to see Wade and Company and it's just ten blocks from here."

"I suppose you've earned a shopping spree. You've been a good patient, Miranda. You've earned a reward."

"No rewards," she said, laughing. "No shopping sprees. I just want to see the store." She glanced up. "Have you been there? Is it very big?"

"My wife is one of Wade's best customers. And yes, it's quite a nice size. Don't let anybody step on you in the elevator. Stores are always crowded on Fridays."

"I'll be careful."

Dr. Wentworth made a notation in Miranda's file, closed it, and tucked it under his arm. "Was there something else, Miranda?"

"I was wondering . . . I know it's sort of a fancy store. Do I—do you think I look all right?"

136

"My dear child, it's a department store, not Buckingham Palace."

"But it's on Fifth Avenue."

"Fifth Avenue," replied Dr. Wentworth with a wry smile, "isn't what it used to be."

Indeed, the Fifth Avenue that so awed Miranda now — the Fifth Avenue of elegant shops and department stores — had once been the private enclave of society. Here the city's oldest and wealthiest families had dwelt, their mansions mute testimony to privileged lives. But in 1906, a merchant named Benjamin Altman had dared to breach custom by opening a department store. Anticipating the outraged protests, he had erected a building whose purpose was decorously hidden behind the facade of a Florentine palace. Other stores had followed: Oppenheim Collins, Mc-Creery's, Best & Company, Tiffany's — palaces all. Lord and Taylor, which opened in 1914, was the first department store that actually looked like a department store; Wade & Company, which opened in 1915, was the second.

Wade & Company had begun as a dry goods store on lower Broadway. Founded by Albert Wade, a cockney from the teeming slums of London's East End, the store had prospered beyond his wildest dreams. By the time of the Civil War it had grown to triple its original size, adding such items as hats, gloves, purses, umbrellas, and women's capes. At the turn of the century, Albert's son Andrew had moved the store to much larger quarters on Fourteenth Street. He had relegated dry goods to a single department, stocking other departments with clothing and accessories for men, women, and children. In 1915, Andrew's son Lionel had moved the store to even larger quarters on Fifth Avenue. When Lionel succumbed to a heart attack four years later, his son Jonah became president of Wade & Company. Jonah made few changes. He had inherited a store known for the quality of its merchandise and the courtesy of its staff; hard as he had tried, he could think of no way to improve on that.

"Here it is," said Lily now. "Wade & Company."

Miranda gaped at the handsome block-long building, at the huge display windows filled with mannequins, at the arched and canopied entrance. "My! The *whole* building? They must sell everything there is to sell."

"That's the idea, I guess. Do you want to go in?"

Miranda smoothed her hair, her dress. She tugged at her new white gloves. "I'm a little nervous. I don't know why."

"If you want to go home —"

"No, Lily. Let's go inside."

The doorman touched his cap as they entered the store. Miranda gazed around, enthralled. She saw wide aisles branching across an expanse of polished marble. She saw well-dressed women strolling the aisles, stopping here and there to examine a silk scarf, a lace handkerchief. She noticed how brightly the glass-and-mahogany display cases shone, how brightly the salesclerks smiled. Voices were low, a gentle murmur drifting toward the carved ceilings; the air was lightly scented with perfume. Her nervousness vanished; she felt calmer than she had in a long time, felt as if nothing bad could happen to her here. She never wanted to leave, for more than any place she had ever known, she felt this was home. "Imagine owning all this," she said, as if to herself. "Imagine what it would be like."

"It's a good business."

"It's not just a business, Lily . . . It's something that will always be here. Like a . . . like a rock." Miranda blushed. It was a ridiculous comparison, but the only one that had come to mind. "Could we walk around? There's so much to see."

"Well, it's getting late, Mrs. Wade. We'll take a walk around this floor, and then we'd better go home. You'll need to rest."

"I feel fine."

"Now you do. Later you might feel you overdid things. You can always come back, you know. The store's open six days a week."

Miranda nodded. "All right, Lily. This floor and then we'll go home. It's a deal."

There were three handkerchief counters, one of them devoted exclusively to wedding handkerchiefs: wisps of silk and lace and chiffon sewn with tiny bows and tiny seed pearls. Farther down the aisle was a spring garden of pastel scarves and shawls; to the left were counters of satiny kid gloves in every possible length. There were hosiery counters, handbag counters. There was a millinery bar, a modern innovation featuring simpler, less expensive hats. Two long counters shimmered with gold and silver jewelry, a third with pearl necklaces and earrings. Toward the rear of the store, near the elevators, were women's toiletries: colored bath salts in swan-necked bottles, dusting powders, fluffy pink powder puffs, scented hand lotions and creams. "It's Christmas every day here," murmured a wide-eyed Miranda.

"For people who can afford Christmas every day. This store isn't cheap."

Miranda's gaze scanned the affluent-looking women laden with packages. "It doesn't have to be. There's a lot of money in New York. And people willing to spend it; that's the best part. Once people walk through the doors, they'll spend their money. It's really very simple."

"Are you ready to leave now?"

"What? Oh yes, Lily. I'm ready."

"Let's go around this way."

Miranda followed Lily up an aisle to a side door. The sun had begun to fade. Patchy gray clouds moved lazily across the sky, a prelude to rain. Traffic had already thickened on the avenue, cars and buses tuning their horns for the usual Friday symphony. At the bus stop perhaps a dozen people waited, some of them reading newspapers, some of them leaning over the curb in search of the doubledecker that was nowhere in sight. "Let's walk."

"Mr. Wade said we could take a taxicab home this one time."

"We'll never find a taxicab. It's only six blocks, Lily."

"All right," she reluctantly agreed. "We'll walk."

Miranda had been so caught up in her own excitement she had not noticed the stares that followed Lily. Now, crossing the avenue, she was ashamed of her thoughtlessness.

139

She saw heads turn, first in admiration and then in shock as the other side of Lily's face was revealed to passersby. She knew that Lily had had to deal with such stares all her life; they were more curious than unkind, but she felt certain that did not ease the pain. She walked faster, fixing her eyes resolutely on the pavement. "I'm sorry I took you from your chores today. I can pitch in and help you tomorrow. It'll get done much quicker with the two of us."

The barest smile flickered at Lily's mouth. "I'll do my own chores, Mrs. Wade. That's what I'm paid for."

"But I can help. I *want* to help."

"No," said Lily with a firm shake of her head. "It's not your place. You're Mr. Wade's daughter-in-law. You can't do housemaid's work. You can't do things like that . . . There are rules."

"Jonah's rules?"

"Rules for the way people live. You can't be palling around with the housemaid, and you can't do the housemaid's work. That's just the way it is."

"You have extra work because of me."

"I'm getting paid for it. I told you I saw to that."

"Then money makes everything all right?"

"What else is there, Mrs. Wade?"

She did not reply; no reply was necessary. She smiled.

"I love your store," said Miranda at dinner that night. "I'm going back tomorrow."

Jonah put down his fork. "I'm afraid Lily can't be spared. She has her duties here. It's high time she returned to them."

"I know. I can manage on my own now. I was thinking I'd take Andrew to the park tomorrow morning, but in the afternoon I'd like to walk over to the store . . . if you wouldn't mind."

"I see no reason to object. Do you, my pet?"

"The stores are so charming in springtime. It's my favorite season. Have you been to Saks yet?"

"Miranda will have no need of Saks." Jonah's rebuke was mild, as were all his rebukes to his wife. She often tried his patience, but not once in twenty-six years had he lost his temper. He was a cold man at heart, and yet he loved Daphne unconditionally. His wife, his store, his money; these were the only things that had ever mattered to him. "Wade and Company is far superior."

"Yes," murmured Daphne. She took a mouse bite of veal, a sliver of carrot. "Skirts are shorter this season."

"Quite shameless, if you want my opinion." Jonah thought of Daphne's smooth, shapely legs. "Of course there are some women who can wear them without ill effect."

Miranda saw the way Jonah looked at his wife. It was an intimate look, intense; she lowered her eyes to her plate. "Now that I can get around," she said quietly, "do you think I should keep Miss Dent?"

"That is entirely up to you," replied Jonah. "You're paying her salary, after all. The boy does seem attached to her."

"Does he?"

"I would say so, yes."

Miranda polished off her cutlet and took another. "It's a big expense."

"Indeed it is. If you wished, you could move into the nursery and look after Andrew yourself."

"Couldn't I move him into my room?"

"Certainly not! Why, the room would be destroyed in no time. And the noise would be intolerable. Children are always making a racket. That's the reason the nursery is on the top floor, the servants' floor."

"I see."

"The nursery isn't large, mind you. Adequate." Jonah speared a piece of meat. "Yes, I'd call it adequate."

"And out of the way."

"Exactly. I dislike having children underfoot."

"I think Andrew is a nice little boy," said Daphne.

"Of course he is. He's a Wade."

He's a McAllister, too, thought Miranda, though she prudently kept the thought to herself. "I'll have to think about what to do. I wouldn't want Andrew to be confused."

"Confused?"

"Well, if he's really attached to Miss Dent. If he'd be sad . . ." Miranda sighed. "I want to do the right thing."

"Children are such mysteries, said Daphne. "One never knows what they're thinking. They're rather like cats. Dogs are different. One always knows with dogs. I had a terrier when I was a girl."

"No birds?" asked Miranda.

Daphne brightened. "Oh my, yes. *Lots* of birds. Parakeets and canaries and the sweetest pair of lovebirds. Their names were Romeo and Juliet."

Jonah, who loathed cats, dogs, and especially birds, who loathed anything that intruded on Daphne's affections, had had enough of this conversation. "Whatever you decide about Miss Dent," he said to Miranda, "Lily will be returning to her own room in the morning. No need to coddle you anymore. No good ever comes of coddling people."

"I'll miss Lily's company."

Jonah's brows shot up. "Her company? She's a *maid.*"

"She's been very helpful."

"Money," he declared tossing his napkin on the table. "You'd be surprised how helpful people can be when there's money in it. But women never understand such things. You women don't know the *value* of money. And that's why I have decided to take charge of your funds."

Miranda bit her tongue to keep from speaking. She knew she would have to hear him out.

"A portion of your funds will be invested," continued Jonah. "The rest will stay in the bank. At the first of each month you will withdraw twenty dollars for your expenses."

"An allowance?"

Jonah inclined his head. "If you wish to look at it that way. It's a generous sum, Miranda. You must remember that your room and board cost you nothing. Twenty dollars a month should be more than enough."

"What will she wear?" asked Daphne.

"Wear?"

"Clothes. She hasn't any spring clothes."

Jonah thought this over while Lily cleared the dishes away. "Yes," he said finally, "you have a point. Miranda, I suggest you withdraw an extra hundred dollars and buy whatever you need for spring. You'll have a ten percent discount at Wade & Company; I'll see you get a card."

"Thank you."

He took a small notebook from his pocket and handed it across the table to Miranda. "This will help you keep track of how you spend your money. Keep a daily record and you'll have no questions at the end of the month."

"Jonah is very organized," said Daphne.

Miranda smiled. "Arrogant" was a better description, she thought to herself. She supposed that Jonah meant well; whether he was right or wrong, she decided it was not worth arguing about, particularly since she had never considered the money hers. She glanced down at the notebook. "Will you be checking my records?" she asked, a twinkle in her eye.

"I believe that would be wise. You've assured me of your thrifty ways, but I would prefer to see for myself."

"Of course. I'll try to keep accurate records, Jonah."

"Bah! Like all women, you'll present a hodgepodge of figures and call it an accurate record."

"Oh, I don't know. You may be surprised."

Lily brought coffee and dessert: a mocha cake thickly frosted with chocolate. Daphne took her customary sliver; Jonah and Miranda shared the rest. When they finished, Miranda excused herself and climbed the two flights of stairs to the nursery.

The hallway was dim, but she could see that there were no adornments here, no soft carpets, no pictures on the drab green walls, no flower vases sitting atop gleaming consoles. The servants' floor, she thought, shaking her head. A band of light showed beneath one of the doors. She knocked. "I hope I'm not disturbing you," she said when Miss Dent appeared.

"Not at all. You're most welcome, Mrs. Wade. Come in."

Miranda entered a small sitting room. The furnishings were castoffs from the Wade attic, but attractive castoffs. There was a deep, pillowed chintz wing chair, a slender writing desk, a velvet loveseat, a pair of butler's tables. There was a braided hearth rug, and above the mantel, a mirror framed in pale oak. Plain blue curtains shaded the

143

single window. A tall, narrow bookcase displayed tattered volumes of Shakespeare and an old Bible. "It's cozy," she said. She settled herself on the loveseat. "Maybe a bit small?"

"I'm quite used to close quarters, Mrs. Wade. And my bedroom is lovely. How does it feel to be up and about?"

"*Wonderful.*"

Miss Dent laughed. She was a fortyish woman with graying hair worn in a neat bun. She was not really pretty, though she had a luminous smile and perfect, very white teeth. "I can imagine how difficult it's been for you. But we must put these things behind us, mustn't we?"

Miranda nodded. "Do you think Andrew remembers anything about the accident? It's worried me that he might have bad memories, bad dreams. I know so little about children. And he's so young."

"Yes, I see what you mean. I wouldn't be concerned, Mrs. Wade. I accompanied your mother-in-law when she fetched Andrew from the hospital. He was a trifle agitated in the beginning. Restless. After the first week, he settled down very nicely. I doubt he actually remembers anything. The noise perhaps. He appears to be sensitive to loud noises. I've noticed nothing unusual apart from that."

"I'm relieved to hear it."

"I'm sure Andrew is relieved to have his mother back."

"Do you think he remembers his mother?" The words had come out before Miranda could stop them. She twisted her fingers together and tried to smile. "It's — it's just that I didn't notice any reaction when he saw me again."

"I believe there's always a special bond between mother and child, Mrs. Wade. Children as young as Andrew may not remember things, but they sense things. They sense the bond. And naturally you'll be spending more time with him now."

"Yes."

"Would you like to look in on him?"

Miranda rose. "Thank you, Miss Dent. You're very understanding."

"I know how mothers worry." She smiled. "Well, there's always *some*thing to worry about, isn't there? In any case,

144

I'm not the sort of nanny who banishes mothers from the nursery." She opened the connecting door. "If you'll just come this way, Mrs. Wade."

The nursery wallpaper was patterned with clouds. The furniture was sturdy and obviously new. A set of toy soldiers sat on a shelf next to a family of toy ducks. A red rocking horse stood against a far wall. "Andrew doesn't have anything to cuddle," said Miranda.

"But he does. He has his teddy. Come see, Mrs. Wade."

She went to the crib. She smiled, for Andrew and a small brown teddy bear lay side by side on the pillow. "I'm glad he has a friend."

"They're inseparable."

Miranda reached her hand to the child's silky hair. She saw glistening copper streaks threading the pale gold. McAllister hair, she thought; there's no doubt he's a McAllister. After a few moments her gaze returned to Miss Dent. "I know you must have a schedule, but I'd like to start spending mornings with him."

"A splendid idea, Mrs. Wade. Andrew has his breakfast at seven."

"I'll be here. Now that the cast is off, I can join you on your outings. Where do you go?"

"There's the park, when the weather is nice. And we always have a long walk. Children need fresh air. Andrew seems to enjoy looking about. He sits in his carriage like a little prince surveying his kingdom."

"We used to carry him around in a basket . . . He's grown so much."

"Yes, they grow quickly at this age."

Miranda turned toward the door. "I'll see you at seven, then."

"Good night, Mrs. Wade."

"Good night."

A little prince, thought Miranda as she descended the stairs. And in a way he really was a prince; he was the heir apparent to Wade & Company, and that was kingdom enough. She wondered if he would want his inheritance or if, like his father, he would choose a different life. She was still mulling this possibility when she entered her room. Lily was there, sorting sheets and pillowcases. "I can make up my bed," she offered.

"That's my job, Mrs. Wade." Lily put a set of sheets on the dresser and deposited the others in a bottom drawer. "If I change the bed tonight, it'll save time in the morning. I'm moving out then."

"Yes, I heard. I'm sorry."

"Sorry?"

"It was nice having company. I don't know anyone in New York, Lily."

"You'll meet people."

"Where?"

Lily shrugged. "The usual places." She sat down on her cot and reached for the mending basket. Deftly, she measured off a length of black silk thread.

"You're always busy."

"There's a lot to do around here, with just Cook and me."

Miranda looked up. "You and Cook take care of this house alone?"

"Cook takes care of the kitchen. I do the rest."

"There isn't anyone else?"

Lily plunged her needle into one of Daphne's gloves. "Have you seen anyone else?"

"No, but I . . . I guess I assumed. This house always looks so perfect. One person couldn't do it all."

"One person does," replied Lily. "Me. There's a woman who comes in Saturdays to do the washing and ironing. That helps. There should be another housemaid, but Mr. Wade doesn't want to pay two salaries. He pays me a little extra instead. It works out." She glanced at Miranda. "If you want to keep on Mr. Wade's good side, don't go throwing money away."

"Thank you for telling me."

Lily shrugged again.

"Do you ever have a day off?"

Now that you're all right, I'll get my Sundays back. I get Sundays and half a day on Thursdays. Unless the Wades are having guests. It doesn't matter to me one way or the other. I don't go out much."

"But don't you see your family?"

"Sometimes." Lily finished sewing the glove and picked up its twin. "Sometimes I see my sister Violet."

"Violet? Violet and Lily; that's nice."

"We were all named for flowers. Rose, Iris, Violet, and me. My mother used to say she had her own special garden. Then I was born, her stinkweed."

Miranda did not know what to say. Lily had never spoken of herself before, and never once had she referred to her disfigured face. Miranda, who long ago had decided that empty words were worse than no words at all, now decided to say nothing.

"You're smart enough not to pretend," continued Lily with a faint smile. "That's what a lot of people do — pretend they don't understand what I'm talking about. I don't pretend, Mrs. Wade. I took this job because I wanted to put some money away. I see my family once in a while and that's enough. I know what I look like. I know my place. That's all there is to tell."

"You think I've been nosy."

Lily finished with the second glove. She rethreaded the needle and plucked a frayed scarf from the basket. "You lost a friend in the train accident," she replied. "I'm sorry about that but I can't help. Give yourself time, Mrs. Wade. You'll meet the right kind of people and they'll be your friends."

Miranda leaned her head against the back of the chair. She smiled. "You're a snob, Lily Olsen."

"I told you I know my place." She held the scarf up, inspecting her handiwork. "There's no disappointments when you know your place."

Those words stayed with Miranda; she had begun to wonder what her place was. During the next weeks she realized that her place was certainly not with Miss Dent and the other nannies who clustered together on park benches, chatting while their charges napped. Nor was her place with Daphne who excluded her from luncheons and teas and shopping trips, who often seemed to forget that she was

147

around. Miranda lived in the Wade house, but she had no place in the household. To the Wades, she was neither family nor friend nor servant; she was simply there, the way an unexpected guest might be there, floating at the periphery of their lives. She had no duties, no responsibilities. She had absolutely nothing to do.

Every afternoon she went to Wade & Company. She wandered from floor to floor, exploring the different departments, studying the merchandise so closely she might have been studying for a test. Now and then she allowed herself to dream, to imagine that an opulent silver fox jacket was hers, or a shimmery evening dress, or a long, billowing white silk negligée. She knew she would never have such luxuries, and yet at Wade's anything seemed possible. It was not the best of the Fifth Avenue department stores, nor even the most stylish, but to her it was magic.

Now, walking a circle around a display of frilly spring blouses, she found herself face to face with Jonah. "I'm here again," she said, a sheepish smile lifting the corners of her mouth. "I keep coming back."

"So I see. Miranda, I don't believe you've met our general manager, Peter Dexter. We're trying to decide if we need extra dressing rooms on this floor."

She turned. She felt her heart thump, for Peter Dexter was a very handsome man. He was tall and dark; his eyes were a stormy blue. He had high, aristocratic cheekbones and a determined mouth; his upper lip was adorned with a dark and dashing brush mustache. He was in his thirties. Quite suddenly, she wondered if he were married. "It's nice to meet you," she said, her face burning bright red. "You — you have a wonderful store."

Peter Dexter took her hand. "Thank you, Mrs. Wade. I gather this isn't your first visit."

Miranda shook her head. All at once her throat was dry; all at once her lips would not move. She smoothed her hair, and as she did so, she dropped her purse.

"Allow me, Mrs. Wade," said Peter Dexter.

"Thank you," she murmured when he returned her handbag. Jonah took his heavy gold watch from his pocket. "We have business, Peter."

"Yes, of course, Mr. Wade." He bowed slightly to Miranda. "A pleasure to have met you."

"Yes, I . . ." She did not finish, for he had already turned away. She followed his progress toward the rear of the store, craning her neck until finally he disappeared from view. Her legs felt wobbly. She steadied herself against the display platform and drew a breath. "Peter Dexter," she whispered with a dazed smile. She knew she must have made a terrible impression on him; she was almost at the elevator when it occurred to her that she had probably made no impression at all. He was handsome and successful, a sophisticated New Yorker; a man like that would never pay her the slightest attention. She glimpsed her reflection in the mirrored elevator panel and she shrank back. *No man will ever pay me the slightest attention,* she thought. *I'm hopeless.*

She took her time walking home, though for once the city failed to stir her. She had a strange, empty feeling, as if she had suffered a great disappointment. Her eyes moved to the blinking traffic lights, then back to the street. She crossed the avenue, turning into Thirty-seventh Street. Trees lined both sides of the street, their branches swaying gently in the breeze. She heard the flutter of leaves, the chirping of sparrows. She thought about Daphne. She sighed, certain that Peter Dexter paid *lots* of attention to the beautiful Daphne Wade.

There was no sign of Daphne when Miranda arrived at home. She glanced at her watch; Andrew would be napping, Miss Dent busy writing letters. She poked her head into the living room. She saw Lily on hands and knees brushing the Axminster carpet. After a moment's hesitation, she went inside and plopped down on the couch. "I need your advice, Lily."

"I don't give advice."

"Break your rule this one time."

Lily put the brush atop the dustpan. She wiped her hands on her apron and looked up. "What's the matter?"

"I'm going crazy; that's what's the matter. I don't seem to belong here. Maybe I don't belong *any*where . . . I'm so useless, Lily. I give Andrew his breakfast and his bath. We play peekaboo, we go to the park, and after all that it's *still* only eleven o'clock in the morning. I have whole days to fill, but with what? I can't spend my life sitting in parks with Miss Dent. And when I come home . . ." Miranda held out her hands, palms up. "Cook won't let me in the kitchen. You won't let me help with chores . . . I sit in my room and read or I go to Wade's and walk around. What kind of life is that?"

"What kind of life do you want, Mrs. Wade?"

Miranda slumped against the back of the couch. She stared into the distance, pulling a lock of straggly black hair through her fingers. "That's a hard question."

"Sounds simple to me. The answer's simple too: decide what you want and go after it."

Wearily, Miranda closed her eyes. It had been seven months since she left Logan Falls. She had had a plan then, a plan altered first by an accidental meeting at Union Station, and later by tragedy. And by New York, she thought to herself, for during these two months in New York she had become oddly indecisive. "You're right, Lily," she said, snapping out the words. "It's time to go after what I want . . . And now I know where to start."

Chapter Nine

Jonah seated himself in the big leather chair behind his desk. He glanced through the mail and put it aside. "Well, Miranda," he said, folding his hands, "I trust you have a good reason for requesting this interview. I've had a hard day. I don't want to hear any problems before dinner."

"I won't keep you, Jonah. It's just that I've decided I ought to have a job. I can work and still spend mornings and evenings with Andrew."

"What about afternoons? You can hardly expect my wife to care for the boy."

Miranda smiled. Daphne visited the nursery once a week, patted Andrew's head, and then made a hasty departure. "No, I wouldn't expect that. Miss Dent will stay on. I had a talk with her earlier today. She's agreed to stay. So if your offer is still open, I'd like to take you up on it."

"I see."

"You haven't changed your mind, Jonah?"

"No, but I wonder if this is the proper time. I'm a busy man. I wouldn't want to arrange things only to find you are having second thoughts. Some women are sentimental about children."

"There won't be any second thoughts," replied Miranda. "Andrew is very young. He's in his own little world. As long as I have mornings and evenings, I won't feel guilty about leaving him during the afternoons."

"In that case, I'm willing to proceed." He leaned back in his chair, pressing his fingertips together. "First we had better discuss finances. Of course you will continue to pay Miss Dent from your own funds; that's understood. There is another point, however. At present, you're withdrawing

151

twenty dollars a month for your expenses. That will stop if you are earning a salary. I believe in preserving capital, Miranda."

She was familiar with Jonah's beliefs. She nodded. "I've always thought of that money as Andrew's. I don't want to keep drawing on it for myself. I'd much rather earn my way."

"Then we are agreed."

"Is your offer still open, Jonah?"

"Certainly. I'm quite prepared to give you a chance. You're a sensible girl; we'll soon see if you are also efficient. Efficiency, Miranda, that's what I demand of my employees. No exceptions will be made for you." Jonah paused, his expression at once benevolent and stern. "Don't expect a free ride. Business is business, after all. I may be soft-hearted, but not when it comes to Wade and Company."

Soft-hearted? Miranda hid her smile behind her hand. "I promise to do my best."

"That's all very well, but your best remains to be seen. You've never worked. You don't know what it means. I'll tell you what it means: responsibility. There's no place in the business world for flighty, irresponsible females. You may count that my one and only warning, Miranda. If you disappoint me, you won't be given another chance."

"Fair enough. I'm sure you're a fair man, Jonah."

He grunted. "Now the question is where to put you?"

Miranda's reply was eager, without hesitation. "Put me behind a counter."

His eyes swept over her. He thought, *That great lump behind one of my sales counters? Never!* "No, no," he said impatiently, "you're not the type for that. We have an image at Wade and Company. But perhaps something in the office . . . Do you have your account book with you?"

She took the notepad from her pocket and passed it to Jonah. If she was hurt by his blunt rebuff, she gave no sign.

"You write a neat hand," he declared. "And I must confess your figures have been accurate to the penny . . . I think the credit department might suit you nicely. Yes, the credit department might be just the place." He returned the notepad to Miranda. "The starting salary for clerks is eighteen dollars a week. A good deal more than you need, since you pay no room and board."

Jonah's frequent references to room and board had not been lost on her. "I'd be glad to make a — contribution — toward my keep here. Say five dollars a week?"

He considered this. He was tempted. Reluctantly, he shook his head. "No, under the circumstances, I couldn't accept any money. Some things simply aren't done." And more's the pity, he thought, his eyes as mournful as a basset hound's. "We won't mention the subject again."

I bet, said Miranda to herself. To Jonah she said, "That's very generous of you."

"Well, one does what one can."

"Yes," murmured Miranda in a perfect, if unintentional imitation of Daphne. "When do you suppose I could start my job?"

Jonah glanced at his desk calendar. "Today is Monday . . . Let's say a week from today. I admire your enthusiasm, Miranda. Apply it to your work and you will do well." He sat back once again, gazing around his study. One wall was lined with books, another with the portrait of mother and child and with several smaller framed watercolors. A third wall was wholly devoted to Wade & Company — to photographs of the store in its various incarnations, to plaques awarded to the store over the years, to mounted and framed newspaper accounts of the store's opening on Fifth Avenue. "My great-grandfather was an uneducated man," continued Jonah. "Certainly an uncultured man. He came to this country with very little. For years he earned his living as a peddler. But he never lost his will to succeed, his enthusiasm. And of course he *did* succeed. Make him your inspiration."

Money was all the inspiration Miranda needed, though she chose not to say so. "You must be very proud of your great-grandfather," she said instead.

Jonah beamed, for he was indeed proud. He boasted about Albert Wade's humble origins, about his early struggles, about his ultimate triumph, about everything except the fact that Albert had been half Jewish. Even more than

153

the Irish, Jonah disdained Jews. "I take pride in all my ancestors."

"I promised I wouldn't keep you," said Miranda, rising to her feet. "It's settled, then? I start work next Monday?"

"That's correct." Jonah uncapped his fountain pen and wrote something on a scrap of paper. "Mr. Houser is in charge of our credit department. Report to him at eight-thirty Monday morning. Take this," he added, holding out the paper. "And remember to use the employees' entrance from now on."

"Yes, I'll remember . . . Does Peter Dexter have anything to do with the credit department?"

Jonah looked up. "Dexter? His title is general manager, but he functions more or less as my assistant. Why do you ask?"

"No reason." She read the words on the paper: *Fifth floor, room 503.* "Thank you, Jonah. I won't let you down."

"We'll see about that."

Miranda smiled. She left the study and walked through the hall to the stairs. *I have a job,* she thought to herself, *a real job.* It was not the salesclerk job she had coveted, but she had to agree that the credit department suited her. She remembered all the bills she had tried to collect for her father. She sighed, wondering if people in New York paid their bills.

"Miranda? I thought I heard you on the stairs."

"Hello, Daphne. I've just had a nice talk with Jonah. He's given me a job at Wade and Company. I start Monday."

Daphne blinked. "A job? Do you need money?"

"Doesn't everybody need money?"

There was a pause, a fluttering of long black eyelashes. "You have such an interesting way of putting things." Daphne looked uncertainly at Miranda. "Yes, very interesting. But never mind. I bought you a present today. You must come and see."

"A present?"

"Come along and I'll show you."

Miranda had never been in Daphne's sitting room before. She had imagined an elegant room, a lot of pale, creamy silk, and in this she was not disappointed. Like all the other rooms in the Wade house, it was quite beautiful.

"My bedroom is just through there," explained Daphne, gesturing toward the connecting doors at the right. "And Jonah keeps a small bedroom through there," she added, gesturing toward the doors at the left. "But he usually . . . Do sit down, Miranda."

"Thank you." She inspected the slender gilt chairs, wondering if they would hold her weight. She sat on the loveseat. "Oh, more birds!" They were everywhere, studding the mantel, the tables, the shelves that were meant for books. "It's a wonderful collection."

"I just adore birds. I put breadcrumbs out on the sills every morning. It's the least one can do. Don't you agree? Don't you agree we must help?"

Miranda could only smile at Daphne's wide-eyed gaze, her childlike gravity. "I'm sure city birds have a harder time than country birds. Finding food, I mean."

"Yes, finding food. I'm so glad you understand." Daphne crossed the room. She took a small package from a drawer and brought it to Miranda. "I'm sorry there isn't a box. It was a Saks box, you see, and I thought . . ."

Miranda folded back the tissue paper. "It's lovely," she said, touching the delicate lace collar. "It's the prettiest thing I've ever had."

"Your gray dress is a bit plain, isn't it? When I saw the collar, I *knew* it would be perfect. Can you sew?"

"Oh, yes. And this won't be difficult to sew on at all. Thank you, Daphne. You were very sweet to think of me. And very generous, too."

"Gray is a good color, but it often needs help."

Like the birds, thought Miranda, smiling. She returned the collar to the tissue paper and stood up. "I'll fix my dress tonight after dinner."

"Lamb chops."

"I beg your pardon?"

"Cook is serving lamb chops tonight."

"Oh, I see." Miranda shook her head, as if trying to clear it, and then slipped out of the room. She went to her own room at the rear of the hall. Through the open door she glimpsed Lily poised atop a stool by the window. "What in the world are you doing?"

"Changing the curtains for spring. Yours is the last room. I wanted to finish today. I'll just about make it."

"Be careful you don't fall."

"I'm all right, Mrs. Wade . . . There, all done." Lily stepped off the stool and folded the discarded curtains into neat squares. "The other Mrs. Wade was looking for you."

"She found me. She gave me a present." Miranda held out the lace collar. "Isn't it pretty?"

Lily nodded.

"And Jonah gave me a present also — a job at Wade and Company."

"Congratulations."

"He won't let me be a salesclerk, though. I'm too ugly."

Lily turned. "You're not ugly, Mrs. Wade. But you keep yourself plain."

"You say that as if I have a choice."

"You do."

Miranda frowned, waiting in vain for Lily to continue. "I must be missing something. *What* choice?"

Lily started to the door. "Get your hair cut," she said, marching into the hall.

Miranda's frown deepened. After a moment she went to the vanity table and sat down. She forced herself to look in the mirror, to examine her face (a pudding face, she thought) and her hair. She tore out the combs and hairpins, tossing them away. Her hair fell in clumps around her shoulders; it had no shape, no shine, no hint of the curls she had prayed for as a child. "Hopeless," she muttered. She opened a drawer, reaching to the back until she found a small envelope she had taped there. She opened the envelope and removed the three crisp ten dollar bills she had saved from her allowance. She stared at the bills. Again, she stared at her reflection in the mirror. "Well," she said with a great sigh, I can't look any worse than I do now."

Michelle's was a small, unpretentious beauty parlor tucked away in a quiet side street. The plate-glass window displayed sketches of various hairstyles; Miranda studied each one in turn and then pushed open the door. She took a few steps, stopping almost in midstride to gape at the funny dome-shaped hair dryers, the counters laden with long metal clips and curlers, the pink swivel chairs facing recessed mirrors.

"May I help you?"

Miranda spun around. She saw an attractive woman wearing a bright pink smock and a bright smile. "Yes, I was wondering . . . I mean . . . do you think you could do anything with my hair?"

"That's what I'm here for. Did you have anything special in mind?"

"I'm starting a job Monday. I — I'd like to look nice." She shrugged; "nice" was the most she dared expect.

"Sit down in that first chair and I'll see what I can do. My name is Michelle. I own the place."

"I'm Miranda Wade."

"Well, sit yourself down, Miranda. Don't be nervous. I'm good at my work. I've been doing it a long time. You'll walk out of here a new woman and that's a promise."

Miranda smiled. "Are you a magician?"

"You have to be, in this business. And I know all the tricks. Just wait till you see the difference."

My transformation, thought Miranda, obediently following Michelle to the sink. Her hair was washed and then rinsed in ice-cold-water "to bring out the shine." A comb was pulled through the tangles. A huge towel was wrapped around her head. "What now?" she asked, drying her damp neck.

"Now we find the new you."

It took two hours. Miranda kept her eyes fixed on the floor but she heard the snip, snip, snip of scissors, the snap of hairclips. Cotton was stuffed in her ears while she baked under the dryer. A light pomade was rubbed into her hair when she emerged. "Are you finished yet, Michelle? I'm not used to all this fussing."

"Soon. You can look if you want."

"No, I'll wait."

157

Michelle brushed and combed and smoothed, inspecting her creation from every angle. She stepped back for a final glance. She smiled. "Meet the new Miranda Wade."

"Do I look silly?"

"See for yourself."

Slowly, warily, Miranda lifted her eyes. If there had been no magical transformation, there had nonetheless been a profound change. She saw a face that appeared to have contours. She saw glossy chin-length black hair rippling with soft waves. "Is it really me?"

"Sure. And I have the perfect finishing touch." Michelle reached across the countertop to a tray of cosmetics. She rummaged around, selecting a tiny pot of deep rose lip rouge. "Here it is," she said, breaking the seal.

"Oh, I couldn't."

"There's nothing wrong with a little makeup. At least try it. What have you got to lose?"

Miranda looked again at her reflection. She smiled. "All right. But just a little."

"That's the spirit! You never know till you try."

Miranda sat patiently while the lip rouge was applied. She agreed to a light dusting of ivory face powder, but waved away the mascara. "No, that's enough."

"Okay. I guess you don't need to try everything at once . . . But look at yourself. You look great!"

Miranda stared into the mirror, her tinted lips parting in surprise. *I'm almost pretty,* she thought. She wished Logan Falls could see her now. "You *are* a magician," she said. "I can't believe it's me."

"Like I promised, you'll leave here a new woman."

Miranda left with two pots of lip rouge, a compact of face powder, a package of long metal hair clips, and a tube of pomade.

She knew she had been extravagant, but she refused to feel guilty. There was a spring in her step as she walked home. Her eyes twinkled, and each time she glimpsed her reflection in a store window she smiled. *It's true,* she thought, *I'm almost pretty.*

She wanted Drew to see her first. She let herself into the

Murray Hill house and dashed up the stairs to the nursery. At the top of the landing she collided with Miss Dent. "Sorry," she said, juggling her packages in her arm.

"Why, Mrs. Wade, I hardly recognized you. You look so different. Your new hairstyle is most becoming."

"Thank you. I was nervous about it, but now I'm glad . . . Do you think Drew will notice anything different?"

Miss Dent smiled. "He's a bit young, isn't he? I wouldn't expect too much. I've just put him down for his nap. Shall we see if he's still awake?"

They entered the nursery. Miranda went to the crib and bent over the railing. "Sound asleep." She stroked his hand, his little wrist. "Well, I suppose it was a silly idea anyway. It's just that I'm in such a happy mood. I wanted to share it with him."

"Of course you did. Perhaps later."

"Yes, later." Miranda straightened up. She turned toward the door. "Thank you for humoring me, Miss Dent. You're very understanding."

Miranda crossed the hall and went downstairs to her room. She deposited her purchases on the vanity table, arranging them in rows. She caught sight of her bitten fingernails and she sighed. No more of that, she told herself, resolving to break her longtime habit. Starting today, no more of that.

It was a few minutes to seven when she left her room and descended the stairs. She wondered what Jonah would think of her changed appearance, what she would say if he disapproved. Briefly, she hesitated outside the dining room. She heard Jonah's voice, and Daphne's murmured response. She squared her shoulders and went inside. "I hope I'm not late," she said, taking her place at the table.

Daphne glanced up. She blinked. "Miranda, how nice you look . . . Doesn't she, Jonah? Doesn't she look nice?"

His dark eyes swept over Miranda. "Yes," he replied after a moment. "Yes, I must say there's been quite an improvement. You know, Miranda, you could be an attractive girl if you tried. If you weren't so fat."

She flinched, as if from a blow. The smile left her face.

159

Crimson, she stared down at the table.

"Jonah, dear," said Daphne, "I know you didn't mean to speak unkindly."

"Unkindly? I spoke the truth. That's always best. I'm certain Miranda agrees."

Daphne touched the pearls encircling her throat. "There are sensitive subjects."

"Bah! Miranda hasn't your delicate sensibilities, my pet. Miranda is quite a sturdy girl."

She wished they would stop talking about her as if she were not there. She had to fight an impulse to run from the room, from the house. *I wouldn't be missed,* she thought, clenching her hands in her lap. Only minutes ago she had been happy, excited; now she knew that nothing had changed. *If your weren't so fat.* "If," she muttered under her breath. "If."

"What's that?" asked Jonah. "Did you say something? Miranda, I'm speaking to you."

She looked at him. "Sorry. I was daydreaming."

"Daydreaming, eh? Waste of time."

"Yes, I'm glad you reminded me."

Jonah favored her with a smile. "You've never seemed the day-dreaming type of girl, Miranda."

"I'm not." She picked up her napkin and snapped it open. "I'm the sensible type. A working girl, Jonah."

"As of Monday."

"Monday," she agreed, her eyes like cold gray steel.

Miranda's determination was apparent to the head of the credit department, Walter Houser. Determined females alarmed him, but in this case he had no choice. Jonah Wade's daughter-in-law had been thrust upon him, upon the department that was his whole world. He had received the news in respectful silence; to himself he had wondered *why me?*

The long-suffering Walter Houser was somewhere in his forties, a small man with thinning brown hair and a small, neat mustache. He was a bachelor, with all the fussy habits of a bachelor. He lived quietly, frugally. He hoped to retire to

160

Florida one day. "Well," he said now, adjusting his necktie, "you're here, Mrs. Wade."

"Yes." She nodded. "Right on time."

"Please sit down."

"Thank you."

"Well, where to begin? Your duties, I suppose . . . Although your duties haven't really been defined. If you see what I mean."

Miranda saw the awkwardness of the situation. "I've had some bookkeeping experience," she said. "My father had a shop and I kept the accounts. But this is your department, Mr. Houser. I'll do whatever you tell me to do. I don't expect special treatment."

Mr. Houser could have wept with relief. "Naturally that makes things much simpler. Your co-workers, you see. One wants to be fair to your co-workers." He turned, glancing at the orderly stacks of folders on his desk. "I have no need of another bookkeeper. Another records clerk, however, would be a great help. Yes indeed, a great help." He raised his mild brown eyes to Miranda. "It's detail work," he explained. "There's something of a backlog right now. We have so many new charge account customers . . . You may find the work tedious. I mention that only as a warning. People who lose interest in their work often try to rush through it. Mistakes are made. We can't afford mistakes."

"I understand. I promise I won't lose interest. I want to work, Mr. Houser. That's why I'm here."

He stood. "Very well. I had a desk cleared out for you. If you'll come with me, Mrs. Wade."

"It might be easier if you called me Miranda."

"We observe the formalities in this department."

"Yes, of course." She gathered her purse and gloves and followed Mr. Houser into a narrow corridor. At the end of the corridor was a large, windowless room. She blinked in the bright lights; she counted seven desks, four of them occupied by middle-aged women, two by middle-aged men. There was an entire wall of filing cabinets, a wall of alphabetized ledgers. The air was musty. "Are all the offices like this?"

"Some of them are decorated with plants and pictures and such." Mr. Houser's nose wrinkled. "I confess I disapprove. Offices are meant for work. Good strong lights and ample supplies — that's all any office needs." He clapped his hands. Six pairs of eyes looked up. "This is Mrs. Wade, our new records clerk. Mrs. Dawber, if I may have a word with you."

The gray-haired woman left her desk. "Yes, Mr. Houser?"

"Would you be kind enough to explain our systems to Mrs. Wade? I feel you're the right person to break her in; you've been here the longest."

"Ten years come July," said Mrs. Dawber to Miranda. "I haven't missed a day's work in ten years."

"That's wonderful."

"We're all very proud of Mrs. Dawber," said Mr. Houser. "And now I'll leave you in her hands."

Miranda nodded. She looked at the woman, at her cap of short, fluffy gray hair, at her eyeglasses dangling from a grosgrain ribbon, at her plain white shirtwaist and black skirt. Ten years in this awful place, she thought. "Well, Mrs. Dawber, where do we start?"

"I'll show you our filing system first. We have all the credit files here. They're confidential," she added, lowering her voice to a whisper. "You understand."

"Yes."

Mrs. Dawber led Miranda across the room to the rows of cabinets. "Are you a relative? I wondered . . . Your name being Wade."

There was a pause. "By marriage," she said finally. "I'm Jonah Wade's daughter-in-law. I hope that won't make any difference. I'm just here to work, like everybody else. I need to earn my living. I'll certainly appreciate your help, Mrs. Dawber."

"Whatever I can do . . . Did you hear that Mrs. Boggs is retiring next year? You'll have a chance for a promotion!"

Miranda smiled. She had bigger plans for herself, much bigger plans. "I'll have to work very hard, won't I?"

Chapter Ten

Miranda was determined to carve out a place for herself at Wade & Company. She was not yet sure where that place would be, but she knew the credit department was merely a stop along the way. It was a useful stop. Working with the credit files every day, studying them, she learned about the store's customers — their average income, their average monthly purchases. She devised her own charts, refining the facts and figures until she had a precise, department-by-department portrait of Wade's.

She gave all her free time to these charts. They were with her during the evenings when she sat with Drew in the nursery, with her late at night when she stretched out in her bed, too excited to sleep. And they were with her every noon when she claimed a small corner of the employees' lounge, bending her head over the table that served as her desk.

She was utterly oblivious to the comings and goings around her, but now she felt a tap on her shoulder and looked up. She saw a young woman with curly dark hair and large, liquid hazel eyes. She returned the young woman's smile. "Yes?"

"I'm sorry to interrupt, but I've been watching this project of yours all week. I'm *dying* of curiosity . . . I'm Natalie Stern, by the way. Ladies' fine handbags."

"Miranda Wade. I'm in the credit department."

"Miranda Wade. Oh, *you're* the in-law. It's the talk of the store, you know. Mr. Wade's daughter-in-law working here. Maybe I should back off while I still have a job."

"Your job is safe," laughed Miranda. "I'm harmless. Sit

down, Natalie. If you sit in that chair you'll catch a little breeze from the fan."

"Okay. Now if you don't mind my asking, what on earth are you doing?"

Miranda smiled again. "When I'm finished, these charts will tell me everything there is to know about Wade's typical customer."

"Why do you *want* to know?"

"It's an idea I have. I've been thinking that if I know all about the typical customer, I'll know what the typical customer will buy."

Natalie Stern shook her head. "I still don't see."

"It's simple. These charts could be my way out of the credit department." She shrugged. "I have a lot of ideas, but they're no good unless I can prove I'm right."

"You're ambitious."

Miranda wondered if she had said too much. She was well aware of the gossip that was a store pastime; it would be a mistake for Jonah to hear of her ideas before she was ready.

"You don't have to worry," said Natalie, reading her thoughts. "I won't tell anybody. I'm ambitious myself. I'm going to be a dress designer. I'm working here to learn about the retail business. Also to put money away, in case I fall flat on my face."

"A dress designer!" Miranda could not imagine a more glamorous profession. "Really?"

"A rich and famous designer. I even have my name picked out: Natasha Starr. In German, Stern means star. My family came from Germany. We're German Jews."

"My!" Miranda was impressed. She had met a young woman who was going to be a dress designer, and who was Jewish. She would never have met anyone like Natalie — or Natasha — in Logan Falls. "You're a real New Yorker, aren't you?"

"Born and raised." She leaned forward, glancing at Miranda's charts. "How long have you been working on those?"

"Two months."

"I'd like to hear about it. I have to get back to the counter now, but maybe we could have a cup of coffee after work."

Miranda was startled by this friendly suggestion. "Oh, I wish I could. I have to go straight home, though. It's my little boy's birthday today. He's one year old. He doesn't understand about birthdays yet, but I planned a party anyway. A small party, just family."

"Another time, then."

"Tomorrow?"

Natalie nodded. "Tomorrow it is. We can meet right outside the employees' entrance."

"I'll be there." Miranda capped her pen and slipped her chart into a manila envelope, tying it closed. "I have to be getting back, too. I'll walk with you to the stairs . . . How's business in ladies' fine handbags?"

A quick smile lighted Natalie's square face. "Can't you tell from your charts?"

"If they're right, I'd say business was down almost eleven percent."

"Hey, that's pretty good. I don't know about percentages, but business is down all right. Just the other day I was thinking it's a good thing I don't work on commission. Some of the saleswomen do, you know. In dresses, coats, furs . . . Furs, that's a cushy spot! But you have to work here a hundred years before they'll promote you to the fur department."

"Yes, I . . ." Miranda left her thought unfinished, for her attention had been drawn to a tall, dark figure at the end of the corridor. "Isn't that Peter Dexter?"

"The mystery man."

"Mystery man? Why?"

"Nobody knows much about him. According to the grapevine, he's from some society family in Boston. He has his eye on the vice president's office — when old man Grayson retires, of course. He's not married and he lives in Gramercy Park. That's it — end of story."

"He's very handsome."

"He doesn't know any of us are alive." Natalie glanced quickly at Miranda. Miranda *Wade,* she thought, the boss's widowed daughter-in-law. Hmm. "But you never know; there's always a first time for everything."

Miranda opened the door to the staircase. "He'll marry someone beautiful."

Natalie's hazel eyes flickered. "Maybe not. You never know with those quiet types. You never know what they're thinking . . . Well, I'll see you tomorrow."

"Bye, Natalie."

Miranda lingered on the stair, hoping for another glimpse of Peter Dexter. After a few moments she gave up and returned to the credit department. Mr. Houser, pocket watch in hand, stood at the door. "You're late, Mrs. Wade."

"I'm sorry."

"I don't like to complain, Mrs. Wade. You're doing a fine job here. But punctuality is important. Why, it's the *cornerstone* of an efficient department. If people come and go as they wish . . ."

Mr. Houser droned on and on. Miranda appeared to be listening, although her thoughts remained with Peter Dexter. She had seen him only a few times during these months at the store; she had dreamed of him almost every night. In her dreams she had felt his arms around her. She had felt the warmth of his lips. "But only in my dreams," she murmured to herself.

"I beg your pardon, Mrs. Wade? I didn't hear what you said."

"I said . . . I said I was sorry."

"You're late, Mrs. Wade. It's nearly six."

"I know, Lily. I was a few minutes late coming back from lunch and so Mr. Houser gave me extra work to do. My punishment . . . I hope I haven't ruined Cook's birthday cake."

"I already took the cake up to the nursery. The presents, too. Mr. and Mrs. Wade are waiting for you upstairs."

"Is *Jonah* home? Goodness, I really *am* late." Miranda dropped her gloves and purse on the hall table. She rushed to the staircase and took the steps two at a time. "He'll be furious."

"Careful," said Lily, following behind. "It won't help anything if you fall and break your neck."

Light streamed from the nursery. Miranda heard Miss Dent's calm, crisp voice. She heard Jonah's rumbling laugh. She went inside. The room had been decorated with balloons and paper banners. Daphne and Miss Dent wore party hats; a shiny paper crown was tilted at a rakish angle on Andrew's small head. "I know I'm late and I apologize," said Miranda, avoiding Jonah's stare. She bent, opening her arms to the child. "Come give Mama a kiss."

Andrew lurched forward. He had taken his first steps several weeks before, but his gait was still uncertain. His short, sturdy legs followed a zigzag path across the room. His knees buckled. He fell, picked himself up, and skidded into Miranda's arms. "That's my good birthday boy. Can you say birthday?"

He grinned. "Bft," he offered.

Miranda hugged him. She straightened his crown and then held him away. "Oh, you're getting so *big*. My great big boy."

"Bft."

Miranda looked up at Miss Dent. "He's very smart."

"Indeed he is, Mrs. Wade."

"Shall we get on with it?" Jonah rose. He lifted the presents from the dresser and placed them on the floor. "I'm expecting a dinner guest, Miranda. I can't dawdle here all night."

There were three boxes and one oddly shaped package. Miranda slid the package closer. "Let's see what this is. Can you help me open it?"

Andrew's hands slapped at the bright red wrapping paper. He was smiling, gurgling words only he understood. His mouth formed an O as the paper was torn away, revealing a tall, white plush goose with long felt eyelashes.

"I do hope he likes it," said Daphne. "I couldn't resist."

"It's wonderful."

Jonah held his watch in his hand. Impatiently, he snapped open the cover. "Can't you hurry, Miranda? Such

167

a fuss for a one-year-old child! The boy doesn't *know* it's his birthday."

"But *we* know," she replied. She wanted to remind Jonah that "the boy" was his grandson, the only grandson he would ever have. Not that he cares, she thought to herself. She had never seen a man less interested in his grandchild, not even on Glenwood Road where men rarely displayed emotion. "Come on, Andrew, let's see what's in this pretty blue box." She undid the ribbon and looked inside. "A caterpillar!" She laughed, uncoiling a long, slender pull-toy striped green and yellow. "You can take him to the park. Won't that be fun?"

Andrew's head bobbed up and down. He touched the caterpillar's back. He giggled.

"A success, Miss Dent. Thank you." Miranda opened Jonah's present: a set of handsome wooden alphabet blocks. She opened her own present last. "This is very special," she said. It was a charming toy carousel with plumed horses, a lamb, a pig, and a swan. A small key in the base sent it spinning around and around, tiny streamers rising and falling in time to the music. It had cost her half a week's salary. "Do you like it, darling?" She saw Andrew clap his hands together, heard his delighted squeal. "Another success! Thank goodness!"

Daphne came over for a closer look. "Miranda, how lovely. Wherever did you find it?"

"At F.A.O. Schwarz. It's imported from Switzerland."

"A terrible waste of money," scoffed Jonah. "He'll break it, you know. Five minutes and he'll tear it apart. What were you thinking of, Miranda?"

She gazed at Andrew, at the wonder in his eyes as he followed the spinning carousel. "I was thinking of my son."

Jonah frowned. He said nothing, for Lily brought in the cake: two layers of devil's food iced with chocolate cream and decorated with two candles. "Happy Birthday" was sung, but not by him. Ridiculous, he thought. All this ceremony for a child still in diapers.

Miranda helped Andrew blow out the candles. She put him in his highchair and gave him a thin slice of cake.

168

"Your very first birthday cake," she said, kissing the top of his head.

Jonah took Daphne's arm. "Come, my pet, we've done our duty. I'd like a few moments to relax before Dexter arrives. We have quite a lot of work to do after dinner. I'm expecting a late night."

Miranda turned. "Dexter? Is that Mr. Dexter from the store?"

"Of course it is. He's bringing the quarterly reports. Don't be late to dinner."

"Me? But I'm never invited when you have guests."

Jonah sighed. Did he have to explain everything? "This isn't a dinner party, Miranda. It's business. But if you prefer to have dinner in your room—"

"No," she said quickly. "No, I wouldn't. I mean . . . I mean—"

"Well, whatever you mean, don't be late to dinner. Come, Daphne."

Miranda grasped the back of the highchair. Peter Dexter coming here, she thought, feeling a familiar weakness in her legs. Coming here!

"Are you all right, Mrs. Wade. You're very flushed . . . Mrs. Wade?"

"What? Oh, I'm sorry. I wasn't listening."

"You're flushed, Mrs. Wade. Do you feel ill?"

Miranda laughed. "Miss Dent, I feel wonderful. Just wonderful. I think I'll change my dress." She kissed Andrew's chocolate-smeared cheek and then hurried to the door. "Thank you for helping with the party."

"Not at all. I enjoyed it. Miss Dent's eyes narrowed thoughtfully on her young employer. "There's something different about you, if you don't mind my saying so. I can't quite put my finger on it. You look—"

"Happy? I *am* happy. My wish came true!"

Miranda changed into her one good summer dress, a stylish black linen with a loose jacket and small jet buttons. She brushed her hair and rouged her lips. She did nothing to her eyes, for they were sparkling.

A little voice told her that she was being foolish. And deep down she knew that wishes and dreams never really came true. Over the years, she had trained herself to expect little from life, to limit her hopes, her vision. But then she had come to New York, a place of infinite possibilities. She had discovered the charm of Murray Hill, the magic of Wade & Company, the lure of a dark, handsome man named Peter Dexter. Inevitably, her expectations had grown. *I'll be sorry,* she thought, though it was a chance she was willing to take.

She was smiling as she entered the dining room. Her eyes went immediately to Peter Dexter, seated at Daphne's right. She blushed.

"Of course you remember my daughter-in-law," said Jonah. "She's in Houser's department now. Doing well, I'm told."

Peter Dexter stood. "Mrs. Wade."

"Please call me Miranda."

"If you'll call me Peter."

She nodded, slipping into the chair opposite him. "Peter," she whispered.

A vague smile drifted across Daphne's face. "Well, here we are. All of us together. It's so nice to have four at dinner. It's . . . balanced. Four is such a *friendly* number. Don't you agree?"

The question had been directed to Peter. He swiftly offered assent, for he had long ago decided that that was the easiest thing to do. He visited the Wade house several times each year, but he had yet to find the clue to the puzzle of Daphne's conversations. He thought she was charming, and very strange. "I always enjoy our dinners together, Mrs. Wade."

"And now we have a fourth! We have Miranda!"

Jonah laughed. "You'd better fill your plate while you can, my boy. Miranda has a hearty appetite."

This boorish comment had also been directed to Peter. He pretended not to hear. His dark gaze fell away, settling upon the bowl of yellow roses.

Miranda was humiliated. Her eyes darted about, as if

170

looking for a place to hide. Jonah's laughter rang in her ears. She stared at a heavy crystal water goblet, fighting an urge to smash it on Jonah's head.

Daphne had winced at her husband's remark, but now her face was devoid of expression. "It's been a terribly warm July, hasn't it? Rain would be such a relief."

Eagerly, Peter seized on this change of subject. The weather was a safe, uncomplicated topic; he decided he could not go wrong talking about the weather. He talked about it through the soup course, through the salad course. By the time the poached salmon was brought, he knew he would have to move on to something else. "How do you like working at Wade's, Miranda?"

She looked up. She had been silent, nursing her hurt feelings, but now she smiled. "I like it very much. The credit department is a good place to learn about the store."

"Is it?" Peter had not understood why Jonah Wade's daughter-in-law should have to work. Jonah's famous stinginess might be the reason, but he was certain it was not the *whole* reason. "In what way?"

"Well, if you study the credit files—"

"What's that, Miranda?" Jonah frowned. "Have you been snooping around in the credit files?"

"Not snooping, no. It's my job to work with those files. I've just noticed a few things, that's all. Patterns. Your regular customers follow regular patterns. When they shop, I mean. You can almost tell beforehand what they're going to buy."

"You can, can you?" Jonah turned to Peter. "That's what comes of hiring women. Harebrained ideas!"

But Peter did not consider her idea harebrained. He saw the logic, surprised he had not thought of it himself. "It could be a kind of research, Mr. Wade."

"Bah! Quality merchandise at a fair price is all the *research* Wade & Company has ever needed. My great-grandfather had no credit files to study. He offered quality merchandise at a fair price and customers flocked to his door."

"There's more competition now," suggested Miranda.

171

"Competition is good! It's the American way! Competition, free enterprise. You mustn't try to discuss things you don't understand."

"I'm sorry, Jonah. I didn't —"

"What patterns?" he demanded suddenly. "Just what patterns do you believe you've unearthed?"

Miranda had barely touched her dinner; she pushed her plate away. She knew she had spoken too soon. She was torn — wary of angering Jonah, anxious to impress Peter Dexter. "I can't really explain," she began.

"Aha!" cried Jonah. "I thought as much."

Miranda took a breath. "I mean that I can't really explain without my charts."

"Charts? What the devil are you talking about?"

"I've been keeping charts."

"Why, how clever of you," said Daphne.

Clever is the right word, thought Peter. He wondered what she had up her sleeve. "Perhaps we could have a look at your charts later on."

"Yes, why not?" said Jonah. "We may have a genius in our midst. A most unlikely genius." He laughed, though he appeared to be more annoyed than amused. "What about it, Miranda? Are you ready to teach us our business?"

"If it sounded that way, I'm sorry."

"You should be. Charts indeed!" Jonah finished his coffee. "What sort of charts are they?"

Miranda shrugged. "I don't know how to describe them."

"Then you must show us. A little after-dinner entertainment, eh?"

Miranda wished she had kept her mouth shut. *I'll never learn,* she thought. She felt Peter's eyes on her. She looked up, seeing a mixture of curiosity and doubt. She turned her head. "All right, Jonah. If that's what you want."

They adjourned to the living room. Brandy was poured and cigars were lighted. Daphne settled gracefully into a chair. She clasped her hands and sat back; her face was expectant, as if she were waiting for a theater curtain to

172

rise.

Jonah exhaled a cloud of smoke. "Well, Miranda? Are you going to keep us in suspense?"

"The charts are upstairs."

"Go and get them. Don't be long; I have *real* business to attend to."

Peter watched her leave. "It's unusual for a woman to take such interest in work," he said when she had gone. "Even as a whim."

Jonah puffed on his cigar. "I don't think Miranda *has* whims. She's not the type . . . I'll tell you something, Dexter: that girl has a good head on her shoulders. I wouldn't tell *her*, of course. You know how women are, especially these days. Give them an inch and they'll take a mile. But I have to admit Miranda's been a surprise. She seems to have a grasp of things. She actually seems to have a mind for figures."

"A clever girl," said Daphne.

Jonah nodded. "And willing to work. Eager, I'd say. Another girl might have tried to take advantage. All in all, I'm rather pleased. Not that I think there's anything to her charts. It's nonsense, sheer nonsense. Still, it shows initiative."

"Yes," agreed Peter. He sipped his brandy, troubled by this praise of Miranda. He had his own ambitions for Wade & Company; now he sensed a threat. It seemed absurd to worry about a young, inexperienced girl, but he knew it was possible that she, too, had ambitions. He knew she had an edge: the Wade name. "Miranda doesn't see much of her son, I suppose."

"Oh, but she does," said Daphne. "She's quite an early riser, you see. Why, she's up and dressed and in the nursery by six-thirty. I know because Cook is upset about having to prepare such an early breakfast."

"Servants!" snorted Jonah.

Peter stared into his drink. It had done no good to suggest that Miranda was neglecting her son, but he could suggest that she was overstepping her place. "Not so long ago, a woman's place was in the home."

"Times change," replied Jonah with a melancholy sigh. "It was the war; nothing's been the same since the war." He glanced up as Miranda returned to the room. "Here's our genius now."

She pretended not to hear. Nervously, she opened the manila envelope and withdrew six large charts.

"All that?" Jonah threw his cigar in an ashtray. He left the couch, walking to where she stood. "I wasn't expecting anything so elaborate. What does it all mean?"

"Well, I think of these charts as a picture of the store's customers. A picture based on numbers." Miranda paused. She felt three pairs of eyes on her, for Peter and Daphne had also come to inspect her work. "The numbers describe things. They tell us things. I can look at this chart and see who your typical customer is."

"I certainly don't need charts for that, Miranda. All one need do is look around the store, look at the customers in the aisles. Our *typical* customer is an older woman."

"A forty-six-year-old woman, as a matter of fact. Married, with grown children. Married to a professional man — a doctor, a lawyer, a stockbroker, somebody like that. Two households, one in the city, one in the country. She has a busy social life. Not counting furs and Christmas, she spends about three thousand dollars a year at Wade's."

"I could have guessed at all that," said Jonah. "We're not a bargain basement store, Miranda. We have an affluent clientele. You're not telling me anything new."

"Maybe not . . . but I could tell you a few things that don't make sense. In numbers, I mean." *There, I've said it,* she thought. *They can laugh at me or cart me off to the crazy house, but I've said it.* "Numbers are all I know," she added.

Jonah's frown had deepened. "*What* doesn't make sense? Give me an example."

"I haven't recorded all the departments yet. It's just a few things I've noticed."

"Yes? Go on."

"Well, this woman, this typical customer, buys all her evening accessories at Wade's. Evening bags, fancy lace

174

handkerchiefs, satin shoes. She buys everything but evening *gowns*."

"We haven't done well with evening gowns for the past five years. Our customers are getting older. They're not running out to balls and cotillions every night of the week."

In for a penny, in for a pound, thought Miranda, gathering her courage. "They're running somewhere. Or else they wouldn't be buying evening accessories. I guess fall must be the big social season in New York. Fall and winter, because that's when you sell evening bags by the thousands."

Jonah looked at Peter. He looked again at the charts. "And just what conclusion have you drawn?"

"Wade's must be selling the wrong kind of evening gown."

"Isn't that interesting," said Daphne, who bought her gowns at Saks. "Miranda's figured everything out."

"Hardly," said Jonah. He put the first chart aside, glancing through the others. "Although I'll grant she's collected some interesting information. What do you think, Dexter?"

It was a tricky question. Charting retail sales was not a new idea, but Miranda had presented her charts in a new way — as a customer profile. She had intrigued Jonah, roused what little imagination he possessed. "I'd like a closer look."

"Yes. Yes, quite right." Jonah touched Daphne's hand. "Will you excuse us, my pet? We're going to continue this discussion in the study."

The discussion lasted more than an hour. Jonah was deeply suspicious of any business procedure that had not originated with his ancestors; as a result, the store was run much the way it had been run fifty years before. There was only a modest advertising budget, and no budget at all for public relations. No effort was made to keep up with changing fashion trends, nor to track customers' evolving tastes. Wade & Company had prospered but it had not grown. While other Fifth Avenue stores saw profits rise

175

year to year, Wade's profits remained the same. Jonah was aware of these things, though in an abstract sense. Now, examining Miranda's charts, the abstract became real.

"Let's cut through all this infernal talk, Miranda. As I understand it, you believe that your research can pinpoint our problem departments."

"If I may, Mr. Wade . . ." said Peter. "The monthly sales reports provide the same information."

"Sales figures don't tell us *why*. Why certain departments are losing customers. Why our profits are flat. They don't tell us about our customers' needs. Perhaps these are things we ought to know. Mind you, I'm only saying perhaps. I am by no means convinced."

But Jonah sounded convinced and that was enough for Peter. He decided it was in his own best interest to offer no dissent. "Miranda has come up with an original approach."

"Yes, an approach. One that might be worth investigating. It might be foolishness, of course. A colossal waste of time." Jonah looked at Miranda. "I'm a busy man, you know. How much faith do you have in this scheme of yours?"

Scheme? She smiled. "Numbers don't lie. It's just a question of the way the numbers are used."

"That's not an answer."

Miranda glanced away. She had not expected the discussion to get this far; now that it had, she knew she had to be careful. Jonah would not forgive a mistake in judgment, nor would he forget. It occurred to her that her future at Wade & Company might well depend upon what was said in this room tonight. "I can't make any promises, not yet. When I've finished recording all the departments, I'll have a more complete picture. A picture in numbers. I think it could be very helpful, but I won't say for sure until I'm finished."

Smart girl, thought Peter. No rash promises, no guarantees. He knew his instinct had been correct: Miranda Wade was going to be competition; she was going to be a threat. He would have to do something about that.

176

"How long will it take you to finish?" asked Jonah.

"Four months, maybe five."

Jonah sat back, making a tent of his fingers. "Too long."

"That's the best I can do. I can't take time from my job. It wouldn't be fair to Mr. Houser."

"I'll decide what's fair, if you don't mind. And I'll decide where you're most useful to Wade & Company. Clerks are a dime a dozen. Really, Miranda, you must cultivate a wider view of things. Priorities. You must learn to set priorities."

Peter looked at the clock. It was nearly ten and still Jonah had not come to the point. "May I assume you want Miranda to put more time into her charts, Mr. Wade?"

"You may indeed. I think she should put *all* her time into this project. The sooner that's done, the sooner we will know if there's anything to it." Jonah nodded, pleased with his decision, for he fancied himself a man of action. "Now that the matter is settled," he continued, "I warn you I will expect results."

"I don't understand," said Miranda. "How is it settled?"

"In the simplest possible way. Starting Monday, you have a new job."

"But—"

Jonah held up his hand. "You needn't expect an increase in salary. That's out of the question. You will, however, have a small office of your own. Fewer distractions that way . . . Yes, now that I think about it, the small office next to mine would be ideal. In my father's time," he explained, "it was customary for the store president to have both an assistant and a secretary. I have no need of an assistant . . . There's Dexter, after all," he added with a curt nod. "And so the office is empty. It's an excellent solution."

"Yes." A thin smile masked Peter's irritation at this abrupt change in Miranda's status. It was bad enough that she had access to Jonah at home; now she would have access to him at the store as well. Life was unfair.

Miranda's smile was genuine, for Jonah's solution meant escape from the drab, airless credit department, from fussy Mr. Houser. It meant an opportunity to prove she was more than a "dime a dozen clerk," to prove she had earned a place at Wade & Company. She refused to consider the possibility of failure. This was her chance and she would make the most of it. "I'd be working on my own, then?"

"In a manner of speaking. I intend to keep a close eye on your activities."

"I'll need the credit files, Jonah."

"Duplicates will be provided. See to it, Dexter, will you?"

"Of course, Mr. Wade." *And now I'm her errand boy,* he thought. "First thing Monday morning. Walter Houser won't be pleased. It's rather short notice."

"That can't be helped."

"If he knew he would have a replacement for Miranda—"

"No," said Jonah. "No replacements until we see what comes of this project. Houser may have Miranda back in his department sooner than he thinks. Time will tell, I suppose."

It was not exactly a vote of confidence but it would have to do. "I'll work hard, Jonah. I promise you that. And you, Peter." Shyly, she raised her eyes to him. Once again, color crept into her cheeks. She wanted to prove her ability to Jonah; to Peter she wanted to prove . . . something more. "I'll try not to disappoint you."

Something in her voice caught his attention. He looked at her, startled by her wistful expression. *The silly girl has a crush on me,* he thought. He smiled, for an idea had begun to take shape. "As Mr. Wade said, time will tell."

"Time," she whispered. She felt that time was on her side.

Chapter Eleven

"Did you ever notice," said Miranda the next day, "that a person's whole life can change in no time at all?"

Natalie Stern reached across the table for a small pitcher of cream. She poured a few drops into her coffee and stirred it. "Has your life changed since yesterday?"

Miranda smiled. "I guess the grapevine doesn't know yet. I'm moving out of the credit department and into a little office of my own. To work on my special project—my charts."

"That's pretty sudden."

"I still can't believe it, Natalie."

"How did it happen?"

"Well, it all started when Peter Dexter came to dinner. I didn't know he was coming. He asked me some question about the credit department and I said it was a good place to learn about the store. One thing led to another until I was telling him about my charts. I was really telling Jonah, I suppose, but it started with Peter Dexter."

"Obviously they liked your ideas."

"Peter didn't have a lot to say. Jonah was probably more curious than anything else. He doesn't think much of me, you know."

Natalie frowned. She shook her head, her dark curls swinging back and forth. "What do you mean? He must think the *world* of you if he's giving you your own office, your own project to work on."

"No, I'm grateful that he's giving me the chance, but I know he doesn't expect anything to come of it. It's up to me to prove him wrong." Miranda glanced around the

179

restaurant — a smaller, more modern version of McAllister's Sweet Shop. She looked down at her jelly doughnut. "I shouldn't really eat this . . . I promised myself I was going to lose weight."

"Good for you."

She pushed her plate away, then drew it back. "Making a promise and keeping it are two different things. I've tried before. I've put myself on diets but I've never stuck to them. It's hard for me."

"It's hard for everybody. It's *my* dream to be a size eight."

"Eight!" Miranda pushed the plate away again. "I'd settle for size twelve. I'd *kill* for size ten."

Natalie laughed. "I know a few tricks that might help. Drinking a big glass of water before meals is one thing you can do. It fills you up. Or you can eat a piece of fruit before meals. But the main thing you have to do is stop eating sweets. You'd be surprised how much weight you can lose by just cutting out sweets."

"I love sweets," said Miranda with a sigh. "And bread and butter and potatoes and all the things I shouldn't love. Food's always been such a comfort. That sounds silly, doesn't it?"

"Not to me. I understand, Miranda. When I'm sad, or worrying about something, that's when I run to the icebox."

"It doesn't show. You have a nice figure."

"Too round. I like that skinny model look. Slinky, you know?"

Miranda pushed the plate to the other side of the table. "Yes, I know."

"But we can't all be models."

"*I* can't, anyway."

"That's not such a tragedy, Miranda. Time catches up with models; when their looks are gone, they're through. I'd rather have a brain. And *you*, kiddo, have a brain."

"Does it have to be one or the other? Some women have both."

"Don't be greedy," replied Natalie. She winked. "Some women have neither. Did you ever think of it that way?"

180

Miranda wondered what way Peter Dexter thought of it. She guessed he would take beauty over brains any day. "But if I had a choice—"

"You don't; none of us do."

"Then I might as well eat my jelly doughnut."

"No, I won't let you. Come on, Miranda, at least give your diet a chance. Just keep thinking size twelve. It helps to have a goal. Whenever you want to dig into something fattening, remember your goal."

Miranda laughed. "You make it sound very simple."

"Mind over matter."

"Then would *you* like my jelly doughnut?"

"I'd like to hear about the project that got you out of the credit department. Unless you're still keeping it a secret."

"It's not a big thing, Natalie. I mean, it's not as if I invented radio."

"So what? It got you out of the credit department, didn't it?"

"Temporarily." There was a twinkle in the gray of Miranda's eyes, for she relished Natalie's practical, straightforward attitude. *We have a lot in common,* she thought, and as she did so, she realized she had found the friend she had been searching for all these months. "Do you want the short explanation or the long?"

"I want *details.*"

"Okay, but stop me when you get bored." Miranda explained her idea and the ways in which it had grown. She talked at length, drawing little diagrams on the paper placemat, scarcely pausing for breath. "You see, it's just a method of gathering information," she concluded. "More exact information than Jonah has now, which is almost none. I think it can help. I *hope* it can, because if I'm wrong—"

"You're not. It makes sense, Miranda. Wade's is so old-fashioned. Some of the styles in the dress department—nobody's worn those styles in five years. Wade's doesn't keep up with the times. But you'll change all that."

"Don't count on it. I'll be supplying information, not suggestions. Jonah doesn't welcome suggestions."

"My money's on you, Miranda. And remember you heard it here first."

"First I have to put everything together and see what I've got. Keep your fingers crossed, will you?"

"Gladly. When's the big day?"

"Monday?"

"To Monday, then," said Natalie, lifting her coffee cup in a toast. "To success."

Smiling, Miranda picked up her cup. "To dreams."

Walter Houser was not interested in Miranda's dreams, nor in anything save his own problems; terrible problems, for he had lost one of his best clerks and he had been ordered — *ordered!* — to deliver duplicates of his files to room 602. He thought the world had surely gone mad; how else to explain this sudden promotion of a young woman with barely three months' experience? There was the family connection, of course. There was an old saying: it's not what you know, but who you know. "Nepotism," he muttered to himself. "Nepotism, plain and simple."

"I beg your pardon, Mr. Houser?"

"I regret to say you've left me in a difficult position, Mrs. Wade. It's not my place to question company decisions, but you were doing so *well* in my department. And with Mrs. Boggs retiring next year . . . Why, you might have moved up to senior clerk."

"I might be back. This is only an experiment. Wouldn't you like to sit down?"

"No, thank you, I'll stand." He looked around the office, a small office with dark paneling, two oak file cabinets, a desk, two chairs, and a window that faced on Fifth Avenue. His nose wrinkled; if he had his way, office windows would be blacked out. "I must caution you again about my files. Guard them, Mrs. Wade. It wouldn't do to have confidential information lying around for anyone to see."

"I'll be careful. I'll return them to you as soon as I'm finished."

"When will that be?"

"I'm sorry, Mr. Houser, I don't know. But I *will* be careful."

He started toward the door. "I suppose I will have to be satisfied with that." He stopped, looking at Miranda. "I wish you good luck, Mrs. Wade, but if circumstances should change, there's always room for you in the credit department."

"Thank you. That's very generous."

He nodded. "Good day, Mrs. Wade."

"Good day, Mr. Houser."

The door closed. Miranda leaned back, spinning around in her swivel chair. "My own office," she murmured as a smile spread across her face. She wished her father could see her; she wished all of Logan Falls could see her. After a moment her gaze fell upon the cartons of duplicate files. They would have to be sorted and organized; for safety's sake, they would have to be coded. Time to get to work, she thought, leaving her chair.

She worked through the morning, wearing a path between the cartons and the file cabinets. Her big yellow notepad filled with numbers and symbols, symbols that she alone understood. Her desk filled with files, each of them bearing a different reference. Glancing around, she felt she had made a proper start.

It was a few minutes to noon when she heard a knock at the door. "Come in."

Peter Dexter entered, stepping nimbly around the cartons. "You haven't wasted any time, have you?"

"Oh, there's so much to do."

"Yes." His dark blue eyes scanned the office. "I see the credit files arrived. Is there anything else you need?"

"Nothing I can think of." Miranda looked into his eyes and then shyly looked away, a blush coloring her cheeks. She could not help herself; when Peter was around, she felt as giddy as a schoolgirl. "I'll probably need more notepads, but I have enough for now."

"Do I make you nervous, Miranda?"

Her blush deepened. "No, not at all. It's just that it's my

first day in a new job. I want to do well."

"There isn't any doubt about that. In the current slang, you'd be called a 'go-getter.' "

Miranda was not certain what he meant; she said nothing.

"I expect you'll do very well indeed," continued Peter. "You've come a long way already . . . I think a celebration is in order."

"A celebration?"

"I had a word with Mr. Wade this morning. I asked his permission to invite you to dinner."

Dinner? She sat down. "Did you say . . ?" She did not finish, for the idea was too fantastic.

"A celebration dinner, Miranda. Mr. Wade has no objections." Peter brushed at his mustache. He could still hear Jonah Wade's rumbling laughter, and the incredulous response that had followed: "You actually want to be seen in public with *her?*" An interesting response, everything considered. "I'm sure you haven't had a chance to see much of New York. You might enjoy a night on the town."

Miranda's hands were clenched so tightly that the knuckles sprang out beneath the skin. Had he really asked her to dinner? "I . . . I'm so surprised . . . I mean, I wasn't expecting . . ." She took a breath. *Idiot,* she said to herself. *Calm down and start again.* "I'd enjoy it very much. A night on the town . . . sounds lovely."

"Good. Shall we say Saturday?"

"Saturday?"

"The day after Friday," offered Peter in a rare display of humor. "If you're not busy, that is."

"No, I'm not busy." She knew her reply had come too quickly, had seemed too eager, but she had never been asked out to dinner before. It was a new experience, like eating oysters for the first time. "Saturday will be fine."

"I'll call for you at seven-thirty."

Miranda could not believe this was really happening. *It's a dream,* she thought. *I'm dreaming. If I pinch myself . . .* "Did you say seven-thirty?"

"I'll make dinner reservations for eight o'clock."

"That sounds . . . lovely."

"See you then," said Peter, opening the door. "I'll look forward to it."

"Yes, so will I."

Miranda stared at the door long after he had gone. Her heart was racing; a dazed smile flitted about her mouth. "A date," she murmured, caressing the word. "And with Peter Dexter." It was impossible, and yet it was true. She looked down at her desk calendar, drawing a circle around Saturday, August 6. Last August she had been sitting at her father's bedside, steeling herself for his death, wondering about her future. A year, she thought, a lot has happened in a year.

She rose and went to the window. She stared out at the traffic moving along the avenue, at the throngs of people walking in their purposeful, New York way. She had not felt herself one of them, but now, with her first dinner date in the offing, she felt a small burst of confidence; she felt she might fit in after all. She looked at her watch. She smiled. There was just enough time to tell Natalie her news.

"Details," said Natalie. "Give me details. And hurry up. Lunchtime is almost over. I can't be late getting back."

They were in the employees' lounge. Miranda sat in her usual corner chair. "Well, he was very casual about it. Smooth. What's that word . . . debonair? He said we ought to have a celebration dinner. He said I might enjoy a night on the town."

"A night on the town, huh? The man has style."

"I thought I was going to faint."

Natalie smiled. "This must be your year, Miranda. Now we have to make sure you're ready."

"Ready?"

"Well, a man like Peter Dexter . . . What are you wearing Saturday night?"

Miranda's face fell. "I didn't even think about that. I have only one good summer dress. I wore it the night Peter came to dinner."

"You'll have to buy a new dress."

Miranda considered what she had spent on Andrew's carousel. She considered her slender bank account. "I hadn't planned on any new clothes until autumn. The expense . . . I'm just not sure, Natalie."

"It's for a good cause. You have to look your best, don't you? Don't you *want* to look your best?"

"But the expense."

"Never mind that now. Think of it as an investment in yourself. There are lots of men who never notice what a woman wears. I'll bet you Peter Dexter notices. I'll bet you he has a very keen eye."

"If he has such a keen eye, why did he ask me out?"

You're the boss's widowed daughter-in-law, thought Natalie, *and Peter Dexter is an ambitious man.* "The reason doesn't matter," she said. "Whatever the reason, take advantage of it. And for gosh sake stop running yourself down. You have beautiful eyes, beautiful skin, beautiful coloring. You could really make something of yourself, Miranda. But you have to try. Cut out the jelly doughnuts and all that kind of stuff. Start wearing the right clothes."

"Don't get excited," said Miranda with a laugh. "I'll buy a new dress."

"But not *any* new dress. I know just the one. There's a clearance rack in the third-floor dress department. There's a perfect black silk—perfect if you'll let me do some alterations."

"How much does this perfect dress cost?"

"It's on sale: twenty-eight dollars."

Miranda groaned.

"Don't forget your discount; that'll help a little." Natalie glanced at the large round clock on the wall. She stood. "I have to get back to the counter. At least *look* at the dress. It's the one with a drape across the shoulder. You may not like it, but it'll be a knockout when I get finished."

"Promise?"

"Promise," called Natalie, disappearing through the door.

Miranda lingered a few moments longer. Finally she got to her feet and went to the staircase. Twenty-eight dollars, she thought on her way to the third floor. Twenty-eight dollars, she thought on her way to the clearance rack. She found the black silk dress draped at the shoulder, the "perfect" dress. She stared at the price tag as if she somehow expected the numbers to change.

"May I help you?" asked a smiling salesclerk.

Miranda hesitated. She debated with herself. She bought the dress.

"Miranda is in an absolute *fever* about her date," said Daphne early on Saturday evening. "It's rather sweet."

"It's nonsense," replied Jonah. "Dexter must be blind, or mad. Or perhaps he's trying to get on my good side. A waste of time, of course."

"I think Miranda is a nice girl."

"Nice? Lily is *nice*, but who would want to be seen with Lily? Who would want to be seen with Miranda? You have a kind heart, my pet. It obscures your judgment."

Daphne smiled. Although she did not say so, her judgment in this situation was accurate. She had assumed that Peter's interest in Miranda stemmed from his interest in Wade & Company. She had assumed that Peter was the sort of man to put his business interests above all else. Like Natalie Stern, she thought this was not necessarily a bad thing. In her opinion, it was just the edge Miranda needed. "A young woman ought to have suitors."

"Suitors?" Jonah laughed. "Impossible! I can't imagine any man chasing after Miranda."

"But Donald—"

"I will always believe she trapped Donald. I don't know how, nor do I want to know. Perhaps she was merely part of his youthful rebellion. He would have come to his senses. Oh, I don't doubt he was fond of her. But to *marry* that great lump." Jonah's gaze darted to the portrait above the mantel. He remembered when it had been painted; it did not seem so long ago. "I had such plans for him."

"Yes," murmured Daphne.

"Well, I suppose it could be worse. Miranda has a good head on her shoulders; I give her credit for that. And Andrew appears to be a bright little chap. Yes, it could be worse."

"Would you mind terribly if I went upstairs, Jonah? Miranda may need help getting ready."

"Must you?"

"Why, no. If you'd rather I didn't . . ."

Jonah's smile was magnanimous. "It's quite all right, my pet. Go on and do your good deed. I'll have you all to myself at dinner."

Daphne rose and turned toward the door. Her step was quicker than usual, for she had been stirred by Miranda's excitement. She had been reminded of her own youth, of summer dances and beaux and chaste kisses stolen in the moonlight. Now, ascending the stairs, she thought again about those happy times. She thought they had ended too soon, thought that, for women, they always ended too soon. "Seize the moment," her father used to say. She wanted Miranda to seize this moment, this chance with Peter Dexter. In her own way, she wanted to help.

Miranda's door was open. Daphne peeked inside. "Is there anything I can do to help?"

"You can tell me if I look all right. I'm *so* nervous."

"Stand up and let me see."

"It's a new dress."

"Yes, and quite lovely. Wherever did you find it?"

"At the store, but a friend of mine made some alterations. She lowered the shoulder drape and did something with the waist."

Daphne blinked. "At Wade's?"

"It was on sale."

"Really?" Daphne took a closer look. The dress was undeniably chic, its fluid lines enhancing Miranda's bosom, narrowing her waist and hips. The stark black matched the color of her hair. It seemed to bring out her porcelain complexion, to enliven the beautiful gray of her eyes. From the first, Daphne had seen possibilities in Miranda; now she knew she had been right. "Charming," she murmured. "A bit of jewelry is all you need."

"I don't have any."

"Pearls, I think. Yes, pearls." Daphne went to the door. "I won't be a moment . . . The summer cotillions were such fun. I always wore pearls."

Miranda's quizzical look followed Daphne out. She shook her head, thinking that she would never understand Daphne's unexpected allusions, her half-finished sentences, her Mona Lisa smiles. Did anyone understand Daphne, she wondered. Again, she shook her head. Women like Daphne—women blessed with grace and beauty—were not meant to be understood; they were meant to be admired.

Miranda returned to her dressing table. She had become less self-conscious about her appearance but mirrors still made her uncomfortable. She ducked her head and glanced sidelong into the glass. She saw highlights glistening in her hair; silently, she gave thanks for Michelle's lanolin hair creams.

"I've collected everything you need," said Daphne, gliding back into the room. "Your purse is all wrong. I brought one of mine."

Miranda took the small, black silk envelope. She touched the beaded clasp. "It's sweet of you, Daphne, but are you sure? This purse probably cost more than my dress."

"I have lots of purses." She reached into her pocket, removing a single strand of pearls and a pair of gold and pearl earclips. "Now you must put these on."

Miranda stared. "Oh, I couldn't. They're beautiful, but I couldn't. What if I lost them? What if something happened?"

"I never worry about things like that. Worrying spoils all the fun. That's why I never go to the races. Everyone seems so *worried* about which horse will win. I don't see what difference it makes. You must wear them, Miranda; I insist. And you must hurry. Peter will be arriving at any moment."

Peter. The thought of Peter Dexter brought a rosy glow

189

to her cheeks. She took the pearls from Daphne and put them on. "What do you think?" she asked, turning. "Do I look silly?"

"You look charming, Miranda. New York has had a good effect on you. You're a different girl."

"I hope so."

"Shall we go downstairs? Jonah will be wondering . . ."

"Does he like Peter?" asked Miranda as they left the room. "He's never said."

"Like him? They're not friends, not social friends. Jonah doesn't have friends at Wade's. I don't, either. I enjoy playing bridge, you see."

Miranda did not see at all, but that was nothing new. She shrugged.

"I think I hear Peter," said Daphne. "No, don't rush. A woman should make a graceful entrance."

"I'll try." Miranda slowed her pace, following Daphne along the hall. She paused at the door of the living room and drew a breath. *This is it,* she thought; *please don't let me make a fool of myself.* She took another breath and cleared her throat. "Hello," she murmured, walking inside. "I hope I'm not late."

Peter stood. "Good evening, Miranda. You look very pretty tonight."

"Thank you."

Jonah's appraising glance swept over her. Grudgingly, he conceded that she did not look bad. "Where did you buy your dress?"

"At Wade's."

He nodded, satisfied. "Very wise. It suits you."

"Thank you, Jonah."

"If you will excuse us," said Peter with a slight bow to Daphne, "I think we ought to be on our way. We have dinner reservations."

"Yes, of course, Peter, you mustn't lose your table. Restaurants are so . . ."

"Don't let us keep you," said Jonah, putting an end to the conversation. "You know the way out."

Peter took Miranda's elbow. "Good night, Mrs. Wade,

Mr. Wade."

"Good night," called Daphne. "Have a wonderful time."

They went to a French restaurant in Greenwich Village, a bistro decorated with striped tablecloths, candlelight, and misty murals of Paris. Vases were filled with mixed bouquets of summer flowers. Somewhere in the background was the romantic sound of violins.

Miranda, seated next to Peter in a fan-shaped booth, gazed around the room as if she wanted to commit it to memory before it disappeared. Her eyes were like a child's; her face shone. She could not believe she was here in this beautiful place, here with Peter Dexter.

He watched her. He smiled, for it was not hard to read her thoughts. His own thoughts were hidden, cloaked by a bland expression that gave nothing away. His reputation as a mystery man was well earned; no one ever knew what he was thinking.

Peter Dexter had been raised in Boston. The only son of wealthy and prominent parents, he had been brought up to respect family, to respect all the virtues preached by six generations of Dexters. His childhood had been predictable — the right schools, the right friends — but not dull. He had thrown himself into sports, into boyish pranks and jokes played on unsuspecting adults. He had been a happy, fun-loving child, a happy young man. At eighteen, as expected, he had entered Harvard. At nineteen, his world had come crashing down.

Peter would never forget the day he had heard the news — the incredible news that his father, staid pillar of society Leander Dexter, had run off with a twenty-year-old chorus dancer named Mamie Malone. Worse news had followed, for within the week it had been discovered that Leander had also run off with the assets of Dexter & Whipple, one of New England's oldest brokerages.

If the scandal shocked Boston, it devastated Peter. He watched his mother age overnight. He watched friends turn away. He watched uncles and cousins and aunts grow coldly distant. He had watched all these things and something in him had broken. By the time the pieces had been put back together, he had become a different man, a guarded and cynical man who trusted no one. He had become especially distrustful of women. The lesson of his father, he decided, was that any man could be destroyed by a woman. Forewarned, he avowed that no woman would ever gain such power over him. He closed his heart to love; little by little, he lost his capacity to love.

Peter's mother had died eight months after his father's disappearance. Everything had been sold by then — the stocks and bonds, the paintings, the antiques, the house on Beacon Hill. Every cent had gone to pay off the legal claims against Dexter & Whipple. Peter had arrived in New York with two suitcases, seventy dollars, and a few pieces of his mother's jewelry, pieces he had hidden from the lawyers and the auctioneers.

His two years at Harvard had been enough to ensure job interviews, but the jobs he was offered were humiliating reminders of what his life had come to. He spent six months selling advertising space for a newspaper, another six months as a glorified tour guide at a museum. After two relatively happy years at a publishing house, he had been fired for having a "superior attitude." His happiest year, in the bond department of a bank, had ended when a colleague raised a forbidden subject: the funds embezzled from Dexter & Whipple.

It had cost him the last of his pride to take a job at Wade's, but gradually he had realized the advantages. He had assessed the situation: Lionel Wade was old and sick; the successor, Jonah Wade, was plodding and weak. In these circumstances, Peter had concluded, a clever, ambitious young man could rise quickly to the top.

He started out as a clerk in the men's furnishings department. Within a year, he was made department manager; within three years, assistant merchandise manager. Five years after coming to Wade's, he had been named general manager. He had envisioned a clear path to the vice president's office, and that goal would soon be reached. Provided there were no complications. Provided there were no surprises. Provided Miranda did not get in his way.

"I'm sorry I can't offer you wine," said Peter now. "The owner observes Prohibition."

"Oh, that's all right. I feel kind of giddy as it is . . . This is a beautiful restaurant, Peter. I'm so glad you brought me here."

"The food's very good."

"I've been peeking at the menu, but I don't understand French."

"Shall I order for you?"

Miranda smiled. "I wish you would."

Peter motioned a waiter over and, in perfect French, ordered their dinner. "The kitchen is slow," he said when the waiter had gone. "You can sit back and tell me all about yourself."

"You'd be bored."

"I doubt that. Tell me about Chicago."

Miranda's gaze skittered away. She studied the play of candlelight on the white plates, the shadows flickering across the striped cloth. "The past isn't my favorite subject," she said quietly. "Coming to New York was the start of a new life. At least I hope it turns out that way." She looked at him. She smiled. "I'd much rather hear about you."

"What would you like to hear?"

"Everything."

Her quick, guileless reply startled him. "Well, let's see . . . I'm from Boston. I came to New York fifteen years ago, after my mother died." He wondered if he should tell her about the family scandal; not yet, he decided. "There were a lot of different jobs. None of them lasted very long. There was the war, but I escaped that. Punctured eardrum," he explained, tapping his left ear. "I think it must have happened when I fell through the ice at the skating pond. I was twelve at the time."

"A lucky accident, if it kept you out of the war."

"I was a lucky child. Were you?"

"No."

Peter lighted a cigarette. "The past isn't my favorite subject either, Miranda. I prefer to look ahead." She was staring at him, hanging on his every word. He took a sip of water. "I enjoy my work," he continued. "Perhaps too much. You know what they say about all work and no play."

"Oh, but that couldn't be true. You must go to parties and nightclubs and all sorts of exciting places."

Peter had his share of invitations, more than his share. He went out with the city's prettiest women, though he was careful to avoid entanglements. "I'm not a hermit. But you'd be surprised how many nights I spend with a briefcase full of sales reports." He smiled at Miranda's earnest expression. "Am I winning your sympathy?"

He was winning her heart, and sympathy had nothing to do with it. She stared transfixed into his dark-blue eyes, thinking once again that he was the handsomest man she had ever seen. She had memorized his face; she longed for his touch. From the time of her fourteenth birthday she had wondered what it would be like to be kissed, to be held in a man's arms. She had wondered about love. "If you had a wife," she began, stopping abruptly in midsentence. "I'm sorry," she murmured, blushing to her fingertips. "I only meant . . . I meant that a wife would keep you from working so hard. I'm sorry."

Peter was amused. "No need to apologize. You're probably right. Although I haven't given much thought to a wife. I expect I will. In time." He had planned to marry when he was forty, and to marry a certain kind of woman — one who would neither bore nor challenge him, one who would make no demands on his emotions. "I'll make my choice, and hope she'll have me."

Miranda was saved from an embarrassing reply by the appearance of the waiter. He brought their first course a velvety pâté with crusty ovals of French bread. It was delicious, but she scarcely noticed. She picked at her food, too excited to eat, too happy. She wished this night would go on forever.

"I sometimes think about children," said Peter, dusting

194

crumbs from his mouth. "How is your little boy?"

"He's wonderful. He's awfully smart."

"Takes after his mother."

Miranda's smile was uncertain. "At his age, it's hard to tell who he takes after. I can't wait till he's old enough to visit the store . . . And not just the store; there are so many places I want to take him. New York is an amazing city."

"And what amazing places have you been to?"

"Parks," laughed Miranda. "Before I started working, Andrew and his nurse and I went to parks. I haven't been anywhere else."

"We must do something about that. Perhaps I can show you the sights."

Her face lit up. "Would you?"

"Where would you like to begin?"

"I'll leave that to you."

An obliging girl, he thought. "How do you spend your time when you're not working?"

"I read."

He could imagine the books she preferred: cheap, flowery romances. "What do you read?" he asked with an indulgent smile.

"Oh, everything. I've just been rereading *Vanity Fair*. I've been wishing I were more like Becky Sharpe. Her spirit, I mean. I wish I had more of her spirit."

Peter tried to conceal his surprise. Was it possible that Miranda read real books? "So you're a fan of Thackeray."

"Yes, but I don't think he was one of the great novelists. He wasn't Dickens. And then there's . . ."

Peter listened in astonishment as Miranda jumped from author to author, book to book. She obviously felt herself on safe ground, for now her stammers and blushes had disappeared. She was suddenly transformed. She was no longer an awkward, unsophisticated girl wondering which fork to use; she was an intelligent young woman with her own opinions. As dinner progressed, he reluctantly conceded that Jonah was right: she had a good mind. He frowned, thinking of the damage that mind

195

could do to his ambitions.

"Is something wrong? I'm sorry, Peter; I've been going on and on. I've been *babbling.*"

"Not at all. I'm very impressed." He fell silent as the waiter cleared away their dessert plates. "I was trying to think where we ought to go next," he said when the waiter left. "I'd planned to show you a little coffee house around the corner. A quaint little place, but not nearly festive enough. It's time you saw some New York nightlife. How would you feel about a speakeasy?"

Miranda's eyes widened; she was a small town girl once more. "A real speakeasy?"

"Are you game?"

"Oh, yes, I'd love to go." First a romantic French restaurant and now a glamorous speakeasy. What had Natalie said? "This must be your year." My year, she thought. "I'd love it, Peter."

He paid the bill. Outside, he bought a gardenia from a flower vendor and pinned it to Miranda's shoulder.

The intimacy of the gesture almost took her breath away. She gazed at him, at his handsome face shadowed by summer moonlight. She knew she was in love.

"Miranda, I think I see a taxi. Shall we?"

"Yes," she murmured. She would have agreed to anything.

The taxi took them to Club Harley, a reconverted brownstone that was one of the thousands of speakeasies flourishing in the city. Prohibition would someday be remembered as "the noble experiment," but noble or not, it was from the start an unqualified disaster. Gangsters grew richer, gang wars grew bloodier, and the law became something to laugh at. The Anti-Saloon League urged people to "Shake hands with Uncle Sam and board the water wagon"—words drowned out by the more popular cry of "Joe sent me."

At Club Harley the password was "roly-poly." Peter spoke the password through a slot in the door and a moment later the door was opened. To Miranda it seemed as if they had walked into a vast party. There was music and laughter; there were more people than she could count, crowds of people clustered in the foyer, on the stairs, around tiny tables in the cabaret. This, she thought to herself, was New York: beautiful women in slinky gowns, handsome men in dinner jackets. This was the city of dreams.

She saw Peter slip a five-dollar bill into the hand of a headwaiter; it bought them the last table in the noisy, smoky cabaret. The show had just begun, and again her eyes widened as a line of chorus girls danced onto the tiny stage. At first glance she thought they were naked; when the spotlights came up, she saw they were clad in spangles and feathers and very small bits of pink net. She laughed, for in Logan Falls they would have been arrested.

Peter ordered champagne, the "good stuff" smuggled in through Canada. She loved the sound of the popping cork, loved the little bubbles that tickled her nose. Most of all, she loved being squeezed so close to Peter. Several times their hands touched and each time she felt a thrill along the length of her spine. Was this really happening or was it a dream?

Peter lifted the candle from the table and held it up to Miranda's face. "A penny for your thoughts."

Her thoughts were tumbling and spinning in a hundred different directions, but they shared a common thread. "I'm having the best time of my life," she exclaimed. "I'll never forget it."

Peter felt an unfamiliar, unwelcome pang of conscience. Quickly, he looked away. He had set out to dazzle Miranda, for he wanted her firmly on his side, at least until he was made vice president. Dazzle her he had. And how easy it had been! Shooting fish in a barrel, he thought to himself. He liked her, but he would never love her; he would never love any woman. Sooner or later she would be hurt, her innocence destroyed. If he continued this charade . . . *But I must,* he silently declared. *For my own sake, I must.* "You're not the only one who won't forget tonight," he said, leaning nearer. "You're a very special girl, Miranda Wade."

A very special girl. She basked in the words, in the soft, intimate tone of Peter's voice. "Thank you," she whispered.

After the show, after more champagne, they left the club and walked back to Murray Hill. As they neared the house Peter took Miranda's hand. Standing outside the door, he kissed her.

A moment later she was stealing quietly into the house and up the stairs. She was flushed with the memory of this night, with the memory of Peter's lips on hers. She thought she could live on his kiss for the rest of her life.

Chapter Twelve

Sunday was cloudy and hot, the air thick with moisture. It had been a cool summer, but now the dog days of August had begun. Miranda fidgeted through church services, alternately mopping her face, tugging at her dress, and shifting around in her pew. The reverend Wisdom's sermon seemed endless; the choir seemed off-key. After the final benediction, she heaved a sigh of relief and bolted into the aisle.

Jonah lectured her all the way home. "Scandalous behavior," he insisted, his dark brows knitting together. "Absolutely scandalous behavior!"

"Not really *scandalous*," offered Daphne. "I wouldn't really say *scandalous*. Unbecoming, I think. Unbecoming behavior."

Miranda looked up at the sky. Clouds shuffled past, heavy summer clouds more gray than white. "I apologize for my behavior," she said. "The church was so hot. And Reverend Wisdom did go on longer than usual."

"Yes," murmured Daphne. "I noticed that."

"Hardly an excuse, Miranda. We were all uncomfortable, but you were the only one making a show of it."

"I'm sorry."

"See that it doesn't happen again."

"It won't, Jonah."

They turned into their street, nearly deserted on this early Sunday morning. Miranda saw the Russells' oldest son wheeling his bicycle along the block, and the Bradley's dog sniffing at a tree, but that was all. Jonah took out his key and opened the front door. He stepped back to let Daphne pass and then followed her inside. Miranda brought up the rear.

"Blueberries have such a short season," said Daphne as they climbed the stairs.

"Blueberries?" asked Miranda.

"Why, yes, we always have blueberry pancakes at this time of year. The first Sunday in August, you know. Cook has a nice light touch with pancakes."

Miranda tried to imagine Daphne eating a stack of pancakes. Impossible, she decided. "I'm sorry I won't be here to taste them. Andrew and I are spending the morning with my friend Natalie. I meant to tell you before we left for church, but I was rushing around."

"You overslept," said Jonah. "There would have been no need to rush if you hadn't overslept."

"Sorry." Miranda counted all her "sorrys" of the morning: five so far, a new record. "I'm not used to staying up late at night."

"That's not a habit I would encourage. You have responsibilities, Miranda. Responsibilities."

"Yes, I know." They had reached the landing. Daphne and Jonah turned toward the dining room. Miranda continued upstairs. The door of her room was ajar. She went inside, surprised to see Lily. "Isn't this your day off?"

"I'm on my way out. I just wanted to get your electric fan set up. We're allowed to use electric fans starting the first Sunday in August."

Another tradition, thought Miranda. "Don't bother about it, Lily. I'm going out, too." She walked to the bureau. Her gardenia, its petals brown and curled at the edges, floated in a small bowl of water. "Aren't you going to ask me if I had a good time last night?"

"That's none of my business, Mrs. Wade."

"Well, I did. I had a wonderful time." She spun around, smiling at Lily. "I went to a speakeasy! I drank champagne, real champagne! Just like Zelda and Scott."

"Zelda and Scott?"

Miranda wondered why she had said that. She sat

down, reminded suddenly of the house on South Crawford Street, of homey conversations in the kitchen, of two stray cats named after two straying expatriates. It seemed a lifetime ago. She asked herself if she had any regrets. No, she thought, none. "What do you think of Peter Dexter?"

Lily shrugged. "He's handsome, I guess."

"Do you like him?"

"I don't know him. I serve him dinner a few times a year, that's all." It was not quite all, for in fact Lily had taken a dislike to Peter Dexter. She had no idea why, nor did it seem to matter, until now. "But you have to watch out for the handsome ones. That's what everybody says."

"Maybe everybody's wrong."

"I wouldn't know, would I?" Lily turned on the fan. "It works all right," she said, turning it off. "I don't know anything about men, Mrs. Wade. But I know a woman's got to be careful."

Miranda glanced up. "That sounds as if—"

"It's my day off, Mrs. Wade. I'll be on my way now."

And with that, Lily was gone. Miranda shook her head. She would never understand the women in this house.

Except Miss Dent; plainspoken, comforting Miss Dent who arrived twenty minutes later with Andrew in tow. Miranda had changed out of her Sunday dress into a simple blouse and skirt. She had located her map of Manhattan and was frowning over it when she heard Andrew's squeals. "There's my big boy," she cried, bending to him. "Are you ready to go exploring?"

He grinned.

"Andrew's all ready, Mrs. Wade. He's been fed and bathed and changed." Miss Dent held out a small cloth bag. "I've packed fresh diapers and a bottle. Oh, and a washrag. It might come in handy."

"You're a treasure, Miss Dent. Did I tell you we were going to the zoo?"

"Yes. And a picnic afterward, I believe. I'm sure you'll have a lovely time."

201

"If I don't get lost. I know where Central Park is . . . I found the zoo on my map, but I can't find the sea lion pool. We're supposed to meet at the sea lion pool."

"That's easy. I'll show you."

Miranda straightened up. She folded the map lengthwise and pointed to an area at the right. "See, there's the zoo."

"And there's the path you want, there at Sixty-fifth. It takes you past the pony rides to the sea lions. You can't go wrong on that path."

Miranda smiled. "You've saved the day. Thank you, Miss Dent."

"I'll leave you, then."

"Yes, I didn't mean to keep you." Miranda knew that Miss Dent had a steady boyfriend, a schoolteacher who took her to Chinese restaurants on Thursday nights and to museums on Sundays. "Don't hurry back. I'll give Andrew his dinner tonight."

"Be a good fellow, Andrew. Behave yourself."

He grinned.

"He'll be fine," said Miranda. "Don't worry about him."

Miss Dent went to the door. She paused, her gaze resting on Miranda. "If I may say so, Mrs. Wade, you're looking especially well this morning. Really quite radiant."

Miranda had been waiting for someone to notice. "I had a date last night," she blurted, her hands fluttering at her sides. "I had the most wonderful time."

Miss Dent smiled. "I thought it might be something like that. It takes a man to put roses in a woman's cheeks, doesn't it? The bloom of romance."

The bloom of romance; Miranda savored the words. "I don't know if it's a romance, exactly."

"I'll be rooting for you, Mrs. Wade. Love is such a happy thing."

Miranda could not help smiling at Miss Dent's classic British understatement. A happy thing? Love was the *only* thing.

202

"I think I'm in love," said Miranda, rushing up to Natalie at the sea lion pool. "I really think I am."

"Most people start a conversation by saying 'hello,' but this is *much* better. Introduce me to your son and then you can tell me all about it."

Miranda scooped the child into her arms. "This is Andrew McAllister Wade, my pride and joy."

"Hi, Andrew. Can you say hi?"

"He doesn't talk yet. He makes sounds; his own language, I guess."

"Oooo," squealed Andrew, as if on cue. He clapped his hands together, his eyes following a sea lion out of the pool and onto a rocky platform. "Oooo."

"I see what you mean," said Natalie with one of her lightning smiles. "He's adorable, Miranda. A little doll."

"He's an angel."

Natalie leaned against the pool railing and gazed around the zoo. It was still early, but people were beginning to stream in. There were parents clutching the hands of small children, adolescents in groups of three and four, well-dressed old women scattering breadcrumbs for the pigeons. Vendors were beginning to arrange their wares: balloons, popcorn, bags of roasted peanuts, ice-cream bars, brightly colored pinwheels. The animals were beginning to stir, pacing and circling in their cages. "So tell me, Miranda. One date and you're in love?"

"I know it's silly."

"I didn't say that. I'm waiting to hear what *you* have to say."

"It was a perfect night. We went to a romantic French restaurant in Greenwich Village, and then we went to a speakeasy. Club Harley." Miranda shifted Andrew to her other arm. "Peter was so wonderful."

"Start from when he called for you, and don't leave anything out. I want *details*."

Miranda related the details. Almost every sentence began with Peter's name, and every time she spoke his name she felt a sudden dizzy pleasure. Her face was luminous with memory, with hopes she dared not express, not even to herself. "And then he took me home," she finished. "He held my hand the last two blocks."

"Did he kiss you good night?"

She nodded, dropping her eyes. A smile played about her mouth. "He's a gentleman, but it was a wonderful kiss."

"And now you're in love."

The sea lion dove back into the pool, sending up a spray of water. Andrew giggled. Miranda dug out her handkerchief and dried his face.

"And now you're in love," repeated Natalie.

"Yes, I really think I am."

"The way you were with your husband?"

Miranda had known that that question would come. She turned her head, watching the sea lions at their games. Absently, she stroked Andrew's hand. "The past is the past," she said. "I'm trying to put it behind me. A new life; that's what New York is all about. That's what I want, Natalie."

"I understand. I only asked because things seem to be happening so fast."

"That's the way things happen to me." She recalled the chance meeting in Union Station that had led to a job and a place to live. She recalled the ill-fated train trip that had changed her life. "It's true," she murmured, her arms tightening around Andrew. "Things always happen without any warning; at least they do to me."

"And to Peter?"

"Well, he invited me to the theater next Saturday night. We were watching the show at Club Harley and he asked me. I've never been to the theater."

"Nor have I. Unless you count the vaudeville down on Second Avenue . . . and I don't think that's what he has in mind. No, next Saturday night you'll be sitting in a Broadway theater with all the swells. Can you afford one more dress?"

Miranda's head snapped up. "Another dress! I

couldn't, Natalie. I couldn't spend any more money."

"It's all right; I have an idea. I'll restyle the dress you wore last night." She nodded, staring off into space. "I can see it now. A velvet insert here," she explained, drawing a diagonal line from shoulder to waist. "And maybe velvet cuffs. I have a big basket of remnants at home—just odds and ends of material. I buy them on Fourteenth Street. I'll bet I have just enough velvet."

"But all the work, Natalie. I can't ask you to do all that."

"I volunteered." She laughed. "It's not work to me, kiddo. Designing is what I do best. So I'll practice a little on you. So why not?"

"You have to let me pay you for the velvet."

"Buy me a hot dog later. If you want to be a sport, throw in a Coca-Cola."

Andrew had begun to squirm and Miranda put him down. "You're spoiling me, Natalie. You're going to get me used to my own personal dressmaker."

"Well, if Peter keeps taking you to fancy places you have to look your best; that's the first rule when you're dating a guy like him."

Miranda did not want to hear the second rule. "Let's walk," she said.

Andrew toddled along between them. He was fascinated by all the strange sights and sounds, waving his hand at a flock of scavenging pigeons, jumping up and down in front of the rhinoceros cage. The giraffes brought a huge grin to his face, for he had a family of toy giraffes at home.

"He's having a good time," said Natalie. She slipped her shopping bag over her arm and looked at Miranda. "If you could be an animal, what animal would you be?"

"I don't know . . . maybe a deer; deer are so pretty. But hunters shoot deer, don't they? Maybe I'd be a dog. Yes, that's it, I'd be a dog. Probably a mutt . . . What about you?"

"A leopard. Or any kind of slinky cat. That's the look I try for in my designs. I'm getting better at it."

205

"Will you show me your designs sometime?"

"When you come to visit . . . Come on, let's find a grassy spot and have brunch."

"Brunch? What's that?"

"Not exactly breakfast, not exactly lunch. Are you hungry?"

"I'm trying very hard not to be. I hope you didn't bring anything too tempting."

"Blame my mother. I just wanted to bring egg salad sandwiches, but then she got into the act. She's a sweetheart, my mother, but she thinks I don't eat enough." Natalie smiled. "She says a bird couldn't live on what I eat. A *bird;* can you imagine that? When you come to visit, she'll give you a five-course meal and still worry that you went away hungry. It's a miracle I don't weigh a ton."

"Why don't you show her your slinky designs? Maybe she'll get the idea."

"Hah! Anything not directly connected to landing a husband is of no interest to my mother."

"Any candidates?"

"Not yet. I was going out with a really nice guy named Phil. But he stopped coming around when he realized I wanted a career. Most men aren't keen on career women. I guess they don't like the competition."

Miranda felt a tug at her skirt. It was Andrew, wanting to be picked up. "Poor little boy. You've done a lot of walking this morning, haven't you? Come on; up you go."

"I'll carry him for a while."

"Thanks, but I'm fine. It's good exercise."

There were crowds gathering outside the primate house — or the monkey house as it was known to generations of children. Natalie steered Miranda away. "You don't want to go inside; it smells. Follow me and I'll show you something beautiful."

Miranda followed Natalie through an underpass. Minutes later, she found herself in a tranquil and exquisite forest. A forest in the middle of New York City.

206

"Where are we?"

"This is the Mall. Like it?"

"It's lovely, just lovely."

There were nearly three hundred trees in the Mall, stately American and English elms and charming Japanese cherry trees. There were birds and butterflies and gray squirrels with long, bushy tails. There was stillness, stillness broken only by the rustling of leaves, the piping of sparrows. It was the most peaceful setting Miranda had ever seen.

Natalie watched her, amused. "I had a feeling you'd approve." She pulled a faded cloth from the shopping bag and spread it on the grass beneath an elm. Soon the cloth was covered with food: hardboiled eggs, fruit, sandwiches wrapped in waxed paper, chocolate chip cookies. "We won't starve, will we?"

Miranda settled Andrew on the grass and gave him his bottle. She sat beside him, taking an egg, a peach, and two cookies for herself. "What did you mean when you said men weren't keen on career women?"

"They're not."

"But lots of women work now. It's practically *all* women at Wade's."

"Behind the counters, not in the executive offices. You're the one and only female on the sixth floor. Haven't you noticed that?"

Miranda tapped the egg against the tree and began to peel the shell. "No, I guess not . . . Do you think Peter's that way? About career women?"

"He's the mystery man, remember? Who knows what he's like? Anyhow, love may change your plans. What are charts compared to moonlight and roses?" Natalie stretched out her legs, pushing her skirt over her bare knees. She watched a robin take a twig in its beak and fly away. "Things do change, Miranda."

"I want my own money; that won't change. I don't ever want to have to depend on someone else for money. I promised myself . . . I made up my mind long ago."

"It's a woman's prerogative to change her mind."

"No."

"Not even for Peter? I know I'm getting ahead of myself here, but what if he asked?"

Miranda leaned back against the tree. Through the branches, she stared up at the leaden sky. She smiled. "You're right, Natalie; you're getting ahead of yourself." But Natalie had given her something to think about. She realized that her work had suffered in the week before her date with Peter. She had made progress, though not the progress she had expected. All during the week she had been distracted, worrying more about what she would wear, what she would say, than about the figures on her big yellow pads. She knew she could not afford to let that happen again. She could not, like her father, get caught up in dreams. "I was getting ahead of myself, too. Thank you for reminding me."

"You're hard to figure out sometimes, you know that?"

Miranda took the empty bottle from Andrew. She laid him on the grass, watching as he fell instantly asleep. "When you're his age, everything is simple. Food, sleep, play. Lots of hugs. It's not so simple later on. Life is confusing. And life in New York is . . . I don't know what it is; kind of crazy. You can get a little lost. Or *I* can, anyway."

Natalie laughed. She lay back, twining her fingers behind her head. "All the handsome men. All the beautiful clothes. All the fancy places. All the *money*. It's all here and it's enough to confuse anybody. Do you ever feel like a kid in a candy store? I do. I see it all and I want it all."

"Love and money."

"That's it, kiddo; that's the whole candy store: love *and* money."

It was eleven o'clock the next morning when the door of Miranda's office burst open. Jonah strode across the room and sat down. "When will you have something to show me?"

"I beg your pardon?"

"A report, a review. Perhaps a set of charts . . . I'm composing my fall schedule, Miranda," he added with an impatient sigh. "We always have an executive meeting in the fall. Will you have anything ready by then?"

She glanced at her desk calendar: three weeks until September. "I won't be finished by then, but I could give you a first draft. Sort of an outline?"

Jonah considered this. "An outline, eh?" He drummed his fingers on the desk. "I warn you it had better make sense. A lot of important business is conducted at executive meetings. We have no time to waste on foolishness."

"When is the meeting?"

"Fifteenth of September."

"I'll have five weeks . . . That sounds just about right."

Jonah studied her for a moment. "You may be called upon to explain your outline. Your premise, if you will."

"At the meeting?"

"Of course at the meeting. Are you ready to back up all your fine talk? I hope so. You're out on a limb now, aren't you?"

And you're holding the saw, she thought. "I'll do my best."

"We'll see about that."

Miranda heard the edge in Jonah's voice. She thought his attitude strange, for at times he seemed to want her to succeed and at times he seemed almost eager to see her fail. "I'll do my best," she said again.

His dark eyes swept over the office. "You certainly have enough information here."

"Mr. Houser has been very helpful."

"Yes, I imagine he has; the mouse."

"If you have another moment, Jonah," she said as he started to rise, "I — there's something I want to suggest. An idea."

He looked suspicious. "What idea?"

"Well, it's about shopping bags."

"Shopping bags!"

A blush crept across Miranda's cheeks. She ducked her head. "It's just that yesterday, in the park, my friend

Natalie had one of Wade's shopping bags. At least I assumed it was a Wade's bag. I mean, it was just a plain white shopping bag and—"

"Get on with it, Miranda."

"Yes. Yes, all right. The point is, it was just a plain white shopping bag and I started thinking it was a waste."

Jonah frowned. "A waste? What the devil are you talking about? Every department store in this city provides shopping bags to its customers."

"Yes, and every store but Wade's has its name printed on them. It's like free advertising. Why does Wade's have plain white bags?"

"Why? *Why?* Because we've *always* had plain white bags. My grandfather felt it was more dignified. My father concurred, as do I. And most heartily!"

Miranda knew she had to choose her words carefully lest she offend Jonah's sainted ancestors. "It's dignified, yes. But there's another way of looking at it . . . A well-dressed woman carrying a Saks or Bloomingdale's shopping bag is the best advertising for those stores."

"And just what would you know about being well dressed?"

Miranda pressed her lips together. She counted to ten. "I know a well-dressed woman when I see one," she replied quietly. "Think of Daphne carrying a Wade's shopping bag. Is there any better advertising? *Free* advertising, Jonah. Or almost free."

He had a sudden picture of Daphne strolling along Fifth Avenue, a Wade & Company shopping bag dangling from her arm. He heard the word "free." "Free? Surely it's expensive to imprint a store logo."

"Well, not really. Your own advertising department could do the artwork. As for the printing . . ." Miranda riffled through some papers on her desk. "I telephoned a few printers this morning. It works out to a few pennies per thousand." She handed a sheet of paper across the desk. "These are the figures."

Jonah stared at her, utterly amazed. He had long

since conceded that she had a good mind, but now he was forced to concede that she had a mind suited to the business world. Studying her, he was even forced to concede that she was looking less lumpish these days. "I will take your suggestion under consideration, Miranda. There may be something to it . . . I suppose you've already decided on the design?"

"You're the decision-maker, Jonah. But now that you mention it, I was thinking of an elegant sort of design. Wade & Company in the same lettering you use in your ads and maybe a pattern of leaves."

"Leaves?"

"I was thinking about different shades of green." Miranda smiled brightly. "Green is the color of money."

Jonah was shaking his head as he left Miranda's office. That blasted girl never misses a trick, he thought. She blushes and stammers her way through life, but she never misses a trick. He saw Peter Dexter walking toward the staircase at the end of the corridor. He called him over.

"Come into my office, Dexter. I want a word with you."

"Certainly."

They passed through Jonah's outer office, a wide, wood-paneled room containing several oak file cabinets, a black leather couch, an aged typewriter, and a handsome dark oak desk. Seated at the desk was Jonah's secretary, Martin Wilkes.

"I don't want to be disturbed," said Jonah. "If there are telephone calls, take the message."

Martin Wilkes, a solemn, efficient man of sixty, nodded his snowy head. "Malcolm Gill left an envelope for you, sir."

Jonah took the envelope and went into his office, Peter following a step behind. "Sit down, Dexter."

There were two leather chairs facing Jonah's massive desk. Peter selected the one that did not squeak. "Is anything wrong, Mr. Wade?"

"Why don't I ever hear any suggestions, any ideas, from my executive staff? I pay them well; what do I get in return?"

"I'm afraid I don't understand."

"Here is a perfect example: why do we have plain white shopping bags?"

A frown touched Peter's brow. "Because we've always had—"

"Yes, yes I know all that. But bags imprinted with the store logo would be *free* advertising. Why haven't any of my genius executives brought that to my attention?"

"We know how much you value tradition, Mr. Wade."

Jonah sat back in his chair. He looked around the office—a monument to tradition. Nothing, not even an ashtray, had been changed since his father's death. "Tradition is important. But occasionally one must improve on tradition. Business is business after all."

"I take it you've decided to improve on our shopping bags. I'll start making inquiries right away."

"No need. Miranda has already done so."

Miranda. Damn her, thought Peter, damn her to hell. "What a clever girl."

"Too clever by half, but that's beside the point." Jonah thrust her neatly written figures at Peter. "Schedule a meeting with the advertising department. See how quickly they can do the preliminary work. You'd best include Miranda in that meeting. She has an interesting idea about the design we should use."

Quite a girl, our Miranda. "Yes, Mr. Wade. I'll see to it . . . Does this mean you also wish to improve our boxes and wrapping paper? Our labels?"

Jonah had not given any thought to the matter; he wondered if Miranda had. He was tempted to ask her, for unlike his executive staff, she presented her views in simple terms, terms he understood. Only last year he had been approached by an advertising agency, by glib, ingratiating men who had talked of "merchandising plans" and "customer surveys" and "radio jingles." His executives had been enthusiastic, but he himself had

212

been mystified. He still was. He granted that radio had created a new breed of advertising man, but why did this new breed seem to be speaking a foreign language? "Schedule the meeting and then we'll see. First things first, you know."

Peter stood. "Will you be attending the meeting, Mr. Wade?"

"Perhaps. Or perhaps Miranda will be my representative." Jonah laughed. "Tell me, Dexter, was Miranda a charming dinner companion?"

"She's a very nice girl. I've invited her to the theater."

"Have you?"

"I hope you don't mind."

Jonah's eyes narrowed. "What are you up to? We both know you can do better than Miranda."

"Better, Mr. Wade?"

"She's not exactly a Ziegfeld girl, is she?"

Peter smiled. "I wouldn't have a great deal in common with a Ziegfeld girl. I'm getting older, sorry to say. I've had my fun, but now I find I'm interested in other things."

"Such as?"

"A woman who understands my work, who enjoys what I enjoy—books, theater."

What rot, thought Jonah. Books and theater will never replace the pleasures of the bedroom. He opened the envelope from Malcolm Gill and glanced through the contents. Smiling, he tucked the envelope into his pocket. "To each his own, Dexter. To each his own. If you find Miranda congenial, then so be it. But I will have no trifling with any member of my household. I hope that's clear."

"Quite clear, Mr. Wade. That wasn't my intention."

Jonah wondered about Peter's intentions. He chose not to ask, for he knew he would not get a direct answer. He thought Peter Dexter was very smooth, almost slippery. "That will be all," he said. "I have work to do."

Peter was used to these abrupt dismissals. He turned and left the office. "Working hard, Martin?" His eye fell upon a group of folders marked for Jonah's attention. "More reports from Mrs. Wade?"

"A most enterprising young woman, if I may say so."

Peter's jaw tensed, for even this modest praise of Miranda irritated him. Until recently, he had been the one who was praised; he had been known as the "enterprising" one. But now the balance had shifted. He would not admit to jealousy, though deep within him resentment was stirring, growing stronger.

He turned again, his step quickening as he passed through the door. He hurried toward the staircase, glad that he had not run into Miranda. "Miranda Wade," he muttered under his breath. *"Damn her."*

Chapter Thirteen

The curtain came down in the darkened theater. There was a brief silence, and then thunderous applause. The curtain rose again; the huge *Follies* cast took their bows. Applause called the cast back to the stage four times more, but finally the houselights went up and the audience began to file out.

Miranda followed Peter to the aisle. She was starryeyed, tingling with excitement at this introduction to Broadway. She rolled up her program and clutched it tightly in her hand. It was a souvenir to put alongside the matchbook from Chez Charles, the champagne cork from Club Harley.

"Well," said Peter, taking her arm. "Did you enjoy it?"

"I loved every moment . . . Wouldn't it be wonderful if life were like that?"

"Like what?"

"Bright and shiny and all dressed up. Wouldn't that be nice?"

"It wouldn't be real, Miranda."

"No. But it would be nice."

He looked into her eyes. For just a moment he saw not the grown-up Miranda but the child she must have been: a child yearning for magic, for make believe. He forced the picture from his mind, remembering his father, undone by a woman; remembering Wade's. His expression hardened. "Ziegfeld always puts on a good show. A month from now, you'll be as blasé as everybody else in this city."

"I don't think so, Peter. There are too many different sides to New York. It's never boring."

" 'Never' is a long time." He steered Miranda through the crowded aisle to a side lobby. "I don't want to fight for a taxi. Would you mind a short walk?"

She shook her head, smiling. "I was hoping to get a look at the Great White Way. That's what it's called, isn't it?"

"That's what it's called."

And for good reason, thought Miranda some moments later. Crossing Times Square, she marveled at the thousands of lights in the signs above Broadway. She could not stop staring; it seemed as if night had suddenly turned to day.

"You look like a tourist."

"I am." She was less than a mile from Murray Hill but she might have been on another planet, for Times Square was a tableau of clichés and contrasts: millionaire playboys in limousines and panhandlers with tin cups, fancy restaurants and dime-a-dance dives, Salvation Army bands and gamblers studying racing forms. She saw a man standing on a soapbox, preaching the evils of Socialism. She saw a cigar store Indian wearing a full, feathered headdress. She saw a peddler selling "genuine gold wristwatches" for a dollar. An amazing place, she thought. "This is better than the county fair."

Peter smiled slightly. "You have me at a disadvantage. I've never been to a county fair."

"Well, I only went to one. When I was little." Miranda's eye was caught by a storefront window filled with odd designs. She looked closer, pressing her nose to the glass. Inside, a man appeared to be painting something on another man's arm. "What in the world are they doing?"

"That's a tattoo parlor," replied Peter, gesturing at

the sign. "And I think we ought to move on." Across the street, an old woman was selling flowers. He stopped, again selecting a gardenia. "Much nicer than a tattoo," he murmured as he pinned the fragile bloom to Miranda's shoulder.

She gazed up at him. She wished he would kiss her, but instead he took her arm, leading her around the corner. "Where are we going? Or is it a surprise?"

It was the Algonquin, a favorite haunt of writers and actors and a popular after-theater gathering place. Seated at a small corner table, Miranda studied the handsome dark woods of the dining room, the chandelier glittering with light. Slowly, her glance moved to the couples at the other tables.

"Looking for anyone special?" asked Peter.

"No, I was looking at the women, at their clothes. They're the kind of clothes we ought to be selling at Wade's."

"Don't you ever forget about business?"

Miranda ducked her head. "I'm sorry. It's just that . . . Well, sometimes I notice things. I'm not smart about business, at least not yet. Not the way you are. But I do notice things. And then I get ideas for the store."

Her ideas invariably turned into ten-page reports, and her reports invariably found favor with Jonah. Thinking about this, Peter shifted around in his chair. "Let's make a pact: no more business talk tonight . . . This may help," he added, reaching into his pocket. He produced a small, flat box. "For you."

Miranda stared at the box. "For me? I couldn't —"

"Of course you could. I insist. It isn't much, just something I thought you'd like."

She opened it, smiling when she saw the filigreed silver brooch. There was an opal at the center, a pale, creamy stone flecked with pink. "How beautiful," she murmured.

"It matches your ring."

"Yes."

"A family heirloom, isn't it?"

"Yes. But, Peter, I can't. You've been spending too much money. I don't feel right about it."

"I wanted to make you happy."

"Oh, I am. I am. But I know what things cost. You work hard; you shouldn't spend all your money on me."

If Miranda had been any other female of his acquaintance, he would have assumed this was an act meant to impress. But it was Miranda and he knew it was not an act. "Don't be concerned. I have an income apart from my salary. A modest income perhaps; still, it provides a few luxuries. I used to be rich, you know."

"No, I . . . Used to be?"

Over a cold supper, Peter told her about his father. He said nothing about Mamie Malone, but he gave an otherwise honest account of the scandal. "After that," he went on, "Mother felt we had to repay the firm's clients. And of course we did." He shrugged. "Not that there was a choice. We were swamped with lawsuits. I managed to stash away a few pieces of Mother's jewelry. When I came to New York I sold it and put the money into the stock market. I have a nice little portfolio now . . . That's all that's left of the family fortune."

The waiter brought their coffee. Miranda reached for the cream pitcher, then pushed it aside. "I'm sorry about your father. Your mother, too. It must have been very hard for her."

"It was. Every family has its black sheep."

Miranda supposed that was true, though she could not imagine her father running off with other people's money. Her father had been just the opposite, she thought; he had given his money away, thrown it away on patients who had laughed at him behind his back. "I guess you could say my father was a black sheep in reverse. He was a do-gooder."

"And you weren't."

"I was angry. Most of time, anyway." She looked

down, gazing at the silver brooch. "People took advantage of my father. He let them do it. I thought that was wrong. But I knew I couldn't change him. You can't change what a person is."

"Your father owned a bar?"

"A bar? Oh yes, a bar. After Prohibition it was a sweet shop."

Peter watched as she lifted the brooch from the box and fastened it to her dress. She took great care. He watched the fluttering of her hands, the small frown of concentration as she fussed with the clasp.

For weeks he had been asking himself how he really felt about Miranda. But the truth was that he felt different things at different times. In private moments away from the store he liked her, liked her enough to overlook the unbeautiful face and figure. At other moments he felt nothing but hostility. He had struggled to build a life in New York, a career. He could not help seeing her as a threat to what he had built, and the worst kind of threat, for despite her protests, she had an innate business sense. She "noticed things"; she had "ideas"; she translated her ideas into dollars and cents, the only language Jonah understood.

And it all comes so easily to her, thought Peter now. *It's as easy for her as it's hard for me.* He knew it was not enough to have her on his side; somehow, he would have to remove the threat.

"It's my turn to offer a penny for your thoughts," said Miranda. "You're a million miles away."

"I was thinking about the future . . . Shall we talk about the future, Miranda?"

Her heart leapt, though she knew "the future" could mean almost anything. She gazed into Peter's eyes. She sat so still she hardly seemed to breathe. "If you want to," she murmured.

"I do. I want to get to know you better, Miranda. I want us to spend more time together, a lot more time . . . Any objections so far?"

She grasped the arms of her chair to steady herself.

219

"No objections."

"Then perhaps you'd be willing to save your nights and weekends for me?"

This had to be a dream; it was the only explanation. "Did you say—"

"You heard what I said, Miranda. I asked you to be my girl." *Well, it's done,* thought Peter. *I got the words out. It's done.* "Will you?"

"Yes," she said when she was able to speak. "Yes, I will."

It was understood between them that no one at the store was to know they were seeing each other. Jonah was the obvious exception to this rule; Natalie was another. Peter was leery of Natalie Stern, but Miranda continued to confide in her. During the next weeks it was Natalie who provided a steadying influence. Miranda was giddy, distracted, her concentration scattered. Often she was tempted to let her work slide, but at such times Natalie brought her back down to earth. "Love *and* money, kiddo." The words echoed in Miranda's mind, spurring her on. Now, preparing for the advertising meeting, she gave silent thanks to Natalie Stern.

The advertising department consisted of three dingy rooms brightened somewhat by the posters, sketches, and fabric swatches tacked to the walls. The department had four employees: an art director, a display director, a copywriter, and a secretary. They were young, clearly delighted at this opportunity to put their creative talents to use.

Miranda took a seat at the battered desk that served as a conference table. She had a folder stuffed with printers' estimates and a big yellow pad filled with her own notes. She glanced at them, hoping she would not make a fool of herself. When she glanced up she saw Peter leaning against a far wall, his arms crossed over his chest. He looked unhappy.

"I guess I'll get the ball rolling," said the man seated

next to Miranda. He was fair and rail-thin. His ash-tray overflowed with cigarette butts. "I'm Frank North, the art director. We're pretty informal around here, Mrs. Wade; just call me Frank." He introduced the others, ending with the secretary who was perched atop a stool. "Mary will take notes," he explained.

"Fine."

"We have some preliminary designs, but maybe you should tell us your ideas first."

"Well," said Miranda, "I only had *one* idea: changing our shopping bags."

"But that opens the door," said the other woman at the desk, a freckle-faced blonde who was in charge of the store's displays. "If we can breathe some life into our packaging, we might be able to do the same with our ads and our windows. We have the dullest windows on Fifth Avenue!"

Miranda smiled. She liked these people. "I'll tell you my idea about the shopping bags and we can go on from there."

She had expected to be nervous but once she began her words came easily. She described the designs she had imagined. She explained the printers' estimates. With surprising wit, she traded suggestions back and forth. It was a lively meeting. Peter's presence was forgotten; no one noticed Jonah slip into the room. He watched and listened, saying nothing. His dark gaze kept returning to Miranda.

"But we have to agree on a budget," she was saying now. "Frank's proposal sounds good, but we have to get the best price. Even if that means waiting a little longer."

There were nods all around.

"I can give you sample layouts," said Frank. "Can you look into the financial end of things?"

Miranda consulted her notes. "I think I know the right printer for the job. He has a small company, so it *will* take longer, but he's anxious to get our business. Maybe we can get a discount."

Jonah smiled. He looked at Peter. "Tell Miranda I want to see her in my office when she's finished here."

"Shall I come along, too?"

"No need. Miranda appears to have everything under control."

It was close to noon when Miranda arrived at Jonah's office. She paused in the doorway, shifting layouts, drawings, and several folders to her other arm. "You wanted to see me?"

"Don't stand there like a goose. Come in and sit down." Sighing, he watched as she struggled into a chair. "Stop fussing with those papers."

"Sorry."

"I assume the meeting was successful."

"I didn't know you were there, Jonah. Peter told me."

"What do you think of my advertising department?"

"They have lots of ideas, good ideas. We started out talking about redesigning the bags, but then we started talking about a whole new look . . . For the ads, the windows, the store displays. In a way, it's all connected with what I've been working on. My charts. I mean, I'm beginning to see the connection."

"Are you?" Jonah drummed his fingers on the desk. "And do you intend to share your vision? Or perhaps you would rather keep it to yourself? After all, I'm only the president of Wade & Company."

Miranda felt his eyes boring into her. She glanced away. "I wanted to get the costs figured out first. The shopping bags won't be expensive because we already have the stock. But if we use that design as a theme—"

"A what?"

Miranda clasped her nervous hands atop the folders in her lap. She took a breath and continued. "It's just a suggestion. Wade & Company has had the same look for a long time. In one way that's good: people recognize our look; they know what to expect. But in another way . . . well, maybe it's not good. I think my

222

charts are going to show we're not attracting new customers. Younger customers. Maybe it's because we have a certain kind of image."

"That's advertising talk."

"Yes."

Jonah leaned forward. "If we have an *image,* it's of quality merchandise at a fair price. That's all the *image* my great-grandfather needed. It's quite enough, in my opinion." But he knew it was not enough. For some years now he had sensed that times and tastes were changing. He had felt powerless to act, to interfere with store policies established generations ago. He had felt confused. From advertising agencies he had heard incomprehensible promises. From his executives he had heard empty echoes of himself. Only from Miranda had he heard the truth. "You have all the answers," he snapped. "Tell me why we aren't attracting younger customers."

"I'm not sure. Maybe they think we're . . . dull."

"Dull!"

Miranda slid down in her chair. Her glance fell away. *Don't let him fire me,* she prayed.

"It's that blasted war, you know. Nothing's been the same since the war. Everything has to be *modern* now . . . I suppose you want me to modernize? Tear the store apart and start over?"

"No, Jonah," she quickly replied, "that's not it at all. But maybe a little sprucing up. Just a few modern touches here and there. Starting with our shopping bags."

"And ending?"

"Wherever you decide. You're the boss."

"How nice of you to remember."

Miranda lifted her head and looked at Jonah. *He's annoyed but he's not going to fire me,* she thought, almost sighing with relief. "I can figure out the costs and give you a report."

"Have it ready by the fifteenth."

"Of September? That's two weeks from today."

Jonah leaned back. He nodded. "It is also the date of the executive meeting. Surely you haven't forgotten?"

"No. It's just that I'm working on the other report for the executive meeting."

"Quite the star of the show, aren't you? Perhaps I should put the entire meeting in your hands . . . Stop squirming, Miranda. It's unbecoming to a girl who has all the answers."

"Jonah, if I've been overstepping my place, I'm sorry."

"Overstepping?" He stroked his chin. "My grandfather would have called it 'gumption.' A nice old-fashioned word . . . I don't know what *I* call it. You've yet to prove yourself. Talk is cheap . . . But you have a certain spirit. You plunge ahead even when you're scared. That's not altogether a bad thing."

It was a grudging admission. To Miranda it was another example of the conflict she sensed in Jonah: he liked her and he hated her; he wanted her to succeed and he wanted her to fail. It was puzzling.

"Spirit has been lacking around here," he went on. "Perhaps it takes an outsider to see things clearly. In any case, I have decided to test my theory. I am reinstating the position of assistant to the president. You will be my assistant, Miranda. It will be announced at the executive meeting."

There was silence. Miranda focused her eyes on the window behind Jonah's desk, watching flecks of sunlight dapple the panes. "Are you teasing me?"

"I wouldn't waste my time."

That's true, she thought; he wouldn't. "You really want me to be your assistant?"

Did he? Yes and no. "We'll try it," he replied. "There is a condition, however. You are not to say one word about this before the official announcement. *Not one word.* If you do, you will find yourself back in the credit department. Are we agreed?"

"I won't tell anyone." But she wanted to tell everyone — Peter, Natalie, the world. "Can — can I at least tell Daphne?"

Jonah frowned. "My wife has no interest in you and your activities."

Miranda studied the floor. "Would it be all right if I told her?"

"If you wish."

"Thank you, Jonah."

"Your salary will remain the same until I see whether you're worth more. But Wilkes will give you a credit slip when you leave. Pick out some decent clothes. I expect you to look the part of my assistant. Pick out some suits and dresses."

"Thank you, Jonah. That's very generous."

He smiled. "One does what one can."

"Yes," she murmured. "Well, I — I have a lot of work to do. Was there anything else?"

"You may go."

Miranda gathered the folders and sketches and layouts. She stood. "I'm grateful to you."

"Of course you are! Where would you be without me?"

The question hung in the air. She turned and left the room.

"Ah, Mrs. Wade," said Martin Wilkes, glancing up from his desk. "This is for you."

She took the credit slip. Her eyes widened as she read the amount: three hundred dollars. "Are you sure there's no mistake?"

"I am indeed, Mrs. Wade."

Three hundred dollars; it was enough for a whole new wardrobe. "Thank you," she called, rushing to the door. "I love you, Mr. Wilkes."

"Did you actually say that?" asked Daphne hours later. "How confusing for Mr. Wilkes. He's probably confessing to his wife right now." She smiled, inspecting a long pink fingernail. "You've brought a bit of excitement to their lives, haven't you?"

225

Miranda sat at the edge of her bed. She clasped her hands, trying to keep them still. "It's only fair. *My* life seems pretty exciting, at least to me."

"Is this promotion what you want? I rather thought you and Peter . . ."

"I haven't told Peter yet. I can't tell anyone until the official announcement. I promised Jonah. It's going to be hard, though. I'm just *bursting* to spill the beans. And that's what I wanted to talk to you about, Daphne. I was wondering if I could have a little luncheon party to celebrate. *After* the announcement, of course. I'd pay for the food. I could do it on a Sunday, and it would just be Peter and my friend Natalie Stern."

Daphne looked up. "Stern, did you say? Is that a German name?"

"Natalie's family are from Germany."

"Well, that's all right, then. I thought it might be a Jewish name."

"Natalie's family are German Jews."

"I see." Daphne sat in the chair beside the bed. There was a rustling of silk as she crossed her slim ankles. "I'm afraid that presents a problem, Miranda. Jonah, you see."

"No, I don't."

"Jonah is not fond of Jews." Daphne leaned closer. "I'll tell you a secret," she said, lowering her voice. "But you must promise never to breathe a word."

"I promise."

"It's so difficult with secrets."

"I promise, Daphne."

"Jonah's family," she began, whispering as if to thwart eavesdroppers hiding behind the furniture. "His great-grandfather . . . or perhaps it was his great-grandmother. Someone way back in his family was half Jewish. It's rather a sore point. Family trees . . . One never knows about family trees. So you see, you really can't have your friend here." She tilted her head. "Although you *could* when we go to Europe."

226

Miranda's forehead wrinkled. "Europe?"

"Oh yes, Jonah and I go every year. Sometimes in summer, sometimes not. This year we're sailing the day after Thanksgiving. You'll have the house to yourself. And you can invite your friend. Lily won't mind, I'm sure. Cook never leaves the kitchen. She doesn't *seem* to leave the kitchen anyway. I don't suppose she sleeps there."

"So you and Jonah are going to Europe the day after Thanksgiving?"

"Hasn't he mentioned it?"

"No, it's news to me."

"Well, you live here."

And that, apparently, explained everything. Miranda felt as if she had slipped between the pages of *Alice in Wonderland*. She was falling through a great dark rabbit hole where nothing made sense. "And Jonah is Jewish, but he—"

Daphne put her finger to her lips. "He has a little Jewish blood," she whispered. "That's not really the same thing."

Miranda's head had begun to ache. She heard Daphne rambling on. She closed her eyes.

"Now that everything's clear, I must ask you again never to breathe a word."

"I promise."

"Well then, it's settled. I feel much better." Daphne rose and glided to the door. "Jonah will be wondering . . ." she murmured, gliding into the hall.

Miranda fell back on the bed. If she lived to be a thousand, she still would not understand the people in this house.

The next two weeks passed quickly. Miranda worked eight hours a day, and after Andrew was tucked in for the night, several more hours at home. She spent Saturdays and Sundays with Peter, lunchtimes with Natalie. She kept her word and said nothing about her promotion, though she could not mask

227

her high spirits. For the first time in her life she was pleased with herself. As the day of the meeting neared, she was floating on air.

She dressed for the meeting in one of her new suits, a smart black-and-gray tweed. Her hair was freshly trimmed and sleek waves framed her face. At her ears were small gold clips, a gift from Daphne. She had splurged on a manicure; her hands were smooth and white, her nails glossy, a soft pink. Walking into the conference room, she looked and felt like an up-and-coming career woman.

The conference room adjoined Jonah's office. It was deep and narrow, furnished with a long table, eight chairs, a brass chandelier, and a portrait of Albert Wade. Pads, pencils, and ashtrays had been set out. Martin Wilkes sat in a corner, ready to inscribe the minutes of the meeting.

"Come in, Miranda," said Jonah from his place at the head of the table. "We are all most anxious to begin. Sit down." He gestured to the chair on his left. "We will begin with your presentation."

She arranged her charts and graphs and folders on the table. She glanced around. Peter was staring at her, taken aback by her polished appearance. Louis Grayson, the ancient vice president, was smiling; she smiled in return. Toward the far end of the table were Harvey Vaughn, the merchandise manager, and Claude Berman, the manager of the accounting department. "Good afternoon, gentlemen," she said.

"Miranda has been working on two special projects," explained Jonah. "One concerns our advertising. Our *image*, so to speak. The other is an analysis of our customers' buying habits. As you know, certain departments have been losing money. Miranda will tell us why." He looked at her. "Well, Miranda? Are you ready to tell us where we've gone wrong?"

"No," she replied, smiling. "But I'm ready to show you lots of numbers. I hope I don't put everybody to sleep."

"We'll soon find out," said Jonah. "You may proceed."

"Thank you." Miranda drew a breath. "I've been doing research on our customers," she began, glancing from face to face, "and I've noticed a couple of things . . . first of all, that we're not attracting many new customers, younger customers."

"We have a select clientele," said Harvey Vaughn.

"Maybe a little *too* select. Maybe that's a mistake. The women who shop here are loyal customers. We want to keep them, but we should also try to add to them. The newspapers are always saying these are prosperous times. More people have more money to spend, and that includes younger people. Why shouldn't they spend their money at Wade's? Why don't they?"

"All right, why?"

"Well, Jonah doesn't like the word 'image,' but there may be something to it. Wade's image is sort of—sort of dull."

Harvey Vaughn gasped at this sacrilege while old Louis Grayson laughed out loud. "She's right, you know! She's hit the nail on the head! What do you say, Jonah? Time to liven things up, eh?"

Jonah smiled and said nothing.

"Go on, young lady, said Louis Grayson. "Let's hear the rest of it."

"Our windows, for example," she continued. "The other store windows on Fifth Avenue jump out at you. Ours are . . ." Could she say it a second time? She could. "Our windows are dull. And our ads. And our shopping bags are plain white." She opened a large manila envelope; an instant later she unfolded a sample shopping bag prepared by the advertising department. "For a few cents per thousand, we could have something like this."

Louis Grayson adjusted his glasses. "Splendid!" he declared. He reached across the table and snatched the bag from Miranda's hands. "Splendid! What do you say, Jonah?"

Jonah was impressed. He studied the handsome design: the familiar block-lettering of Wade & Company colored in dark green and set against a background of falling leaves. The leaves were different shapes and sizes, different shades of green, yet they formed a distinctive pattern. A stylish pattern, he thought to himself; it catches the eye.

Harvey Vaughn murmured his approval. Claude Berman asked for the printers' estimates. Peter was silent.

"Well, Dexter?" said Jonah. "Cat got your tongue?"

"It's very attractive, Mr. Wade. A great improvement."

Miranda smiled; more than anything else, she wanted Peter to be proud of her.

"Shall we vote?" cried Louis Grayson. "I say we vote!"

"Are the figures in order, Berman?"

"Yes, Mr. Wade. It looks to me like you're getting a bargain here."

The new shopping bags were unanimously approved. Miranda took a moment to savor her little victory, and then went on to explain how the design could be used in ads and window displays. She was questioned about costs and she replied without hesitation, for she had memorized them. In no time at all, a new advertising budget was approved.

The second part of the meeting began. Miranda felt she was on firmer ground now and she breezed through her presentation, expertly shuffling charts and graphs, expertly fielding questions. She defined the typical Wade's customer of five years before and the typical customer of today. Within this contrast, she offered reasons for strenghtening certain departments and eliminating others.

"That's right," crowed Louis Grayson at the end of the presentation. "Women don't want corsets anymore. Women want black satin scanties. Can't do a Charleston in a corset! Can't do—"

"I believe you've made your point, Louis," interrupted Jonah. He sat back, a smile twitching about his mouth. "Shall we give someone else a chance?" His gaze moved around the table. "Vaughn, we'll start with you."

Harvey Vaughn suggested that Miranda's information would be useful to his buyers "as a guideline." Claude Berman agreed, suggesting that the information would "help keep inventory down."

Peter spoke last. He knew what had to be said; he hoped he would not choke on the words: "Congratulations, Miranda. You've done a fine job, a truly fine job."

She smiled, basking in his compliment. The months of work had been worthwhile. The risk had been worthwhile. She had succeeded; she had taken the first step.

"Yes, congratulations are certainly in order," said Jonah. "I'm pleased to announce that the position of assistant to the president has been restored. As of today, Miranda is my new assistant." He looked at the stunned faces turned in his direction. He rose. "The meeting is adjourned."

Miranda is my new assistant. To Peter, the words had been like a sudden sharp kick in the stomach. Somehow he had managed to keep his composure, to congratulate Miranda yet again. Alone with her in the corridor, he had insisted they have a celebration dinner. There had been no doubt of her answer: weeknight or not, she eagerly accepted.

He took her to the Edwardian Room at the Plaza. During dinner, he showered her with attention, with ardent compliments that sent her world spinning. She thought this would surely be the night he swept her into his arms and kissed her, really kissed her.

She was lightheaded as they left the Plaza. The air was crisp, the sky an expanse of shimmering, twin-

231

kling stars. There was a huge silver moon, a beacon in the darkness. "Isn't it beautiful, Peter? Look," she said, stopping at the fountain in front of the hotel, "you can see the moon shining in the water."

"And in your eyes."

"What's come over you tonight?" she asked with a flustered smile. "You're different."

"Am I? How?"

"All this flattery . . . Not that I want you to stop. I love it, but it isn't like you."

Peter took her hand, drawing her away from the fountain. "Perhaps I'm in a romantic mood tonight. And it's all your fault."

"I hope so."

"Let's take a carriage ride through the park. Have you ever seen the park by moonlight?"

Miranda's heart thumped. "You *are* in a romantic mood."

"And it *is* your fault."

Happiness bubbled up in her. She had been seeing Peter for six weeks, but this was the first time she felt close to him, close to the man behind the smooth, patrician facade. The watchful look in his eyes was gone. He seemed relaxed, as if he had solved some troubling problem.

"This way," he said now, leading her across the street to a long line of horse-drawn carriages. "Your chariot awaits."

The driver tipped his shiny, slightly battered top hat. He helped Miranda into the cab and gave Peter a worn lap robe. "Once around the park, sir?"

"Slowly."

"Yes," said Miranda. "We want to see the moonlight."

The driver climbed atop his high seat and grasped the reins. The horse, a Central Park veteran, lifted his head and trotted off.

Peter slipped his arm around Miranda's shoulder. He heard her sigh, a soft murmuring as gentle as the

232

breeze that ruffled her hair. He stared into the shadowy night, thinking that there was still time to change his mind. He had not committed himself yet, nor did he have to. He thought, *I don't have to do this . . . But if I don't, Miranda will keep moving up at Wade's and I'll be left in the dust. I have to get her out of the store. This is the only way.*

He glanced sidelong at her. She was not the woman he would have chosen, but he consoled himself with the knowledge that she met at least one of his criteria: she never bored him. Small consolation, but it would have to do.

He gazed up at the starry sky, at the tall trees silvered with moonlight. It was very quiet, the silence broken only by the steady clip-clop of the horse's hooves. It was very peaceful, a place for lovers. He took a breath. "Do you remember . . ." he began, whispering against Miranda's ear, "when I said I hadn't found the right girl to marry?"

She nodded, for all at once her voice was frozen in her throat.

"You're the right girl, Miranda. Will you marry me?"

She had never expected to hear those words. She had imagined them, dreamed them, but never had she expected to hear them. Tears sprang to her eyes and splashed down her cheeks. Her heart was beating so fast she thought it would explode. "Peter," she sniffled. "Oh, yes, Peter, I'll marry you. Yes, yes, yes . . . I love you so much. I'll be a good wife, really I will."

He fished out his handkerchief and dried her tears. He kissed her. "You mustn't cry. This is supposed to be a happy night."

"It *is*," she insisted, her eyes welling again. "Oh, Peter, it's the happiest night of my life!"

233

Chapter Fourteen

"*Marry* her?" Jonah stared across the desk at Peter. It was after ten and the two men were alone in the study. "Is this some sort of absurd joke?"

"No, Mr. Wade. I wouldn't intrude on your evening for the sake of a joke."

" 'Intrude' is exactly what you did. I was enjoying a quiet evening with my wife until you barged in, demanding an interview."

Peter had neither barged nor demanded, though he let it pass. "I suppose I was anxious to tell you the good news. Miranda and I are anxious to have your blessing."

"Blessing! You can't be serious, Dexter. You can't possibly *want* to marry her."

"But I do."

"*Why?* Surely you're not in love with the girl? You're a man of the world. Miranda is . . . well, whatever she is, she's no match for you."

"She's the perfect match. I'm fond of her. We have a great many things in common. I expect she'll be a very pleasant companion."

Jonah puffed on his cigar. "You talk like an old man. Pipe and slippers and hot chocolate by the fireside. Is that what you would have me believe?"

Peter smiled. "Nothing quite so dreary."

"Sounds dreary to me. Where's the excitement?

The spice?"

"I won't pretend to be desperately in love, Mr. Wade. But then I'm a little past the age for that."

"No man is ever past the age."

My father certainly wasn't, thought Peter to himself. "I've waited a long time to marry. You might say I've played the field. Now I'm ready to settle down. Miranda has all the qualities I want in a woman. I believe we'll be happy together."

"She hasn't any money of her own, you know. She has a salary, and a modest sum set aside for Andrew. There's nothing more."

Peter's smile was chilly. "If you're suggesting that I'd marry for money—"

"I'm merely trying to understand this. Miranda is a member of my household. In a way, she's my responsibility. I need to know the facts."

"I've given you the facts, Mr. Wade."

Jonah's eyes went to the portrait above the mantel. He had married Daphne because he had wanted to possess her, to own her in every sense of the word. He felt that was a good reason for marriage. Money was also a good reason, and social position, but Miranda had neither. "She's Irish. Her father was a saloon keeper."

Peter almost laughed. How could he worry about marrying a saloon keeper's daughter when his own father had run off with a chorus girl? And with the company funds? "In Boston that would have been an impossible problem," he gravely replied. "This is New York."

"Yes, so it is." Jonah tossed his cigar in an ashtray and sat back. "There is the matter of the child. Andrew is a Wade. He is the heir to what my great-grandfather began, the heir to this house. He must be raised here. Traditions are important, Dexter. All our traditions are here. Do you follow what I'm saying?"

"Andrew must be raised in this house. Yes, I've thought about that."

"Have you indeed?"

Peter nodded. He had known from the beginning that Andrew's life could not be disrupted. Carefully, he had balanced the pluses and minuses of living in the Wade house. The pluses were obvious. It was a beautiful house, filled with beautiful things. The kitchen was excellent. Most importantly, he would have free access to Jonah. There was only one minus: the effect on his privacy. For years he had been visiting a brownstone in Turtle Bay, a brownstone owned by the charming Madame Felice and inhabited by her "nieces," an ever-changing group of lovely, accommodating young women. He did not intend to end these visits after his marriage, but certainly he would have to be discreet. A man can always find reasons to duck out for a few hours, he thought to himself.

"Well?" asked Jonah. "How do you propose to solve this problem?"

"It's awkward. I can hardly invite myself to live in your house."

"No, you can't. And I don't relish the idea of another stranger under my roof; I'll tell you that. Still, it *is* the only answer . . . Don't think I'm going to support you, Dexter. Put any such notion out of your head."

Again, there was a chilly smile. "I would insist on paying rent, Mr. Wade. All our other expenses as well. I'm sure we can make a satisfactory arrangement."

"Perhaps." Jonah stroked his chin. "Perhaps we ought to talk about your finances in general. I know you earn a fine salary for a man of your age. I trust you have savings?"

"Yes, and a tidy brokerage account. The stock market's been good to me. I'm more than able to

236

support Miranda and her son. And our own children, if we have any."

"In that case, I have no objections to your marriage." Jonah paused, his dark eyes fast on Peter. "But you had better be very certain this is what you want. I don't believe in divorce. Any nonsense about divorce will put an end to your career at Wade & Company. I know you're waiting for old Louis to retire, or drop dead. I know what you're after. Take a wrong step and you can forget all about it." He laughed suddenly. "You don't take many wrong steps, do you, Dexter?"

"Not many, Mr. Wade."

"No, I thought not." He stood. "Shall we join the ladies? I suppose we ought to drink a toast to the occasion. And I suppose you ought to start calling me Jonah . . . strange, the way things turn out."

Peter smiled. "Yes," he said. "Strange."

"Do try to be calm, Miranda," said Daphne. "I'm sure Peter is doing very well. It's sweet of him to observe the formalities. Don't you think so?"

"I guess." She sat down, but in the next moment she was on her feet again, pacing back and forth. "What if Jonah says no?"

"But why should he? He knows Peter. If he trusts him to work at the store . . ."

"Yes, that's true."

"Would you like a bit of brandy for your nerves? Or I could ask Lily."

Miranda stopped pacing. She turned. "Lily?"

"To bring tea."

"No, thank you, Daphne. I just wish they'd hurry. What's taking so long?" She sank into a chair and started nibbling at her fingernail. She remembered her expensive manicure and pulled her hand away. "What do you think they're talking about?"

237

"Oh, I never know what men talk about. Birds seem to understand each other. It must be the same with men . . . Birds of a feather and all that."

Miranda glanced at Daphne's aviary. She noticed a new addition, a porcelain thrush. She was staring at it when she heard voices in the hall. She leapt up, spinning around toward the door. Jonah entered the room first. Anxiously, she searched his face. "Is everything all right?"

"Quite all right. You seem to be engaged."

"I'm going to faint," she murmured, but an instant later she was flying across the room to Peter. Her arms were outstretched, her eyes misty with tears. *"Peter,"* she cried.

He knew he had to give Miranda this moment. He let her wrap her arms around his neck, let her cling to him, let her sprinkle tears on his shirt. He smiled indulgently and stroked her hair. "There, there," he murmured, as one might murmur to a child. She *is* a child, he thought, feeling a small pang of conscience. He untangled her arms and held her away. "I have something for you."

"For me?"

"Now that our engagement is official," he said, reaching into his pocket, "you have to have a ring." He produced a tiny velvet box and lifted the lid. "I hope you like it, Miranda. It was my grandmother's."

She gasped as he slipped the ring on her finger. "Peter, it's *beautiful*. A diamond!" It was a diamond solitaire, a perfect stone set on a thin band of yellow gold. "It's a diamond!"

"Of course it is," said Jonah. "A diamond is traditional. Come over here and let us see."

Miranda ran to them and thrust out her hand.

"Yes, very nice. Very nice indeed. What do you think, my pet?"

"Lovely. Look how it sparkles in the light. Congratulations, Miranda. And congratulations to you, Peter. Do you feel any different?"

"I imagine I will," he replied with a smile. "I may hate myself in the morning."

Jonah poured four brandies and passed them around. "To Miranda and Peter," he said, raising his glass. "May they have a long and happy life together."

"A long and happy life," echoed Daphne.

Jonah drank, and then put down his glass. "We have a few things to discuss, Miranda."

"Oh?"

"It has been decided that you and Peter will live here after your marriage. There is a guest suite upstairs. It's rarely used. After your honeymoon trip, the suite will be yours and Peter's. It's not grand, mind you, but it will do. I assume you have no objection?"

Miranda glanced from Peter to Jonah. "I—everything's happened so fast. I haven't had time to think."

"You may leave the *thinking* to me. This is my house after all."

"Yes, Jonah, but—"

"The important thing is that Andrew will be raised in this house. He will be raised to take his place at Wade and Company. It's never too soon to consider the future. The boy is young, but time goes quickly. All that aside, he belongs here. And your fiancé agrees."

Miranda looked at Peter. He nodded.

"There is one more thing," continued Jonah. "The wedding date. We're coming into our busiest season at the store; neither of you can be spared. Nor do I want you distracted with arrangements."

"What date would you suggest?" asked Peter.

"Any date after the January clearance sales."

"Valentine's Day!" cried Miranda. She turned to

Peter and clasped his hand. "Isn't that a wonderful idea?"

Her excitement was almost contagious. Almost. "Yes, wonderful," he replied.

"Is that enough time, my pet? I'm afraid the real work of this wedding will fall to you. You must make it easy on yourself."

Daphne's long lashes fluttered. "Weddings are fun. I don't mind at all . . . Winter flowers. That *is* a bit more difficult. We'll have the reception here, won't we, Jonah?"

"A small reception, yes. We needn't worry about that now. In fact, we needn't worry about any of it now. It's late. Do you plan to spend the night in my living room, Dexter?"

The abrupt change in Jonah's tone caught Peter by surprise. "I apologize. I forgot all about the time. I'll be on my way."

"A fine idea."

"I'll walk downstairs with you," said Miranda.

"Good night," called Daphne.

"Good night. And thank you, Jonah."

They walked into the hall. "Why did you thank him?" asked Miranda as they reached the staircase.

"Jonah could have complicated matters. He didn't."

She laughed. "He took over instead. He had everything decided before I even had a chance to think."

"Watch where you're going, Miranda. You don't want to fall down the stairs."

She gripped the banister. "But didn't you notice how he took over?"

"He's top dog. He owns a department store. He owns this house . . . He owns us."

"Peter, what a thing to say!"

"With bonuses, my salary will double when I'm made vice president. And with the stock market rising every day, that extra money will make me a rich

240

man. So you see, Jonah has my future in his hands."

They reached the hall. Miranda entwined her arms around Peter. "I promise you a wonderful future," she murmured, gazing into his eyes. "I love you." He kissed her, though it was hardly the passionate kiss she had been yearning for. "You do love me, Peter? I mean—"

"You're a very special girl, Miranda. The girl who's going to be my wife."

"Yes, but—"

"No buts." He smiled, once again untangling her arms. He kissed her cheek lightly. "You've had a big night and you're tired. Off to bed with you."

"Tired? I won't sleep a wink."

He brushed a strand of hair away from her brow. "I want you to get into your bed and close your eyes and dream of me."

"I always dream of you, Peter."

There was nothing to say to that. He turned and opened the door. "Good night, Miranda."

"Good night."

The door clicked shut. After a while she left the foyer and walked back to the staircase. She felt a curious letdown, an emptiness she did not understand. Climbing the stairs, she wondered why Peter had not said he loved her, wondered why he had never even mentioned the word love. She wondered why his kisses had been so restrained. He's a gentleman, she reminded herself, a proper Boston gentleman who "observes the formalities." That explanation seemed to cheer her. She was smiling when she tiptoed into the nursery to peek at Andrew, smiling when finally she returned to her own room on the floor below.

She sat beside the tulip lamp and held her hand up to the light. She stared at the fiery diamond, moving her finger back and forth. "Miranda Dexter," she whispered, trying out the name that would soon be hers. "Mrs. Peter Dexter."

It was almost a year to the day since she had boarded the train in Logan Falls. Not a long time, she thought, and yet so much had happened. As if in a dream, she saw the rainswept cemetery, the sagging houses on Maple Street, the small train station. She saw herself the way she had been then, watched herself bidding good-bye to the town and the people she had despised. All the old, familiar angers stirred in her. They flared quickly, like a rush of flames, but just as quickly they subsided. She felt cleansed. In some strange way she felt she had closed the door to the past.

The anger and hurt and conflict were behind her. She really was Miranda Wade, a Miranda Wade of her own creation. She gazed at her shiny diamond ring. She smiled.

Miranda's engagement became the talk of Wade & Company. At first no one believed it, but after a time suspicion gave way to surprise and then to speculation. Virtually all the store's employees had theories about the unlikely pairing of Miranda Wade and Peter Dexter. It was assumed that she had been the pursuer, that she had set the bait and reeled him in. It was the nature of the bait that caused the juiciest speculation. Had she seduced him? Had this quiet, artless young woman lured him into her bed?

Natalie appointed herself gossip monitor. She listened to the talk, the wild conjectures, and laughingly reported back to Miranda. "So according to just about everybody," she said now, "you're a femme fatale."

"Good for me!" It was the Sunday after Thanksgiving. Daphne and Jonah were well on their way to France; Miranda, temporary mistress of the house, was presiding over her first luncheon — a simple meal of salad, roast lamb, and chocolate tarts. "Tell everybody I'm having a wonderful time."

Natalie took a last bite of dessert. "You should be. You've got the world by the tail, kiddo. A great little boy, a great job, a handsome fiancé, and this house into the bargain. What I wouldn't give to live in a place like this." Her hazel eyes traveled around the dining room. "Classy. Peter will fit right in."

"Better than I do."

"You're doing fine. And the best is still to come. A wedding, a honeymoon, presents. Oh, that reminds me. I'd like to make your wedding dress, Miranda. It will be my present to you."

She smiled. "You're a good friend, Natalie."

"Is it all right, then?"

"All right? It's *marvelous*. It's going to be a very small wedding, you know. Jonah and Daphne aren't asking any of their friends. Peter's asking only four or five people." Miranda lowered her eyes to the table. She picked up her fork and put it down again. She shifted around in her chair. "Natalie, I don't know how to say this . . . I wanted to ask you to be my maid of honor, but I can't. It's Jonah. He—well, he has a lot of rules about religion. I mean, he thinks everyone should be Episcopalian. I tried, but—"

"Stop worrying. It's no secret how he feels about Jews. There's sort of a quota at the store. Did you know that? Ten percent of the sales staff is Jewish; never more than ten percent. He's not the only one, Miranda. Some businesses won't hire Jews at all. It's an old story."

"A terrible story," said Miranda, meeting Natalie's level gaze. "I'm so ashamed of myself. I was afraid to make Jonah too angry. I was a coward."

Natalie could not help smiling at Miranda's forlorn look. "It's not the end of the world, kiddo. I wouldn't want to throw a monkeywrench into things,

243

either. And just between you and me, my mother wouldn't be crazy about my taking part in a church ceremony. My father wouldn't care, but my mother . . ." She shrugged. "It's not only Christians who have *rules*."

"No, I suppose not. But I'm sorry, Natalie, really sorry."

"Forget it."

Miranda pushed her chair back. "Let's take a walk. I could use some air."

"What about the dishes?"

"Lili told me to leave them until she got home. And Cook won't let me in the kitchen anyway."

Natalie laughed. "You'll never get dishpan hands," she said as they left the dining room. "That's one good thing."

"There's another: no midnight snacks. Whenever I'm tempted, I remember Cook's sharp tongue."

"You're doing pretty well with temptation. You've lost more weight, haven't you?"

A proud smile lighted Miranda's face. "Five pounds. This dress is a size fourteen. I'm determined to be a size ten by my wedding day."

They walked downstairs and took their coats and purses from the cloakroom. "Want to do some window shopping?" asked Natalie.

"I want to stop next door and look in on Andrew first. He's never been to a birthday party before. I hope he's behaving himself. Mrs. Selkirk is very brave to have a house full of one-year-olds. Jonah would be horrified."

The wind was gusting when they stepped outside. Natalie turned up the color of her coat. "What happened to the sun? Maybe we should go to the movies instead. There's a new John Gilbert movie playing at the Royal. He's gorgeous."

"Not as gorgeous as Peter."

"Well, I'll admit Peter looks a little like him."

"I'll tell him you said so."

"Do that," replied Natalie with one of her quick smiles. "Maybe he'll give me a raise." She waited outside while Miranda disappeared into the Selkirk house. She pulled on her gloves and hunched her shoulders against the wind. The street was deserted; a few dry brown leaves, the last of the season, scraped along the pavement. She turned, looking at the handsome dwellings, the windows sheathed in silk. She felt like a trespasser, for she knew that the people behind those windows also had "rules" about religion. Her own Bronx neighborhood was far more hospitable, but still she yearned to escape, to live in an elegant house on a quiet, tree-lined Manhattan street. "Someday," she murmured, "and damn the rules."

"Talking to yourself?" asked Miranda, coming up beside her. "Don't worry, I do it all the time."

"How's Andrew?"

"Happy as a lark. He's playing with Jimmy Selkirk's trains."

"Then let's get going. A warm movie theater sounds good to me."

"Could we go somewhere for coffee instead? I wanted to talk to you about something."

"Sure. There's that little place on Third—Angelina's." Natalie glanced at Miranda. She frowned. "What's the matter?"

"Nothing."

The traffic light changed. They crossed the street.

"You look very serious all of a sudden."

Miranda tucked her purse under her arm and jammed her hands into her pockets. "There are some things you don't know about me, Natalie. Things nobody knows. And that's the way I want to keep it . . . But I need your advice."

"You're not in trouble, are you?"

Miranda shook her head. "No, it's nothing like

245

that. It's more complicated," she said as they turned a corner. "You may have second thoughts about being my friend after you hear what I have to say."

"How bad can it be? You didn't murder anybody—"

"In a way I did. A girl named Jenny Porter."

Natalie's mouth fell open. "*Who* is Jenny Porter?"

"Let's wait until we get to Angelina's."

"Miranda—"

"Let's wait."

Natalie looked doubtful. "Okay . . . but let's hurry."

Angelina's was a bakery with tables in the back where coffee and pastries were served. It was small and homey, fragrant with the aroma of cinnamon muffins and fresh-baked bread. One table was occupied by a man reading the newspaper and munching on a sugar doughnut; another table was occupied by a woman and two young children. Miranda and Natalie took a table in the rear. Angelina, smiling and round, dusted flour off her hands and took their order.

"Okay," said Natalie. "Tell me. Who is Jenny Porter?"

"Well, first I better tell you about a place called Logan Falls." The words spilled out, tumbling and bumping and rushing together. Every few moments she paused for breath; she paused when Angelina brought their cappuccino, but not for long. She talked about the town, about her father, about Glenwood Road. She talked about Union Station and a flame-haired young woman who had dropped a handbag and thus started a chain of events. She talked about South Crawford Street, about the Sheens. Tears glistened in her eyes as she talked about the train wreck and the grim weeks in the hospital. "Everybody thought I was Miranda," she said, dabbing at her eyes. "I'd been identified . . .

246

Everybody kept calling me Miranda. And then one day I thought, Why not? I didn't want to be sepa-rated from Andrew. I didn't want to lose him. I was so scared, so angry. I just decided to *be* Miranda. And that's when I murdered Jenny Porter."

Natalie was stunned. She stared at her friend, shaking her head from side to side. "That's the most incredible story I ever heard. It's — it's *incredible.*"

Miranda glanced away. "Do you hate me?" she asked in a small voice. "Because the truth is I'd do it again."

"Of course I don't hate you. But you have to give me a minute to get used to all this."

"Do you think I did a terrible thing?"

Natalie took a gulp of her cappuccino. "Hell, I don't know. Not a terrible thing, no. Maybe it was wrong . . . maybe it wasn't. I don't know, Miranda. But I can see why you did it. I can see nobody was hurt. Miranda — the other Miranda — was dead. An-drew was just a baby. I mean, there was no *harm* done to anybody . . . And maybe I would have done the same thing in your place. Maybe it was meant to be this way."

A weak smile flickered about Miranda's mouth. "Thank you for the kind words."

"Kind? No, I'm not being kind." She frowned. "I'm thinking what I would have done. I really can put myself in your place, because we both grew up feeling like outcasts. The reasons were different; it was the same result. When you're a Jew, the whole world might as well be Glenwood Road. So I under-stand how it was for you. But what happens next?"

"Nothing."

"You said you wanted my advice. About how to tell Peter?"

"I'm not going to tell him, Natalie. You're the only one who'll ever know. I *am* Miranda now. I'm Andrew's mother. I made my decision and there's no

247

looking back. People who look back always see the bogeyman."

"And what about Jenny Porter?"

"She doesn't exist anymore. She was a fat, unhappy girl with rats-nest hair and lots of worries and *no* future. I've started a new life. I thank God I did. Whether that's right or wrong—Natalie, I just don't care."

"Then what's bothering you?"

Miranda glanced down. A shadow fell across her face. "The honeymoon," she quietly replied.

"The honeymoon? Why?"

"Papa explained about the marriage bed. But I was wondering . . ." Color flooded her cheeks. She ducked her head. "I never had a boyfriend before. I never . . . There's never been anybody. I was wondering if Peter would know I'm a . . ."

"A *what?*"

"A virgin," whispered Miranda.

Natalie laughed. "*Now* I see what you're talking about. I'm a little slow sometimes. Yes, I see the problem. A widow with a child can hardly be a virgin."

"Will he know?"

"Well, let me tell you what *I* know," said Natalie. "It's not much, but I was dating this guy last year— Jerry Owens. I thought I loved him. Worse, I thought he loved me. He said he did; I guess they all say that. Anyway, to make a long story short, we went out to the beach one night and had our fling. That's what it was, too, at least to him. The rat never called me again after that night."

"I'm sorry."

She shrugged, running her hand through her dark curls. "I nursed a broken heart for a while. I nearly went crazy worrying that I was pregnant. But I wasn't, and my heart mended good as new." She smiled. "Now back to your problem. What I started

248

to say was that Jerry never noticed I was a virgin. I told him afterward and he was surprised . . . Maybe he was just stupid. Or it could be he was too busy to notice. I only had the one experience, Miranda, but I think when things get started, men don't stop to take inventory . . . Look at you, you're one big blush."

"This is very embarrassing."

"Why? Sex was God's idea, not yours."

Miranda laughed despite herself. "Natalie, you're impossible."

"I just think you should stop worrying. Even if Peter notices something different, he'll never put two and two together. How could he?"

"I hope you're right."

"Forget about it, Miranda. We have more important things on the agenda. Your wedding dress, for example. I already have a few ideas. I'll sketch them, and then you can make up your mind."

"A simple afternoon dress, Natalie. That's really all I want."

"Simple but elegant. Trust me, you're going to be a beautiful bride."

"A bride! It still doesn't seem real."

"Wait till you're knee-deep in wedding plans. It'll seem real enough then."

"I had to write to Chicago for a copy of Miranda's birth certificate. To the Hall of Records. I thought I might need it for the wedding license. Of course I have to make sure Peter doesn't see it."

"Why?" asked Natalie.

"You'll laugh at me."

"No, I won't. I promise."

"Well, I wanted to keep *something* of Jenny's. So I kept her birthday: January twenty-second . . . Does that sound silly?"

"Brides are allowed to be as silly as they want," replied Natalie. "Silliness is part of the fun. Enjoy it, kiddo. Soon you'll be an old married lady."

"I'm counting the days."

Happily for Miranda, the days flew by. She was working hard — refining her charts, writing departmental reports, studying Wade's from top to bottom. With Jonah away and Louis Grayson running the store, she became something of a sounding board for the old man, listening to his ideas and occasionally venturing an opinion of her own. She was called to meetings in the advertising department, called all over the store to check the new Christmas displays. As crowds of shoppers thickened, she was called to fill in wherever help was needed: at a wrapping desk, a gift counter, an information booth, and even at the chaotic central switchboard. No matter what job she was given, she kept her eyes opened and she learned.

Her evenings were quiet. She bathed Andrew, read him a story, tucked him into bed. She took her own dinner on a tray in her room and then buried herself in paperwork until Peter's nightly ten o'clock phone call. Her heart always soared at the sound of his voice, but too often she felt something was missing, for he never sounded like a man in love. Each night she raced to the telephone, hoping that *this* call would be different; each night she came away disappointed.

Their dates were no better. Peter was attentive to her, even thoughtful, yet he seemed detached, as if his mind was elsewhere. He gave her gardenias and books of poetry. He held her hand and kissed her good night. He did all the right things, but without any hint of passion. He's a gentleman, she told herself, an explanation that grew less reassuring as time passed.

She was relieved when Jonah and Daphne returned, for the silent house had begun to grate on her nerves. Daphne returned with a trunk full of new clothes, Jonah with a gross of hand-carved angels for the store's Christmas shop and invoices for merchandise that would be shipped in the spring. "If I still *have* a store in the spring," he said now. "If you and Louis and Dexter haven't ruined me."

"I left a copy of the sales figures in your study," said Miranda. "I thought you might want to see them as soon as you got home. You'll be pleased, Jonah. The first two weeks of December are are up twenty percent over last year. If next week is as good, it will be your best Christmas. Our new ads have been very successful."

"Too early to judge." He poured a brandy and lifted the glass to his lips. "Time is the real test."

"We had such a nice time in Europe," said Daphne. "I brought back some lovely antique lace for your wedding dress . . . You look thinner, Miranda. It's most becoming."

"Thank you. And thank you for bringing the lace. A friend of mine is making my dress."

"What is this friend of yours charging?" asked Jonah.

"The dress is a gift."

"Is it? Excellent! That's one less expense." He finished his brandy and started to rise.

"I'd like to talk to you for a moment, Jonah. It won't take long."

He resumed his seat. "Very well. What is it?"

Miranda had once promised herself that she would choose her battles carefully. She had promised to avoid thorny subjects, but in the last couple of weeks she had decided there was one thorny subject that could not be avoided. "I—I wanted to talk about the wedding guests. About my friend Natalie Stern."

Jonah frowned. "I've heard that name before . . . Oh, yes, I remember now. And I distinctly remember telling you the answer was no. I haven't changed my mind. Your friends are your affair, but Jews are not received here. Nor are they received at our church."

"I spoke to Reverend Wisdom. He said it was perfectly all right for Natalie to come."

Jonah's face was like a thundercloud. "Did he?"

"Yes."

"I'm not surprised. The reverend Wisdom is a liberal thinker. That's the new trend in clergymen. It's the modern thing . . . and it's absolute rubbish! I'll have no part of it, Miranda."

She looked away. There was a rustle of silk at the windows, a roar of flames on the hearth. She looked back at Jonah. She cleared her throat. "Maybe Peter and I should be married at City Hall."

"City Hall!"

She shrugged. "It would solve a lot of problems."

Jonah knew there would be talk if a Wade abandoned St. Matthew's for a civil ceremony. He was certain that Miranda knew as well. *She's forcing my hand,* he thought. *That upstart girl is trying to maneuver me.* "Your friend Natalie Stern is my employee. But not for long, not if you persist in this foolishness."

Miranda shook her head. "It would be bad for the store if you fired Natalie," she replied in a quiet voice. "Natalie is a talented designer. I've seen her sketches; they're very good. She's still learning, but one of these days she could be designing for us."

"Us?" Jonah's eyes flashed. *"Us?* Have you become a partner in Wade & Company, Miranda?"

"I didn't mean—"

"You're a nervy girl. And ungrateful." And always one step ahead of everybody, he silently conceded. "I brought you to New York, gave you a home, a family, a job, and *this* is my reward. A nervy girl who defies me at every turn!"

"Weddings," murmured Daphne.

Jonah turned. "What's that, my pet?"

"I was thinking that weddings put a great strain on people. Especially the bride-to-be." A smile touched Daphne's lips, lingering there for just a moment. "Do you remember how muddled I was before our wedding?"

Jonah's face softened. "You were charming, as always . . . But perhaps you have a point." He turned to Miranda. "Under the circumstances, I'm willing to give you the benefit of the doubt. I will assume you meant no disrespect."

"I didn't, Jonah. Thank you."

"We will say no more about it."

Miranda drew a breath. "But Natalie is my only friend and I want her at my wedding."

Jonah threw up his hands. He rose. "If you will excuse me, my pet, I want a look at the sales figures before we go upstairs."

"Yes," she murmured.

He strode to the door. He paused, casting a murderous glance at Miranda, and then strode into the hall.

"Jonah is like his mother," said Daphne when his footsteps had faded. "He has Eleanor's little quirks."

Miranda sighed. She was in no mood to listen to family history. "We all have our little quirks."

"Eleanor couldn't bear to be contradicted. She *hated* it when people disagreed. She was suspicious of anyone who was different from herself . . . Of course she was devoted to St. Matthew's; she was very religious. And very thrifty. Jonah's father was the soul of generosity, but Eleanor . . ." Daphne lowered her voice to a whisper. "Eleanor was a pinchpenny."

"Daphne, I really don't see —"

"The interesting thing was that Eleanor could always be brought around by flattery. She could be . . . persuaded."

Miranda looked sharply at Daphne. "Are you saying Jonah can be *persuaded?*"

Daphne picked up a magazine and began leafing through it. "It's so helpful to have time on one's side."

Time? Miranda frowned, but a moment later a smile lighted her eyes. *Time,* she thought. *I have almost two months to bring Jonah* around, to persuade, to cajole, to flatter. She laughed. "You're amazing, Daphne."

"I?"

Miranda went to Daphne and kissed her cheek. "Yes, you. You've just given me a wonderful present. My wedding!"

Chapter Fifteen

Miranda became Mrs. Peter Dexter on Valentine's Day of 1927. A long white carpet covered the center aisle of St. Matthew's. The altar was decorated with white candles and sprays of gardenias; immense white satin bows were affixed to the pews. On the groom's side of the church sat several Wall Street friends and their wives, several of Wade's buyers, and most of the executive staff. On the bride's side sat Daphne and Jonah, Louis Grayson and his wife, the advertising department, Walter Houser, Miss Dent, Andrew, Lily, and Natalie Stern.

Miranda walked down the aisle on the arm of an elderly Wade uncle. She was radiant, clad in an ankle-length dress of ecru silk trimmed with antique lace. Daphne's pearls were clasped about her neck; atop her head was an exquisite confection of ecru silk and chiffon. She carried a bouquet of roses and orange blossom encircled by lacy ruffles. Her eyes were misty, for this was surely the happiest day of her life.

Peter stood at the altar, watching his bride approach. He thought she looked lovely, lovely and very young. He felt a stab of conscience, but it passed quickly. Once upon a time, he, too, had been young and vulnerable. He had survived his disillusionment and so would Miranda. Everyone has to grow up eventually, he thought.

She was smiling as she joined him at the rail, smiling as he took her hand in his. She gazed into his eyes. "I love you," she whispered.

Peter's lips parted, but he said nothing. He turned his attention to the minister.

"Dearly beloved," began Reverend Wisdom.

Miranda gazed at Peter throughout the ceremony. When the time came to speak her vows, she spoke them in a soft, clear voice. After the blessing, after the exchange of rings, she heard the words that filled her heart with joy: "I now pronounce you husband and wife."

"Well, we've done it," said Peter.

"You may kiss the bride," said Reverend Wisdom.

It was a chaste kiss and it concluded the ceremony. Arm in arm, Peter and Miranda left the church. They paused on the steps for photographs; moments later they ran through a shower of rice to the waiting limousine. "Mrs. Peter Dexter," she murmured when they were settled in the backseat. She held out her hand, staring at her slender gold wedding ring. Her gaze moved to Peter. "I'm so happy."

"It shows. You're a beautiful bride, Miranda."

She nestled her head on his shoulder. "And you're my handsome groom. Oh, Peter, we're going to have a *wonderful* life."

Thirty people attended the reception at the Wade house. There were canapés: minced shrimp, deviled ham, pâté, caviar. There was champagne from Jonah's cellar. There was a wedding cake, three tiers of genoise frosted with vanilla cream and decorated with tiny pink and white rosebuds. There were two toasts, one offered by Jonah, the other by Peter, who raised his glass to "my beautiful wife, and my new son Andrew."

The child heard his name and looked up. Miranda scooped him into her arms. "You have a papa now," she said, hugging him close.

"Papa."

"That's right, Andrew. You're a very lucky little boy."

"Papa."

She laughed. "Miss Dent, I think Andrew's had enough excitement for today. And enough cake," she added, brushing crumbs from his mouth.

"Yes, I'll just take him upstairs."

Miranda watched them go. Soon she would be leaving on her honeymoon, leaving Andrew behind. She thought about that. There was a sudden tightening in her chest.

"Do I see a frown?" asked Natalie. She wore a dress of beige crêpe, another of her own creations, and a small beige hat. In each hand was a glass of champagne. "Here," she said, giving a glass to Miranda, "I brought you a refill."

"Thanks. Are you having a good time?"

"Terrific. I was talking to Mrs. Wade. She's a little . . ."

"Yes," laughed Miranda. "She certainly is. She loves my dress, by the way. Everybody does. You're a big hit."

"So are you. You look great, Miranda, no kidding. Your hair, your makeup, your size ten figure." Natalie smiled. "Excuse me — your *perfect* size ten figure. I have to give credit where it's due."

"And I'll take it. I've earned a little credit for starving myself. I haven't had a bite of chocolate in a month!"

"Poor thing."

Miranda glanced around the room. Peter was deep in conversation with Harvey Vaughn. Daphne and Jonah were talking with the Graysons. Her friends from the advertising department were trading jokes with the store's buyers. Walter Houser and Claude Berman stood off to one side, watching. Peter's friends were a group unto themselves — handsome, prosperous, assured. She saw Lily standing alone in a corner. "Come on, Natalie, let's mingle."

"I want more champagne. I may never get this chance

again."

"There's plenty of champagne. Come on, I want you to meet Lily. You've heard me talk about her."

Natalie turned, following Miranda's gaze. "The gorgeous Amazon over there? We introduced ourselves in the car . . . It's a shame about her face, isn't it? Half of her is absolutely stunning."

"That's what's so sad. If she were ugly, it probably wouldn't matter as much.

They threaded their way through the crowd. Natalie plucked a glass of champagne from the tray of a passing waiter. "Three cheers for Prohibition," she said.

"Are you getting drunk?"

"Maybe." *Why not,* she thought. *When I leave here I go back to a lousy flat in a lousy building in the lousy Bronx. Why the hell not!* "But I promise not to disgrace myself. Or you," she added with a wink.

Miranda laughed. She caught Natalie's wrist and dragged her along to where Lily stood. "Here you are," she said. "You don't look very happy."

"It's a nice party, Mrs. Dexter. Thank you for inviting me."

"I like your dress," said Natalie, expertly appraising the navy blue wool, the white satin cuffs. "It's not from Wade's."

"Macy's basement. It was on the bargain rack. I made the cuffs myself."

Natalie inspected the stitches. "Good job."

"Thanks." Lily sipped her champagne. Her eyes moved slowly around the room and came to rest on an ormolu clock. "It's getting late, Mrs. Dexter; Mr. Dexter said he wanted to leave by seven."

"I have to change my clothes."

"Your traveling clothes are all laid out upstairs. Your suitcases are in the cloakroom."

"May I ask you a favor, Lily?"

She shrugged.

"It's about Andrew. I know he'll be fine with Miss

258

Dent, but I'd feel much better if you could spend a little time with him. If you could play with him a little? Give him a hug once in a while?"

Lily almost smiled. "I'll see to it he isn't lonely, Mrs. Dexter."

"I left a list of his favorite bedtime stories. It's on the bureau in the nursery."

Lily nodded.

"You're only going for a week," said Natalie.

"Nine days."

"All right, nine days. It's not nine *years*, Miranda."

"It's the first time I've left him alone."

"He won't be alone."

Miranda glanced across the room to Daphne and Jonah. "His grandparents don't spend any time with him. He's sort of isolated up there."

"Will you stop worrying? A bride's entitled to a honeymoon, you know. Just think, nine romantic days and nights at Lake Placid. Snow and roaring fires and walks through the woods . . . Hell, if you want to stay here, *I'll* go."

Miranda shook her head. "That's very kind of you," she replied, laughing. "But I'll force myself."

"I thought you might."

"I'd better change." Miranda put her glass down. She turned, about to walk away, and then turned back. Impulsively, she threw her arms around Natalie. "Thank you," she said. "For everything."

"Anytime, kiddo."

Miranda turned next to Lily, who held out her hand. "I hope you have a nice trip, Mrs. Dexter."

Formal to the end, thought Miranda. "Thank you, Lily. I hope so, too."

She left them, slipping past the guests on her way to the staircase. She blew a kiss to Peter. Smiling, she started up the stairs. Her hand slid along the banister. She glimpsed her wedding ring and her heart thumped. "It's not a dream," she murmured to herself. "I'm married!" *Nine romantic days and nights,* she thought as color rose in her cheeks. *My honeymoon,* she thought, and now she was flying up the stairs.

"Off we go," said Peter, starting the engine of his Pierce-Arrow. "Happy?"

"I'm floating in the clouds . . . I'm over the moon."

He smiled. "I take it that means yes."

"I've never been happier, Peter."

"Did you enjoy the reception?"

"It was wonderful. The whole day was wonderful . . . I think your friends had a good time. It was nice meeting them after all these months. I was beginning to wonder if I ever would."

Peter kept his eyes on the road. "They aren't *close* friends. I've been concentrating on my career, not friendships. I want that promotion, Miranda. It's the key to everything."

"You'll get your promotion. There isn't the slightest doubt."

"No, but there's Louis Grayson. He doesn't seem to be in any hurry to retire."

Miranda snuggled her head on Peter's shoulder. A light rain had started to fall; she watched the little drops slip down the windshield. "Louis is such a sweet man. He's been so kind to me."

"Yes, you two are great pals."

"Not pals, exactly. He's more like a kindly old grandfather."

"Old grandfathers ought to know when to retire. Perhaps you should offer a few subtle hints."

She lifted her head. "You don't mean that, Peter?"

"The sooner I get that promotion, the sooner I'll be able to add to my investments." He took one hand from the wheel, fumbling for his cigarettes. "The market is booming; I hate to miss out. This is a golden opportunity, Miranda. I know I'll never recoup the family for-

260

tune, but I can build a tidy fortune of my own. My stocks have been doubling, tripling. There's no end in sight."

"I don' t understand. If you're doing so well—"

"I am. The catch is that I've put almost every cent I have into the market and it's not enough. Not for a real killing. There'll be an immediate bonus when I'm made vice president. With that money . . . Do you know what buying on margin means?"

"No."

"It means I only have to put down ten percent. If I buy twenty thousand dollars worth of stock, I only have to put down two thousand dollars."

Miranda frowned. She sat up. "That sounds too easy."

"Easiest thing in the world, as long as you know what you're doing. I happen to have a talent for the market . . . I'd be working in Wall Street now, if it weren't for my father."

"People can't blame you for your father."

"They'd be looking over my shoulder every minute, thinking 'like father like son.' But that's water under the bridge . . . I have a chance to make my own fortune. But old Louis has to step aside."

Miranda leaned her head back. She thought about the money she had put away for Andrew. She knew she could borrow from it, but what if something went wrong? What if the money were lost? The market was risky, no matter what anyone said. It was gambling, and she was not a gambler. "What if your stocks started going down instead of up?"

Peter's eyes were fast on the road. "You don't understand these things, Miranda."

"But it could happen."

"Not in today's market . . . You simply don't understand."

"No I don't. I think I should, though. When we get back, I'll go to the library and—"

"The library!" Peter laughed. "You can't learn about

261

investments that way."

"It's the way I've learned everything else."

He glanced at her. "You're serious, aren't you?"

"I don't want to feel stupid, Peter. I want you to be proud of me."

"I'd be very proud if you had a word with Louis Grayson. Drop a few hints." He shook another cigarette out of the pack. "Wade's is in a little world of its own, Miranda. I want to be vice president of that world. And I want to be rich."

Something cold and hard had come into his eyes. Her frown deepened. "Peter—"

"Just think about it. Just tell me you'll think about it . . . Remember," he added, smiling through a haze of blue-gray smoke, "you promised to love, honor, and obey."

"All right, I'll think about it," she reluctantly agreed. "If that's what you want."

"Good. There's a long drive ahead. Why don't you lie back and get some sleep."

It was after midnight when they arrived at Lake Placid. Miranda had dozed for most of the journey, but now, opening her eyes, she gasped with pleasure. Snow blanketed the grounds of the resort, smooth, pristine snow that glittered in the moonlight. There were no people about, no cars, but she saw two old-fashioned sleighs, the reins draped with shiny bells. Smoke curled from the chimney of the main lodge; lamps glowed at either side of the door. The gravel path, white with snow, crunched underfoot. "Peter, how wonderful! It's like something out of Currier and Ives! Can we take a sleigh ride?"

"It's a little late," he said, taking her arm as they walked to the door. "But I'll ask. Are you hungry?"

"Starving."

The lobby was deserted, save for a clerk who smiled

262

pleasantly behind the desk. "Mr. and Mrs. Dexter? We've been expecting you."

"Good evening, or good morning, I should say. What are the chances of getting some food?"

"The kitchen is closed, but I'll have sandwiches and coffee sent to your rooms. We have early nights here. Sleigh service stops at ten o'clock; the kitchen closes at eleven." The clerk held out a pen. "If you'll just sign the register, sir."

"Of course."

Miranda glanced around the lobby, which was divided into two wings. There were cozy chairs and couches, tables piled with magazines. There were bowls filled with pinecones, vases filled with fragrant pine branches. The draperies were closed. A fire crackled in one of the stone hearths.

"Come along," said Peter as the clerk stepped from behind the desk. "Our rooms are ready."

They were shown to a charming suite on the second floor. The furnishings were country pine and maple; the wallpaper was a woodsy green and white. Walking into the bedroom, Miranda saw feather quilts and braided rugs and two rockers bracketing the fireplace. She smiled, squeezing Peter's hand. "I love it," she cried. "It's just perfect!"

A maid appeared. She turned down the beds, plumped the pillows, lighted the fire. A bellman brought their luggage, returning a few minutes later with sandwiches and coffee and a basket of fruit. He bid the newlyweds good night and left the suite.

"Alone at last," laughed Miranda.

"Yes."

They got out of their coats and mufflers and gloves. Miranda kicked off her shoes. She took a quilt and spread it in front of the fireplace. She saw Peter's questioning look. "A romantic supper by firelight," she explained. "Isn't that a nice idea?"

A comfortable chair is a much nicer idea, he thought,

but he was reluctant to spoil the moment for Miranda. He opened his suitcase and pulled out a bottle of brandy, pouring some into their coffee. "I came prepared," he said with a smile.

They sat together on the quilt, eating roast beef sandwiches and drinking brandied coffee. The fire blazed, rushing, roaring up the chimney, showering golden sparks. Peter draped his arm around Miranda, drawing her to him. "Tired?"

She nodded, gazing up at him through her dark lashes. Almost before she knew it, he was pulling her to her feet. He kissed her. He started to stroke her hair, and then abruptly he held her away. There was an odd look in his eyes. "Peter, what's wrong?"

"Wrong? I suppose no man is quite himself on his wedding night. It's nothing to worry about . . . Go on, Miranda; I'll just finish my coffee while you change."

"I won't be long," she murmured.

She left him, going over to the luggage stacked on a bench. She found the smaller of her two suitcases and carried it into the bathroom. Quickly, she unpacked her things. Her hands were trembling as she held up her new nightgown, a fluid column of shimmering ivory satin edged with lace. She held the gown against herself and looked in the mirror. She took a breath. "Mrs. Peter Dexter," she murmured to her reflection.

Peter was in his robe when she returned to the bedroom. He had dimmed the lamps, but the fire cast a rosy glow that seemed to follow her every step. She seemed to be bathed in light; her hair had the shine of polished onyx and her face was luminous. Her gown was not sheer, but he could see the curves of her body straining against the cloth. His breath caught. He went to her, slipping the straps from her shoulders. His hands moved over her naked breasts. Slowly, he lowered her gown over her hips to the floor. He threw off his robe and led her to the bed.

Miranda's arms encircled him. "Peter," she cried softly

as his lips moved from her mouth to her throat to her breasts to her thighs. She felt his hand move between her legs, slowly at first, very slowly, and then faster and faster until she again cried his name. His breath quickened and now his hands were everywhere, impelled by her lush young body. He made no sound, whispered no endearments, but his eyes glittered with desire. His hands went beneath her. Their bodies joined. She felt a brief moment of pain, but in the next moment she felt wave after wave of pleasure, engulfing her, drowning her. "Peter," she murmured as their bodies trembled. "Peter."

He fell back on the bed, his chest heaving. He said nothing. His breathing began to slow and he reached for the blanket, pulling it to Miranda's chin.

"I love you, Peter," she said. "I love you so much."

He knew that she wanted to hear those same words from him; he knew he was incapable of saying those words. He kissed her cheek, tucked the blanket around her, and left the bed.

Miranda raised herself on her elbow. "Peter? Did I — is anything wrong?"

"Everything is exactly right," he replied. "Or didn't you notice?"

She felt the blood rush to her face. "I noticed."

"I once said you were a very special girl, Miranda. And so you are . . . We're going to be very happy," he added, throwing back the covers on the other bed.

"What are you doing?"

"I'm a restless sleeper. I'm not comfortable sharing a bed."

"But—"

"It's best this way. Please don't make a fuss." He smiled at her in the shadowy light. "You're not going to turn into a nagging wife, are you?"

"No."

"I'm glad." He slipped between the sheets and rolled on his side. "Good night."

265

"Good night, Peter."

The fire was dying out. Miranda watched the last bursts of flame, the last vivid flashes of red and gold and blue. After a while she settled her head on the pillows and stared up at the ceiling. She recalled the strange letdown she had had on the night of her engagement, on so many nights since that time. She had sensed something missing; she sensed something missing now. She looked across at Peter. He was asleep, peacefully, soundly asleep. She returned her gaze to the ceiling. Why hadn't he said he loved her?

Miranda was awakened hours later by bright sunlight streaming through the windows. She opened her eyes. She blinked, stretching her arms high above her head. When she turned, she found a note on her pillow. It said, "Wanted to get an early start on the slopes. Will join you for lunch at 12. Peter." She crumpled the note and sailed it toward the fireplace.

Her nightgown had been neatly folded, placed at the foot of her bed. She snatched it up, then thrust it away. "An early start on the slopes," she muttered, hurt and angry and confused. "How *could* he?" She wrapped herself in the quilt and swung her legs to the floor. She stomped over to her suitcase, pulling out underclothes, her new wool slacks, and a heavy sweater. The bathroom door was ajar; she flung it open, slammed it shut. There was a loud hissing sound as she turned on the taps. She dropped the quilt and stepped into the tub, splashing about in the water. "Happy honeymoon," she muttered, reaching for the soap.

Twenty minutes later, she walked into the lobby. She found the dining room and was shown to a small table beside a wide picture window. Her spirits lifted, for the view was dazzling. Powdery, pure white snow cloaked the ground, the trees, the rooftops. On the paths were people in jaunty wool stocking caps and long mufflers,

266

ice skates slung over their shoulders. In the distance, a horse-drawn sleigh climbed a hill. Somewhere out there Peter was skiing. *Well, let him,* she thought, opening the menu.

Miranda was tempted to soothe her hurt feelings with a huge breakfast. Her mouth watered as she read the selections: apple pancakes with butter and maple syrup, waffles with syrup and Canadian bacon, country-style ham and eggs with hashed-brown potatoes, muffins and popovers and cinnamon toast. She settled for a popover and coffee.

"Coming up," said the waitress, scribbling on her pad.

"I was wondering if you know anything about the — activities — here? I'd like to go skating, but I haven't any skates."

"You can rent 'em out at the pond. It's half a mile from the gate. You can walk, or you can take the sleigh."

"Oh, the sleigh!"

The waitress smiled. "Yeah, that's what everybody says."

Miranda enjoyed her breakfast. She slathered the popover with apple butter and ate every crumb. She drank two cups of hot black coffee. It was nearly ten when she left the dining room and plunged into the frosty Adirondack air.

Bundled in a gray wool jacket, a red wool tam, leather gloves, and thick socks, she made her way along a winding path. She stopped once or twice to scoop up a handful of snow, letting it trickle through her fingers. She ran the last few steps to the sleigh barn; moments later, she was heading off to the pond.

There were three other passengers in the sleigh and she was glad to have their company. She felt less alone, though no less angry. She did not even try to explain that her husband of one day had disappeared to get "an early start on the slopes."

But Miranda forgot her anger when she arrived at the pond. She donned a pair of skates and glided onto the

267

ice, spinning and circling in time to the music that came from sound boxes in the trees. She was a good skater and she did not want for partners. She skated with young men, old men, with anyone who asked. She was almost sorry when a flashing blue light signaled the noon hour.

Miranda and her new friends shared a crowded sleigh on the ride back to the lodge. They sang all the way there — several choruses of "Jingle Bells" and several choruses of "To Grandmother's House We Go." The driver, amused, joined in.

Peter was standing in the lobby when Miranda and her merry band spilled through the door. He looked and then looked again, for once more she seemed to be bathed in light. She was radiant, her hair windblown, her cheeks rosy with cold. She was laughing. "Miranda?"

She turned. "Come meet my friends," she called cheerfully.

He crossed the lobby, shaking hands as the introductions were made. "If you'll excuse us," he said, "our table is ready."

"Let's get one big table for all of us," suggested an eager young man.

"Perhaps another time."

Miranda glanced at her husband. "Yes, another time," she agreed. "Maybe tomorrow. Maybe I'll see you back at the pond this afternoon."

Peter took her elbow and led her away. "Where on earth have you been?"

"I went skating. I used to love to skate. It's one of the few happy memories of my childhood." Miranda knew he would not pursue the subject. Long ago she had realized that neither Peter nor the Wades had any interest in her past. "Besides, I was feeling kind of . . . abandoned."

"Abandoned!"

She shrugged. "Well, when I found your note . . ." She paused, for she really did not want to be a nagging wife, a complaining wife. "I was a little surprised, that's

268

all."

"But you said you didn't want to learn to ski. You said you were afraid of hurting your leg."

"Yes, I know."

They were shown to their table, the same table Miranda had occupied only hours before. Peter held her chair as she sat down. "I don't understand," he said. "Why were you surprised?"

"This is our honeymoon," she replied quietly. "I—I thought we'd spend our time together."

He smiled. "Being married doesn't mean we have to live in each other's pockets. I'm not a dewy-eyed boy, Miranda. I'm thirty-five and set in my ways."

"But this is our *honeymoon*."

"A very good reason for enjoying ourselves."

"Separately?"

"There are things that are good to do together, and things that are good to do separately. You musn't confuse the two." He picked up the menu. "Marriage isn't prison, you know. We're not chained at the wrist."

His tone had been light, amiable, but his words had carried a sting. Miranda felt the sting, for all at once she understood that there would never be any real closeness in her marriage, any real intimacy. She began to see that those were the the things that had been missing, that those things were alien to Peter. And it has nothing to do with his being a gentleman, she thought.

"Have you decided what you want?" he asked.

She glanced up. "I thought I had, but now I'm not so sure."

"I'll order for us, then."

"Yes, I'll leave it to you."

"That's my girl."

But as the days passed, Miranda knew she would never be his girl, not in the ways that mattered to her. He was always pleasant, always thoughtful about small gestures, always strangely aloof. He was there, and yet not there, as elusive as the wind. He came to her bed every night, later returning to his own. He disappeared from their suite with the first rays of morning sunlight, reappeared for lunch, and then was gone again. Often he brought Miranda touching remembrances of their trip — a lovely picture book of Lake Placid, a gold pine-cone brooch, a tiny glass sleigh — but just as often he forgot to kiss her, or seemed to forget. She noticed that his conversations verged on the impersonal; he was talking to her, but he might have been talking to anybody. By the time of their third night together, she noticed the same thing about his lovemaking.

She stopped trying to find excuses. Peter was what he was, and if he was not exactly the husband of her dreams, he was nonetheless the man she had married for better or worse. She doubted they would be happy in the true sense of the word, but she was certain they would not be *un*happy. She refused to look too closely into her own heart, to probe her feelings. She told herself she would forget her dreams, her romantic notions, and build a life with Peter. She dared not ask what kind of life it would be. She knew very well that life played tricks.

It was snowing as they left Lake Placid, snowing as they arrived in the city. She was not sorry to be back, for instinctively she sensed that this was where she belonged. Like Peter, she was no longer dewy-eyed. The city's hard edges suited her now. She could, she thought, use them to spur her on. She could hardly wait to return to her office. She wanted to spend a few days with Andrew, making up for lost time, and then she wanted to bury herself in work. "Do you suppose they missed us at the store?"

"No one is indispensable."

"No, I guess not."

"When do you plan to give notice?"

Miranda's head snapped up. "What?"

"No one is indispensable, but you can't just walk out."

"Walk out? Why would I walk out?"

"You're a married woman now. You don't need to work."

"Maybe not for money, but I do need to work. It's what I do best, Peter. You know that."

"I know you're a wife and mother. You have responsibilities, Miranda, and they come first. Surely you didn't expect to go on working?"

She heard the words, but she could not, would not, believe them. She studied his handsome profile. It was calm, unchanged; no clues there. "You're teasing me, aren't you?" she said after a moment. "You're playing a joke."

Peter turned the car onto Second Avenue. He was not concerned, for he had expected resistance. They would argue perhaps, but he would win. "I've never been more serious," he said. "You're my wife now and I naturally assumed—"

"Assumed! But how could you? I don't understand any of this. I mean, it's out of the blue. We went out for months before we got married. We had nine days at Lake Placid. Why did you wait until now to tell me how you felt?"

"It didn't occur to me that you'd have to be told. Why did you marry me if you didn't want to be my wife?"

"Peter—"

"You're putting Wade & Company ahead of me."

"I'm *not*."

"What else do you call it?" He turned an aggrieved look on Miranda. "No man wants his wife to work. And especially not at the same company. I'd be a laughingstock."

"Wade's is a family company."

"You're not a Wade anymore; you're a Dexter. You keep forgetting that."

"*Forgetting?*" Amazement was stamped on Miranda's face. Suddenly she was in the midst of an argument she had not anticipated and did not understand. "Do you actually want me to quit my job?"

"It's not such a tragedy, you know. Millions of women are perfectly happy to stay at home and look after their families."

"But don't you see there's nothing for me to *do* at home? I'd go crazy. How would I spend my time?"

"How does Daphne spend her time?"

"She shops and plays bridge and lunches with her friends."

"That doesn't sound so terrible."

"Not for Daphne, no. Peter, I can't believe you mean this. I'm happy at Wade's. I feel useful."

"Don't I make you happy?"

"Yes, of course, but why does it have to be a contest between you and my job?"

"Because it is." He took his hand from the steering wheel and rested it on her knee. "Maybe I'm selfish, but I want a wife, not a business associate. I want to come first with you."

It was an appeal and it had the desired effect. Miranda began to wonder if her job had been standing between them all along. She realized that she, too, had been guilty of assuming; she had assumed she could have both marriage and a career. If she had to choose . . . Dear God, if she had to choose. "I wish you'd said something sooner," she murmured. "I'm so confused. You caught me by surprise."

Surprise was what he had intended. He smiled. "Did I?"

"Let me think about it, Peter."

"Look, if the store is more important to you than I am—"

"How can you say that?" interrupted Miranda, shaking her head. "Wade's is important to me, but you're my husband."

"Then what is there to think about? It's simple."

It was anything but simple. Miranda turned and rolled down the window, staring vacantly at the passing streets. The car slid into the flow of crosstown traffic. In a few minutes they would reach Murray Hill; they would be home. "You have to give me time, Peter. Please. I need time."

His hands tightened on the wheel. "How much time?"

"I don't know. Time enough to figure things out."

"So you're going to be stubborn, are you? Stubborn people are very often stupid. I hope I didn't marry a stupid woman!"

She heard the anger in his voice. She was hurt, frightened; her head was spinning. "I'm sorry, Peter. I didn't mean —"

"Never mind what you meant. I want this settled by morning . . . I want to know if we have a marriage, if *I* have a wife."

Miranda's throat was thick with tears. She swallowed. She took a breath. "I wish you'd . . . try to understand how hard this is for me."

"We won't talk about it any more tonight. And for heaven's sake, dry your eyes. I don't intend to parade a tearful bride in front of Jonah."

"I'm sorry."

He brought the car to a halt, easing it into a parking place a few steps from the Wade house. He shut off the motor. "Are you all right?"

"Yes," she murmured, returning her compact to her purse. "Fine."

Lily greeted them at the door. "Mr. and Mrs. Wade are out," she announced as she took Miranda's bags. "They'll be home at ten."

"How's Andrew?"

"He's okay, Mrs. Dexter. We tried to keep him up for you, but he was too tired. Do you want something to eat or do you want to go to your rooms?"

"We stopped to eat along the way," said Peter. "I'm rather anxious to see our rooms. Did my things arrive?"

"Safe and sound. Everything's unpacked, Mr. Dexter. I followed your instructions."

273

"I appreciate that. Just please remember I don't want anyone going into my bureau drawers. Not for any reason. My laundry can be left on the bed; I'll put it away myself . . . I'm fussy about my things."

"I understand," replied Lily when they reached the landing. "I'll keep out."

They climbed the second flight of stairs. The door to Miranda's old room was closed. She glanced at it, and then continued down the hall. "I was hoping that would be Andrew's room one of these days. What do you think, Lily?"

"You know how Mr. Wade is; he doesn't like children underfoot. Maybe when Andrew's older, five or six . . . Here's your new place." She opened the door to their suite. The sitting room was charming, decorated in polished cherrywood and pale, creamy silks. To the left was Miranda's bedroom. "We just moved the furniture from your old bedroom," she explained. "But the wallpaper is fresh. Roses instead of birds."

Miranda smiled. "Yes, it's very pretty. It's a nice change."

"And that's your bedroom through there, Mr. Dexter."

"Will you excuse me, Miranda? I want to have a look around."

"Go ahead."

"I'll help you unpack, Mrs. Dexter."

They laid the suitcases atop the bed. Miranda snapped open the locks. Nestled amongst her sweaters were several boxes from the Lake Placid gift shop. "A little present," she said, giving one of the boxes to Lily, "and let's not argue about it. I'm too tired."

Lily opened the box, removing a pair of leather gloves lined with cashmere. "Thank you. They're beautiful."

"They're warm. I bought the same ones for Daphne and Natalie. I bought a toy moose for Andrew." Miranda opened the smallest of the boxes. Inside was a silver keyring trimmed with tiny silver skis; a gift for Peter. She looked across the sitting room into his bedroom. He was

274

taking some papers out of his briefcase, depositing them in his bureau. "I think I'll surprise him and hide his present in his handkerchief drawer."

"Mr. Dexter said not to go into his bureau."

"I know, but . . ." But a surprise gift might take the edge off his anger, she thought. It might bring a smile to his face; he looks so grim. "I'm sure he won't mind, just this once."

"Miranda?" he called. "I'm going downstairs to wait for Jonah."

She watched him go. She looked again at the keyring. After a moment she closed the box and tucked it in her pocket. "Don't bother about the rest of the unpacking, Lily. I'll see to it in the morning."

"If you say so." She picked up her gloves and went to the door. "Good night, Mrs. Dexter."

"Good night, Lily."

Miranda sat at the edge of the bed, clutching the toy moose. She felt a great lethargy, a terrible heaviness in her arms and legs. She puffed out her cheeks, glancing around at the familiar furnishings. She was home, but what did that mean now? What did anything mean if she had to give up her job?

Somewhere a clock was chiming. Still clutching the moose, she rose and left the room. The hallway was bathed in soft light. A vase of winter roses sat atop a slender gilt pedestal. She sniffed the roses, and then, slowly, she mounted the stairs to the nursery. *No matter what happens,* she thought, *I have Andrew.*

She tiptoed past Miss Dent's room, entering the nursery from the hall. Andrew was curled beneath the blankets, sound asleep. In the glow of the night light, his hair was burnished copper, thick and straight and falling onto his brow. Miranda gazed down at him. She smiled. All at once she felt better. She bent and kissed his cheek. He stirred, but did not waken. "Sweet dreams," she whispered, placing the moose in a corner of the crib.

She tiptoed out of the room and closed the door. Her

275

step was lighter as she descended the stairs. There had to be a way to make Peter understand. She would think very carefully tonight. She would find the right words, and tomorrow she would plead her case.

Miranda took the little box from her pocket, pausing before Peter's door. Quietly, she went inside. It was a masculine room, all dark woods and leathers and antique brass lamps. Most of these furnishings had been brought from his bachelor flat on Gramercy Park. The beige curtains and bedspread were new.

She ran her hand across the top of the bureau. She opened the drawer, reaching under a pile of handkerchiefs to hide her present. Something was wedged at the back—postcards, she thought, feeling around. She pulled them out, expecting to see views of Lake Placid. What she saw were views of naked women in obscene poses, of naked men and women joined together in obscene poses. She froze. The cards fell from her hand and scattered on the floor. "Dear God," she murmured. She had been Peter's wife for eleven days, but what kind of man had she married?

Her eyes strayed to the pictures. There was no love in them, no tenderness. It was raw sex; the mating of animals. Peter had never spoken of love. He had never once used the word. Looking at the pictures, she thought she knew why.

"Miranda," called Peter, striding into the room. "Jonah is . . ." His voice faded away when he saw her pale, shocked face. He saw the open drawer; an instant later he saw the pictures strewn on the floor. He saw them through her eyes, and he was filled with shame. He saw clearly the man he had become; the pictures, like Madame Felice's brownstone, were all part of that man. He blamed his father, and his father's whore, Mamie Malone. It was not something he could explain—not to Miranda or anyone else. He could only take refuge in anger. "Damn you," he cried, "I *told* you to keep out of my things. You damn women are all alike. Always in the

276

wrong place at the wrong time! Always causing trouble!"

Miranda's lips parted. Angry color flooded her cheeks as shock turned to outrage. "Don't talk to me like that. You have no right. I wasn't snooping. I was hiding a present for you and I happened to find . . . If you want to collect dirty pictures, that's your business. Just don't talk to me as if I were—"

"You're my wife, Miranda. I'll talk to you any way I please."

"Oh, really? Is that your idea of marriage? You almost had me fooled, Peter. All your fine talk about wanting to come first with me. About wanting a wife. You don't want a wife. You want a . . . a . . . Maybe you should have married one of the women in those pictures."

He slapped her with such force that she reeled backward. She caught hold of a chair, steadying herself. Her eyes, when she looked at him, were like cold gray steel.

Peter had never hit a woman before; he had never hit anyone before. He felt sick, for his violent act was the final proof of what he had become. He stared at his hand, stared at Miranda. A muscle twitched in his jaw. "I'll never forgive you for making me do that."

She brushed past him, heading toward the door.

"It's no use to go running to Jonah. I happen to know he has his own handkerchief drawer."

She whirled around. "Don't worry, Peter. Your nasty little secrets are safe with me. I'd be too embarrassed . . ." She paused, thinking that she had gotten what she deserved. She had fallen in love with a handsome face, an urbane manner; she had not looked beyond those things to the man himself. "There's no point in making matters worse."

"Where are you going?"

"To bed. I have to be at work early in the morning."

"Nothing's changed, Miranda. I don't want you to work."

"Everything's changed. Everything. Work is something I trust and understand. That's more than I can say for you. I dont know who you are."

"Jonah will—"

"Tell Jonah I'll be at work as usual." She touched the side of her face. She could still feel the sting of Peter's slap. "Tell him the honeymoon's over."

Peter stared after her. The door closed with a sharp click; he was alone. He turned. The postcards lay where they had fallen. He kicked them out of the way. He sank into a chair, dropping his head to his hands. It was all for nothing, he thought bitterly. For nothing!

Chapter Sixteen

The coolness between Miranda and Peter lasted several months. They were careful at the store, so as not to cause talk, and they were careful in front of Jonah and Daphne, but in private they dropped all pretense. They were civil to each other, nothing more. Peter resumed his visits to Madame Felice's brownstone; Miranda filled her days and nights with work.

Work was an escape, though it was small consolation for the bitter disappointment she felt. Once again everything had happened very quickly; in only a few moments the last of her dreams had been destroyed, the last of her storybook notions about love and marriage. Her first reaction had been cold, hard anger, but with time, that anger had become sorrow. It was as if she were in mourning — for lost dreams, lost promises, for the betrayal of love.

Andrew was her solace. He was a happy, good-natured child who seemed to take things in stride. When the adults in his life wanted to play games, he played games. When these same adults deserted him for their own pursuits, he was content to play by himself. He had his carousel, his rocking horse, his huge family of toy animals. He had a toy drum, and often he paraded it through the nursery, a one-boy, one-drum band.

Peter was the newest adult in Andrew's life. And with Andrew, Peter was a changed man. His reserve melted away, thawed by the spontaneous, unthreatening affection of a child. He roughhoused with Andrew; he made up silly games and sillier stories. He began to think of Andrew as his own son, lighting up when the boy called him Papa. Marriage meant nothing to him, but fatherhood meant a great deal. It was yet another side of Peter, and in a way it was this side that brought about a truce with Miranda.

"It wasn't anything dramatic," she explained to Natalie one warm June afternoon. "Peter just came into my room a few nights ago and said he was sorry. He said he was what he was, but couldn't we try to make the best of the situation."

"You agreed?"

"Yes."

Natalie poured sugar into her iced tea. She reached across the table for a straw. "You did the right thing, Miranda. You couldn't go on the way you were."

"Well, I didn't want to be at war with Peter. I certainly didn't want to keep brooding over things I couldn't change. He's a good father to Andrew; I can settle for that."

"You know what they say about time healing all wounds."

"Not these wounds, Natalie. Talking to me the way he did. Slapping me . . . He made me see what a fool I'd been. I guess that was the worst part. I suddenly realized our marriage was a fake."

"I wouldn't go that far."

"I would."

"But you were in love with the guy."

"For all the wrong reasons." Miranda shrugged. She stared down into her coffee cup, stirring her spoon around and around. "I remember the first time I met Peter. I thought he was the handsomest man I'd ever seen. He was the kind of man I'd always dreamed about, handsome and sophisticated and . . . sort of elegant. One look and I was head over heels. Like a schoolgirl, Natalie. And when he started paying attention to me, it was a schoolgirl's dream come true. It took a slap in the face to wake me up."

"Yes, but wake you up to what?"

"Facts," replied Miranda. "Fact one, I never should have married Peter. Fact two, whatever his reason for marrying me, it wasn't love. He's afraid of love. Not sex, love." She sipped her coffee and then put the cup down, returning her gaze to Natalie. "But he's wonderful with Andrew. That's what matters."

"You matter, too."

"Oh, I'm all right. Now that the stars are out of my eyes, I think Peter and I will get along very well. I'm a sensible girl," added Miranda, laughing. "I have character. Haven't you noticed?"

"I think you're putting on a good act."

"Listen, Natalie, nobody gets *exactly* what they want. In a lot of ways, I'm doing better than I ever expected I would. If I'd stayed in Chicago, I'd be a file clerk somewhere. A *spinster* clerk . . . Wade's has been lucky for me."

"When do you get your raise?"

"Next paycheck. I'll be getting fifty dollars a week! Jonah's been pleased with my ideas about a bridal department. And that's not the only news . . . Louis Grayson told me he's retiring in July. Peter will finally get to be vice president."

"Does he know?"

"Not yet. Jonah wants to make the announcement."

Natalie shifted around in the booth. Her hazel eyes flitted about the restaurant and lighted on Miranda. "Speaking of announcements, I have one of my own. That job at Milady Dresses came through. I'm going to be an assistant to an assistant to an assistant, but it's a start."

Miranda clasped her hand. "That's marvelous, Natalie. I'm so happy for you. We have to have a celebration! How about Saturday night? Peter and I will take you out to dinner."

"I have a feeling Peter's not too crazy about me."

"Who cares? When we talked the other night, we agreed I'd have some say in the marriage. And *I* say we all go out to dinner. Someplace expensive," she laughed, "since Peter is going to be a millionaire."

"Is he?" asked Natalie.

"He sounds pretty sure. The stock market, you know."

"Well, I hope he's right. Think what you could do with a million bucks. Hell, you could open your own department store!"

Miranda smiled. "I'm happy at Wade's." She finished her coffee and sat back. "Someday we'll be selling your designs at Wade's. Natasha Starr originals."

"You have big plans, kiddo. I can see the wheels turning."

"Can you?"

"You bet I can."

Miranda's smile widened. "*Very* big plans," she said.

A bridal department for Wade & Company was foremost among Miranda's plans. Jonah had expressed interest and that was all the encouragement she needed. With her usual zeal, she gathered facts, figures, odd bits of information, and her own observations into one preliminary report. It took her the better part of three months, but she felt the results were worth the effort. She was confident when she presented the report to the executive staff, overjoyed when it was approved. Peter was astonished; Wade's had not unveiled a new department since 1918.

He bought Miranda a pearl necklace to celebrate her triumph. Outwardly, he was a proud and enthusiastic supporter of his wife; inwardly, he seethed. He could not understand—would never understand—how she always managed to succeed with Jonah where he himself had failed. Her ideas were not new to retailing, yet she made them sound new, giving them novel twists that impressed everybody. Like a master chess player, she always seemed to anticipate the next move. She anticipated questions before they were asked, objections before they were raised. Most annoying of all, she seemed to know precisely when to argue a point and precisely when to remain silent. He had no doubt that he was smarter than she. Certainly he was more experienced. He counted at least a dozen other things in his favor, but to no avail. It was Miranda who won all the honors.

Peter kept his feelings to himself. He had blundered once with Miranda, blundered badly, and he was determined not to repeat his mistake. He granted that he would never get her out of Wade & Company, but he was certain that she could still be useful to him. In the meantime he did everything he could to regain her trust. She had a weakness for romantic gestures and he exploited this weakness — leaving little presents under her pillow, sending flowers to her office, taking her to intimate candlelit restaurants. When the leaves began to turn, he spirited her away for Sunday drives in the country. When winter came, he took her ice skating in Central Park. In spring and summer, he took her to charming outdoor cafes.

Miranda enjoyed these times with Peter, though she was careful to read nothing into them. She knew he had not changed, knew he never would. His visits to her bed were little more than brief interludes, pleasurable but meaningless. After two years of marriage he had yet to tell her he loved her; they never spoke of love, for they both knew it was no use.

Miranda had accepted the situation, but beneath the tranquil surface there was anger. She had been cheated again, deprived, and now she gave her trust to very few — to Natalie, to Lily, to old Louis Grayson. She trusted her love for Andrew. She trusted her work, the one constant in her life that was wholly her own.

She received another raise early in 1929. It was a reward for her part in the successful debut of the bridal department. She gave full credit to Harvey Vaughn, her partner in the project, but the energy behind their work was pure Miranda. She put in long hours, cutting through scores of problems large and small. She guided, suggested, urged. She fought for extra money in the advertising budget, and with Harvey's help, she won. "Brides by Wade & Company" was scrolled across the ads announcing the new department, double-page ads that featured misty young brides in clouds of lace and satin and tulle. It had been her idea to offer everything from wedding handkerchiefs to wedding gowns within one department; it was a shrewd idea, immensely popular.

By July of 1929, Miranda was busy at work on another project: the redesign of Wade's fashion departments. Again in concert with Harvey Vaughn, she was following Jonah's order to "explore the possibilities." The project excited her, but this time she had trouble getting started. She tired easily, could not seem to concentrate. Her stomach was always upset, and twice she had suffered dizzy spells. The doctor confirmed her suspicions; she was pregnant.

It was happy news, for she wanted a child of her own body, wanted another child to love. She thought that Peter would be happy, too, but now, alone in her bedroom, she was so nervous she couldn't sit still. She jumped when she heard a knock at the door. "Come in, Peter."

"Lily said you wanted to see me. Is it important? There are some things I wanted to talk over with Jonah."

"It's important."

He nodded. "All right, I'm here . . . Nothing's wrong, I hope."

"Nothing's wrong." She took a breath. "I—I saw the doctor today. He did a test last week—"

"A test?" Peter frowned. "What sort of test? Why on earth didn't you tell me?"

"I'm trying to tell you now. And I might as well just say it—I'm going to have a baby."

284

"A baby!"

"Yes." Miranda watched him. In other circumstances, this would have been a joyous occasion; in these circumstances, she was not sure. She saw his startled expression, heard his sharp, quick intake of breath. At the very last she saw his smile. She relaxed. "You don't mind, then?"

"Mind!" He went to her, clasping her hands in his. "Miranda, it's wonderful. I'm . . . I don't know what I am. Overwhelmed. It's absolutely wonderful." He kissed her cheek. "When?" he asked.

"February. It may be a Valentine's baby"

"Are you all right, Miranda? Do you feel all right?"

"Fine. The doctor said I was in perfect health."

"Well, come and sit down." Peter led her to a chair. "You must start taking care of yourself. Proper rest, exercise. And no more dieting; you're eating for two."

She smiled. She was pleased by his concern, pleased and a little amused. "I'm not sick, just pregnant."

"Have you told Jonah?"

"Not yet. I thought you should be the first. We can tell Daphne and Jonah after dinner. I don't know what they'll say . . . They're not fond of children . . . We have to tell Andrew, too. That could be tricky."

"Tricky?"

"He's been an only child for almost four years. He's been king of the hill." Miranda laughed. "How would *you* like to share your kingdom with a howling baby?"

"My child won't howl."

Peter dragged a chair alongside Miranda. He sat down and lighted a cigarette. "Andrew will be thrilled to have a brother or sister. Why, it's like having a built-in playmate."

"Yes, I suppose so."

"The timing couldn't be better. Another two years and I'll have all the money we'll ever need. We'll be in clover, Miranda. Our children will have the best of everything."

"A millionaire by forty. Is that your goal?"

285

Peter watched a ribbon of gray smoke curl toward the ceiling.

"Perhaps not a millionaire, but we'll be *extremely* comfortable. We can sit back and clip coupons."

"If the stock market holds out."

"Good Lord, are you going to start that again? The stock market is the backbone of American business. What could be safer than investing in General Electric? Or U.S. Steel? My money is in good, sound stocks—blue chips . . . Think about it, Miranda. I began with a stake of eight thousand dollars and I've run it up to well over a hundred thousand. That will double in two years; there's an excellent chance it will triple. In this market, the sky's the limit."

She glanced away, her lashes casting wispy shadows on her cheeks. "I did a lot of reading on the stock market. I read about the 'panics' and the huge sums of money that were lost each time." She looked at him. "Peter, I'm not saying you shouldn't invest, but why can't you take some of your profits and put them in the bank?"

"Because my money won't double and triple in the bank. Profits earn *more* profits in the market. That's the point."

"Yes, but some of your profits are only on paper. That's really what buying on margin means, isn't it? In a way, you owe many thousands of dollars to the brokerage."

"That's merely a technicality."

Miranda shrugged. "We see things differently, Peter."

"You're a worrier."

"I've had to be . . . Money in the bank gives me a nice secure feeling."

"I promise you there's no need to worry anymore. Remember, I have a talent for the stock market."

Miranda decided to drop the subject, for she knew it was a waste of time. Peter was convinced that the boom would go on forever, and he was by no means alone. The whole country seemed to be in the grip of stock market fever; who was she to argue? "Jonah will be expecting us downstairs," she said, rising from her chair. "Shall we?"

Peter rose also. "I hope you're happy about the baby, Miranda."

"Very happy."

"Things will be better now."

It was all he could think of to say. Miranda understood. She linked her arm in his, smiling brightly. "Things will be fine," she said.

"A *baby*." said Jonah as if he had never heard the word before. "Are you certain?"

Miranda glanced at Peter. She nodded. "Quite certain."

They were seated in the living room, after-dinner brandies in hand. The windows were open, but no breezes stirred the humid summer air. On the table near Daphne was a delicate silk fan, peach-colored to match her dress. She turned slightly. "Have you ever seen baby birds? They're so helpless. There's a nest in the tree outside my window."

"Very interesting, my pet, but perhaps this is the wrong time."

"Yes," she murmured.

Jonah drank off his brandy and sat back. "I suppose congratulations are in order . . . Of course *my* concern is Wade & Company. There are projects underway. What's to become of them? Really, Miranda, it's most unfair. You should have been more considerate."

She bit down on her lip to keep from laughing. "The store won't be affected," she replied after a moment. "The doctor said I could work almost up to the end. And that's what I plan to do. There's no reason for any of our projects to be delayed."

"There is one very good reason: propriety. How would it look for a woman in your condition to be running around the store? It's out of the question."

"There's another reason," said Peter. "Think of the strain on your health. I'm sure Dr. Wentworth doesn't realize how hard you work. The long hours. This is a time for you to relax, to save your strength."

"Save my strength!" Miranda's gray eyes twinkled. She smiled. "Peter, I'm not working on a chain gang. I sit in a nice, comfortable office and write reports. I work with figures, not a pickax." Her gaze moved to Jonah. "And as for my *condition*, when it becomes obvious, I can work from here. Harvey won't mind bringing files and whatever else I need. We can have our meetings here too, if *you* don't mind."

Jonah lighted a cigar, puffing on it as he considered Miranda's suggestion. He was not surprised that she had offered a solution to the problem, but he was surprised at how relieved he felt. To himself he admitted that he had come to depend upon her; she was imaginative, something he was not, and she was so often right. "This house has never been used for business purposes."

"It's only temporary, Jonah."

"What do you think, my pet? Would such an arrangement inconvenience you?"

Daphne blinked. "Why, no. There's the study, you see."

Jonah nodded. "I suppose you could use the study, Miranda . . . If you didn't touch anything."

"I'd be very careful."

Peter slouched in his chair. He had been forgotten and that was nothing new. At Wade's he did all the boring, everyday work that kept the store running, but he received little credit. He was the invisible man, excluded from major projects, rarely asked for his opinion. And it was the same way at home. To Jonah, he was still "Dexter," a hired hand of no particular importance. "I take it the matter is settled?"

"For now."

"Well, Miranda, I hope you're pleased."

She heard the edge in his voice. She looked at him.

288

"Try to understand, Peter. I'd go crazy sitting in my room day after day with nothing to do. I need to keep busy."

Daphne glanced up from her magazine. "If you learned to play bridge . . ."

"Oh, I'm terrible at games. I always get the cards mixed up."

"Yes, one needs a clear head."

Again Miranda wanted to laugh. A clear head? *Daphne?* "It's a talent," she replied. "We all have different talents."

Peter could stand no more of this conversation. "Jonah, may I have a word with you about the Mayhew consignment? I left the correspondence in the study. If you remember, it's rather a sticky situation."

"Yes, of course. Will you excuse me, my pet? I won't be long."

"Certainly, Jonah. Business is so complicated, isn't it?"

The two men rose and left the room. Daphne picked up her magazine, slowly turning the pages; Miranda watched. She had not expected a cozy chat about babies, but she had hoped that her news could elicit some sign of interest, woman to woman. Instead there was silence. "You—you won't mind having a baby around the house, will you?"

"Oh, I think babies are lovely. Such tiny little ears. Like seashells, really. Do you want another boy?"

"A girl would be nice, a sister for Andrew."

"Yes, Andrew will have to cope." Daphne put down her magazine and took up her fan. "I'm afraid it will be a bit awkward. Only Wades can inherit from the family trust, and this child will be a Dexter."

"I'm not worried about inheritances; I just want a healthy baby. Anyway, Peter is going to be rich someday."

"Is he? How wonderful! Life is much easier when one has . . . resources."

Miranda laughed. "Much easier," she agreed.

"And when Peter's rich, you won't have to work."

"But I'll always work, Daphne." Hadn't she been listening? "I enjoy it. My job is what I do best."

"Well, you're a clever girl. And times are different now, aren't they? It's quite all right for a girl to be clever . . . I wouldn't go too far, though, if I were you."

"Too far?"

"You were so happy when you married Peter. I noticed that. Of course there are disappointments in marriage. There are unpleasant moments. Still, marriage is a woman's only refuge. It's very comforting."

With the right man, thought Miranda. *If only I had married the right man.* She sighed, glancing off toward the windows. "This awful heat," she murmured. "I wish it would rain."

It was a torrid summer. Day after day, a fiery yellow sun beat down on the city until waves of heat seemed to rise from the sidewalks. The air was oppressive, heavy with moisture. The sky flashed with lightning every night, but no rain fell. During the first week of August, temperatures soared into the nineties and stayed there. Sweltering New Yorkers grumbled that the summer would never end.

Miranda was miserable. Plagued by morning sickness, by stifling heat, even the simplest task became an effort of will. She dragged herself to the office each day, sitting between two fans that did little more than move the sultry air from place to place. Her clothes stuck to her body; her brow streamed. Like everyone else, she was cranky.

September brought the first break in the weather. Rain came, two days of rain that washed away the heat. When finally the skies cleared, the sun was gentler, the air cooler, almost brisk. It was a preview of autumn, and to Miranda, it was a blessed relief. Her energy returned; her morning sickness stopped as suddenly as it had begun. She was able to look at food again, able to resume her dinners out with Peter, her Sunday brunches with Natalie. On one Sunday, Natalie took her to Orchard Street, a sprawling pushcart market that was a landmark of the Lower East Side. There, amidst the carts, amidst the tiny stores crowded side by side, they shopped for baby clothes. Miranda, ever practical, bought little shirts and sleepers in plain white and plain yellow, but at the last moment she snatched up a pair of little pink booties "Just in case it's a girl," she laughingly explained, crossing her fingers.

She had names picked out: Grace and Jonathan. They were names without any ties to family or the past, for both she and Peter felt their child should have a fresh start. She was still hoping for a girl child, but she seemed to be the only one who was. Jonah had long ago declared the superiority of boys. Andrew, after mulling over her announcement, had declared that he wanted a brother. Peter desperately wanted a son. She supposed that all men wanted sons.

Now, staring across the desk at Jonah, she wondered what his feelings had been when his own son had been born. It was hard to imagine him as a father. Had he wanted a son, or was it true that he had just wanted an heir to Wade & Company?

"I'm waiting, Miranda."

"What?" She blinked, coming out of her reverie. "Oh, I'm sorry, Jonah. I guess I was daydreaming. You wanted the figures on the new display cases."

"If it isn't too much trouble," he replied, scowling. "Can't you keep your mind on your work? I have no time for daydreams; this is an office, you know."

"Yes, I'm sorry." She took a sheet of paper from her folder and placed it on the desk. "Those are estimates, but the final figures won't run more than ten percent over."

"You're certain?"

"Yes."

He glanced at the neat rows of figures. "Highway robbery," he snorted.

"The cost will be higher next year."

"I don't doubt it. Labor unions! They'll be the ruin of this country."

"You needn't decide today, Jonah. Frankly, I prefer the old display cases. It's just that they look awfully beat up." She took another sheet of paper from her folder. "That's the cost for refinishing and new glass."

"Hardly a saving."

"No, but the old display cases are so handsome. They're part of Wade's tradition."

Jonah looked up. "You're a fine one to talk of tradition. Every week you suggest changing something else, adding something else. Out with the old, in with the new; that's your motto."

Miranda smiled. "Not exactly. We're trying to make the store more fashionable. And it's working . . . Daphne does some of her shopping here now, doesn't she?"

He had no answer to that. He put the papers at the side of his desk and sat back. "I will think about it, Miranda. It's a large sum of money either way. There's the store budget to consider . . . I must have time to think."

"If you need any more information —"

"That won't be necessary. You're a difficult girl, Miranda, but I give you credit for being thorough."

"Thank you." She closed her folder and stood up. "We can talk next week about the display —"

"We will talk when I'm ready."

"Of course."

"Well, don't stand there like a goose. Go on about your business."

Miranda turned. She was almost at the door when she felt a sharp pain in her stomach. She drew a breath, but in the same instant there was another, sharper pain. She doubled over. The folder dropped from her hand, spilling its papers on the floor. They blurred before her eyes; the room began to spin. She felt something sticky on her leg — blood. *"Jonah,"* she screamed.

His head snapped up. "What . . ." He did not finish, for Miranda had fainted. He left his chair and hurried to her. "Miranda?" He saw her ashen face, saw the trickle of blood on her stocking. "Martin!" he shouted, throwing open the door. "Martin, call an ambulance and have Dexter paged. Immediately!"

"I'm very sorry, Miranda," Dr. Wentworth was saying, "but sometimes these things happen for the best."

The best? I've lost my baby; how can that be for the best?

"We have a more serious problem now," he continued. "We can't stop the bleeding. You mustn't be alarmed; you're going to be fine, perfectly fine. But we *must* stop the bleeding and the only way is surgery."

Surgery? Miranda tried to rise. The nurse eased her back onto the pillows. "I want to go home."

"That's quite impossible, Miranda. You're going to be perfectly all right, but you have to cooperate. Dr. Jessup is a fine surgeon, the best. There's nothing to worry about."

"I want to go home."

Dr. Wentworth leaned over the bed and clasped Miranda's hands. "Now you listen to me. If we don't stop the bleeding, you'll die. The only way to stop the bleeding is surgery, and surgery is what you're going to have."

"Is Peter here?"

"He's in the waiting room. I'd rather you didn't see him until after the surgery. I want to give you a sedative now, and in a few minutes Nurse will prepare you for the operation."

"Andrew won't understand why I'm not home."

Dr. Wentworth smiled slightly. "If you do as I say, you'll be back home in no time at all." He nodded to the nurse. She handed him a syringe. "You'll feel a little sting, Miranda . . . There, that wasn't so bad, was it?"

She felt nothing. She was numb with sorrow for the child she would never know, never love. "Why did it happen? Why did I lose my baby?"

"We can't really be sure why these things happen. There's no particular reason . . . Something goes wrong. Nature makes the decision. Or God, if you view events in that light. We simply can't be sure."

"Why would God want to take my baby?"

"Miranda, the best advice I can give you is to accept this loss and then put it to rest. You're a young woman. You must look ahead."

"Because people who look back . . ." The sedative was taking effect. Her eyes felt heavy; her thoughts kept slipping away. "People who look back . . . always see . . ." Her eyes fluttered closed. "So tired," she murmured.

"Good," said Dr. Wentworth. He checked Miranda's pulse, held his stethoscope to her heart. "Nurse, you can start getting her ready. I'm going to have a word with the husband."

"Yes, Doctor."

He left, striding through the corridor to the waiting room. There was a young man pacing back and forth, and an older couple seated near the windows. Peter, looking haggard, sat near the door. He jumped up as the doctor entered. "Now take it easy, Peter. I—"

"The baby?"

"I'm very sorry. Miranda lost the baby on the way here."

Peter sank down into the chair. He stared blindly at the floor, passing his hand across his mustache. His head slumped, and his shoulders. He said nothing.

Natalie burst through the door then. "Peter . . . Oh, Doctor, I'm Natalie Stern, a friend of Mrs. Dexter's. Is she . . . Is she all right?"

"She lost the baby, Miss Stern. I'm afraid there's been quite a lot of bleeding. We're preparing her for surgery."

"My God, will she be all right?"

"I don't anticipate any complications. But surgery is always a risk . . ." Dr. Wentworth's gaze returned to Peter. "You haven't asked about your wife," he said, frowning. "Miranda's had a terrible time and there's more to come."

Slowly, Peter rose to his feet. "Was the baby a boy?"

"For heaven's sake, that's not the—"

"Was the baby a boy?"

"Yes."

The last glimmer of light died in Peter's eyes. Wordlessly, he turned and left the room.

"Where the devil are you going?" Dr. Wentworth followed him out, stopping abruptly when Peter disappeared into an elevator. He shook his head. A poor excuse for a man, he thought.

"Has Peter gone?" asked Natalie.

"Flown the coop, as they say."

"Bastard," she muttered under her breath. "Is it okay if I hang around?"

"I have to warn you it could be a long wait."

"I don't mind."

"Then make yourself comfortable, Miss Stern. I'll let you know when there's any news."

"Thank you, Doctor." She pulled off her gloves and sat down. Every few moments she glanced toward the door, hoping Peter would return. After an hour she gave up hope. "Bastard," she muttered again.

Miranda awoke from the anesthetic to find Dr. Wentworth sitting at her bedside. "I didn't die," she said.

"Of course you didn't die. You're going to be fine; right as rain."

"I don't feel fine. I have an awful headache . . . And my tongue feels fuzzy."

"That's the anesthetic. It will pass. You're a very healthy specimen, Miranda."

"Am I?"

"Certainly."

"Then why are you here? Why do you look so sad? There's something you're not telling me."

He sighed. "Yes, I'm afraid there is." He preferred to have the husband present at a time like this, but obviously Peter was not coming back. Shameful, he thought. Shameful. "The surgery was more extensive than we'd anticipated. There were tears in the womb that couldn't be repaired. We performed what is called a hysterectomy. That means . . ."

She knew what it meant: she would never be able to have children. The doctor went on talking; she buried her head in her pillow and wept.

Her tears flowed for days, but apart from the hospital staff, there were few people to see them. Daphne visited once, bringing a satin bedjacket and an armful of roses. Lily visited once, bringing magazines and a book of crossword puzzles. Peter did not visit at all.

"But he sends a big bouquet of flowers every morning," said Miranda now. "It must be a standing order."

Natalie's hazel eyes swept across the room. "Expensive flowers, too."

"He's very generous . . . Generous with everything but himself."

"He's a rat, Miranda."

She shrugged. "It was my idea to marry him; nobody held a gun to my head. I wanted a handsome husband . . . I wonder how many people get married because they've fallen in love with a face."

"There was more to it than that."

"I'm not so sure." Miranda smoothed the blankets, tucking them around her waist. "I was looking for Prince Charming. All fat, lonely girls look for Prince Charming . . . I was grateful. I didn't care about anything else."

"What was Peter looking for?"

"Who knows? I suppose he married me because of Wade's. Maybe he thought I could do him some good. With Jonah or Louis. Or maybe he just wanted me out

296

of there . . . I feel sorry for him in a way. Things don't seem to work out for Peter."

"Well, I always figured Wade's was part of the package. But I never figured he was a rat. He fooled me."

Miranda smiled. "You're too hard on him."

"Hard!"

"At least he never lied. He never said he loved me. And I think he would have tried to make something of the marriage. If I hadn't found the pictures; if we hadn't quarreled. If I'd quit my job—"

"In other words, everything would have been peachy if he'd had his own way."

"That's what men want, don't they? Especially men like Peter. He was king of the hill for the first eighteen years of his life."

"Fine, but where does that leave you?"

"Out in the cold."

"That's nowhere to spend the rest of your life, Miranda. Divorce him."

She shook her head. "I wouldn't do that to Andrew; he loves him. And Jonah would have a fit. No, that's impossible . . . We'll just have to muddle along. People do, you know. Besides, I have work to keep me busy. I get out of here next week, and in another three weeks I can go back to the store."

"Work's not enough, kiddo. Not for you, not for any woman."

Miranda lay back against the pillows. She looked around at all the flowers. Some were from people at the store; most were from Peter. They were beautiful, but they meant nothing to her, for Peter meant nothing to her. "We'll see," she said.

Chapter Seventeen

"You're supposed to have bed rest, Mrs. Dexter," said Lily, straightening the blankets again. "Doctor's orders."

"I haven't forgotten. I've had *two weeks* of bed rest and I hate it."

"Only one more week to go." Lily opened the windows, letting in the crisp October air. She picked up the breakfast tray and carried it to the door. "Do you want any books from the study?"

"I've read them all twice."

"Do you want anything else?"

Freedom, thought Miranda. "Harvey Vaughn's dropping off some reports. Will you bring them upstairs right away?"

"I'll see to it, Mrs. Dexter, but I don't think Dr. Wentworth would approve." Lily glanced around. Miranda's desk was stacked with reports. There were more reports stacked on a small table next to her bed, and lying atop her bed were the morning newspapers and two big yellow pads. "This place looks like an office."

"Nothing wrong with that. The doctor said I had to stay in bed; he didn't say I couldn't work."

Lily shrugged. "But that was the idea," she said, marching out.

Miranda switched on her new bedside radio. She reached for the *Times* and turned to the business section. She read an account of strong retail sales across the country. Smiling, she made several notations on her pad. After a while, she moved on to the stock market listings.

The market had soared to an all-time high on September 3, but in the ensuing weeks, key stocks had fallen off. On October 4, the market had lost thirty points in brief but heavy waves of selling. On October 21, a selling avalanche had been checked only moments before the tickers closed. A small group of economists had warned that trouble lay ahead, warnings quickly dismissed by Wall Street and by President Hoover, who declared the economy sound. It was reported that the nation's bankers had amassed a pool of 240 million dollars to shore up the market; to some, this was a sign of faith, to others, a sign of panic.

Miranda was concerned, and in her nightly meetings with Jonah, she sensed that he was concerned as well. Peter remained confident. Foolishly confident, she thought now, putting down the newspaper. She knew he had borrowed money to cover the first margin calls, knew he had lost thousands of dollars when the second and third calls had come. She frowned, wondering where it would end.

"Mama!" Andrew bounded into the room, a vast smile splitting his freckled face. "Mama, are you feeling better?"

It was his usual morning question, prompted, Miranda was certain, by Miss Dent. "I'm feeling fine, darling. Come give Mama a kiss."

He ran to the bed and into her outstretched arms. "There was jam this morning. Did you have jam, too?"

"A little." She smiled down at him. He was a handsome child with thick, coppery hair and clear blue eyes. At four, he was tall and sturdy, not a bit shy. Miranda thought he was very smart; he had learned the alphabet in nursery school, and he could count almost to a hundred. "Are you going to be a good boy at the museum today?"

"I can see the dinosaurs. They're *big.*"

"You can't touch, you know."

He nodded.

Miranda opened the drawer of her nightstand and removed an envelope. "Here's your permission note for your teacher. Remember to do as she says. And stay with the other children; don't wander off."

"I won't, Mama."

"If you're a good boy, I'll read you a special story tonight."

"I'll be good," he earnestly replied. He loved stories. "Can I have my dinner in here, too?"

"Of course you can." Miranda saw Miss Dent standing in the doorway. "But now you'd better scoot. You'll be late for the dinosaurs."

"Bye, Mama."

"Good-bye, Andrew. Don't wander off . . . Remember to keep your coat buttoned outside."

"I will," he called, skipping away with Miss Dent.

Miranda listened to his light, quick steps. When they faded, she leaned over and plucked a sales report from the stack on the table. Her pad filled with notations—things to ask Jonah and Harvey and Claude Berman, reminders for the advertising department, reminders for the lingerie department. At eleven, Lily brought a new set of reports. At twelve, she brought a lunch tray which Miranda put to one side.

It was after two when she heard the news flash on the radio: the stock market had suffered sharp declines. Later, she would learn the enormity of those declines. She would learn that thirteen million shares of stock had been sold off, and that market losses had exceeded ten billion dollars.

It was only a prelude, for now even the bankers with their huge pool of money could do nothing to stem the tidal wave of selling. The next day, a day that would forever be known as Black Tuesday, the market crashed.

There was bedlam in the canyons of Wall Street, bedlam on the trading floor as desperate men shouted and cursed and wept. According to a Stock Exchange guard, "They roared like a lot of lions and tigers. They howled and screamed. They clawed at one another's collars.

300

They were like a bunch of crazy men. Every once in a while, when Radio or Steel or Auburn would take another tumble, you'd see some poor devil collapse and fall to the floor."

The toll was stupendous. The selling off of twenty-three million shares let loose a panic that would destroy thirty billion dollars in market values. Great corporations were struck a mortal blow, as were the great investment trusts. And now the market's big men went down with the small investors, with the clerks and shopkeepers and cabdrivers who had put their last dollars into the golden dreams of Wall Street.

Nobody knew how many people were invested in the stock market on the day of the crash. Estimates ran from a million people to twenty-five million people, but whatever the true number, the effects of the crash would be felt by an entire nation. Because the stock market ultimately affected jobs, the stock market ultimately affected everyone, and the crash drew no distinctions. It was a whirlwind buffeting rich and poor. It was a disaster.

Miranda's first concern was Peter. She felt no love for him, but she felt sympathy and, instinctively, she felt his pain. All through that terrible Monday he had continued to hope the market would recover; on Tuesday, he had staggered home a broken man. Ashen, his mouth trembling, he had gone into his room and locked the door.

Miranda had turned away Jonah's questions and stationed herself in the sitting room, close to Peter's door. She spent Tuesday night there, starting at every sound, for the radio had broadcast more than a few reports of distraught men jumping out of windows or putting guns to their heads. Did Peter have a gun? She had no idea; she had not been in his room since the long ago night they had come back from Lake Placid. Was Peter likely to do something desperate? Again, she had no idea. She

301

realized how little she knew him. They had lived under the same roof, lived as man and wife, and yet they were strangers.

Now she heard the sound of glass shattering and she leapt to her feet. She raced to his door, pounding on it. "Peter? Peter, are you all right?"

"Go away, Miranda."

"I want to talk to you. Let me in."

"Go away."

She sighed. "I'm not going anywhere until I talk to you. Let me in."

The door was flung open. "You're supposed to be in bed, Miranda."

"Never mind me. It's you I'm worried about." She stared at him, at the shadowy patches beneath his eyes, at the deep lines etched around his mouth. His clothes were wrinkled; he was unshaven. He looked suddenly old, as if he had aged overnight. "Sit down, Peter." She glanced at his bed, which had not been slept in. "You must be exhausted."

"I'm ruined, that's what I am. Not that that comes as any surprise to you. Miranda Wade Dexter, the girl who sees all and knows all. How does it feel to be so damned smart?"

"Let's both sit down." She went to him and took his hand. He reeked of Scotch. On the floor near his bureau were shards of glass from a smashed whiskey bottle. "Here, sit in this big comfortable chair," she said, drawing another chair alongside. "That's better; I was afraid you were going to fall over."

"What do you want? Did you come to gloat?"

"Peter, I want to help. I just don't know how."

"I'm beyond help, thank you very much. I've lost everything. Wiped out, and if that's not enough, I owe ten thousand dollars . . . Throwing good money after bad, as you would say. It's the money I borrowed to cover the margin calls."

"I'm sorry."

"Are you?"

"Oh, of course I am, Peter. We're not enemies, you know. Of course I care about what's happened."

"More than two hundred thousand dollars," he said, dropping his head into his hands. "Almost a quarter of a million. Gone . . . I'm coming up on forty and I'm penniless. Not only penniless, but in debt."

Miranda had not lost her distaste for easy, empty words of consolation. She knew it would do no good to say that everything was going to be all right when in fact everything was all wrong. "At least we have our jobs. We have two salaries and—"

"Salaries? Jobs? I had a *plan*, Miranda. It didn't include being a job slave for the rest of my days. Christ, what a dreary prospect!"

"I can remember when all you talked about was being vice president of Wade & Company."

"Did you ever ask yourself why? I wanted that job so I could put my own stamp on the store. It would have been an accomplishment, Miranda. Something to prove I was alive. In those days I even dreamed of easing Jonah into an early retirement. I would have became president then. But you came along and ruined it all. You and your charts and your numbers and your damned ideas. Oh, I got the job, but thanks to you it wasn't worth anything. You had taken over."

"I wish—"

"Of course I still had the other half of my plan: money. I'd never get the family fortune back, but I could make my own fortune. A killing in the market." He passed his hand across his face, staring at the floor. "I was so close, so bloody *close*. Another year . . . Why couldn't the market have held out one more year?"

"I don't know what to say, Peter. Isn't there anything I can do to help?"

"Not unless you have a few hundred thousand bucks hidden in your mattress."

"Sorry. You didn't marry a rich woman."

"I couldn't. I had the bloodlines, but not the bank account. So I did the next best thing: I married Jonah's

303

right-hand man. And lived to regret it."

Miranda's eyes flashed. She stood. "I'm obviously not doing any good here, Peter. I'll go back to my room."

"By all means."

She went to the door, pausing at the threshold. "Jonah will want to know what's wrong. He was asking questions last night, but I put him off. I gather you never told him about your investments."

"He knew I was in the market; he knew all along." Peter shook a cigarette out of a crumpled pack and lighted it. "I didn't tell him the extent of my investments. I didn't want another lecture on the subject of risks . . . There's a man who never took a risk in his whole damned life. Of course he never had to. That makes a difference, doesn't it? The old windbag probably has thousands stashed away in *his* mattress."

"Are you going to work today?"

"You're not my boss, Miranda. Not yet."

"Lucky for you," she quietly replied.

He looked up, coughing on the smoke from his cigarette. "What did you say?"

"Nothing, Peter." She studied his gray, haggard face. She felt sorry for him, but in the detached way one feels sorry for the unknown victim of an accident. "I guess there's nothing more to say."

"At last I agree with you. Close the door on your way out, Miranda."

Peter returned to work the following day, Miranda the following week. A meeting was called to discuss the changing economic climate; the faces gathered around the conference table were uniformly grim.

"We have to be prepared for the worst," said Claude Berman.

"What does that mean?" asked an edgy Harvey Vaughn. "You know how far ahead my buyers work. They're placing orders *now* for next spring. Meanwhile, this year's Christmas merchandise is already being

304

shipped. Six months ago we didn't know the market was going to go to hell. We ordered on the basis of last Christmas, which you'll remember was up twenty percent over the year before. I can show you the figures."

"I have the figures, Harvey."

"Then you understand the situation. If our customers decide to hold back this Christmas, we'll be sunk. And what about right now? What about today? Do I tell my buyers we're cutting certain departments? How much do we cut?" He turned his head to Jonah. "I need guidelines, Mr. Wade."

Jonah sat back in his chair and pressed his fingertips together. "Dexter, we'll hear from you. What do you have to say?"

"In my opinion, there's nothing we can do until we have a clearer picture. There's nothing we can do about Christmas at all. Harvey, I'd say a ten percent cut across the board is safe, at least for now."

"Miranda?"

She shook her head. "I don't know, Jonah. I'd like some time to see if any patterns develop in the sales figures. They were way down the week of the Crash, then they picked up again. They've been off this week." She riffled through her folder, holding up a sheet of paper. "Toiletries is the only department holding steady. All the others are up and down . . . Oh, except for the fur department, which has been dead."

Jonah looked at his new general manager, a craggy, fortyish man named Tom Guthrie. "No one is willing to go out on a limb. What about you, Guthrie? Are you more courageous?"

"It's not courage, Mr. Wade," he briskly replied, "it's a matter of perception. My perception of circumstances is that we're in for hard times. I'd cut fifteen percent at the high end, ten percent at the low, and be ready to cut deeper on all nonconsignment merchandise. The days of prosperity are over."

"President Hoover seems to disagree with you."

"That's his privilege, sir."

305

There was silence as everyone waited to see how Jonah would react. He laughed. "Someone has climbed out on a limb after all!"

"I'd still like some time," said Miranda. She lifted her eyes to Tom Guthrie. "I don't think a month will make any difference."

"Probably not. Providing we're ready to make quick decisions, and to cancel orders if need be. You'll have to stay on top of things, Harvey."

"I know my job, Tom."

"We all know our jobs," said Peter.

Jonah tapped his pen on the table. "That will do. We have business here, in case you've forgotten. Miranda, you will have your month, but keep Guthrie informed of your progress. As for you, Vaughn, I'm authorizing a five percent cut across the board . . . I don't believe the future is as bleak as Guthrie suggests. I *do* believe we must be prepared to move quickly. Five percent is a starting point, nothing more. It has never been Wade & Company policy to cancel orders placed in good faith, but we may be forced to alter our policy. Notice I said may, only time will tell. For now, we must avoid panicky thinking. It serves no purpose."

"We can't avoid reality," said Tom Guthrie.

"What a profound observation," said Peter.

Miranda looked up from her notes. "It's silly to argue. I'm sure we all agree that things are different now. We'll have to make adjustments. This is just the beginning."

"Of the end," added an unsmiling Tom Guthrie.

Indeed an era had ended, for the Crash ushered in the Great Depression, as dark a time as the country had ever known. Unemployment was the immediate consequence, and it worsened from year to year. Fourteen million men were unemployed by 1932, one out of every four American workers. Millions more had only part-time work to sustain them. People lost their homes, their farms, their businesses. Factories closed by the thousands, and bank failures were rampant. Desperate men sold apples on street corners, while others, even more desperate, begged coins and rooted around in garbage cans. President Hoover continued to affirm the soundness of the economy, declaring that "prosperity was just around the corner," but anyone looking around the corner in 1932 was likely to see yet another breadline, yet another soup kitchen.

Miranda knew how lucky she was, but she took nothing for granted. In the early years of the Depression, all the city's department stores had suffered heavy losses and Wade's was no exception. Jonah, faced with his first true business crisis, seemed unable to make decisions. Peter, still mourning what might have been, seemed uninterested. She knew something had to be done.

"It's up to us, Tom," she said one rainy autumn morning in 1933. "We've been sitting back, waiting for someone to take charge." She shrugged. "No one has. I nominate us. And Harvey. Harvey will go along with anything we suggest."

"How do we get past Jonah? He's in no mood for suggestions. He has that glazed look in his eyes. 'Quality merchandise at a fair price'; that's all I've heard him say this whole year."

"He's scared."

"Everybody's scared, Miranda."

"Look at it from his point of view. Wade's has been in his family for four generations. He doesn't want to be the one to lose all that his family's built up. I think that scares him more than anything else—failing his sainted ancestors."

Tom smiled. He stood, pacing around Miranda's office. "And we're going to save Jonah. Is that it?"

"We're going to save ourselves. Another year or two like this one and we're all in trouble. You know the figures as well as I do, Tom. Only a handful of departments are showing profits: the bridal department, the baby department, lingerie, toiletries. Toiletries has been our biggest profit maker; the stuff just flies off the shelves.

307

That's given me an idea."

"Cosmetics?"

"Exactly!" She was not surprised that Tom Guthrie had anticipated her. Their minds were alike: quick, sharp, open to ideas. "We wouldn't have to put much money into a cosmetics department. We can get the merchandise on consignment."

"I'm thinking about the counter space. Cosmetics should be at the very front of the store."

"To lure customers," agreed Miranda.

"Right. The three big handkerchief counters would have to go."

"That's no loss, Tom. These days, we're lucky if we sell three handkerchiefs a *week*. But I suppose you're wondering about Jonah. He *is* sentimental about those counters. His great-grandfather started his business selling handkerchiefs and gloves, you see. It's been a tradition ever since."

"Every time I turn around I run smack into another tradition."

"I'm pretty sure I can handle Jonah. He's gone against tradition before, almost always with good results."

Tom shrugged. "I'm all for the idea, Miranda, but Jonah I leave to you."

"Fair enough . . . My other idea is a bit more complicated."

"Oh?" Tom resumed his chair. He picked up his coffee cup, staring at Miranda over the rim. A very pretty woman, he thought. Shapely, well dressed. Wonderful gray eyes. *Shrewd* gray eyes. "I'm listening," he said with a smile.

"I want to introduce a new dress department. No, don't say anything until I've finished. I know dresses aren't doing much business; a lot of women are making do with what they have. But there are also a lot of women working now — single women working in offices, married women helping to support their families. Those women need clothes to wear to work. Not expensive clothes, but nice clothes. And if they're stylish, all the

308

better . . ." Miranda paused, studying Tom's uncertain expression. "The catch is they have to be reasonably priced." She shook her head. "What the hell, they have to be *cheap!*"

Tom laughed, and the corners of his eyes crinkled. "To say the least. There are manufacturers turning out cheap dresses, Miranda. The cloth frays and the seams split after the first cleaning. Do you want Wade's to sell that kind of merchandise?"

"No, of course not. I don't want to cheat our customers."

"Then what's the answer?"

"Natalie Stern."

"Who?"

Miranda reached under her desk, producing a large portfolio. She opened it and removed several sketches. "Look at these," she said. "Tell me what you think."

"Natalie Stern's handiwork?"

"Yes. What do you think, Tom?"

"Impressive." He put on his glasses and had a closer look. "Very impressive. But I don't see how these sketches solve our problem. Who is this girl?"

"Natalie was a designer at Milady Dresses before they went out of business. She's good, Tom. When she started there she was a lowly assistant. She worked her way up."

"A friend of yours?"

Miranda nodded. "She used to work here. Natalie was in women's better handbags when I was in the credit department. We learned the retail business at the same time. The point is, I think she can design a line of dresses for us. Cheap dresses that have style and that won't fall apart. I'd like to give her a whole department — Today's Woman, or Modern Woman, or something of that sort. If we back it up with advertising —"

"Hold on a minute. Let's say she designs these miraculous dresses. Who's going to manufacture them?"

"Well, that's the complicated part. Natalie wants to start her own business. On one hand, it's the worst possible time, but on the other, it's the perfect time. She can

309

rent space and equipment dirt cheap. She can get all the employees she needs at a modest wage. She can do it; she's managed to save some money." Miranda took a deep breath. "And I've saved some money, too. You know I'm no gambler, but I've decided to invest in Natalie's company."

"I sense an 'if' in there somewhere."

Miranda glanced down at the sketches. "This will work only *if* she has a substantial order."

"From us."

A smile flickered around her mouth. "That's right. We'll have an exclusive."

"I should hope so!"

"It's risky, Tom, I know that. I honestly believe everyone will profit. We have to go after younger customers, young working women. I believe this is the way to start."

"You must, if you're risking your own money. Sorry I can't get in on it. All *my* money is tied up in alimony payments. Why do women keep divorcing me, Miranda?"

"Poor Tom. Your wives don't understand you."

He laughed. "I'm not going to get any sympathy from you, am I?"

"Not a bit. You and your roving eye."

"The flesh is weak."

"Umm." She smiled at Tom. "Among other things."

"Is that why you always turn down my dinner invitations?"

"I always turn down your dinner invitations because I'm married. You may know my husband. Peter Dexter?"

"Speaking of weak —"

"We're not," interrupted Miranda. "We're discussing ideas."

"All right," said Tom, nodding his sandy head. "I'm all for the cosmetics idea. And the new dress department as well, providing we can agree on the size of the order. Deal?"

"Deal."

"But there's something you have to do first."

"I know," sighed Miranda. "I have to convince Jonah. Wish me luck!"

Jonah was alone in his study when Miranda arrived home. She stood in the doorway, watching him, thinking that the past few years had taken a terrible toll. His dark hair was streaked with white, his brow scored with deep lines. He was still heavy, yet there were sunken hollows in his cheeks. In his eyes was a strange look at once vacant and confused; the look of a sleepwalker, she thought to herself. She knew he had been totally unprepared for the economic ruin that had followed the Crash. To the very end he had believed President Hoover's rosy forecasts; when finally he had accepted the truth he had been devastated, for the truth was that Wade & Company could be lost. "Jonah, may I come in?"

"It's been a long day, Miranda."

"I won't keep you," she replied, sinking into the chair beside his desk. "I'm a little tired myself."

"You're a young woman. Why should you be tired?"

She smiled. "Worries take a lot out of people, Jonah. I'm as worried about the store as you are."

"I doubt that."

"Tom and I had a meeting this morning. We came up with a few ideas."

"Ideas?" Jonah waved his hand as if he were waving away an annoying fly. "What good are ideas? My great-grandfather had only one idea: quality merchandise at a fair price. If he were here now . . ."

"We're here now, Jonah. And we have problems your great-grandfather couldn't even have imagined. It's our responsibility to find solutions."

"In harebrained ideas? In gimmicks? Should we copy the movie theaters and give away free dishes? Or perhaps we should sponsor contests like the newspapers do. Or we could hold raffles, I suppose. Or two-for-one sales . . . Have I left anything out?"

"Jonah, you know very well I'm not talking about

things like that. I'm talking about adding two new departments."

"New departments? Think of the cost. How can you consider such an expensive project in these times? Everybody is cutting back. Why, you of all people should understand the *need* to cut back. You work with sales figures every day."

"Yes, that's just it." Miranda opened her briefcase, extracting a thick file. "These figures prove my point, which is that women are still buying small luxury items. Big luxuries are beyond the reach of a lot of people now, but a woman can still treat herself to a jar of handcream or a pair of silk stockings. Little things that make her feel good. That's why I want to introduce a cosmetics department."

"Cosmetics!"

"Women do wear cosmetics, Jonah. A woman may not be able to afford a new hat, but a new lipstick is an affordable luxury. We should sell what people can afford to buy, what people want to buy. There's another thing— cosmetics will draw customers into the store."

Jonah sat back, stroking his chin. "The wrong kind of customers."

"I disagree. In the first place, we're in no position to be choosy; there aren't as many rich people anymore. Besides, rich women wear cosmetics, too. It's perfectly respectable. *Daphne* wears cosmetics." Miranda saw his expression soften, his eyes go to the portrait above the mantel. He smiled; a little wistfully, she thought. She realized that it had been a while since she had heard his loud, lusty cries coming from Daphne's bedroom. Quickly, she glanced away. "I'd like to show you the research, Jonah. I have quite a lot of information here."

"If you must."

Miranda opened the file and sorted through her papers. She selected five, arranging them on the desk. "These will give you some idea," she began. She talked for ten minutes, often referring him to her notes. He asked only a few questions and scarcely seemed to listen to her answers. "The important thing to remember," she concluded, "is that cosmetics are almost pure profit."

Jonah looked up. "Profit, you say?"

"Cosmetics are cheap to manufacture. We can take a very nice markup and still offer our customers a bargain. Cosmetics is a volume business. And it's *not* seasonal," she added, saving the best for last. "I really don't see how we can go wrong."

Jonah sighed. He knew Miranda expected him to make a decision. He was tired; he wished she would leave him alone. "All these changes." He shook his head. "There are times I hardly recognize my own store."

"Change can be healthy."

"Perhaps."

"My other idea — and Tom agrees — is a new dress department. Inexpensive dresses for young working women. It would replace resort wear. No one is buying resort wear."

Jonah leaned back in his chair. His head had begun to throb. "My father started the resort-wear department."

"It was a wise move, but the world is different now. When this is over — "

"Will it ever be over? There is a soup kitchen three blocks from here. A soup kitchen! That's what the world has come to."

"I have faith in President Roosevelt."

"Have you? He's a Socialist, you know."

Miranda laughed. "Jonah, he's no such thing! Can we get back to the subject of the dress department? It's safer."

"I don't want to think about new departments, Miranda. I suppose you're right. You're usually right, aren't you?" He turned as a knock came at the door. "Yes?" He brightened, for Daphne was gliding into the room. "I've neglected you, my pet. Blame Miranda; she's kept me here listening to more of her schemes."

"Jonah, I'm afraid I have bad news. Helen Grayson just telephoned. It's Louis . . . He died this morning."

"Died?"

313

"Yes, I'm sorry. He was having breakfast . . . Poached eggs," Helen said. "And he just slumped over. It was quick, you see."

Miranda felt tears mist her eyes. "Dear sweet Louis," she murmured.

"Yes," agreed Daphne, "he *was* sweet, wasn't he? Of course he was almost ninety."

"The last of my father's associates," said Jonah. Once again his eyes were strangely vacant. His mouth was pale. "Well, it's all done now."

"What is?" asked Daphne.

The past, thought Miranda. Jonah's lost his last tie to the secure, comforting past. She watched him rise unsteadily and walk to the door. "Jonah—"

He held up his hand, silencing her. "I'm very tired, Miranda. Do . . . do whatever you want."

"It can wait, Jonah."

He turned. "Is that a kindness, Miranda? Don't waste your time . . . Time is all there is."

Chapter Eighteen

Miranda threw down her briefcase, kicked off her shoes, and dropped gratefully onto her bed. The fire had been lighted; she stared at the shifting flames and tried to make her mind a blank.

"Mrs. Dexter?"

She sighed. "Come in, Lily."

"Mrs. Wade ordered dinner on trays tonight. Because of Mr. Grayson, I guess. Here's yours."

"Thanks. Just leave it on the desk. I'm not hungry."

"You're getting thin."

A smile hovered around Miranda's mouth. "I can remember when I would have killed to hear those words." She sat up, massaging her neck. "Has Peter gone?"

"Over an hour ago. Mr. Dexter changed his clothes after work and then went right out again . . . And you gave Andrew permission to spend the night at Jimmy Selkirk's, so now you won't have any company at all."

"Well, I want Andrew to have friends."

"Did you see your mail? I put it —"

"Mail?" Miranda glanced up. "I never get any mail."

"You got a letter today." Lily took the letter from the bureau and gave it to Miranda. "From Ireland."

"Ireland!" She studied the bold, black handwriting. Frowning, she tore open the envelope. "Dear God . . . It's from a Daniel McAllister. He's coming here next month. He . . . Dear God, he wants to *meet* me."

Lily was very still, her gaze fixed on Miranda's astonished face. "That would be around Thanksgiving," she said. "Mr. Wade might let you invite him to dinner—a relative and all."

"He's not a . . ." Miranda stopped herself. "Well, I mean, he *is* a relative. A cousin. *My* cousin, but we've never been in touch . . . There are lots of cousins in Ireland. Dozens. But, they're strangers, really . . . I can't imagine how he found me."

Lily started toward the door. "It's nothing to be nervous about, Mrs. Dexter. It's just family."

Miranda swallowed. "Yes, family." She glanced again at the letter. For one desperate moment she wondered if she should write back to Daniel McAllister, making some excuse, any excuse, to avoid the meeting. Would he accept an excuse? Probably not, she thought. If he had taken all the trouble to track her down . . . "It's a little awkward," she murmured. "A long-lost cousin."

"Just be yourself," suggested Lily.

"Myself?"

"You'll be fine, said Lily sailing through the door.

Miranda crumpled the letter and tossed it into the wastebasket. An instant later she fished it out and smoothed it carefully on the bed. "Daniel McAllister," she murmured, shaking her head. "Dear God, what am I going to do?"

"What am I going to do, Natalie?" asked Miranda the next day. "I thought about it all night, and I just *know* it's going to be a disaster."

"Not if you keep your head. It's like you said: you're strangers to each other. He doesn't know what to expect, either. Stay off the subject of family history and everything will be okay."

"What a terrible time for this to happen. I have so much on my mind now."

"You're at your best under pressure."

"I used to be." Miranda looked around the conference

316

room, her eyes settling on the portrait of the founder, Albert Wade. "I bet he's glad to be out of it."

"Out of what?"

"*Life.* Life is so damned complicated."

"I'll drink to that," said Tom Guthrie, walking into the room. "Troubles, Miranda?"

She shrugged.

"This must be the famous Natalie Stern. Hello, Natalie, I'm Tom Guthrie. It's nice to meet you. I understand we're going to be doing business together."

"I'm keeping my fingers crossed."

Tom sat down. He put his coffee cup and notebook on the table and turned to Miranda. "What's the story with Jonah?"

"He's not himself, Tom. We talked, or at least *I* talked. At the end, he told me to do whatever I wanted. Those were his words and I'm taking them as approval to go ahead."

"What if he changes his mind?"

"Once everything is in motion, he won't be able to. That's why we have to move quickly."

Tom smiled. "Nerves of steel," he said, looking at Natalie. "Your friend has nerves of steel."

"I wish," said Miranda. "Anyway, it will save time if we divide the work. I'll get started on the cosmetics project. You and Natalie can start planning the dress department."

Tom sipped his coffee. "Are we bringing anybody else into this? Harvey? Peter? *Any*body?"

Miranda nodded. "At the executive meeting next month," she replied. "We'll be more organized and we won't sound like idiots."

"We're going to spring it on them; is that it?"

"No, it's not. Harvey has a general idea of what we're doing. And Peter . . . Well, he has his hands full with the personnel budget. Claude and the accountants are after him to cut staff. Peter's trying to find ways around that . . . He always gets the dirty work. It's really not fair."

317

"He wanted to be vice president, Miranda. It was his choice."

"There were reasons . . ." she began. "Oh, never mind. Where were we?"

"Dividing up the work," replied Tom. "Do you have target dates for the new departments?"

"I want cosmetics in by spring; it's the ideal time. The dress department . . ." Miranda looked at Natalie. "That's more or less up to you," she said. "You don't even have work space yet."

"I can have a loft tomorrow morning, fully equipped. But I'll have to leave here today with a firm order."

"What about staff? Fitters and cutters and pressers? And the women operating the sewing machines are going to have to be good. We don't want uneven seams or bunched hems or any of that."

Natalie smiled; little gold flecks danced in her hazel eyes. "So you're an expert now? Don't worry, Miranda. My uncle Sy's been cutting dresses for thirty years. He knows everyone in the garment district. He can get me all the people I need by the end of the week. Good people who need the work. But I have to have a firm order."

"Well, you and Tom can thrash that out." Miranda laughed. "Tom is much tougher in negotiations than I am, so be warned."

"Don't believe a word of it," said Tom. "I'm a pushover."

"Just my type," said Natalie, smiling into his crinkly brown eyes.

Miranda pushed her chair back and stood up. "Obviously you two are going to get along very well. I'll leave you to it."

"Don't you want to sit in?" asked Tom.

"I have a meeting with advertising and I can't put it off. We're closing the store tomorrow for Louis's funeral," she explained to Natalie. "I have to get all my meetings in today . . . Tom, I'd like a memo outlining what's decided here. Okay?"

"Okay, boss lady."

"I've never seen her in action before," said Natalie when Miranda had gone. "She's a whiz at this stuff, isn't she? I'm impressed."

"Tell her she works too hard," replied Tom. "Because she does."

Miranda was working twelve-hour days and taking work home with her at night. She spent one evening a week at the Ladies Relief Society, assembling food and clothing packages for needy families, but the rest of her time she gave to Wade's and to Andrew. She had no social life, no outside interests. Away from the store she saw little of Peter, for he was seldom home. She had no idea where he went or what he did. She assumed there were women, probably bought and paid for, but that part of his life he kept to himself. His absences were not questioned. Neither Daphne nor Jonah appeared to notice, and Miranda no longer cared. Peter drifted at the edges of her life. Occasionally they went to the theater together, to neighborhood dinner parties, but that was all and that was enough.

She saved her love for Andrew. She had managed to be at home for the important moments in his life, but still she began to worry that she was missing his childhood. She wanted to spend more time with him and so she began taking him to Wade's on Saturday mornings. She gave him small chores to do — sharpening pencils, stamping envelopes, carrying messages back and forth. In the corner of her office was a small table that served as his "desk."

"Is this really my store?" he asked one morning in early November. "Is it *mine?*"

Miranda looked up from her sales reports. "It will be yours someday." *If we make it through the Depression,* she thought to herself. "Why do you ask?"

"It's a big store."

"Yes."

"If I have this whole big store I'll be *important.*"

Miranda frowned. Why would an eight-year-old care

319

about that? "Do you want to be important?"

He shrugged. "I don't know. It's what Papa said."

"Oh, I see." She would have to have a talk with Peter. "Do you know why he said that? To get you thinking about things. About school, for example. You have to pay attention in school if you're going to run this store someday. A lot of people will be counting on you."

"Why?"

"Because you'll be the boss."

"Like you?"

"Like Grandpapa," replied Miranda, smiling. "So you have to stop cutting up with Jimmy and Clark and start paying attention at school."

"School is hard."

"Not if you put your mind to it, Andrew. You're a smart boy."

He grinned. "I am?"

"Yes, you *am*."

He giggled. "You're funny, Mama."

"Have you finished those envelopes? Let me see . . . Very nice," she said when he brought them to her. "Shall I pay you your salary now? All right, here you are. One dime . . . And one kiss."

The door opened; Peter entered. "Ready for lunch, sport? Where would you like to go today?"

"The ice-cream place."

"The ice-cream place?" asked Miranda.

"He means Rumpelmeyer's."

"Are you going to go all the way up there?"

Peter took Andrew's coat from the closet and helped him into it. "Why not? We'll hop a cab." At that, Andrew began hopping around. Peter laughed.

Miranda watched, thinking that Peter was a different man when he was with Andrew. He was happy, or as close as he ever came to being happy. He was utterly relaxed. It was true that he sometimes filled the child's head with foolish ideas, but most of the time he was an ideal father — interested, caring, patient. At moments like this, she

320

could not help wondering what Peter would have been like if his own father had been stronger. "Enjoy yourselves," she said as they walked to the door.

"Want to come along?" asked Peter.

"I wouldn't dream of intruding on boy talk. But remember, *lunch* before ice cream. Oh, and Andrew's due at the Russells at two. Diane is taking all the children to the movies."

"I'll have him there on time."

"Good-bye, Andrew."

"Bye, Mama."

Miranda returned to her reports, but after a while she rose and went to the window. There were fewer cars on Fifth Avenue now, fewer trucks. Crowds of people still rushed from place to place, though many of these people were not as well dressed as they used to be. She saw a policeman shooing a panhandler away from the store entrance. She shook her head, for the city was filled with men who could not find work or even a bed for the night, men who lived on the occasional nickels and dimes of passersby.

"Mrs. Dexter?"

She whirled around. Standing there was a dapper, white-haired man carrying a briefcase. "Yes?"

I didn't mean to startle you. Your door was open."

"Can I help you?"

"I'm Sumner Hale. Of Baxter, Craig and Hale? We have an appointment, I believe."

"Oh, yes, yes, of course. Please sit down, Mr. Hale. I'm afraid I'd forgotten all about it. You're Louis Grayson's attorney, aren't you?"

"I was. I represent the estate now."

Miranda slipped behind her desk. "I'm sorry I wasn't able to go to your office. I had several meetings that day. Jonah — Mr. Wade — said he would take care of everything."

Sumner Hale put on his glasses and opened his briefcase. "The matter concerns a bequest in Mr. Grayson's will."

"Yes, but Jonah—"

"Excuse me, Mrs. Dexter; Jonah Wade is not involved in the matter. If I may begin?"

She nodded.

"Mr. Grayson bequeathed to you the sum of ten thousand dollars."

"Ten thousand dollars! There must be some mistake, Mr. Hale. Ten thousand dollars is . . ."

"Quite a lot of money for these times, yes. Nonetheless, the money is yours. I have a check here. There is, however, a second bequest, and for that I will need your signature."

Miranda had heard nothing after the words "the money is yours." She had recently put most of her savings into Natalie's new company. It had been a gesture of friendship as much as a business investment, but still she was nervous about risking her carefully accumulated nest egg. Money in the bank meant security, perhaps the only security, for she knew how quickly things could go wrong.

"Are you listening, Mrs. Dexter?"

"What? Oh, I'm sorry. It's just that I wasn't expecting such a . . . generous gift."

"There is more."

"More?"

"The second bequest. If I may have your attention, I shall proceed."

Miranda blushed. "You have my full attention, Mr. Hale."

"Excellent. This bequest concerns Wade and Company. As you probably know, Wade and Company is almost wholly owned by the Wade family trust, which holds ninety percent of the shares. The remaining ten percent was given to Mr. Grayson by Lionel Wade many years ago. The sole stipulation was that these shares were to revert to the Wade family upon Mr. Grayson's death. Put simply, Mr. Grayson was free to bequeath his shares to any member of the Wade family. He bequeathed his

322

shares to you, Mrs. Dexter."

"To *me?* I'm not a Wade."

"You are a Wade by marriage. For our purposes, that is sufficient."

"I don't think I understand, Mr. Hale."

"You are a member of the Wade family, even if not by blood. Lionel Wade's gift to Mr. Grayson stipulated only that the shares revert to a member of the Wade family. Mr. Grayson's bequest is entirely legal. Therefore, you now own ten percent of Wade and Company."

Miranda's mouth fell open. *"I* do?"

"Yes, Mrs. Dexter."

"But I . . . I . . . Does Jonah know about this?"

"He has made inquiries as to Mr. Grayson's shares," replied Sumner Hale. "I was not at liberty to discuss the terms of the will until probate was cleared."

"Then he doesn't know."

"He will be informed as soon as the formalities are completed. I need your signature on several documents first."

"I actually *own* ten percent of Wade's?"

"That is correct."

"Dear God!"

"If I may say so, Mr. Grayson was quite fond of you, Mrs. Dexter. He felt you would lead Wade and Company into the future . . . Naturally your shares have limited value in these very difficult times, but when the economy recovers, they will have great value indeed. Mr. Grayson felt strongly that the store's best years were still to come. You may consider his bequest a vote of confidence."

Miranda was too stunned to consider anything. She watched the old attorney remove two sets of papers from his briefcase and place them on the desk. She stared at the typewritten words, but they all seemed to blur together.

"These documents merely confirm the transfer of shares from the estate to you. If you will sign both copies, please."

Her hand trembled slightly as she took up her pen. She signed "Miranda Dexter"; only half a lie, she thought,

and maybe only half a crime. "Do — do these papers go to
. . . a court?"

"A formality, Mrs. Dexter . . . And here is your check
for ten thousand dollars."

She gazed at the check. She reached for it, then pulled
her hand back — a gesture she repeated twice before finally and firmly shaking her head. "I wonder if I might
ask a favor, Mr. Hale?"

"A favor?" His eyes blinked behind the polished lenses
of his glasses. "What sort of favor?"

"Well, I wonder if you could make this check over to my
husband? As if it were Louis's bequest to him. I mean,
without his knowing I had anything to do with it . . . You
wouldn't have to *say* it was a bequest, exactly. A few vague
phrases would be enough."

"But why?"

Why? Miranda sighed. Because she was feeling guilty,
feeling greedy. Because she felt she owed Peter something,
for Andrew if for nothing else. Because she knew he was
deeply in debt. Because it was what she wanted to do.
"My husband's had his problems since the Crash . . . But
it would be awkward if he thought the check came from
me."

"His pride, I suppose."

"More than money was wiped out in the Crash, Mr.
Hale."

"Yes, quite true. Of course what you suggest is most
irregular. And extremely complicated."

"I appreciate that. I realize it's a lot to ask. Still, it really
wouldn't do any harm."

Sumner Hale removed his glasses and rubbed the
bridge of his nose. "What you suggest is deceitful."

"A small deceit." Miranda glanced at her signatures on
the documents. She ducked her head. "Where would we
be without out small deceits?"

Jonah took the news of Miranda's inheritance very

well. She had expected bluster, sarcasm, anger, but instead he shrugged and murmured a few words about loyalty. His muted reaction concerned her; a week later she persuaded Daphne to call Dr. Wentworth.

He came to the Murray Hill house, and after a careful examination he pronounced Jonah healthy but despondent. "It's a common condition these days," he explained, addressing both Daphne and Miranda. "People feel they've failed."

"What shall we do?" asked Daphne.

"I'll leave a prescription for a tonic. It may help a little. I advised a trip, a change of scenery, but Jonah refused."

"We haven't been away in three years. We used to go to Europe, you know."

"I'll take that drink now, Miranda. Isn't it nice that alcohol is legal again? So much easier."

Miranda went to the drinks table and mixed a whiskey and soda. She poured a small brandy for herself, and a sherry for Daphne. "There has to be something we can do, Doctor."

He sat down. "This isn't a medical problem," he replied, sipping his whiskey. "It can't be cured with pills or surgery or splints. Jonah's sickness is in his spirit. He believes Wade & Company will go under. He believes he's failed his father, his grandfather—the whole damned family tree. And the trouble is, he may be right, at least about the store." Dr. Wentworth looked at Miranda. "Jonah's own money is secure, as far as I can tell. This isn't about money; it's about Wade and Company."

"Yes, I thought so."

"His fears aren't unreasonable."

"The store's always been run for a certain kind of customer," said Miranda. "Well, in a way it had to be; you have to know who your customers are. But you also have to keep . . . broadening the base. We'd started to do that, and then came the Crash. We drifted for a while. Now I think we're starting to move in the right direction. I'm *sure* we are."

"Convince Jonah of that and his spirits will improve."

"Oh, I'll never convince him. I'll have to *show* him."

"Miranda is such a clever girl," said Daphne. "Why, she practically runs things!"

"That very flattering, but it's not true."

Daphne picked up one of her porcelain birds and absently stroked its head. She was past fifty now, though she still looked years younger. She had not gained an ounce; no gray hairs were visible. She was stylish, serene, her beauty untouched by time. "I know you'll make everything right," she said, smiling at Miranda. 'There's always an answer, isn't there? If one looks for an answer. The effort . . ." Her voice trailed off. She put down the porcelain bird and picked up a crystal swan. "Think how hard it is for swans in wintertime."

Dr. Wentworth laughed. "You're as charming as ever, Daphne. I'm glad the Depression hasn't affected *your* spirits."

She blinked. "The Depression? Oh, no, of course not."

Miranda finished her brandy. She rose. "If you'll excuse me, I want to look in on Andrew. He isn't used to his new room yet. He might disturb Jonah."

"Nothing will disturb Jonah tonight," said Dr. Wentworth. "I gave him a sleeping powder. Insomnia is very often a problem in these situations."

"I think I'd better warn Andrew anyway. Good night, Daphne, Dr. Wentworth."

"Good night, Miranda."

She left the room and went to the stairs. She could not forget Daphne's words: "I know you'll make everything right." How, she wondered. Wade's was in trouble, Jonah was in despair, and in two weeks' time Daniel McAllister would be standing on her doorstep. How could she possibly make everything right?

"Thanks for meeting me, Natalie," said Miranda the next day.

326

"I never turn down a free lunch, especially at the St. Regis. What's going on? You look a little green around the gills."

"Only a little?"

Is anything the matter with Andrew?"

"He's fine, thank heavens. He's too young to realize the world is falling apart."

The waiter brought their cocktails and then swiftly departed. Natalie plucked the onion from her Gibson and popped it into her mouth. "Okay, tell me. What terrible thing has happened now?"

Miranda told her about Jonah's slow, steady decline, about Dr. Wentworth's visit, about Daphne's remark. "I suddenly started to feel I was in over my head. This isn't a Sweet Shop we're talking about. It's Wade and Company; it's hundreds of employees who count on getting a paycheck every week. I can see why Jonah's sunk in gloom. There's so much at stake."

"This isn't the time to lose your nerve, Miranda. And it's sure as hell no time to take all the work on your shoulders. What's Peter doing? Let him have some of the headaches for a change. What's Tom doing?"

"Both Peter and Tom work hard."

"They could work harder. Why should all the problems land on *your* desk?"

"I'm afraid they belong there. I'm the one who pushed for the new cosmetics and dress departments. They're my idea, my responsibility." Miranda took a sip of her drink, then set the glass aside. "I appreciate the sympathy," she said with a smile, "but what I need is reassurance. Natalie Inc. has a firm, substantial order. Is Natalie Inc. ready to go into production?"

"I'm on schedule."

"What does that mean?"

"Miranda, I've got workrooms and equipment. I've hired a few people and I'll hire more as soon as my designs are approved. And we'll all work like hell, I promise you. You'll have an exclusive spring line on April 2. I'd say

327

April 1, but that's April Fool's Day and this is no joke."

Miranda laughed. "That's what I wanted to hear. God bless you, Natalie Stern."

"Now what's the rest of it?"

"You know the rest: Daniel McAllister."

The waiter returned for their lunch orders. "Very good, ladies," he said, collecting their menus.

"So what about Daniel McAllister?" asked Natalie when the waiter had gone.

"He'll be here in two weeks. Expecting his long-lost cousin."

Natalie shrugged. "That's you."

"What if he trips me up?"

"On what? Tell him your father never talked about the old country, about family. Keep him talking about himself. A man's favorite subject is himself."

"I wish I had your confidence."

"Confidence! For gosh sake, Miranda, look how far you've come. If that doesn't give you confidence, I don't know what will. Look at what you've accomplished."

"I had a lot of help, Natalie."

"You saw the opportunities and you grabbed them. It's not like anything was handed to you on a silver platter. You want my advice? Forget about this McAllister guy. He's probably never been off the farm. He'll be so dizzy with New York he won't give you a second thought."

"He's not a farm boy," said Miranda, toying with the stem of her cocktail glass. "He's from Dublin. He has a pub, the Fiddler."

"What's Dublin compared to New York? Believe me, he'll be bowled over by this town."

"You may be right."

"Sure I am. You're worrying for nothing. Or is worrying your hobby?"

Miranda smiled. "I'm getting good at it." The waiter brought their omelets. She picked up her fork, looking at Natalie. "Are you going to be one of my worries? According to the grapevine, you've been seeing Tom."

"We've had a couple of dates."

"Why didn't you tell me?"

"I knew what you'd say. Tom's much older than I am. He's had two wives. He's not exactly the reliable type."

"Yes," agreed Miranda, "that's what I would have said."

"Well, it's all true, but I don't care. I like Tom." Natalie took a bite of her omelet and dabbed her napkin to her mouth. "We have fun together. He knows my business has to come first for now and he doesn't mind. That's a *big* plus . . . My mother fixed me up with the nephew of Mr. Morris, the dry cleaner. That's what my mother does. She goes around the neighborhood asking people if they have anyone for her Natalie. Anyway, to make a long story short, I went out with the nephew. A nice, steady, sober CPA. Real husband material, you know? Well, we hadn't even finished our appetizers when he started telling me how women have no place in business because the female brain is different from the male brain. He had a whole theory about it. Basically, his theory was that women are stupid. He didn't come right out and say so, but that's what he meant. We're okay for darning socks and baking pies, but when it comes to serious decisions—"

"It's a man's world?"

Natalie smiled. "That's about the size of it. Tom doesn't think that way. He's very open-minded."

"Don't misunderstand me; I like Tom. Just don't rush into anything. Tom has an eye for the ladies."

"Hell, they all have something. Men are men."

Miranda finished her omelet. She lifted her napkin from her lap and tossed it on the table. "I wonder what my Irishman is like."

"*Your* Irishman?"

"In a way," laughed Miranda. "I'm stuck with him, aren't I?"

"Who knows, you may be in for a pleasant surprise."

"Or I just may be in for a disaster. There are always *two* possibilities!"

The Irishman, Daniel McAllister, would have said there were hundreds of possibilities, for that was the way he thought about life — as a challenge, a puzzle, a great and glorious game. He had a sense of adventure, an ironic appreciation of the absurd. His first glimpses of New York had inspired not awe but exhilaration; this was a city to be enjoyed, and enjoy it he would.

Daniel was twenty-seven, a year older than Miranda. Like his four brothers, he was blessed with the kind of strong, masculine good looks that made women's heads turn. Tall and lean, he had the coppery hair of the McAllisters, the slow, seductive smile. He had a temper, he had his moods, but there was nothing dark in him, nothing hidden. His words were direct, often blunt; it was said that people always knew where they stood with Daniel Patrick McAllister.

He had been born into a happy family. His parents had been strict, his brothers quick with their fists, but the McAllisters had loved each other, and family had mattered above all else — above politics, religion, drink. They had been prosperous by Dublin standards; the McAllister boys had been educated at Trinity College, and three of the four had chosen to enter the family business, which included several pubs and a small brewery.

It was business that brought Daniel to New York, but he had other things in mind as well. He wanted to see the sights: Broadway theater, bohemian Greenwich Village, fancy restaurants and shops, St. Patrick's Cathedral, and the Empire State Building. He wanted to meet the people who lived in America's largest city, to learn what they were like. Most of all, he wanted to meet his American cousin.

Now, striding briskly along Fifth Avenue, he glanced at the Christmas displays in the store windows, at the sidewalk Santa Clauses collecting money for the poor. He dropped a dollar bill into a large kettle and moved on. He crossed the street, stopping in front of Wade & Company.

A panhandler stood beside the entrance. Again, Daniel reached into his pocket and made a contribution.

The store was not crowded. Daniel browsed his way to the elevators, his gaze taking in the gleaming counters, the display cases filled with expensive blouses and scarves and gloves. He glanced at the price tags and he thought about the panhandler shivering in the cold outside.

"Going up," said the elevator operator.

Daniel stepped into the car. "I've an appointment with Miranda Dexter. Would that be the sixth floor?"

"Yes, sir. Mrs. Dexter's expecting you."

Miranda looked at her watch. She stood up and then sat down again, clasping her nervous hands atop the desk. After a moment, she opened her purse, digging around for her compact and comb. She repaired her makeup, ran the comb through her hair. She took a breath, jumping when she heard the knock at the door. "Come in."

"Cousin Miranda?"

She saw the thick coppery hair, the handsome features. She saw a crisp white shirt, a dark tie, a dark, double-breasted suit, a Burberry raincoat. Slowly, reluctantly, she met his gaze. Now she saw blue eyes the color of the sky and framed by red-gold lashes; Irish eyes, though they were not smiling. "Yes," she murmured. "I'm Miranda."

Chapter Nineteen

"Well then, let me look at you. I've traveled a long way." Daniel spoke in a soft brogue touched here and there with the clipped accents of London. He spoke deliberately, as if measuring his words. "And I'm thinking I'm glad I did."

"Won't you sit down?"

"I will, thanks . . . D'you mind if I smoke?"

"No, not at all." Daniel offered his case to her. She shook her head. "English cigarettes?"

"We do business in England. The family, that is. You don't know much about the McAllister family, then?"

Miranda colored. "Not as much as I should."

"I'll warrant you never expected to find a McAllister knocking at your door."

"No, I suppose not." She ducked her head. "I — I was wondering how you managed to track me down."

"It was a bit of luck, it was. I wrote to your address in Chicago. Of course you weren't there anymore, but there was a neighbor, a Mrs. Sheen. The dear lady wrote me a long letter, pages and pages. She wrote that Miranda had gone to her inlaws in New York City. To the Wades. She wrote about the little lad, Drew. And about the terrible train crash."

Miranda shifted uneasily in her chair. "I'd rather not . . . That was a difficult time for me, Daniel. I'd rather not relive it."

He nodded. "That was the way Mrs. Sheen saw the situation. She's sorry she doesn't hear from you, but she understands about memories. It's best to leave the past alone, isn't it?"

Miranda sensed he was feeling her out, studying her reactions. She warned herself to keep a clear head but she was nervous, and handsome Daniel McAllister was a very distracting man. "Would you like a cup of coffee? Or tea? I can call downstairs. It won't take a moment."

"I've a better idea. Have lunch with me."

"Lunch?"

"It's close on noon," replied Daniel. "And I'd fancy a nice long chat. I'm wondering about your life here in America. A fine life it is, I'm sure. You've done well for yourself."

Miranda glanced at her watch, at her desk calendar.

"Are you going to tell me you have engagements?"

She smiled. "No, as a matter of fact, I have nothing scheduled this afternoon. There's paperwork, but it can wait. It's not every day my cousin comes all the way from Ireland. This is a special occasion."

"It's kind you are to say so."

She loved the sound of his voice. She looked into his eyes and her heart seemed to skip a beat. "Well, I suppose that's settled," she said, quickly averting her gaze. "Lunch, I mean. There's a Longchamps not far from here. It's very pleasant."

"I'll take your word on the subject."

"I'll just get my things."

Daniel helped Miranda into her coat. His hand brushed the back of her neck and now her heart thumped. *Don't be a fool,* she chided herself, though she was sorry when his hand fell away.

"Are we off, then?"

"My purse, she said, snatching her purse and gloves from the desk. She picked up the telephone and left word with the switchboard that she was going to lunch. *"Now* we're off," she smilingly declared.

"What's your job here, if you don't mind my asking."

333

"No, I don't mind, but it's hard to explain. A little bit of everything, I guess. My title is assistant to the president. No one pays much attention to titles."

"And who looks after the little lad?"

"Andrew's in school until three o'clock," explained Miranda as they walked to the elevator. "Then there are all his activities. Two afternoons a week are taken up with riding lessons and dancing lessons. Thursdays he goes skating with his friends. Fridays—"

"And when do you see him?"

Miranda's smile vanished. "Whatever you may be thinking, we spend a lot of time together. We have breakfast together every morning, dinner together most nights. Andrew comes here on Saturdays, and there's always a special outing on Sundays . . . I check his homework and listen to his prayers. I take him to doctor's appointments. He's not deprived."

The elevator door slid open. Daniel stepped back to let Miranda pass. "It was a fair question," he said. "And no insult intended."

"Don't women work in Ireland?"

"Some do. But not in the way of having careers. Not in the way of being assistant to the president."

Miranda looked at Daniel. He was smiling and his smile melted her anger. "If that's an apology, I accept."

"Do you, now? I admire your forgiving nature. It's your Irish blood, no doubt."

Miranda glanced away. "No doubt," she murmured.

They sat across from each other in a small booth. Their drinks had been brought—a whiskey sour for Miranda, an Old Bushmills for Daniel. He tasted his drink and set it aside. "Are you comfortable? Is everything all right?"

"Yes, Daniel, fine."

"Then perhaps you'll do me the kindness of telling me who you really are."

There was a sharp intake of breath "I—I don't understand."

"You've fooled everyone else, lass, but you'll not be fooling me. You're no McAllister and that's the truth. Who are you?"

The room seemed to blur. She put her hand to her head. "If this is your idea of a joke," she said, her mind groping for words, "it's not very funny."

"Do I look like a man who's joking?"

"Well, I . . . I can see why you might be confused. I mean, if you were expecting an Irish colleen . . . I was born and raised in America, Daniel."

"Born with black hair and gray eyes. In hundreds of years of McAllisters, there's never been a one with black hair and gray eyes. Nor with such porcelain skin." He saw that her hands were trembling; he took them in his own. "You mustn't think I mean you harm," he said quietly. "I don't, and that's the truth, too . . . I've an idea about all this. It was the train crash—"

"Please don't say anymore."

"Tell me who you are."

"I'm Miranda Dexter," she said as tears welled in her eyes. "But I used to be Jenny Porter . . . I suppose I ought to start from the beginning." She started the only place she could—with Logan Falls. In a halting voice she described the town, the people, the good intentions of her father. She talked about a rainy cemetery, and a train ride to Chicago's Union Station. Her voice broke when she talked about the beautiful young woman who had befriended her. She recalled the house on South Crawford Street, the Sweet Shop, the Sheens, the decision to move to New York. "I don't remember much about the accident," she said. "The snow just got heavier and heavier. The wind . . . Everything happened so fast. In an instant, really."

"And my cousin?"

"She—she'd gone to another part of the train. It was early in the morning; she wanted coffee. I stayed in the compartment with Andrew . . . Dear God, I knew we were going to crash. I *knew* it, but there was nothing I could do . . . I put a lot of pillows around Andrew and covered him with my body . . . The train was just *racing* along the track. There were people screaming, and there were . . . All of a sudden, the train was plunging off the track. I don't know what happened then . . . The next thing I remember is waking up in the hospital."

Daniel signaled the waitress for another round of drinks. "You told them you were Miranda, did you?"

"They told me. The Wades made the identification . . . From this ring Miranda gave me," she added, holding out her hand. "It's a Wade heirloom. They'd never seen their daughter-in-law, and since I'd been found in her compartment, wearing the heirloom ring . . . well, I guess it was a natural assumption. When I realized what had happened, I tried to explain. But the doctors kept telling me not to talk, to save my strength . . . And then I started thinking. I thought if I just said nothing, I could have a new life."

"A prosperous new life," remarked Daniel as the waitress served their drinks. "Would that be the idea?"

"Only part of it. All my money had been lost in the accident — burned or torn to shreds or just lost. I had nothing, nobody. It was terrifying. As Miranda Wade, I knew I'd at least have a roof over my head . . . But there was more to it. There was Andrew. I loved him; I couldn't let strangers take him. I wanted a son, Daniel. And Andrew *is* my son now, in all but blood. Can you understand? Can you try to see it from my point of view?"

Daniel sipped his whiskey. "Has your stolen life made you happy, lass?"

"Andrew makes me happy. My work makes me happy . . . No one's been hurt by what I did."

"I'm taking that fact into account."

"I suppose you think I'm a terrible person."

He smiled. "No."

"What *do* you think?"

"There's an old saying — be careful what you wish for. You can wish up a new life, but *living* it — ah, that's something else again. You can't live another woman's life."

"I'm living *my* life, Daniel."

"Miranda Dexter's life, y'mean."

"That's who I am now. Are you going to give me away?"

"And why would I do that? As you say, no one's been hurt, and maybe it's been a good thing for the lad. The right and wrong of it I'll leave to the priests."

"Andrew is being raised an Episcopalian."

"Is he now?" Daniel lit a cigarette and sat back. "Well, that's a nice respectable religion. I'll drink to it," he said, lifting his glass. "And I'll drink to you, Miranda Dexter."

She smiled, for she knew the worst was over. "I think we're going to get along very well."

Daniel smiled also—his slow, seductive McAllister smile. His eyes twinkled. He was glad she was not his cousin.

"I can't stay, Peter," said Miranda several hours later. "I'm having dinner with Daniel McAllister."

"Oh, yes, the Irish cousin. Why don't you have him over here? It'll be an earlier evening and you'll have time to look over my budget projections."

She sat down at her vanity table, running a comb through her hair. "Have him over here?" she asked, smiling. "Last-minute company? Cook would have a fit. And I don't think Jonah would care much for the idea."

"I wouldn't worry about that. Jonah's bark isn't what it used to be. It's more like a whine now."

"Exactly why I don't want to upset him. He's upset enough as it is."

"Very noble. But then you're the soul of nobility, aren't you, Miranda?"

"I don't want to spar with you, Peter. I'm sorry I can't stay, but I can't and that's that. I didn't know you were going to be home tonight; it happens so rarely. The budget will have to wait until morning." She opened a little pot of rouge and dipped her finger into it. "Or you could call

337

Tom."

"You're the one with the head for figures. A strange trait in a woman, I always thought." Peter sat down and stretched out his legs. He was past forty now, still slender, still handsome, though the Depression had etched permanent lines across his brow and around his mouth. The ten thousand dollars from Louis Grayson's estate had repaid his debts; he was solvent again, but he would never stop mourning all that he had lost. "How late are you going to be?"

"I don't know. We have a lot to talk about."

"Talk fast."

"Peter, the world won't come to an end if the budget waits another day. Now will you excuse me? I want to get dressed."

"Go ahead. I've seen you without your clothes."

"Not lately."

"By mutual agreement."

Miranda finished applying her lipstick. She capped the tube and tucked it into a small black velvet purse. She turned when she heard a knock at the door. "Come in."

"Here's your dress, Mrs. Dexter," said Lily. "I found a button that's almost a perfect match to the others. See, you can't tell the difference."

"Yes, very nice. Thanks, Lily."

Peter's eyes swept over the elegant black velvet dress. "Is that one of Natalie's creations?"

"Yes. You remember; I wore it to the Russells' dinner party. You said you liked it."

"The girl has talent. She ought to do something about her personality, though. That big mouth of—"

"Good night, Peter."

"Give my regards to your cousin," he said, leaving the room.

"Do you need anything else, Mrs. Dexter?"

Privacy, thought Miranda. "No thanks, I'm fine." She looked up, her mascara brush frozen in midair. "What is it, Lily?"

338

"Can I ask you a personal question?"

Miranda was surprised; Lily never asked personal questions. "It must be important; ask away."

"How much money did you put into Miss Stern's company?"

Miranda stared at Lily's reflection in the vanity mirror. "Five thousand. Why?"

"Are you a partner, then?"

"Not an equal partner, no. I have a share in the company . . . What's this all about?"

Lily shook her head. "There's no time now. I have to help Cook with dinner. Could I talk to you tomorrow?"

"You can talk to me whenever you want; you know that."

"Tomorrow, then. Good night, Mrs. Dexter."

"Good night."

Miranda shrugged. She leaned toward the mirror and swooped the brush across her lashes. She dabbed perfume on her throat and wrists, affixed pearl clips to her ears. She sat back and gazed at herself. "Not exactly Joan Bennett," she murmured, "but not bad." Quickly, she got out of her robe and into her dress. She smoothed her stockings, picked up her purse and gloves, and hurried to the hall.

Light streamed from beneath Andrew's door. She knocked and went inside. The child was sprawled on his bed, reading a comic book. "Did you finish your homework?"

He nodded. "You look pretty, Mama."

"Thank you. I'm having dinner with your cousin Daniel. You'll probably meet him this weekend." Miranda sat down at the side of the bed. "You have lots of cousins in Ireland, you know. Aunts and uncles, too. Maybe we'll go to Ireland one day."

"To live?"

"To visit." Miranda smiled. She reached out her hand, sliding Andrew's coppery hair off his forehead. "Would you like to visit Ireland?"

339

"Are there horses?"

"Of course."

"Okay."

It was the kind of exchange Miranda had come to expect, for Andrew had always been an easy, uncomplicated child. At the age of six, he had insisted on walking to school by himself, and a few months later he had insisted he no longer needed a governess, but such stubbornness was unusual. Looking at him now, she could imagine the man he would grow up to be — a good-natured man who nonetheless knew his own mind. "Papa will be staying home tonight," she said. "And I won't be late."

"I can stay alone, Mama. I'm not a baby."

"I know, but isn't it nicer to be with people?"

Not grown-up people, thought Andrew. Grown-ups were always patting his head and asking if he had a clean handkerchief and telling him to mind his manners. "Well, *some*times it's nicer," he granted. "If people don't treat me like a baby."

"Yes, we'll have to watch that." Miranda kissed his freckled cheek. She stood. "Good night, darling."

" 'Night, Mama."

She returned to the hall just as Jonah emerged from his room, Daphne at his side. "You seem to be dressed for a big evening, Miranda," he said. "Where are you off to?"

"I'm meeting my cousin, Daniel McAllister. I told you about him."

"Did you? Oh, yes, the Irishman. I suppose you have no choice. It's family after all."

Daphne took Jonah's arm. "We were going to have a cocktail before dinner. Will you join us?"

"I'm sorry, I can't. You know how hard it is to get a taxi at this hour. I'd better be on my way."

"Dexter was going to work on the budget tonight," said Jonah.

"Yes, he's working on it now."

"I expect we'll be firing more staff."

"Not necessarily," replied Miranda. "Peter's trying to

340

find other solutions."

Jonah's shoulders sagged. He looked down at the floor. "Is your cousin in business?"

"Yes. I'm sure he's having problems, too."

"But he's young, isn't he? Young people can start over."

"Come, Jonah," said Daphne. "Lily is mixing our cocktails."

"Tell your cousin to be grateful . . . Life is so simple when one is young."

To Daniel, life suddenly seemed anything but simple. He had been unprepared for Miranda's revelations, even more unprepared for Miranda herself. The facts of her deception he put aside, considering the circumstances instead. Desperate circumstances, he thought, and yet she had found a way out. She had courage; he gave her credit for that. Obviously she had imagination. And spirit. And strength. And the most extraordinary gray eyes.

Now he gazed into her eyes and his smile widened. "I've heard enough about Wade and Company for one night. Tell me about the important things . . . Tell me about your husband."

Miranda glanced down at the table, moving her water glass back and forth. "He's very handsome. He was almost very rich. He's been a marvelous father to Andrew." She shrugged. "Peter and I lead more or less separate lives."

"More or less?"

"We live in the same house, in separate rooms. Peter comes and goes as he pleases. I have no idea what he does, and I can't say I really care."

"Why did you marry him, then?"

"I loved him, or I thought I did." A faint smile touched Miranda's lips. "In Logan Falls, the neighborhood kids used to call me Jenny Porker. They said I looked like Mr. Hawthorne's pigs. They exaggerated of course, but not by much; I really was a mess . . . Then I came to New York

341

and met Peter. When he started paying attention to me, I was in seventh heaven . . . Maybe I did love him for a while. I could have loved him forever. There are good things in Peter, but those are the things he keeps buried. I won't bore you with details. The truth is that our marriage was over years ago. End of story."

"Not quite. You haven't said why he married you."

"I don't know why. I suppose it had something to do with the store, or with Jonah. It wasn't love. Peter can't love."

Daniel frowned, for he could not imagine a life without love. In the McAllister clan, love was as necessary as food and drink. "I'm thinking it's a lonely life for you, Miranda."

"Oh, I'm too busy to be lonely."

"I don't believe that" came Daniel's blunt reply.

Miranda reddened; for the second time today, he had seen through her lies. "All right," she said, "I *do* get lonely every now and then. Do you know anybody who doesn't? I remember reading something about 'the human condition.' Loneliness is the human condition."

"Not for a beautiful woman."

Miranda's lips parted in surprise. Had he called her a beautiful woman? She felt the blush creep back into her cheeks, but now she was blushing with pleasure. "Was that a compliment?" she asked in a small voice.

"It was." Daniel smiled, reaching across the table to take her hand. "D'you know the tale of the ugly duckling who turned into a swan? That's you, Miranda Dexter. I'll buy you a looking glass and you can see for yourself."

"It better be a magic looking glass."

"I promise you all the magic you'll ever want."

There was something caressing in Daniel's voice, something intense in his eyes. Miranda drew her hand away. "It's your turn now. Tell me what's brought you to New York."

"Business . . . Though I've no objection to mixing business and pleasure," he added with a glittering smile.

342

Miranda spilled her wine. "You have a pub, don't you?" she asked, mopping up a stream of chablis. "The Fiddler?"

"The Fiddler, the Hare and Fiddler, the Dog and Fiddler, the Crow and Fiddler. The last two are in London. We'll be opening a third one there — the Hen and Fiddler."

"Oh, you have a chain of pubs. I didn't realize."

"The first of the Fiddlers was a coaching inn," said Daniel. He fell silent as the waiter brought their salads, and then went on. "That was two hundred years past, if you're interested in history."

"I'm curious; how does an old Irish family come to be doing business in England? I thought the Irish and English were enemies."

"All but sworn," agreed Daniel. "There are those who want their revenge in blood. I'll take mine in £sterling. It's the old saying, y'know — living well is the best revenge. I'd rather have money than blood on my hands."

"Very sensible."

"Were you expecting a raving, wild-eyed Irishman?"

Miranda poked at her salad. "I didn't know what to expect. But I think I would have recognized you anywhere. You'll know why when you meet Andrew."

"And when will that be?"

"How about Sunday morning after church? Peter's taking him to a football game in the afternoon, but the morning's free."

"Sunday morning it is. I'm leaving Sunday night for a place called Milwaukee, Wisconsin."

"Leaving?" Miranda's heart sank. "But why?"

He saw her disappointment and he smiled. "Business. We brew our own ale; there's Fiddler's Best and Fiddler's Nut Brown. We're thinking it's time to start selling our ale in the States. So it's a brewery I'm after."

"In Milwaukee?"

"Or here in New York City. There's one gone out of business in a place called Yorkville."

Miranda brightened. "Then you'll be back," she exclaimed before she could stop herself.

"That I will. And will you be glad, lass?"

Her cheeks were burning, but she met his gaze. "Yes, Daniel. I'll be glad."

After dinner they went dancing at the Savoy. The loud, often raucous music of the twenties had been replaced by gentler sounds, by the love songs of Gershwin and Rodgers and Hart. Daniel and Miranda danced to these songs, drifting across the polished floor as if in a dream. Miranda felt the fluttering of her heart; wrapped in Daniel's arms, she felt a quickening desire. She had lost all sense of time. What was the day, the hour? She could not be sure. She could not be sure of anything but Daniel's arms holding her close.

She was still in a daze when they left the Savoy. The night was clear, the sky strewn with frosty December stars. A breeze scraped at the bare trees along the avenue. Footsteps echoed on the pavement. Here and there, lights were winking off in hotels and apartment buildings. "It must be late," she murmured.

Daniel was silent, for he knew that what he said next, did next, could well change their lives. Shortly after meeting Miranda he had decided he wanted her in his bed, but during the course of this evening he had realized she was not a women for a casual affair, a fling. Until now he had managed to avoid serious involvements, nimbly sidestepping all the subtle and not-so-subtle traps set by Irish lasses. In Dublin and London, he had enjoyed the affections of more worldly females; he had had his fun, and no harm done. Always, he had played within the rules. But without warning, the rules had changed; he thought he was falling in love. "The very witching hour of night," he said. "Are you a witch, Miranda Dexter? Have you cast your spell on me? I'm thinking you have. I'm thinking I don't want this night to end."

His voice settled around her like a warm cloak. She

slowed her pace, smiling up at him. "Why does the night have to end?"

"You ask dangerous questions, lass."

"Give me a dangerous answer."

"We've two choices: I can see you home, or I can take you home with me." Daniel stood still, his hands gripping Miranda's shoulders. "If I take you home with me, it won't be for tea and biscuits. I want you, Miranda. I want to make love to you." He pulled her into his arms, crushing his mouth on hers. "I've been wanting to do that all night," he said moments later. "And more."

Miranda had to catch her breath, had to calm her racing heart. "Daniel," she murmured when she could speak. "Oh, Daniel."

"Two choices, lass."

"There's only one choice . . . Take me home with you."

"I've no right, y'know. Your life is here, mine is across the ocean. We can't be talking about tomorrows or —"

Miranda put her finger to Daniel's lips. "Let's not worry about tomorrows," she said. "We have tonight."

He slipped his arm around her. "My flat is just a few streets away."

It was a borrowed flat on a quiet street near Central Park. It was small — three rooms in a reconverted brownstone — and indifferently furnished, for its bachelor owner was seldom there. The only personal touches were books, an empty goldfish bowl, and a philodendron plant. The only items in the pantry were two jars of olives, a jar of mustard, a tin of sardines, and three bottles of gin.

Miranda scarcely noticed her surroundings. She clung to Daniel's hand, walking with him into the bedroom. She felt no shyness, no embarrassment. She did not reproach herself, for she was where she wanted to be.

Daniel took her coat and dropped it on a chair. Again, he pulled her into his arms. His hands tangled her hair; he kissed her, a long, fiery kiss that made her gasp. There was a roaring in her ears. Little lights seemed to dance before her eyes. "Daniel," she whispered.

345

He undressed her, brushing his lips against her naked flesh. He carried her to the bed. His own clothes fell to the floor and then he was beside her, caressing her breasts, her thighs, the sweet darkness between her long legs. "My darling," he murmured again and again. "Darling lass."

Their bodies were locked together, arching, swaying to the ancient rhythms of love. Their pleasure in each other was infinite. Their passion blazed, a white-hot fire rushing toward some secret and rapturous place. For them there was only this moment, this blissful moment stolen from the world; there was only this truth. "Daniel," she called softly as her body trembled and shook, as she was carried off to that secret place.

It was the place where love dwelt, and she was a woman in love.

Part III

Chapter Twenty

The first purple rays of dawn were streaking the sky when Miranda arrived home. She crept into the house like a thief, removing her shoes before she tiptoed upstairs. One of the steps creaked; she froze for an instant, and then continued on her way. All the bedroom doors were closed. She saw no light, heard no sound. She slipped into her own room and offered silent thanks; she had not been caught.

She got out of her things, leaving them scattered on the floor. She ran a bath and sank happily into the warm, jasmine-scented water. She closed her eyes, thinking of Daniel. A slow smile spread across her face. She knew now what love was, what love could be. She knew the mystery of it, the power, the sheer magic. "Daniel," she whispered, and even his name filled her with joy.

Miranda climbed out of the tub, wrapping herself in a thick terry-cloth robe. She sat down at the vanity table and examined her reflection in the mirror. Her eyes sparkled; her skin seemed to glow. And what's that silly smile? she wondered. But she knew what it was, for if love was magic, it was also silly — wondrously, sublimely silly.

She crawled into bed. She dozed, though not for long. Her head had barely touched the pillow when her alarm clock shrilled; a second or so later, Lily knocked at the door. "Come in," she called, reaching to turn off the alarm. "Good morning, Lily."

"Good morning, Mrs. Dexter. Here's your coffee, nice and hot."

"Just what I need."

"It's going to snow."

Miranda rubbed her eyes. "Is it?"

"You could do with a hot breakfast. Cook will be starting the oatmeal soon. She's making popovers, too."

Miranda had a weakness for popovers, but she shook her head. "I'm not hungry. Coffee is all I want."

"It's up to you," replied Lily with a shrug. She bent, gathering Miranda's discarded dress and shoes.

"Don't bother about that."

"It's your good dress."

"I know. I'll take care of it." Miranda stretched. "I've told Andrew that when he makes a mess, he has to clean it up himself. The same rule applies to me, so stop fussing. You're not happy unless you're fussing, are you? You never take a minute to relax."

"I have a few minutes now. Can I talk to you?"

"Of course."

"It's about Miss Stern's company."

Miranda sipped her coffee. "Natalie Inc.? What about it?"

"You put your own money into her company. I figure that makes it a good investment." Lily drew a chair to the side of the bed and sat down. "It must be or you wouldn't be in it. You're pretty careful with money, like I am." She folded her hands in her lap. Her steady gaze was fixed on Miranda. "I've been saving my money," she continued. "My room and board is free here; I've been able to save. I always had it in the back of my mind that I'd use my savings to get started in something. A little business maybe. Or maybe some kind of investment. I don't plan on working here the rest of my life."

Miranda knew nothing of Lily's plans, for Lily had never spoken at such length before. Miranda had tried to draw her out, but in vain. Lily had kept her distance all these years, kept her "proper place." "If you're think-

350

ing about investing in Natalie Inc., I have to warn you it's risky. It's a new business, and the Depression makes everything more complicated. It's hard to judge a new business when times are hard."

"You risked your own money, Mrs. Dexter."

"That's not a good enough reason for *you* to risk yours, Lily."

"I didn't say it was. It's just one of the reasons I'm thinking about it." Lily glanced at the clock, then looked back at Miranda. "I've seen all the clothes Miss Stern's made for you. They're as fine as the clothes Mrs. Wade has in her closet. The designs and the workmanship too. I never saw a crooked seam or a loose stitch. The buttons are always sewn on just so. Miss Stern is particular."

"Yes, she's that all right."

"And women notice things like that. Especially now, when everybody's watching their pennies. You want to buy something that isn't going to come apart."

"True," agreed Miranda.

"Would Miss Stern let me invest? If I decided?"

"She'd be delighted. Natalie needs all the money she can get her hands on."

Lily glanced again at the clock. She stood. "I have two thousand dollars in the bank. Would it make me a partner?"

Miranda's head snapped up. "Two thousand!"

"I have a little more than that, but I'm leaving something for myself, just in case."

"Lily, two thousand dollars is a lot of money these days. You could buy a shop—a candy store, a small grocery. Or you could buy a small house and rent it out. That would give you a regular income."

She almost smiled. "I have my eye on bigger things, Mrs. Dexter. You could say Miss Stern's company is my one chance. Would two thousand dollars make me a partner?"

"Not an equal partner."

"But a partner all the same?"

"Yes, certainly."

Lily nodded. "Then that's what I'll be." She went to the door. "I have to help Cook in the kitchen now. Could you arrange for me to talk to Miss Stern?"

"I'll see to it today."

"Thank you, Mrs. Dexter."

"Lily —"

"I have to help Cook now."

The door closed. Miranda sat back, pondering this new development. There was a great deal riding on Natalie Inc.; there were a great many unknown factors. Once again she wondered if she were in over her head, if she had started something that would bring trouble to everyone.

She wished she could forget about business for a while. She wished she could curl up in bed, pull the blankets to her chin, and dream about Daniel.

Miranda arrived at her office to find a bouquet of violets sitting atop her desk. Tucked inside the florist's box was a card signed "Cousin Daniel." She laughed, but she hurried down to the gift department and bought a crystal vase. All through the day, she kept the violets near; when she left the store at the end of the day, she took the violets with her.

She took them to Daniel's borrowed flat.

"I've been counting the hours," he said, sweeping her into his arms. He kissed her, kissed her again as they sat together on the couch. "Let me look at you . . . Such beautiful eyes. A man could get lost in those eyes."

"Are you lost, Daniel?"

"You know I am." He held his hand to her cheek. "I love you, lass. And I'm thinking you love me."

"Yes," she murmured. She nestled her head on his shoulder. "Oh, yes, I do . . . But I have to be careful. I can't spend another night away from home. I can't make anyone suspicious."

" 'Anyone' being Peter?"

"He's the only one likely to notice. Daphne and Jonah live in a world of their own. But Peter . . . He's not beyond making trouble, if the mood struck."

"And what kind of trouble would that be?" asked Daniel.

"I don't know. He wouldn't hurt Andrew. At least he wouldn't mean to. Nasty things are said in arguments; nasty things are overheard. I just have to be careful."

Daniel stroked her hair. He hated the idea of sneaking around, hated it even more for Miranda. He knew what the priests would say: Father Rooney would say it was what they deserved, and Father O'Dean would have quite a lot to say about the fires of hell. "It's all right, darling. We'll find a way. I swear it."

"But if—"

Miranda said nothing else, for Daniel was kissing her, lifting her into his arms, carrying her into the bedroom he had filled with violets and champagne, with love.

Daniel and Miranda learned to steal time—an hour at noon, a couple of hours when work was done. On Sunday morning they took Andrew to the Empire State Building, but they had the afternoon to themselves, a long, lazy afternoon spent partly at a romantic café and partly at the flat.

Daniel left for Milwaukee that night; Miranda was at Grand Central Terminal to see him off. She watched the train pull away, watched Daniel disappear from sight, and her heart sank like a stone. They had had a week together, only a week. A thousand weeks wouldn't be enough, she thought as she walked toward the exit; ten thousand weeks.

It was a cold night, the moon hidden behind masses of dark clouds. She started to flag a taxi, then changed her mind. She turned up the collar of her coat and kept on walking. She was a block from home when she changed

353

her mind again. A few moments later she was standing in a telephone booth, depositing a nickel in the slot; an hour later she was sitting in a coffee shop with Natalie.

"That's the whole story," she said, taking one of Natalie's cigarettes. "That's why I've been so busy this week."

"I was beginning to wonder."

Natalie smiled. "You've never looked better, if that means anything. Love agrees with you. But why did you have to pick a guy who lives an ocean away?"

"I didn't pick him; it just happened. Things always happen to me when I least expect them, and they always happen quickly." Miranda shrugged. "No time to think . . . Not that time would have made any difference. All the time and thought in the world couldn't have kept me from Daniel. Wait till you meet him, Natalie. He's handsome and funny and strong . . . Funny in that sort of droll Irish style. And he's a good man. I know he is."

"When do I get to meet this paragon?"

"When he comes back from Milwaukee. After the first of the year."

"After the first? He's spending the holidays in Milwaukee?"

"That's the way it worked out. It won't be so bad. He knows people there. He seems to know people everywhere." Miranda drew on her cigarette and dropped it into the ashtray. "But when Daniel comes back, he'll have at least a month here."

"And then what?"

Miranda turned her head to the plate-glass window. A light rain had begun to fall. The sidewalks looked shiny, as if they had been given a coat of gloss. Wisps of steam rose from the grates. Cars glided past, dark, blurry shadows in the night.

"And then what, Miranda?"

"I haven't planned that far in advance. He'll go back to Ireland, I suppose. But not forever. He'll go back there and come back here and . . . Oh, I don't know. I didn't say it was an ideal situation. It's complicated." She called the waitress over and ordered a jelly doughnut. "No lectures Natalie," she said when the waitress had gone. "I'm feeling very lonely all of a sudden. I need comfort."

"I wasn't going to say a word. You could use a pound or two." She stubbed out the burning cigarette in the ashtray. "When did you start smoking?"

"I'm also feeling very pressured. The store, Jonah . . . I have all these responsibilities. I know I asked for them, but this week I realized how little time I have for myself."

"It didn't matter before this week."

"I guess not."

Natalie sipped her coffee. "I had a meeting with Lily Olson today."

Miranda looked up. "I forgot all about that. What happened?"

"Lily is our new partner. She drives a hard bargain, too. She now has ten percent of Natalie Inc. You have twenty, she has ten, my employees have five. There's my fifty-one percent, so that leaves fourteen percent. If you know anybody else with a few bucks in the bank, send them my way."

The waitress brought Miranda's jelly doughnut. She refilled their coffee cups and left. Miranda bit into the doughnut. She smiled, wiping jelly from the corners of her mouth. "This is wonderful."

"Did you hear what I said?"

"Jonah's the only one I know with any money. I can't ask him. What about Tom?"

"He doesn't have a sou. Alimony."

"It's probably just as well. I'm not even sure *I* should have invested. Don't get excited," laughed Miranda. "It's not a lack of faith or anything like that. But sooner or later someone is going to accuse me of conflict of interest, which it is."

"You know I couldn't have started my company without your investment."

"Of course. All I'm saying is that it's kind of tricky. I'm approving orders for a company in which I have a financial stake. Wrong conclusions could be drawn . . . That's why your spring line has to be a smashing success. If it is, no one can accuse me of bringing you into the store for my own personal gain. It will *still* be a conflict of interest, but as long as the store comes out ahead, it's all right. No one can say my first loyalty isn't to Wade's."

"How could anyone doubt that?"

"Peter takes great joy in needling me. And given Jonah's state of mind, who knows what he'd believe? Now that I think about it, it's just as well Tom isn't involved. Peter isn't especially fond of Tom, either. Let's not rock the boat."

Natalie was frowning. "It never occurred to me that this could cause you trouble. Why didn't you say something?"

"Because I'm convinced we need you. There are dozens of dress manufacturers who could supply us. But I couldn't be sure of the quality and I refuse to sell junk. You're very particular, as Lily would say. I know our customers will get their money's worth. More than their money's worth. That's in keeping with the tradition of Wade and Company."

"Thanks for the vote of confidence. I just wish you'd stop worrying."

"I will, when the dresses are in the store. You're on a tight production schedule, Natalie. You have a small staff. Anything could happen."

"But nothing will. I had a production meeting last week. We all sat around imagining every possible problem. We're covered. Unless there's an earthquake or a tidal wave, we're covered."

Miranda smiled. She finished her doughnut, licking the powdered sugar from her finger. "You always cheer me up."

"Now that you're in such a cheery mood, I have a question. I want longer skirts in the spring line; Tom doesn't. It's a standoff. My question is, who breaks the tie?"

"I do," replied Miranda. "Go ahead with the longer

356

lengths. Skirts have been inching down for the past two years. Besides, a slightly longer length is easier for working women . . . But nothing extreme. We're in no position to gamble."

"Agreed. How's the cosmetics department coming along?"

"So far, so good. I plan to introduce both new departments April 2."

"Then you have everything under control."

"Knock on wood," said Miranda, doing just that. "First I have to get through the holidays . . . We *all* have to get through the holidays."

In years past, Jonah had supervised the holiday decorations at the Wade house. Almost reverently, he had examined the ornaments that had been handed down from generation to generation, directing where each one should be placed. He had spent hours fussing over the Christmas tree, the mantels, the windows, and even the wreath for the door. No new ornaments had been permitted, no departures from the Christmases of his youth. Christmas had always been a time of memory, but this year his memories haunted him, mocked him as a failure. This year, the sight of his treasured ornaments filled him with pain.

Daphne and Miranda decorated the house. They selected the tree, the branches of silver birch; they freshened the wreaths, restrung garlands of crystal beads, polished tiny, hand-carved angels. Lily helped them wrap presents. Cook made the traditional eggnog and gingerbread men. It was, to all appearances, an ordinary Christmas, and yet sadness hung in the air.

Daphne scaled down her Christmas Eve party to include only family: several distant cousins and their spouses, an ancient uncle and his nurse. Daphne was her charming self, but Jonah was subdued, staring off into space; the guests left early.

357

Neither Daphne nor Jonah was downstairs the next morning when Andrew rushed in to open his presents. Miranda watched her son, smiling occasionally at Peter, but she, too, was distracted; Wade & Company had had the worst Christmas in its history.

"To a better year" was Miranda's toast on the first day of 1934. It was a modest wish, all she would allow herself, for the year did not begin well. Daniel had to extend his stay in Milwaukee—indefinitely, he said. Andrew came down with chicken pox. Peter ran his car into a mailbox and was hospitalized for three days. The figures on Wade's post-holiday clearance sales were tabulated, showing a drop of forty-six percent below the year before.

Miranda dared not think where it would end. The Depression had deepened and, with it, unemployment. For those lucky enough to have jobs, average paychecks hovered around fifteen dollars a week. For those not so lucky, there were meager charity baskets and less than meager assistance payments from the Home Relief office.

Like millions of other Americans, Miranda put her faith in Washington, where President Roosevelt and his numerous "alphabet agencies" were fighting to turn the tide. The WPA was charged with creating jobs, while the NRA sought formulas to boost wages. The FDIC insured depositors' bank accounts, and thus the banking system. The SEC was established to regulate the dangerous and greedy excesses of Wall Street. It was a massive assault on the complacency of the past, aptly called the New Deal.

Miranda believed passionately in the reforms of the New Deal, but she knew they would take time. Time was the problem, for she was not certain how much longer Wade's could go on losing money. She was working hard. She was tired. She was worried. "It's discouraging," she wrote in a letter to Daniel, "because there doesn't seem to be anything we can do. It doesn't matter how hard we work, how long. We're all putting in fourteen-hour days and we all feel absolutely useless. Still, we're the lucky ones. We have places to live and food on the table. That's more than a lot of people have. Every day I see more beggars on the street, women as well as men . . . It's heartbreaking.

I need you, my darling. I need your smiles and your comfort. I need your arms around me. When are you coming back? Soon? Please, please, please come back soon. I'm so lonely for you. I *want* you, Daniel Patrick McAllister. Hurry."

Daniel returned to New York on a blustery afternoon in March. Miranda left work early and raced to his borrowed flat. "Daniel," she cried as he opened the door. "Oh, Daniel, you're really here."

He took her in his arms. "My darling lass," he murmured, covering her face with kisses. "My own darling lass, I've missed you so much."

"I was afraid you'd forget me."

"Never in this world. Nor in the next. You've stolen my heart, you have. I'm yours and that's the truth of it. I love you."

Those were the words Miranda wanted to hear. Happiness washed over her, vast waves of happiness that seemed to lift her off the ground. She felt weightless, as if she were floating on air. She felt wonderful. She touched her hand to Daniel's face. Moment by moment his eyes grew more intense; his breathing quickened. "Daniel," she sighed, answering his unasked question.

Almost before they knew it, they were in the bedroom, their clothing strewn all about. They fell onto the bed, consumed by their hunger for each other, by their great need. Somewhere, music was playing but they did not hear. They clung together, two people with one heart and soul, two people scaling the fiery crests of love.

The last rays of twilight faded; darkness gathered at

359

the windows. Miranda lifted her head from the pillow and squinted at the clock. Daniel was asleep beside her, his arm thrown over her leg. She gazed at him for a moment, and then slipped out of bed. She collected her scattered clothing, reaching under a chair to retrieve a shoe. Quietly, she went into the bathroom and closed the door.

The lights were on when she emerged several minutes later. Daniel, wearing tan slacks and a black pullover, was in the living room. "I didn't mean to wake you," she said.

He looked up, scraping his coppery hair from his forehead. "You're leaving, then?"

"I have to. It's almost seven."

"Yes."

"I'm sorry, Daniel."

"I'm thinking it's a sorry way to live — rushing about, never a moment to ourselves. It's a sorry way to be in love . . . I want to smash all the clocks, be done with them for good and all." He sat down. His eyes skipped around the room, coming to rest on Miranda. "Would that change things, d'you suppose?"

"I *can't* change things." She sat next to Daniel and took his hand. "I can't change my life. It's sort of like a house of cards; one wrong move and the whole thing collapses in a heap. I can't risk it . . . Because that would be risking Andrew."

"The lad isn't the problem. It's everything else. It's the store and the husband and the inlaws. They're the clocks, lass. They're the clocks you're forever watching, forever worrying over. And they're taking you away from me."

"Only for a little while."

"What is it you call a little while, then? All your days and your nights?" Daniel drew Miranda into the circle of his arms. He smiled slightly. "There's more to us than the bedroom. I want more. That's what you've done to me; you've made me want more. It's you I'm blaming.

360

Luring an innocent Irish lad into—"

"Innocent!" Miranda laughed. "I'll bet you've left a trail of broken hearts from one end of Ireland to the other. England, too."

"I'll confess to a few disappointed hearts, but no worse. I never give promises I don't intend to keep. That's the secret of an uncomplicated life. Or so I thought until I came to New York City. There aren't any uncomplicated lives in New York City, are there?"

"It's not fair to judge the city by me."

"Fair?" Daniel reached away from Miranda and lighted a cigarette. He leaned back, blowing smoke rings toward the ceiling. "We've different ideas of what's fair."

Miranda ducked her head. A shadow fell across her face. "You're scaring me. This conversation is scaring me. You know the way things are, Daniel. What do you want me to do?"

"You're not ready to hear the answer to that question."

"Probably not, but tell me anyway."

Daniel aimed his cigarette at the ashtray. It dropped in with a soft plunk. He turned to Miranda and gazed into the gray depths of her eyes. "I want you to marry me," he said after a while. "I want you to be my wife." The words seemed to surprise him as much as they surprised Miranda. He had never spoken of marriage before, and he had known from the start that marriage to Miranda was impossible. But it was what he wanted; he wanted her for a lifetime, not a night or an afternoon or random hours stolen here and there. "Ah, you mustn't cry, lass," he murmured as tears welled in her eyes. "I was dreaming out loud, I was." He held her, stroking her hair. "I was dreaming about tomorrows, and I've no right. I knew—"

"No," she sniffled, "you didn't know how it would be with us. I didn't know, either."

"And how is it, then?"

"We love each other. We need each other. Oh, God, I *want* to marry you, Daniel. I wish I could grab Andrew and run off with you to Ireland. I wish . . . Oh God, I

361

wish."

"But you can't."

"I can't even stay here." Through a blur of tears she looked at her watch. "I have to go home."

Daniel found his handerkchief and dried her tears. "Tell me it won't always be this way. Tell me we'll have our tomorrows. Dream with me, lass, if only for a moment."

"The Irish are great ones for dreams . . . That's what Mrs. Sheen said." Miranda remembered the backyard on South Crawford Street, the pewter skies, the laundry fluttering on the line. She could almost see the cats Zelda and Scott slinking around the shrubbery. "Dreams can break your heart."

"And d'you know what's worse than a broken heart? An *empty* heart. It's dreams that fill the spaces, Miranda. The world's a cruel place, and love is fragile. It's dreams that keep love safe."

Miranda's arms tightened around him. She nestled her head on his shoulder. "Oh, Daniel, what are we going to do?"

"We're going to find a way, lass. A way to our tomorrows."

Peter was waiting for Miranda when she returned home. "Where the devil have you been?" he asked, following her into her room. "You knew I had theater tickets."

"I told you I had to see Natalie. There were some details to go over."

"Strange there was no answer at Natalie's office. I've been telephoning for close to an hour."

"We didn't meet at her office. We went to a coffee shop."

"Not a very comfortable place for a business meeting."

"Well, we wanted a bite to eat." Miranda took a black silk dress from her closet and laid it across the bed. "We had things to discuss, but we were both hungry and we decided to have a hamburger."

Peter frowned. "You certainly took your time about it. You must have had a four-course meal."

"Hardly."

"Natalie isn't falling behind schedule, is she?"

"No, everything's all right. We just lost track of time."

"But how—"

Miranda slammed her purse on the vanity table. "Will you *stop* cross-examining me? I didn't mean to be late; it just happened. I'm sorry, but I really can't see what difference it makes. I can't see why you need a minute-by-minute account of my afternoon."

"I have theater tickets, Miranda."

"Yes, I know. If you'll leave me alone, I'll change my clothes and we'll go. All these questions!"

Peter's frown deepened. "What on earth's the matter with you tonight? All *what* questions?"

Color flooded her cheeks. She looked away. "We can stand here arguing or you can let me get dressed. Which will it be?"

"You'd better be careful," said Peter, turning toward the door. "You're beginning to show signs of strain . . . Rather like Jonah, if I'm any judge. You've taken too much on your plate, Miranda. It's not good for you, not good at all."

"Your concern is touching. You'd like to see me fall apart, wouldn't you?"

"Frankly, I wouldn't have thought it possible." He smiled, glancing over his shoulder at Miranda. "Until now," he added, closing the door.

Miranda sat down at the vanity table and massaged her throbbing temples. Her head seemed to be filled with voices: *I want you to marry me . . . Where the devil have you been . . . Tell me it won't always be this way . . . You've taken too much on your plate . . . I love you, lass.*

She heard her own voice trying to explain to Peter, to Daniel, to herself. She bent her head and wept.

363

Chapter Twenty-one

There were more tears during the next three weeks, for Miranda was torn between the things she had to do and the things she wanted to do. When she was with Daniel she dared to share his dreams, dared to believe in tomorrows, but these interludes were all too brief. Time was her enemy, calling her to Wade's, calling her to meetings, calling her home. She could not linger in Daniel's arms, could not spend a whole night in his bed. Clocks kept ticking the days away; soon Daniel would be going back to Ireland.

She tried not to think about it, though as the date of his departure drew nearer she could think of nothing else. She desperately needed to believe that their dreams would survive, that this was not the end. She prayed it was not, for how could she face all the years ahead without him?

They spent their last night together in the little flat near the park. Daniel had had dinner brought in, a romantic dinner complete with candles, starched white tablecloth, and champagne. He had placed a bouquet of violets at the center of the table, and off to the side, a small velvet box. "It's not a ring," he said as she took the box in her hand. "People have a way of noticing rings. It's something to wear close to your heart."

It was a gold locket, engraved with both their initials. She opened the tiny lock; tears misted her eyes as she gazed at his picture. "Oh, Daniel . . . I'll wear it always. I promise."

He clasped the gold chain about her neck. He held her

364

for a moment and then let her go. He sighed. "I'd stay if I could; you know that, lass?"

"Yes, I know."

"And I'll be coming back, I will."

"To see your brewery."

Daniel laughed. "Well, that's the excuse. *You're* the reason . . . We can have our wee visits, Miranda. I can visit here; you can visit Dublin. But that's not the answer for us. It's not enough and it never will be . . . When the lad's a few years older, I'll be asking you to decide." He stroked her cheek, traced the line of her mouth. "Is it your Wade and Company you want? Or do you want to come home to me? That's what I'll be asking, lass."

"A fair question."

"A hard question for you, I'm thinking. You've turned yourself into Miranda, but it's Jenny who'd be coming to me."

"Jenny's dead."

"No." Daniel smiled. "She's in there somewhere. Hiding till you're sure it's Miranda you really want to be. Ah, she's a patient lass, Jenny is."

"Do you believe in the 'little people,' too?"

"And why wouldn't I? I believe in magic."

Miranda smiled also. She wrapped her arms around Daniel. "What am I going to do without you?" she murmured. "I miss you already."

He dried her tears. "It's not forever."

"Daniel—"

"I love you, my darling. And love always finds a way."

Miranda was in her office when Daniel's ship sailed out of the harbor. She stared at the clock until the numerals blurred, and then quickly she glanced away.

"Is anything wrong?" asked Tom Guthrie. "You look pale."

"No, I'm fine. I suppose we've all been working too hard. You *are* working hard, aren't you, Tom?"

"You know me."

"That's why I asked."

"Oh, come on," he said laughing. "I do my part around here. I haven't much choice. You're a slave driver, Miranda."

"Well, things will be easier once the new departments are set up. We have only two days left." She opened a folder, making tiny check marks. "Natalie's dresses were delivered this morning and so we can . . . Oh, that reminds me. I was down in the receiving department this morning and I happened to pass Malcolm Gill's little office. The place is an absolute mess! It's probably a health hazard. I know he's been here a thousand years and Jonah seems fond of him, but can't we give him his pension and send him into happy retirement?"

"Malcolm Gill isn't as old as you think. He started working here when he was just a kid — thirteen, maybe fourteen."

"An early retirement, then. He's a terrible janitor. Caleb and Sam and the others do all the real work. And his office is a pigsty. I tried to talk to him but . . . There must be something we can do."

"I wouldn't pursue it, Miranda. Malcolm Gill has his supporters."

"God knows why."

"God has nothing to do with it." Tom shifted around in his chair. "Quite the contrary."

Miranda frowned. "Can you be more specific?"

"I can; I'm not sure I should . . . Do you know what pornography is?"

"A fancy name for dirty pictures."

"Yes, well, Malcolm Gill is the local supplier . . . I don't mean to suggest that Wade's is a hotbed of . . ." Tom laughed. "Excuse the unfortunate choice of words. The point is, he has a few select but steady customers . . . Like Jonah."

"Jonah!" And yet she was not surprised. Her mind skipped back through the years to the night she had re-

366

turned from her honeymoon. She remembered Peter's handkerchief drawer, and the dirty pictures that had spilled out of it. She remembered Peter's words: "I happen to know Jonah has a handkerchief drawer of his own." She shook her head. "Of course Jonah's not his only customer."

"That's a leading question. And I've done enough ratting for today. It's not cricket, you know. Men aren't supposed to tell on other men."

"Your secret is safe with me."

"All kidding aside, I just thought you ought to know what you were getting into. We're going to need everybody's goodwill, especially if our new departments get off to a poor start."

"Bite your tongue."

"We're on the line, Miranda. We pushed for those departments."

"Nervous?"

Tom shrugged. "I'd rather not lose my job. There isn't a hell of a lot of future in selling apples on street corners. And anyway, the best corners are taken."

Miranda smiled. "You won't lose your job, Tom. These departments are going to work very well. I can feel it. They're the right departments at the right time. Natalie's designs are wonderful."

"She's pretty wonderful herself."

Miranda looked up. "Yes, she is."

"You don't approve of me, do you? Seeing Natalie, I mean."

"It's none of my business." She closed the folder. She gazed at Tom and her expression softened. "I know you're not one of the bad guys," she conceded. "And I know Natalie is happy. That's all that counts. Besides, I'm . . ." *In no position to give advice,* she silently finished. "I think I should stay out of this."

"You wouldn't boycot a wedding if there were to be one?"

"A wedding?" Miranda smiled. "Really?"

"I said *if* . . . We're both having trouble with our families. The religious thing, you see. My people are staunch

Methodists. Natalie's are staunch Jews. It's complicated."

"Elope."

"That's one way," laughed Tom. "Or there's always City Hall. We do have choices."

"Are you and Natalie *engaged?* Why didn't she tell me?"

"There's nothing to tell yet. I'm thinking about it. I've made two mistakes, Miranda. I'm not anxious for a third. I'm trying to figure things out."

"Well, if there *is* a wedding, I'll be there. You couldn't keep me away."

"Good. Natalie would feel much better if she had your blessing."

"My blessing!" Laughter burst from Miranda. "You make me sound like Natalie's mother!"

"It's worse than that; you're her best friend."

"Stop worrying, Tom. Natalie has my blessing in anything she wants to do. I'm on her side."

"And mine?"

"If you behave yourself," replied Miranda, her brows arching in amusement. She picked up her folder and left her desk, pausing in front of the advertising layouts arranged on a shelf. "I hope these ads do the trick. I like the ones for the Today's Woman department; Natalie's dresses photographed beautifully . . . I'm just not certain about the cosmetics ads. They still look a little too artistic."

"They catch the eye, Miranda. That's important. Have the counter displays been delivered yet?"

"The last of them came in this morning. Annie should have them unpacked by now. Come downstairs with me, Tom. I want you to see how we've decided to arrange the counters."

"You and Annie?"

"She's the most talented display person in New York."

"The Tiffany guy is damned good."

"Annie's better than the Tiffany guy. Wait till she unveils the new windows. You'll be dazzled. They're so feminine and romantic . . . Lots of lace and perfume bottles, and big swirls of different-colored lipsticks. Oh, and roses.

Huge paper roses, because we're featuring the Jobina Rose line."

"That's Jobina Grant's company, isn't it?"

"She's been extremely cooperative."

"Why not?" asked Tom, rising to his feet. "You're putting money in her pocket."

"Money in her pocket means money in *our* pocket. The profits on cosmetics are enormous."

"I can't quarrel with that," said Tom as they walked to the elevator. " 'Profits' is one of my favorite words."

"I won't ask what the others are."

"Coward."

They stepped into the elevator. Miranda glanced at Tom. "Do you think we could at least tell Malcolm Gill to clean up his office?"

"Forget about Malcolm Gill."

"Yes. Yes, I guess you're right."

There were about two dozen people strolling around Wade's main floor, and another dozen or so at the wrapping desk. Miranda knew business would pick up during the noon hour; the sparse crowd would thicken but then thin out again . . . One more lost day. She walked toward the front of the store, Tom keeping pace beside her. The front counters had been emptied, cleaned, and polished, though now they were almost hidden under the display department's heavy cloths. "I see Annie's already begun," said Tom.

"No use waiting until the last minute."

Annie Wolfe looked up as they approached. She was in her late twenties, a freckle-faced blonde wearing a gray smock over her red wool dress. A tapemeasure was draped around her neck; her pockets were stuffed with marking crayons and odd bits of fabric. "Nothing to worry about here," she said, glancing from Tom to Miranda. "We'll be ready."

"What are all these boxes?"

"Be careful, Miranda. That box has the mirrored panels for the Chanel counter. *This* counter," said Annie, tapping the glass. "I want to be sure they fit . . . We'll have the elegant, tailored look for Chanel, and the soft, romantic look for Jobina. Silk flowers and little lace fans. The idea," she explained to Tom, "is for each of the six cosmetic counters to have a look of its own."

Miranda peered inside another box. She saw a garden of silk roses, different shades of pink and red. She saw scarlet anemones and tiny sprigs of freesia. Nestled in the corner of the box, she saw a silken bouquet of violets. Gently, she lifted the bouquet and pressed it to her cheek. "Violets," she murmured. Tears sprang to her eyes. She turned away.

The cosmetics department was an immediate success. The advertising, the lush window displays, brought hordes of women into the store, women eager for some small touch of luxury. For the first time in years, the counters were swamped with customers; lipsticks and eye shadows and perfumes seemed to fly off the shelves. Miranda studied the sales figures, charting them week to week. By the end of the sixth week she knew that Wade's had taken a great step forward.

She was not as certain about the new dress department. Sales were modest, falling well below the figures she had projected. She told herself, and Natalie, that everything would work out, but still she worried. She authorized more advertising, authorized different advertising, but in vain. As the spring season drew to a close, less than half the inventory had been sold.

"Wade and Company can't afford another department running in the red." Peter's remark had been addressed to Jonah, who sat in his usual place at the head of the conference table. Jonah was silent, as were the other members of the executive staff. "We've all seen the sales figures," continued Peter. "Only one conclusion can be drawn."

"I disagree," said Miranda.

Peter smiled. "If you'll forgive me, I'm afraid your personal interest in Natalie Inc. has clouded your judgment."

"Again, I disagree."

"I'm not surprised."

Nor was Miranda, for Peter was clearly enjoying this chance to put her on the spot. "Everybody here knew about my investment in Natalie Inc.," she replied. "I didn't keep it a secret. And I didn't make any special deals, either. I believed we needed a department like Today's Woman. I believed Natalie Stern was the right designer. I still believe those things."

"But the department is a failure."

"It's been disappointing. I'm not ready to call it a failure, not yet."

"You have your investment to protect."

"You're out of line," said Tom. "Both Harvey and I have been involved in the decisions and not once has a decision been made to favor Natalie Inc. over Wade's. There's never been the slightest suggestion of that."

"Until now." Peter turned to Jonah. "In my opinion, we should cut our losses and close the department. We can put the space to much better use."

"Such as?" asked Tom.

"*Anything* would be better than Today's Woman and you know it."

"The department is only three months old," said Miranda. "We have to give it time. We're trying to bring in new customers, a different kind of customer. That doesn't happen overnight."

"It did in the cosmetics department. The cosmetics department is bringing in *all* kinds of customers."

Harvey Vaughn cleared his throat. "That's a start, Peter. Getting them through the door is a start."

"Right," agreed Miranda. "And the next step is to get them to the third floor. When they're comfortable shopping here — when they're *used* to shopping here, they'll start exploring."

"We'll all be dead by then," said Peter.

"Speak for yourself," said Claude Berman.

"All right, I will. For the record, I vote to close Today's

371

Woman. Obviously, Miranda and Tom are opposed. Claude, what about you?"

"Going by the figures, I'll vote to close the department."

"Harvey?"

"No, I'm opposed, too."

Peter looked at the newest addition to the executive staff, the new head buyer, Jeff Woodrow. He was a cautious man, anxious about his job and his future, anxious not to make a mistake. He sensed that he could earn points with his first vote, but points with whom? He had not been at Wade's long enough to know where the power lay. He had to guess, and he guessed that Peter was more important than Miranda, for men were always more important than women.

"Close it," he said finally, hoping he had made the correct choice.

Peter nodded. "We have a tie. The decision is yours, Jonah."

Jonah clasped his hands atop the table. He sighed. He had been afraid it would come down to him, and now that it had, he felt trapped. His thoughts were disjointed; his voice seemed to be stuck in his throat. He tried to think what his great-grandfather would have decided, but inspiration eluded him. He glanced around the table, looking last at Miranda. His eyes almost pleaded for help.

"Maybe you'd prefer to reserve your decision," she quietly suggested. "The picture will be much clearer three months from now, won't it?"

"Clearer, yes." Jonah felt as if he had been rescued. "Without all the facts—"

"We *have* all the facts," said Peter.

"Not *all* the facts," said Miranda. "Why make a hasty decision?" She smiled at Jonah. "You've always resisted hasty decisions, and rightly so."

"Yes, rightly so." He brightened at this unexpected testimony to his good judgment; for just a moment the mists of his mind seemed to lift. "I've never thought it wise to act in haste. I will, therefore, reserve my decision. Patience is a virtue, after all."

The meeting adjourned. Peter left quickly. He was furious, for Miranda had won again. His job was all he had now, but what was his job? What was his place at Wade & Company? *I'm a lackey,* he thought to himself, *a yes man carrying out Miranda's plans. Jonah doesn't know it, but she's running this damned store. She's running all of us.*

He was too old to start over; too old, too tired. The Crash had taken the last of his money, but he blamed Miranda for taking the last of his self-respect. He scowled as he saw her coming toward him. He would gladly have wrung her neck. "Another victory," he said, biting out the words. "Congratulations."

"This isn't a contest, you know."

"What I *know*," he replied with an icy stare, "is that one of these days the gods are going to stop smiling on you. One of these days your luck is going to run out."

But Miranda's luck held. In July, sales figures for the Today's Woman department suddenly started to climb. They soared during the month of August; every dress, every skirt, was snapped up and Natalie Inc. began working overtime to fill reorders. A fashion columnist for the *Tribune* wrote an article praising the "fresh new American look of Natalie Stern's designs." There were mentions in other columns, and each one brought new customers into the store. Wade's lost a few customers — staid dowagers who found the new clientele "common" — but for every five customers lost, a hundred came along to take their place.

Miranda was elated. "You're a hit, Natalie," she crowed one sunny autumn afternoon. "You're going to be rich and famous!"

Natalie poured sugar into her coffee. She shrugged. "I still can't believe it. Six months ago, I was ready to slit my wrists. And then . . . Well, it's you, kiddo. Your golden touch rubbed off on me."

"No false modesty please. There's the little matter of

373

your talent."

Natalie shook her head. "Talent's no guarantee of anything."

"It helps."

"Sometimes, not always. Luck. Talent's nothing without luck."

Miranda laughed. "I'm glad to see your press clippings haven't gone to your head."

"My mother started a scrapbook. It has about two hundred pages, so you can figure she's expecting big things."

"I am, too. I'm thinking of enlarging the department. Can you handle that?"

"I've hired more people." Natalie sipped her coffee. She put the cup down and looked at Miranda. "I've been getting calls from other stores. The switchboard has been jammed."

"That's wonderful!"

"I feel a little funny about it . . . Disloyal, you know?"

"Don't be silly. You're in business, Natalie, and businesses have to grow. I'm delighted for you. Of course I fully intend to hold you to your contract. Your designs for Wade's have to be exclusive to Wade's. As long as that's understood, we have no problem. None at all." Miranda paused while the waitress refilled their cups. "It won't be easy," she went on when the waitress left. "You'll really be designing two separate lines."

"If I'd wanted 'easy,' I would have stayed behind the handbag counter. I love my work. And I have a soft spot for Wade's. I won't let you down . . . Not even when I'm rich and famous," added Natalie with a quick smile. "I owe you."

"It's mutual. The store was in terrible trouble. For a while there, I was afraid we'd have to close our doors. But with the cosmetics department, and Natalie Inc., and a few others, we're headed back in the right direction. We're not exactly breaking records, but we're beginning to see profits again. Jonah's beginning to show flashes of his old self."

"Is that good or bad?"

"Both," laughed Miranda. "But what about you? Now

374

that you're the darling of the fashion world, isn't it time you moved out of the Bronx?"

"Past time."

"Well?"

Natalie ran her fingers through her dusky curls. She had changed little during the years. She wore the same hairstyle, the same deep rose lipstick, the same tiny pearl earrings, but now the scent of Chanel swirled around her and now she dressed only in silk. "As a matter of fact, I'll be leaving the Bronx this summer. That's what I wanted to tell you about. I've been keeping a secret: Tom asked me to marry him."

Miranda leaned forward. "And you said?"

"I said yes. We'll be married in June. A June bride; corny, isn't it?"

"It's *marvelous*. Congratulations, Natalie. I'm just delighted!"

"Are you? You had your doubts about Tom."

"But he's reformed," replied Miranda, her eyes twinkling. "He's behaving himself. And he happens to be a damned nice guy. You know how closely I've been working with him. I've had a chance to see different sides. He doesn't hide anything, Natalie."

"I had to be sure."

"Sure of what?"

"First, that he really didn't mind my career, because I'm not going to give it up. And then there was the money problem. It looks like I'll be earning more than he will. I had to be sure we could deal with that."

"And are you?"

"More or less. Tom's no kid and neither am I. A June bride at thirty? Imagine!"

"It sounds fine to me."

"Will you be my matron of honor?"

"Of course I will. Where is it going to be? Tom said there was some conflict about religion."

"Conflict! It's like a holy war! My mother is carrying on about having a rabbi and Tom's mother is carrying on

375

about having a minister. It's *crazy*. I mean, this is the third time around for Tom. And *I'm* not even wearing white. So why is everyone acting like this is the wedding of the year?"

"Weddings bring out the best and worst in people," said Miranda. "Pay no attention."

Natalie held a small gold lighter to her cigarette. "We'll probably wind up at City Hall." She laughed. "But wherever we wind up, I'm going to look great. I'm making my own dress."

"Somehow I'm not surprised."

"I found the most beautiful rose-blush silk. It's actually an ivory color with a pink undertone . . . I'll show you; I have a swatch in my bag." Natalie opened her purse and dug through the contents. "Oh, my God."

"What's the matter?"

"I'm sorry, Miranda. Another letter came for you from Daniel. I completely forgot. It was a good idea to have him send his letters to my address, but—"

"Where's the letter, Natalie? Give it to me."

"It's here. I just have to find it. I know I put it in my bag and then . . . I *know* it's here."

"*Natalie*—"

"It's all right . . . I found it."

Miranda snatched the letter away and tore it open. A smile leapt across her face as she saw the familiar handwriting. Her heart leapt as she read the familiar words: "My darling lass." She forgot about Natalie, about everyone and everything but Daniel.

He had written two pages. She read them slowly, savoring them. When she came to the end, her smile disappeared. "He won't be back till next year," she murmured.

"Next year is only a few months off."

Miranda glanced again at the letter. She folded it carefully and slipped it into her purse. "It will be longer than that. He—they're expanding the brewery. Business is very good. It's a good business to be in, I suppose. People drink when they're happy; people drink when they're sad."

"You look like you could use a drink yourself."

"No, but I'll take one of your cigarettes."

"Sure." There was the rustle of paper, the click of a lighter. "Have you thought about taking Andrew to Europe during the holidays? He could visit his relatives in Ireland."

"I think about it all the time. But I can't do it now. Maybe when this Depression is over. Maybe . . ." Miranda exhaled a stream of bluish smoke. She sighed. "I keep saying 'maybe' and time keeps flying by."

Another Christmas passed, another winter. Miranda took Andrew and two of his friends for a week at Lake Placid, but that was as much of a vacation as she could manage. When she returned, she was swamped with work. She reorganized many of Wade's departments, initiated new displays and advertising campaigns. She added more cosmetic counters, more space for Natalie's designs. After a four-month battle with Walter Houser, she succeeded in introducing new accounting systems, systems which Claude Berman was forced to accept as well. By the spring of 1935, Miranda had acquired a secretary, an intercom device, a dictating machine, and control of store policy. Jeff Woodrow no longer questioned where the power lay at Wade & Company, for now there was no doubt.

Jonah could have intervened at any time but he remained silent, tacitly giving his support to Miranda. He felt he could do no less, for he had watched her steer Wade & Company away from disaster, watched her take all the necessary actions that he himself had been unable even to consider. His spirits, the state of his mind, had improved, and yet he had little desire to reclaim his responsibilities. He had come too close to losing what had been entrusted to him; he would not risk such a loss again. He would keep the symbols of his authority—his place at the head of the conference table, his large office, his title—but the work, and the problems, he would leave to Miranda.

Once again she buried herself in work. It was her way of avoiding the things she did not want to face, did not want to

377

think about. Work got her through the days, but there was nothing to get her through the nights. She tossed in her bed, listening to the ticking clock and wondering about Daniel. She knew there were women in his life, probably quite a few, probably beautiful. She hated these unseen women; at times she hated Daniel. Why wasn't he here with her? Why did he have to leave? Why hadn't he come back? The questions were always the same, and the answers. He would not give up his life in Ireland for stolen moments in New York; she could not give up the life she had chosen so long ago.

"Natalie and Tom are being married tomorrow," she wrote to him, "but in my dreams *we're* the bride and groom. I see us standing there. I hear us saying the words. Dreams are so treacherous . . . Or are they real? Tell me what's real, Daniel. Oh, my darling, tell me dreams come true."

Natalie and Tom were married in the Sterns' Bronx flat — five rooms filled with overstuffed furniture, knick-nacks, crocheted doilies, and exquisite Austrian crystal that had been passed down from generation to generation.

The flat was immaculate. Sunlight poured through windows draped with sheer white curtains. Roses were massed in two white porcelain urns; mixed roses and white tulips were entwined around the mantel and the wide arch of the living room. Sixteen small white chairs were arranged in straight, perfect rows. Seated at the spinet piano was Natalie's aunt Fran, the "musician" in the family.

Mrs. Stern, plump, pretty, and middle-aged, was crying. The Guthries, plump and in their sixties, looked confused. The other guests were chatting quietly, though they fell silent as Aunt Fran played the notes of the Wedding March.

Andrew, wearing his first pair of long pants, was the ring bearer. He passed beneath the arch, biting his lips to keep from giggling. Miranda, wearing pale-rose silk, entered next. She was smiling. She glimpsed all the upturned faces, glimpsed Peter's bored expression. Her eyes swept to the mantel, where Tom waited. It was indeed his third time around, but it might have been the first, for he was obviously nervous.

Natalie entered the room on her father's arm, and now there was no trace of the swaggering New York facade. She was dewy-eyed, pink with blushes. Her smile was almost shy. Her lashes fluttered over hazel eyes wide with wonder.

She was a lovely bride. Her ivory silk ankle-length dress was softly gathered at the bosom and sewn with glistening seed pearls. The sleeves were long and full, the cuffs edged with old lace. She wore flowers in her hair, white roses that matched her bouquet. She wore Miranda's pearl necklace — something borrowed — and tucked in her pocket was a little blue handkerchief.

The music stopped as Natalie took her place beside Tom. She gazed into his eyes and drew a tiny breath.

"Dearly beloved," began Judge Klugman.

Miranda listened to the words of the marriage ceremony. She listened to the vows, thinking not of her own wedding years ago, but of Daniel. *Tell me what's real, Daniel. Tell me dreams come true.*

Chapter Twenty-two

Daniel returned to New York in the winter of 1936. Miranda was at the pier to meet him. Fighting her way through the crowds, the confusion, she flew into his open arms. "You're here," she murmured, her throat choked with tears. "Oh, Daniel, you're here."

They had a week together. Miranda made excuses to be away from the store — imaginary dental appointments, imaginary meetings with Andrew's teachers, imaginary meetings at Natalie Inc. She was believed, for there was no reason not to believe her, but still it was difficult. The rushing around, the deceptions, the juggled schedules; all these things took their toll. She felt as if she were leading her life on the run, a fugitive who dared not look back, dared not look ahead.

It was no easier for Daniel. He was a man accustomed to taking matters into his own hands, to finding solutions, but in this case he realized there was nothing to be done. He had never known a woman like Miranda, a woman so complex, so tangled up in the choices of the past. He wanted to undo those choices. He wanted to sling her across his shoulder and carry her off to Ireland. He wanted the impossible.

They both wanted the impossible, but they settled for seven wintry days in New York. They took long walks through a deserted Central Park. They went to little out-of-the-way cafés. They went to the Battery, strolling the path by the sea wall, laughing as gulls swooped and soared

380

against the pale sky. They took a ferry ride across the bay. Alone on the windswept deck, they gazed at each other while the Manhattan skyline blurred and then receded from view. They heard the cry of sea birds, the hollow clang of buoys, and it was like a melody playing just for them.

Daniel had borrowed another flat, a small penthouse on Beekman Place. Each afternoon they went back to the flat, and in the gathering twilight they shared the endless mysteries of love, the endless depths of passion. For a little while they were the only two people in the world. They were utterly happy, utterly lost.

"I promised myself I wouldn't cry," said Miranda on their last night together. "But what am I going to do without you?"

"It needn't be that way, lass. Come home with me. Marry me."

A shadow brushed her face. Her lips parted; her words came slowly, quietly. "We've been all through this, Daniel. You know I can't."

"I know nothing of the sort. There's 'can't' and there's 'won't.'"

"Well, I *can't*. At least not yet."

"Andrew will be going away to school soon. Have you thought about that?"

"Of course I have."

"Ireland has fine schools. And England, to give the devil his due . . . The lad could see a bit of the world, a bit of history. It's clear you don't intend to bring him over for a holiday. But if he were in school—"

"I can't do that, either," sighed Miranda. She rested her head on Daniel's shoulder, looking up at him through her lashes. "Jonah's made all the arrangements. He enrolled Andrew at Groton years ago. Groton and then Yale; that's a Wade tradition."

"We McAllisters have a few traditions of our own. And the lad is half McAllister."

"He's been raised as a Wade. It's too late to do anything about that now. He's a typical American boy, Daniel. Ex-

381

cept that he's going to inherit a department store one day."

"And if he doesn't want a department store?"

"It will be up to him to decide," said Miranda. "But it's up to me to keep his inheritance safe. That's what I've been trying to do. The store is almost out of the woods. In a couple of years, Wade's will be stronger than ever. *Richer* than ever . . . I'll have more freedom. Including the freedom to divorce Peter."

"A couple of years is it? You're asking a lot of me."

"Yes. I'm asking you not to run off with some beautiful coleen. I'm asking you not to stop loving me."

"Never in this world, and that's the truth." Daniel's arm tightened around Miranda. "But I'll be holding you to your word. I'll be marking the calendar."

"Calendars and clocks." She sighed again. "What a terrible way to live."

"It's not forever, lass."

"It will *seem* like forever. You'll be gone tomorrow, Daniel. I can't bear the thought."

He tilted her face to him. He kissed her. "We still have tonight," he murmured. Slowly, he opened the buttons of her blouse. "A night made for love."

"The nights are the hardest," said Miranda a few months later. She was walking with Natalie along Lexington Avenue. Snow was falling in big, chunky flakes. The streets were slippery; traffic had slowed to a crawl. "Sometimes I toss and turn for hours — missing Daniel, wondering what he's up to."

"Whatever he's up to isn't serious. The guy's crazy about you."

"The guy's thousands of miles away." Miranda hunched her shoulders against the wind. She smiled. "And he's no monk!"

"You wouldn't want a monk."

They crossed the avenue. Natalie skidded on a patch of ice and Miranda caught her arm. "Careful. Pregnant ladies have to watch where they're going."

"Don't you start on me too, Miranda. Tom calls ten times a day to see how I am. And the grandparents-to-be are treating me like I was made of cake. I'm fine. Strong as a horse. Soon I'll be fat as a horse."

Miranda laughed. "Only temporarily . . . You're not overdoing things, are you?"

"Tom wouldn't let me. We've been real homebodies lately. We used to go out after work, but now we both go straight home . . . I'm kind of glad Tom had to stay at the store for the inventory. I'll have some time to myself. You have no idea what a luxury that is."

"Oh, I think I do."

"Sorry," laughed Natalie. "Of course you do. Your life's pretty damned complicated . . . And I'm about to make it worse."

Miranda looked up. "Don't tell me you're having production troubles. Please don't tell me that."

"No, we're on schedule. I'm there every day cracking the whip. But it may be a different story a few months from now. I may not be able to work till the end. Even if I am, I'll still have to take time off when the baby comes. I've been worrying about it, Miranda. I've been talking to Lily about leaving the Wades and working at Natalie Inc. I need someone I can trust. Someone who can keep things running smoothly. I figure anyone who's worked for Jonah Wade can put up with a lot."

"True," agreed Miranda.

"So I've been talking to Lily. She wasn't easy to convince; she's a very cautious woman. But she called today just as I was leaving and said she was giving notice. I wanted you to know beforehand . . . I hope you're not angry about all this."

"Why should I be angry?"

"Lily is the only sane one in that house. It's going to be hard on you. Without her there, I mean."

"Oh, I'm happy she'll have a life of her own. And she can afford it now, thanks to her investment in Natalie Inc. We're all going to be rich!"

383

Natalie smiled. "The two of us have done all right, haven't we? Remember when we met? In the employees' lounge at Wade's? Did you think it would turn out this way?"

"I remember how impressed I was with you. A true New Yorker. And all those glamorous plans! I was absolutely dazzled . . . What ever happened to Natasha Starr?"

"Some day I'm going to do a high fashion line. Under the Natasha label. Natasha *Starr* is a little too much, but Natasha is just perfect."

"Wade's has to have an exclusive, at least at the start."

"So what else is new?" They reached the canopied entrance of Natalie's apartment building. "Want to come up for a drink?"

"I'd better get home. I have some things to go over with Jonah. Now that he's back to his old self, he's making pronouncements again. I can't seem to do anything right."

"Baloney! Everyone knows you're running the show, Miranda."

She shrugged. "Jonah *owns* the show," she replied, turning up the collar of her coat. "Good night, Natalie. I'll call you tomorrow."

The snow was heavier, mounding rooftops and window sills, spreading a long, thick carpet of pure white. Miranda slowed her pace, enjoying the hushed night air, the powdery crunch beneath her feet. She knew that Andrew would be hauling his sled down from the attic. She smiled.

She was in a good mood when she arrived home, but her mood changed when she heard Jonah's angry voice coming from upstairs. She left her things in the cloakroom and went to the staircase. What now? she wondered, glancing at her watch.

Jonah's voice grew louder, angrier. "This is all your fault!" he cried as Miranda entered the living room.

She saw Daphne seated on the couch; standing quietly near the window was Lily. "My fault?" she asked, looking at Jonah.

"Lily has just given her notice."

384

"Yes," murmured Daphne. "I really don't know how we'll manage. It's really . . ."

"I blame you, Miranda. Putting foolish notions in Lily's head. Risking her hard-earned money. Never giving a thought to the consequences."

"Consequences?" Miranda frowned. "But Lily's done very well with her investment."

"That's right, Mr. Wade," said Lily. "The profits—"

"Profits! What are profits compared to loyalty? Why, we *depended* upon you. We *trusted* you to stay with us and do your job."

"I don't know how we'll manage," murmured Daphne.

Miranda sat in a small chair by the fireplace. "Now I see what this is all about. Surely you don't expect Lily to spend the rest of her life here. She's been offered a better opportunity, Jonah."

"And so the ungrateful girl leaves *us* in the lurch!"

"I said I would stay to train a new girl, Mr. Wade."

Daphne sighed. "But it isn't the same, is it? We know you, you see."

Lily took a step toward the door. "I have to set the table for dinner, Mrs. Wade."

Daphne blinked. "Dinner?"

"It's past six, Mrs. Wade."

"Oh for heaven's sake, go ahead," said Jonah. "We will discuss this later."

Lily took several more steps, pausing when she reached the door. "I've accepted the other job, Mr. Wade, but I want you to know Mrs. Dexter had nothing to do with it. Nothing at all."

"I suppose that makes everything quite all right," snapped Jonah when she had gone.

Miranda watched him, thinking that life had been much easier when he had been sunk in gloom. Now she had to deal with petulant outbursts, with sarcasm and bluster. In her own way she was fond of Jonah, and certainly she was grateful to him, but he was a difficult man. "If we can forget about Lily for a moment—"

385

"Forget? She's disrupting the life of this house. Perhaps I was wrong to blame you, Miranda, but I can and do blame your friend Natalie Stern. Stealing my employee! And after all I've done for her."

"What have you done for her, Jonah? I got Natalie's designs into the store, and I kept them there when Peter and the others wanted to close the department. Wade's gave her a showcase, but she repaid that debt a thousand times over. Natalie's designs helped save the store."

Jonah flushed with anger. "It's like you to take all the credit."

"No, it's not. I don't care about credit . . . But I'm starting to care about respect." Miranda wondered if she should go on. She had never been this blunt with Jonah before; she had always measured her words. Out of fear, she thought to herself. She shook her head. "You talk about Lily as if she were your property. You talk about Natalie as if—"

"That will do," said Jonah. He stared at Miranda, waiting for her to back down, waiting for her to apologize. She did neither. A minute passed, two. Daphne stirred beside him on the couch. He clasped her hand. Very slowly, a smile spread across his face. "So you've grown up, have you?"

"Yes, Jonah, I think I have."

Daphne looked from her husband to Miranda. "But how are we going to manage?" she asked.

The new housemaid was young, pretty in a bland sort of way, eager, chatty, and efficient. Within weeks, she learned the Wades' many rules and idiosyncrasies; within months, the household was once again running smoothly. "We can all relax," Miranda jokingly wrote to Daniel, "the domestic crisis is over."

The crisis at Wade's appeared to be over as well. By summer, Miranda knew she could stop worrying, for sales figures were steady and most departments were showing increases. She was convinced that a strong fashion image

386

was the key to the store's success, and so she sought out new designers, designers with fresh, exciting ideas. She continued to make subtle changes in the look of the store; she continued to make the store's ads warmer and more welcoming. Wade & Company had once catered to the carriage trade. In Miranda's hands it catered to a wide cross section of New Yorkers. If there were ten-thousand-dollar sable coats in the fur department, there were also thirty-nine-cent stockings in the hosiery department. And no matter who the customer was, the customer was always right.

Now, on a steamy August afternoon, she opened a file folder and gazed across her desk at Tom. "Jonah and Daphne are going to Europe next month. He can do some buying while he's there. The question is—"

"The question is, why aren't *you* going to Europe? You could sign up a few European designers for us."

"God knows I'd love to go. But Jonah and I can't both be away, and he's the boss."

"Hah!"

"He's going and that's that. He won't be doing any fashion buying, but I was thinking about our Christmas Shop. Jonah always used to find marvelous one-of-a-kind decorations and ornaments. Expensive, but marvelous. What would you say to giving fifteen percent of the shop to Jonah's finds?"

"Ten percent is enough."

"All right, ten percent. Annie Wolfe can set up a special display."

"Annie wants a raise."

"Yes, I know. Of course what she's asking is way too much. See if you can reach a compromise."

"And if not?"

Miranda smiled. "You're a persuasive man, Tom. I have confidence in you."

"She's no pushover."

"Look, I'd hate to lose Annie. I honestly believe she's the best. But we have a budget. I'm not going to open the floodgates on salaries just because the store is profitable again. We all had to take cuts when times were bad. A lot of people deserve raises. And they'll get them, but *no one* is going to get more than we can afford. Including Annie, including you, including me."

"May I quote you?"

"Please do."

Tom glanced through the papers in his folder. "You know, we should probably do a complete personnel review. Hank Nelson can start putting the figures together. He might be able to have a report ready for next month's executive meeting. Then we can decide on a policy for salary increases."

"Good idea. Will you follow up?"

"Sure."

The intercom buzzed. Miranda picked up the telephone. "Yes? Yes, just a minute . . . For you," she said, handing the phone to Tom.

"Guthrie here . . . What? When? Are you . . . Yes, I see." He jumped to his feet. "Yes, yes, I'll be right there . . . I'm leaving now."

"What's wrong?" asked Miranda, for Tom was suddenly pale.

"That was the housekeeper. Natalie's pains have begun; I have to get her to the hospital. Good Lord, I'm going to be a father!"

Miranda laughed. She left her desk and put her hand on Tom's shoulder. "Everything's going to be fine, just fine . . . Give my love to Natalie and I'll see you both at the hospital right after work. Maybe there'll be a new little Guthrie in the world by then."

"Good Lord, I hope so. I couldn't stand a long wait. Will it take long, do you think?"

They walked into the corridor. "Stop worrying, Tom. Everything really *will* be fine. Here," she said, kissing his cheek. "For luck." She watched him hurry away. Smiling, she crossed the corridor to Peter's office. "Oh," she exclaimed as the door opened, "I was just coming to see you.

388

Tom's gone to take Natalie to the hospital."

"It's about time."

"I'm sure Natalie feels the same way. Will you have time to go to the hospital after work?"

"I suppose. There's a membership dinner at my club tonight, but it isn't until eight . . . Shall I order flowers? No, on second thought, *you* can order the flowers. You're the one with all the money. You can buy the kid a solid gold teddy bear."

"Why do you have to be so nasty?"

Peter's smile was cold. "Allow me my small pleasures, Miranda. Compensations for a wasted life."

She sighed. "You're in a wonderful mood today," she said as they walked toward the staircase. "Any special reason?"

"No, just my usual wonderful mood."

"May I help?" She regretted her words, for they were followed almost instantly by Peter's derisive laughter. "We can't even have a civil conversation anymore."

"It's no great loss." Peter opened the door to the staircase. "As I recall, we never had much to say to each other. As I recall, we never had much of anything."

The door slammed in Miranda's face. She stood there for a moment and then turned back in the direction of her office. *We never had much of anything.* She thought back through the years of their marriage, empty years, futile years. She had decided to ask him for a divorce as soon as Andrew went away to school. She felt no qualms, no doubts, but still she could not help wondering what their marriage would have been like if they had tried. If they had made allowances, compromises. If they had let their defenses down. If he had been able to trust. If she had been able to have children.

Natalie had twins, a girl she named Jenny, and a boy named David. The Guthrie household was thrown into chaos, for only one child had been expected, but it was a happy chaos and Miranda was often there to share in it. She visited during her lunch hours; at least twice a week

389

she stopped by on her way home from work. Sunday mornings she brought Andrew along. He had no interest in babies, but he was delighted with Tom's collection of model trains. During these Sunday visits the "men" played with the train sets while the women cooed over the twins.

Natalie returned to work when the twins were three months old. Andrew's former nanny, Miss Dent, was located and hired to care for them. They kept her busy. In the first six months of their lives they seemed to cry all the time, their voices blending into one loud, continuous shriek. They were always hungry, always wet. They hated baths. When they learned to crawl, they raced off in opposite directions, stopping only to pull lamp cords out of sockets, plants out of pots; when they learned to walk, nothing in the Guthrie apartment was safe.

"I never thought we'd get through it," said Natalie on a summer day in 1938. "Two years of sheer hell. But look at them now."

Miranda looked. Jenny and David sat at the kitchen table eating birthday cake. They were calm, scrubbed, smiling. Every few moments they put their dark heads together in the whispered, secret conversations of twins. "They're angels," she said.

"*Now* they're angels," laughed Natalie. "After being devils for two years."

"They had to get it out of their systems."

"Whose side are you on? I want sympathy, Miranda, and I deserve it too. You never had such craziness with Andrew."

"He spent most of his first year sleeping." Miranda sipped her drink. "When he woke up, he had the run of the nursery. That was a big help."

"That's why we're moving: the kids need more room. Four bedrooms on Central Park West! My mother's thrilled. Central Park West was always her dream."

"You'll be able to buy her a nice chunk of it, if Natalie Inc. keeps rolling along. And I see no reason why it shouldn't. You and Lily are a wonderful combination . . .

390

Where is she, by the way? Didn't you invite her?"

"Sure I did. She'll be here . . . Jenny, wipe your mouth . . . On your *napkin*, Jenny. That's the girl." Natalie leaned over and kissed her daughter's head. "Have you had enough?"

"Yes, Mommy."

"How about you, Davey?"

His bright brown eyes slid to his plate. "Ice cream," he said.

"No, the ice cream's for later. Why don't you go find your uncle Andrew? Maybe he'll give you a piggyback ride."

The twins clapped their hands together. They jumped down from their chairs and skipped away.

Miranda watched them go. She smiled. "They're great pals, aren't they?"

"You look tired. Problems at the store?"

"The store's fine. I just haven't been sleeping well . . . Andrew's going off to Groton next month, and I'm starting to feel sad about it." Miranda glanced down at the table. "In the middle of the night I start remembering him as a tiny baby in his basket. And now . . . Thirteen years old, Natalie. *God*, the time's gone quickly . . . He's practically grown up."

"When are you going to talk to Peter?"

"As soon as Andrew's settled at school. I'm not looking forward to that, either. It *should* be a simple matter. I mean, we should have divorced long ago . . . But something tells me he's going to make it complicated. And very nasty."

"That's all right," replied Natalie. "Daniel will be here to hold your hand."

"He's coming in November." She smiled, and the light returned to her eyes. "If everything works out the way I hope it will, I'll be going to Ireland in the spring. I'm going to take a month off. I think we need time over there . . . To see how I fit in, or *if* I fit in. I'm sure it's an altogether different life."

"Mother?"

Miranda looked up. Andrew was standing in the doorway. He was tall for his age, almost as tall as she. His hair, thick and straight, was a deep copper color. His freckles had faded; his braces had been removed. He was a handsome boy. "What it is, darling?"

"Can I take the twins for ice cream?"

"No," said Natalie. "They're stuffed full of cake already. Those kids never stop eating!"

"Well, I sort of promised."

"You did? I'll bet they tricked you into it, the little stinkers. Okay, but only half a scoop of ice cream in each cone. Don't forget."

"I won't, Aunt Natalie. Thanks."

"You have a brave boy, Miranda," she said when he had gone. "I don't know anyone else who has the nerve to take my kids to an ice-cream parlor . . . Miranda?"

"I was wondering if he overheard our conversation." She shrugged. "I suppose not."

They left the kitchen and walked through the hall to the living room. Tom was sprawled on the couch. The Sunday papers were strewn all around him, comics and crosswords mixed in with the business pages. In the corner were the twins' birthday presents, stacks of presents from the grandparents who had come and gone, from Miranda, from other friends. The angora cat Snowflake sat atop a bookcase and washed her paw.

It was a cozy scene; to Miranda, it was everything she had missed in her own marriage. "Home sweet home," she murmured.

"You always say that."

"And I always mean it. Why do you think I'm here so often?"

Tom lowered the newspaper and glanced at Miranda over the top of his glasses. "I thought you came for the pleasure of my company."

"Yes," said Natalie, moving his leg as she sat beside him, "you're a real pleasure. Another Cary Grant." He swatted her with the paper. She laughed. "Would you like to see some new sketches, Miranda? The new spring line. *Maybe.*"

392

"No offense, but I don't want to think about business to-day."

"What!" cried Tom in mock surprise. "Natalie, I think this woman must be an impostor. She's not the Miranda Dexter *I* know."

The doorbell rang. They heard the housekeeper's brisk footsteps in the foyer, and then the sound of voices. A moment later, Lily entered the room. The Wades would not have recognized her. She was smartly, expensively dressed, her disfiguring birthmark partially disguised by makeup and an artful new hairstyle. She was more breathtaking than ever, but the greatest change was in her attitude. She had gained a measure of self-assurance, a stronger sense of who she was. She had learned to smile, and even to laugh. She had learned to appreciate life. "Did I miss the party?" she asked now, looking around the room. "Where are the twins?"

"Andrew took them for ice cream," replied Natalie. "It wasn't much of a party; just us and our folks."

Lily put her presents with the others. Gently, she lifted Snowflake from the bookcase. She stroked the soft fur. "Whenever I see a cat I think about Mrs. Wade's aviary. Does she still have all those birds?"

"Hundreds, said Miranda. "Thousands, for all I know."

Tom sat up. He took off his glasses and rubbed the bridge of his nose. "Help yourself to a drink, Lily. We have a head start on you."

Lily poured a small sherry. "Anybody else? Miranda?"

"No, thanks. I'm just waiting for Andrew and then I'm off. Is that a Natalie original you're wearing?"

"A special design."

"That silk is from France," explained Natalie. "It cost the earth. I'm doing the cheap version in cotton."

Again the doorbell rang. The twins tumbled into the room, and like hounds on the scent, they made straight for the new presents. Wrapping paper and ribbons went flying. Snowflake jumped out of Lily's arms, chasing a shiny red bow.

393

Miranda watched for a moment. A happy family, she thought, rising to her feet. "Are you ready, Andrew? We ought to be going."

He nodded. With all the dignity of his thirteen years, he held out his hand to Natalie, Lily, and Tom. "I had a very nice time," he said.

"Very nice of you to come, old chap," replied Tom, hiding a smile.

Miranda kissed the twins and said her good-byes. Andrew held the door as they left the apartment. They rode downstairs in silence, though he kept glancing quizzically at Miranda. "Are you going to Ireland?" he asked when they emerged into the bright sunlight.

She realized he had overheard at least part of her conversation. She frowned. "I've been thinking about it. I haven't had a vacation in a long time, Andrew. I'd like to visit Ireland."

"Without Father?"

"Yes. Your father and I . . ." She paused. What could she say that he would understand? That wouldn't worry him? "Your father and I have different interests now. It happens sometimes with married people. Sometimes it's best to . . . to be apart."

"Are you and Father going to get a divorce?"

The bluntness of his question surprised Miranda. She believed it was wrong to lie to children, and yet she knew she had to be careful. "Why do you ask?"

"Chip Lockwood's parents are getting a divorce. It's terrible at their house. Everybody's always mad. And Mrs. Lockwood cries a lot. She always says she has a cold, but she doesn't. I can tell."

"Your father and I aren't mad at each other, darling. It's nothing like that . . . I can't predict the future. The thing to remember is we both love you *very* much. No matter what happens, our love for you won't change. Parents never stop loving their children."

"Never?"

"*Never*. No matter what." Miranda wanted to gather him

394

into her arms, to cradle him the way she had when he was little. Instead she put her hand on his shoulder, smiling into his clear blue eyes. "You're stuck with us, young man. Like it or not. Now how about a kiss for your old mom? Just one?"

"I'm not a baby, you know."

"Oh, I know. But humor me. I really need a kiss."

Andrew looked around to see if anybody was watching. He turned and pecked Miranda's cheek. "I love you, too," he mumbled, flushing.

"Thank you, darling. I'll remember that when you're away at school . . . When I'm missing you."

Peter and Miranda drove their son to Groton. They unloaded suitcases filled with clothes and books, unloaded skis and ice skates and tennis rackets and an old baseball glove. They saw Andrew's room, had a few words with the headmaster, and then, after a tearful farewell, they drove back to New York. They hardly spoke during the ride home. The last bond between them, perhaps the only bond, had been broken; there was simply nothing to say.

Things were no cheerier at the Wade house, where they found Jonah staring fixedly at a newspaper. "Here," he snapped, thrusting the paper at them. "See for yourselves."

Miranda saw the big black headline: Hitler Invades Poland. "Dear God," she murmured.

"It's just the beginning," declared Jonah. "Mark my words, it's just the beginning. The bloody fool is out to conquer the world."

"I remember the last war," said Daphne.

"War!" exclaimed Miranda. "But surely you don't think there'll be a war?"

Jonah threw his cigar into an ashtray. "If there is, it's no concern of ours."

"I remember the songs," said Daphne.

Songs? Miranda frowned. "What songs?"

"It was such a romantic time."

Miranda glanced at Peter. He shrugged.

"I remember too, my pet," said Jonah. His voice had grown softer, infinitely more gentle. He clasped Daphne's hand and his eyes seemed to glitter. "Shall we have an early night?"

She rose and walked with him to the door. "Cook left some sandwiches for you," she said, looking back at Miranda. "Addy will bring a tray . . . Good night."

"Good night, Daphne."

Miranda looked again at the newspaper headline. "There won't be a war. There can't be."

"Not over Poland, anyway. Of course crazy Adolf may not stop at Poland. Have you seen him in the newsreels? Did you notice his eyes? The guy's nutty as a fruitcake, but he has big plans. Jonah's right — Hitler's out to conquer the world."

Miranda was not thinking about the world; she was thinking about Daniel. If there were war, he would be in it. "I'm going upstairs now."

"Don't you want to eat?"

"No, I'm not hungry. Good night, Peter."

"Good night."

Wearily, Miranda climbed the stairs. She walked through the silent hall, stopping outside Andrew's room. She opened the door, switched on the lights, and gazed around. Most of the shelves were empty; all the familiar clutter was gone. With a sigh, she switched off the lights and closed the door.

She went to her own room. The bed had been turned down and her nightgown had been folded atop the quilt. The latest Agatha Christie waited on the nightstand. A single light burned. She kicked off her shoes and went to the vanity table, pulling open the drawer. Toward the back was a small trinket box which she used for hairpins. She dumped the pins out, reaching into the secret compartment for a folded sheet of paper. It was a page from one of Daniel's letters; it was the comfort she needed tonight. By the light of the tulip lamp she read his words.

". . . I've bought a cottage near the sea. It's just two hours from Dublin—a wee village, Carley by name. I come here alone and I try to come at night, when the moon turns the waves to silver and the sand is white beneath my feet. Do you remember our ferry ride? This is better, lass. There are mists rolling off the high cliffs. There are fishing boats nestled by the cove after the day's work is done. There are gulls drunk on moonlight and the Irish Sea. Why aren't you here with me now? Why . . ."

Miranda looked up as she heard Peter enter his room. His door closed and she continued reading.

"Why aren't you with me when the moon is shining and the waves are crashing on the shore and the gulls are dancing a jig. This is our kingdom by the sea. It's . . ."

Miranda did not finish, for suddenly she heard a woman's screams. She realized they were Daphne's screams, and quickly she jumped to her feet. She stuffed the letter in her pocket. She rushed to the hall, almost colliding with Peter. "It's Daphne," she said.

They sprinted to her room, but the door was locked. They pounded on it and Daphne's screams grew louder.

"What's happened?" cried Addy, running down the stairs. "Is it murder?"

"Do you have a key to this room?"

"No, sir. You'd have to go through Mr. Wade's room."

The three of them rushed to Jonah's room and burst through the door. It was dark; they could not find the lightswitch. "Damn," muttered Peter as he banged into a chair.

They stumbled into the sitting room. "We're coming, Daphne," called Miranda, and now the screams turned to shrieks.

It was Addy who found the lightswitch in Daphne's room. They all blinked when the lights came on. In the very next instant they froze, for they saw Jonah's nude body slumped atop Daphne. She was still shrieking. She seemed to be pinned underneath him, unable to move, unable to shift his heavy, lifeless form.

"Christ," murmured Peter. He rushed to the bed,

Miranda and Addy following a step behind. He grabbed Jonah's wrist, feeling for a pulse. "Christ," he said again.

"Is Jonah . . . Is he . . ."

"As a doornail." Peter turned and drew Addy away. "It's too late for an ambulance. I guess you'd better call the police."

"Yes, sir," she said, hurrying off.

Miranda picked up Daphne's nightgown from the floor and threw it on a chair. She reached for a blanket. "Peter, I need your help. We have to—"

"Yes, I know what we have to do. It's damned awkward."

Peter tugged and pushed at Jonah's inert body. Daphne's shrieks ceased as Miranda pulled her out of the bed and wrapped her in a blanket. "I'm so sorry, Daphne. I—I don't know what to say . . . Come into the other room and sit down. I'll get you some brandy."

"I couldn't breathe, you see."

"Yes, I . . . I'm really so sorry. Is there . . . Are you all right?"

"I think it was his heart."

Chapter Twenty-three

Wade & Company closed on the day of Jonah's funeral. More than six hundred people crowded the church to pay their last respects. Daphne was seated in the front pew, her head bowed, her face hidden by a heavy black veil. Beside her was Miranda, pale and still. Beside Miranda was Andrew, hastily summoned back to New York after only twenty-four hours at Groton. Beside Andrew was Peter, looking tired, looking drained.

The reverend Dr. Wisdom eulogized Jonah as a man of "decency and conviction, a man, who like his fathers before him, sought always to do good. Jonah Wade's good works are known to us. We celebrate them, for in them is the measure of the man who today resides with God."

When the service concluded, limousines carried fifty people to the burial at Woodlawn Cemetery, and afterward to a cold buffet lunch at the Wade house. Daphne seemed a bit puzzled, but in all other ways she was a thoughtful and serene hostess. Her guests murmured condolences, murmured the polite phrases that were expected and that meant nothing. They were not sorry when the time came to leave, nor was anyone sorry to see them go.

"You ought to lie down for a while," said Miranda to Daphne. "Let me take you upstairs."

"Upstairs?"

"To your room."

"Oh, yes, I see. But Mr. Harrington says there must be a reading of the will." The will. Miranda's eyes swept across the living room to the attorney, Porter Harrington. He stood apart from the others who had been asked to stay. She noticed that Lily was among the group, as were several cousins and several long time employees of Wade's. "It's probably best to get it over with," she conceded.

"Money, you know."

"Money?"

"Why, yes. There's always a fuss over money, isn't there?"

Miranda had no chance to reply, for Mr. Harrington had stepped forward.

"If you will all be seated," he said, settling into a chair by the fireplace. He removed a folded document from his coat pocket and turned to the second page. "I apologize for what might appear to be undue haste, but there are business matters pending. In the circumstances, it's necessary to ensure a smooth transition. If that is understood, we may proceed."

"By all means," said Peter, lighting a cigarette.

"There are various charitable bequests—to the church, to foreign missions, so forth and so on. We can dispense with those for now." Mr. Harrington cleared his throat. " 'I, Jonah Wade . . .' " he began.

It was a surprisingly generous will. Cook, Lily, and four of Wade's oldest employees, including Malcolm Gill, each received five thousand dollars. Jonah's recently retired secretary, Martin Wilkes, received fifteen thousand dollars. As had been arranged, these people left the room immediately after their bequests were read.

The cousins' bequests were read next. "And the will also specifies," added Mr. Harrington, "that your incomes from the Wade trust are to continue as before."

The cousins took their leave. Remaining in the room were Daphne, Miranda, Andrew, and Peter. Peter lighted another cigarette. He was tense, for he knew they were coming now to the heart of the matter: the future of Wade & Company.

"The last portion of the will is extremely complicated," continued Mr. Harrington. "Perhaps if I simplify—"

"Anything," said Peter, "but get on with it."

"Very well . . . 'To my most beloved wife Daphne, I bequeath the house in Murray Hill, and all its contents, for the duration of her life.' The attorney looked up. "That is known as a 'life trust,' Mrs. Wade. It simply means that this house remains yours to enjoy during your lifetime. It may not be sold or mortgaged. Upon your death—in the very distant future, we all hope—the house passes to your grandson Andrew. If Andrew is not of legal age at that time, his named trustee is Miranda Wade Dexter . . . Do you understand?"

Daphne blinked. "I always thought it was quite a nice house."

"Yes . . . Yes, well, to continue . . . You are of course the sole beneficiary of Mr. Wade's life insurance, which is in the amount of two hundred thousand dollars. In addition, you are the sole heir to Mr. Wade's personal assets: a bond portfolio currently valued in excess of fifty thousand dollars, and four bank accounts with a current worth in excess of two hundred thousand dollars . . . Do you have any questions, Mrs. Wade?"

Daphne shook her head.

"As to the Wade trust; Jonah Wade held the majority position in the trust and that now passes to Andrew Wade. His trustee is Miranda Dexter." Mr. Harrington turned a page. He took a tiny sip of sherry, replaced the glass on the table, and again cleared his throat. He read' " 'The best interests of Wade and Company must be considered above all else. I therefore bequeath my holdings, in equal shares, to my grandson Andrew Wade, and to Miranda Wade Dexter, for the duration of her life.'" The attorney paused. He looked at Miranda. "This is another life trust. Upon your death, your holdings will pass to Andrew . . . Do you understand?"

Her lips parted but she said nothing. She had had no inkling of Jonah's plans for Wade & Company; in the confusion of the last few days, she had had little time to speculate. Now she felt Peter's eyes on her. She heard Porter Harrington's impatient sigh. "Yes, I understand."

"Then I will proceed. 'Further, I name Miranda Wade Dexter to succeed me as president of Wade and Company, to serve until such time as she judges Andrew Wade ready to assume his duties.'"

Peter leaped up. He looked at the attorney, glared at Miranda, and then turned and stalked out of the room.

"Mr. Dexter," called Porter Harrington, "there is a final bequest to you . . . Mr. Dexter?"

"What's the matter with Father?" asked Andrew. "Did he want to be president instead of you?"

"Yes, maybe he did . . . I'm sorry, Mr. Harrington, but it's been a long day. Are we finished here?"

"The final bequest to Mr. Dexter is in the amount of twenty thousand dollars. Mr. Wade has also stated his wish that you retain Mr. Dexter in his present position . . . That concludes the will."

Daphne rose. "Thank you for coming, Mr. Harrington. Shall I see you out?"

"Don't trouble; I'll find my way. Good afternoon, Mrs. Wade, Mrs. Dexter. Andrew."

"Good-bye, Mr. Harrington."

The attorney left. Miranda took a breath, trying to absorb the fact that she was the new president of Wade & Company, that for all intents and purposes she *owned* Wade & Company. Her emotions were mixed. Half of her was deliriously happy, but the other half felt trapped. She thought about Daniel, about the plans they had made. She thought about a wee village in Ireland, Carley by name.

"Mother?"

"What?" She looked around. "Oh, I'm sorry, Andrew. I was . . . daydreaming. Are you all right, darling?"

He nodded. "But it's getting late."

Miranda glanced at her watch. "Yes, of course. Run along upstairs and collect your things. Tom should be coming back with his car any minute."

"I could take the train to school."

"I'd rather Tom drove you. Run along now, Andrew." She watched him go. He had shown little grief over Jonah's death and she thought that was understandable; despite all the years he had lived in this house, he had scarcely known his grandfather. Harder to understand was Daphne. There had been the hysteria on the night Jonah died, but it seemed to have had more to do with the circumstances of his death than the death itself. Since that night there had been no tears, no signs of sorrow. A faintly puzzled expression was the only hint that something might be wrong. "How do you feel, Daphne? Would you like to talk?"

"Why, that would be lovely."

"I mean about Jonah."

Daphne's long lashes fluttered. "Jonah?"

"Well, you haven't said much. You haven't actually said anything."

"Jonah was very good to me. He *was* a good man, you know. In his own way. That's why I was glad."

"Glad?"

"There was no suffering, Miranda. It was so quick. A blessing, really." Daphne lifted her exquisite topaz eyes, smiling serenely. "We all have to die, don't we?"

Miranda called an executive meeting two days later. Added to the participants were Frank North of the advertising department, Hank Nelson of personnel, and the display director Annie Wolfe. They were all seated when Miranda entered the conference room. She saw the empty chair at the head of the table, Jonah's chair, and a lump rose in her throat. She had not forgotten her many disagreements with Jonah, nor how difficult he had sometimes been, but now she realized she would miss him. She approached his chair warily, as if she were trespassing. She opened her folder and glanced around at the faces turned in her direction. "This will be a short meeting," she said. "I have a few announcements and then I'll let you get back to work."

"Before you begin," said Harvey, "we'd all like to welcome you as our new president. We know you're the right person for the job, Miranda. You have our support one hundred percent."

She colored. "Thank you, Harvey. Thank you all." Her eyes strayed to Peter. He was twenty thousand dollars richer, but no happier. He slouched in his chair, smoking a cigarette and studying the ceiling. "I'll do my best," she said, "and the first thing I want to tell you is that there won't be any personnel changes. Please reassure all the people in your departments; everybody's job is safe . . . While I'm on the subject of personnel, I want it understood that the quota system is over. Starting today, we hire people on their merits, not their religion or their sex or anything else. All right, Hank?"

"You're the boss."

"Also I'd like to announce that starting today Tom will be doing two jobs: general manager and assistant to . . . and my assistant. We'll be working closely together — as a matter of fact, I expect we'll *all* be working closely together. That includes advertising and display. They've been the orphans around here, but from now on they'll be involved in executive decisions."

"Hallelujah," laughed Frank North.

"Lastly," continued Miranda, "there's the problem of Malcolm Gill." There was a chorus of groans. She shrugged. "I've given up trying to get him to retire. He's happy as a clam in his little office downstairs, so that's that. He's one of Wade's *traditions* and I guess I'm stuck with him. But I *do* want his office cleaned up. It's a disgrace! He doesn't even throw out his old whiskey bottles."

"He doesn't bother anyone, Miranda," said Claude Berman.

"He bothers *me*. And if I start seeing roaches or mice or worse, I'll know where they're coming from."

"I'll talk to him," offered Tom.

"It won't do a bit of good. He doesn't like you any better than he likes me. But Claude may have some influence. What do you think, Claude?"

"I'll try."

Miranda nodded. She closed her folder. "Unless there are any questions, that's all for today."

There were no questions. Several of the staff stopped to chat with Miranda, but Peter left immediately, brushing past the others on his way to the door. He was silent; the look in his eyes was murderous.

"Peter isn't taking this well, is he?" asked Tom, following Miranda into her office.

"I can't say I blame him. It's not an easy situation . . . And it was a tremendous disappointment after all. He never expected Jonah would leave the store to a woman. He thought he'd inherit Wade's by default. I was ready for that myself." Miranda sat down behind the desk that had been Jonah's. She sighed. "Somehow, Peter's plans never seem to work out."

"How about *your* plans?"

"Mine?"

"Does Ireland ring a bell?"

Her shoulders slumped. She lowered her gaze to the desk, moving a stack of papers from side to side. "My plans" she murmured.

"Yes, what about them?"

"I'm afraid the answer is obvious."

It was not obvious to Daniel. He had learned of Jonah's death shortly before his ship sailed for New York.

He had assumed that now Miranda would be free to live her own life, but when he arrived in the city he found she was busier than ever. All his high hopes came crashing down. His temper flared, for he felt betrayed.

"There's no reason for me to stay," he announced a few days after his arrival. They were in the apartment he had sublet on Gramercy Park. Rain drummed at the windows; a fire crackled in the hearth. Two tumblers of whiskey stood untouched on a table. "I'll be off to Milwaukee tonight. I can get a ten o'clock train."

"Oh, Daniel, how can I make you understand? How can I explain to—"

"And what would there be to explain? You want Wade & Company and New York and me. You want everything. Well, you can't *have* everything. You're lying to yourself if you think you can. You're leading me a merry chase, Miranda, but here is where it stops. I'll not waste my life on lies."

"I love you."

"So you say."

"It's the truth; you know it's the truth."

Daniel started to pace. His head bent, his hands thrust in his pockets, he paced from one end of the room to the other. "I'm thinking we have different ideas about love."

Miranda tensed. She was pale, tired. She was afraid, for there was something very final in the tone of his voice. "I—I didn't know this was going to happen, Daniel. How could I have known? Jonah was perfectly fine."

"It's a true shame the man's dead, but he has no part in our troubles. You don't seem to realize there'll always be someone or something keeping you tied to Wade's. You have to break the ties, or loosen them. If you don't, we have nothing."

"The store won't run itself, Daniel."

"And are you ready to give your whole life to the store? That's what you're doing. That's the top and bottom of it . . . You love me, but you've no time for me.

406

You've no time for *love*. You'd rather be worrying about profits."

"Sarcasm aside, that's my job. Daniel, we both have jobs. Why is mine less important than yours?"

"It's not. But I don't give all my days and nights to business. I don't deny myself holidays, trips. I don't . . ." He shook his head, exhaling a great breath. "It's no use, is it?"

"Daniel —"

"I didn't expect you to quit the store, you know. In the back of my mind I had it that you'd get things straight with Peter, and then marry me — that we'd spend half the year in your New York City, half the year in Dublin." He stopped pacing. He turned, staring at the leaping, whirling dance of flames upon the hearth. "That we'd have a life," he continued. "But you've no time for me here in New York City. And you've surely no time to go sailing off to Ireland. The clocks keep ticking, don't they?"

Miranda felt a chill. She clasped her hands together, hunching her shoulders as if against an icy wind. *I have to stay calm,* she warned herself. I have to stay calm or I'll go crazy. "Daniel, I know I haven't been fair to you, to us . . . But things will change. I promise you they will."

"No. You have the store and you won't trust it to anybody else."

"I can't, not yet. It's my responsibility . . . It's Andrew's inheritance."

"You've made your choice, then."

Miranda flung herself from the couch and ran to him. "Please, Daniel," she cried, her hands fast on his shoulders. "Please give me more time."

"It's a strange pair we are, Miranda Wade. We've got it all backwards, haven't we? Most men would be happy to have a mistress instead of a wife. And most women see it the other way round. But here *we* are, turning everything upside down." He stroked her hair. He sighed. "There's no more time, lass." He took her hands from his shoulders. He took a step, two, and then her hands were on him again. She kissed him, pressing her lips, her body, to his. *"No,"* he said, stepping back. "I want you, Miranda. I'll want you till I'm dead and buried in my cold grave. But we can't solve anything this way. It's false."

"What's going to happen to us?"

Daniel could not think clearly when Miranda was so close. He walked a safe distance away. "I'm leaving for Milwaukee tonight."

"I see." She stood very still, hugging her waist. "And then?"

"When my business is finished, I'm going home. To Dublin. To Carley. Home."

Through a mist of tears she searched Daniel's face. "Don't — don't you love me anymore?"

"I'll always love you, lass. You're in my blood. But I won't settle for bits and pieces of time, for stolen moments . . . I want what I want; I'm not a man to take less."

Silence fell between them, silence broken only by the hiss of the fire, the steady tattoo of the rain. Miranda was white. Her eyes were vacant, staring at the floor, staring at nothing at all. She groped for a chair and clung to it, as if for dear life. "In a year or two, the store won't need so much attention. My attention, I mean."

"We may not have a year or two. The world may be caught up in war. Todays are what matter now, lass, not tomorrows."

The room seemed to blur. She touched her hand to her temple. "Yes," she murmured. "Yes, you're right. I . . . suppose I should go."

Daniel wanted to sweep her into his arms. He wanted to sweep away the words that had been spoken here, but he knew it would do no good. It would change nothing, for change had to come from Miranda. He looked at the streaming windows. He felt a tightness in his throat, in his chest. He felt utterly alone. "I'll put you in a taxicab, then."

"No, you mustn't bother."

"Miranda—"

"Please don't say any more. I couldn't bear it."

She snatched up her coat and purse and ran out the door. She thought she was going to be sick. She lurched down the flight of stairs, lingering briefly in the foyer. Crying, gasping for breath, she pulled open the door and ran outside.

The rain soaked through her clothes. She shivered, walking blindly in the direction of Murray Hill. She stumbled, almost colliding with a lamppost. She crossed the street against the light, oblivious to the screeching brakes, the angry chorus of car horns. The cold, the wet, seeped into her bones. She hoped she would get pneumonia. She hoped she would die.

She came down with a cold. For a week she sneezed and sniffled and coughed and wearily refused the various remedies offered to her. She showed no interest in her health or anything else. She was like a sleepwalker, devoid of emotion, moving by rote.

"You have to snap out of it, Miranda," said Tom a month later. "I'm worried about you. We're *all* worried."

"I'm fine."

"The hell you are! I can't remember the last time I saw you smile. All the life's gone out of you."

She glanced around the study that had been Jonah's and now was hers. "You had some memos for me to sign?"

"Don't you want to read them?"

"I read the first drafts. They were all right."

Tom sat back in his chair and lighted a cigarette. "What about the bridal department?"

"What about it? We could stock wedding gowns made of paper bags and they'd still fly off the racks. The bridal department is money in the bank." Miranda's voice was flat. Her gaze wandered idly across the desk. "I told Annie she could order new carpeting, but that's all. There's no need to redesign the department."

"Okay." Tom took several memos and reports from his briefcase and placed them before Miranda. She initialed them. "Thanks," he said. "I'll get these to Harvey and Jeff first thing Monday morning."

Miranda rose. "Daphne's waiting for me upstairs. She has some sort of surprise . . . Do you want to stay to dinner?"

Tom shook his head. "Natalie and I have plans. What with work and the kids and the grandparents dropping in all the time, we try to save Saturday nights for ourselves. Why don't you join us, Miranda? It's just dinner, and maybe a movie. A night out would do you a world of good."

"No, I don't think so. Would you mind letting yourself out?"

Tom picked up his briefcase. "See you Monday."

"Good night, Tom."

Miranda went upstairs. She knocked at the door of Daphne's sitting room and went inside. She saw Daphne. She saw the surprise: two yellow canaries in a large and ornate brass cage. "They're charming," she said. "Do they sing?"

"Oh, yes," replied Daphne. "I expressly asked for songbirds. Come and see them, Miranda."

She walked over to the cage and peered through the bars. There were two of everything: birds, perches, feeders, fountains, and even two tiny swings. The birds were about the same size, though one of them was much brighter in color.

"That's Jonah," explained Daphne. "I think his namesake would be pleased, don't you?"

"And the other one?"

"Why, Daphne, of course."

Miranda nodded. "Yes, of course. They've certainly found a good home."

"You may come and see them whenever you wish."

"Thank you, Daphne. But if you'll excuse me now, I'd like a bath before dinner." She started toward the door, stopping when she glimpsed a frilly box of chocolates. "Is that yours? I've never seen you eat candy."

"Oh, I haven't for years and years. But I don't have to watch my figure anymore, do I? I don't plan to marry again; I can eat whatever I want. Isn't that nice?"

"Yes, very nice."

A happy widowhood, thought Miranda; birds and chocolates. She left Daphne and went directly to her own room. She switched on the lights and sank down on the bed. Next to her, sitting atop the bedside table, was a dried, faded bouquet of violets—the bouquet Daniel had sent before he returned to Dublin. There had been a card, simply signed "Good-bye." She had torn the card to pieces, but she had kept the flowers. A remembrance, she thought now, of what might have been hers.

"Miranda?"

She turned her head. Peter was standing in the doorway. "What is it?"

"I just ran into Bob Selkirk. He asked if we'd like to come to dinner. It's all very last minute. An old friend of theirs arrived unexpectedly. They're having a small dinner party."

"No, I don't think so. You go along, if you want."

Peter took a step into the room. "You've been acting strangely, Miranda. What on earth's the matter with you?"

"Nothing. I'm fine."

"You *should* be fine. You've got everything you wanted. Everything you touch turns to money."

"Lucky me."

"I'd say so, yes."

"Do we have to argue?"

"I wasn't arguing; I was stating facts. You were born lucky."

"Born lucky," said Miranda with a frigid smile. "Born

411

lucky." She sat up, fixing her eyes on Peter. "I've made my own luck, and not all of it good. You're right about one thing: I wanted Wade's and I got it. My great and glittering prize, except now my whole life has to revolve around the store. Except now the store has to come first. You know the old saying—be careful what you wish for."

"Poor Miranda. You're breaking my heart . . . This new pose of yours isn't very attractive. You actually seem to expect sympathy. Sympathy!"

She glanced up. "Is that what you think?"

"What *should* I think? You mope around, looking like death. Christ, you even keep dead flowers." He plucked the bouquet from the vase, scattering dried petals across the floor. "Positively morbid," he said, throwing the rest in the wastebasket. "Would you care to trade places? I'm willing. Wade's would have been mine if you hadn't come along . . . You and your damned charts," he went on, growing angrier with each word. "You and that damned adding machine you have in your head. You and your damned luck. You're always in the right place at the right time, aren't you?"

"Peter—"

"You were nothing when you came to New York. *Nothing.* A fat, ugly girl. A *lump.* That's what Jonah used to call you, you know: 'that great lump of a girl'—that's what he used to say . . . And now you have everything. Everything but love. Love is *so* important to women, isn't it? How does it feel to know that no one will ever love you?" Savagely, Peter kicked the wastebasket, sending it flying. *"No one,"* he roared, slamming out of the room.

Tears stung Miranda's eyes and rolled down her cheeks. She fell to her knees, gathering the scattered petals. "Daniel loved me," she murmured. "Oh, God, Daniel loved me."

Peter's cruel, sudden words had wounded Miranda,

but they had jolted her, too. They had broken through her lethargy; like a splash of cold water, they had roused her. She stopped feeling sorry for herself, and though she could not, would not forget Daniel, she tried to continue with her life.

It was a life composed largely of work. She was at her desk every morning by eight, and often she remained past the store's six o'clock closing. Most nights she took work home, but she also made time for dinners with Natalie and Tom, and parties at the Russells and the Selkirks. She looked forward to Andrew's school holidays and she spent hours planning the activities he would enjoy. It was not an easy task, for Andrew was growing up. He had lost his interest in cartoons and cowboy movies. When Miranda took him to the theater, it was the long-legged chorus girls he noticed, though he was still young enough to blush.

"He's at that in-between age," said Miranda shortly after his fourteenth birthday. "Too old for toys, too young for girls."

"Don't be so sure," replied Natalie. She stood beside a mannequin, adjusting the sleeve on one of her designs. A moment later she stepped back and looked at the other displays in the Natalie Inc. department. "Kids have secret lives."

"Not Andrew. At least not yet. He turns beet red around pretty girls. He gets tongue-tied . . . I wish he could stay fourteen for a while."

"Afraid he'll cut the apron strings?" asked Natalie with a quick smile.

"Oh, he's cut them already. It's not apron strings I'm worried about; it's war. I hate to read the newspapers now. There are all those stories about Hitler on the march."

Natalie took a last glance at the displays. "It'll be over by the time Andrew's old enough to fight. Even if America *does* get into it, and I don't think we will."

"War is contagious."

413

"I've seen enough here, Miranda. I wouldn't put in more displays. It's fine as it is. But *when* do I get a window?"

"Next month. Natalie Inc. is scheduled for the prize summer window of the season: the lawn party window."

"And I deserve it! C'mon, let's go have lunch."

They walked through the crowded aisles to the elevator. Miranda pressed the button. "I wish someone would shoot Hitler," she said.

But Hitler and his armies continued to inflict death and destruction. All during the next year, newspapers were filled with increasingly dire predictions. These predictions were proved true, for in the summer of 1940 the Third French Empire ceased to exist and the Battle of Britain began.

By August, after devastating attacks on British airfields and radar stations, the battle shifted to London. For fifty-seven nights Luftwaffe planes blitzed the city, killing thousands of people and destroying, in whole or in part, more than a million buildings. There was no longer any doubt of Hitler's intentions. There was no doubt that worse was yet to come.

Early in 1941 Natalie brought Miranda a letter from Daniel. He was a lieutenant serving with his regiment in an undisclosed location. He was married.

". . . I knew Sally long ago, when we were both very young. We met again after the Blitz. She lost her husband in the bombings, and a while later she came to Ireland with her daughter. Jane's a darling lass, almost seven now, and just starting to get over what happened to her da. Sally may never get over it. She needed somebody, and so did I, and so did the little one.

"Sally and I have no secrets between us. I told her about you—about the great love of my life . . ."

Miranda could not read any more. The letter slipped from her hand and drifted to the floor.

Natalie picked it up. "Are you okay?"

"Daniel's married."

"I know. He put a note in with the letter. A note to me. He was worried about your reaction."

"I'm fine." Miranda stood. She wandered across her office to the window. Snarled lines of morning traffic moved slowly along Fifth Avenue. Pedestrians crowded the sidewalks. A long-haired woman in a black cape carried a sign that said Beware the End of the World. "I should have known he'd marry sooner or later. I guess I didn't want to think about it."

Natalie read the letter. Frowning, she laid it on Miranda's desk. "He still loves you; married or not, he still loves you."

"I had my chance."

"You had a choice to make. I don't see what else you could have done."

"Don't you?"

Natalie shrugged. "It's a wartime marriage. They don't last."

Miranda turned. She went to her desk and sat down. She glanced again at the letter and then tore it to shreds. "To show you what a rat I am, I hope you're right . . . Only I want Daniel to be happy. Like you and Tom. I've always envied you and Tom." She looked up. "You are happy, aren't you?"

"Yes. But it's not a grand passion. What's the expression? A fire in the blood? It's not that. I love Tom and he loves me, but it's no blazing fire; it's comfortable. It's exactly what I want. And Tom. After all his years of catting around, it's exactly what he wants, too . . . You and Daniel are different. With you two, it'll always be a love affair. Weak knees, fluttery hearts. Moonlight and roses all the way."

"Violets."

"Okay, moonlight and violets, then. That's what you two were made for. I'll give you odds he doesn't have it with Sally."

Miranda swept the shredded letter into the wastebasket. A faint smile hovered about her mouth. "I'm keeping you from work."

"True," agreed Natalie, looking at her watch. "But remember what I said. Wartime; what happens in wartime doesn't count."

"Go on to work, Natalie. Go make me rich."

"Guaranteed," she replied, turning toward the door. "How about dinner tonight? Tom is cooking his famous spaghetti."

"Thanks, but I don't think so."

Natalie paused at the door. "You're not going to get yourself into another funk, are you?"

"Only one to a customer. I've already had mine."

"Good girl!"

The door opened. Peter brushed past Natalie. "The ladies' fang and claw society is meeting early this morning," he said.

"I love you, too," she snapped, closing the door behind her.

"What does she want now, Miranda? More space? More advertising? What?"

"We were talking about war."

"War?"

"You know: that little mess in Europe?"

"*Europe* is the operative word," said Peter. "This is America."

"Oh, we won't escape. We'll be part of it . . . We'll be part of it; just wait and see."

Chapter Twenty-four

They did not have long to wait; for on December 7, 1941, Japanese planes bombed American naval bases at Pearl Harbor.

Miranda was working in her study when the first news bulletins came over the radio. She called to Daphne and Peter, motioning them inside. "Listen," she said, turning up the volume.

Early reports were horrifying. Later reports were worse. They told of bombs raining from the sky, of battle-ships going down in flames, their crews trapped aboard, of chaos and destruction and death.

In the Wade house there was profound shock. There was grief, and at the last, anger. "The bastards!" cried Peter. "The dirty sneaking bastards!"

Even Daphne appeared shaken by the news. "What a terrible thing to do," she murmured, a rare frown touching her smooth brow. "I really don't understand it at all."

Miranda was as silent as a statue, and as white. Her fingernails dug into the palms of her clenched hands. Her mouth was a taut line. She had only one thought: Andrew. He was in his last year at Groton, due to enter Yale in the fall. But would he? He was young, and wars always took the young.

"There's no need for Andrew to go right away," said Peter, as if reading her thoughts. "There's no need to rush into anything. We'll insist he finish his schooling. No nonsense about enlisting. We'll insist and that's all there is to it."

Miranda knew that Peter was trying to reassure himself, but she also knew her son — an easygoing young man who could dig in his heels when he chose to. "Maybe we're jumping to conclusions," she said, though without much conviction. "You can't be sure he'll want to enlist."

"Boys his age think war is romantic. A great adventure."

Daphne stirred in her chair. "The last war . . . It *was* a romantic time, you see. Of course we didn't have radio then."

They looked at her.

"To hear all these unpleasant things," she continued. "It was different." She rose. "There's comfort in what one doesn't know," she added a moment before she left the room.

"Daphne finally said something I agree with," muttered Peter.

He and Miranda remained in the study. Every bit of news, whether from Hawaii or Washington, was debated and analyzed, for there was a desperate need to believe that things were not as grim as they seemed to be. But the truth, as news reports became less emotional and more hard-edged, was inescapable. A formal declaration was still a day away, but America was at war.

Addy brought coffee and sandwiches. Peter smoked cigarette after cigarette. At six o'clock they tried to telephone Andrew, but the phone lines were hopelessly jammed. They tried again at seven, and at eight.

"We'll have to wait till morning," said Miranda.

Peter nodded. He was almost fifty and he looked every one of his years. "You'd better give some thought to the store, Miranda. Contingency plans."

"I can't think about it tonight."

"You might as well. There are going to be a lot of problems." He ran his hand through his graying hair. He reached for the brandy, pouring some into his coffee. "A

418

mountain of problems, and they're all yours."

A personnel shortage was the first problem Miranda faced in the early months of the war. More than a dozen of Wade's younger male employees enlisted immediately. Others followed, nearly emptying the shipping department and leaving stockrooms in disarray. "The real trouble," said Hank Nelson in March of the new year, "is going to come with the draft. Thirty percent of the guys who are left are of draft age. There's talk that some of the kids at the warehouse already received their notices."

"They'll take the single men first," said Miranda. "We don't have many single men left. And the ones we have . . . Well, you know . . . sissy boys. The Army won't take sissy boys."

Miranda sighed. "I'll keep that in mind, Hank."

"We don't have to worry about salesclerks. I can hire enough women to cover the counters. But looking ahead, we have problems in shipping and receiving—"

"You can hire women to process orders. That will free some of the men to do the heavy work."

"Possibly. Possibly . . . I don't know, though. Men and women working together in the basement."

Again, Miranda sighed. "Oh yes," she said. "A very seductive place, the basement."

"You know how people talk."

"Let them. We have a store to run."

"I *hope* we have a store to run."

"We got through the Depression; we'll get through this."

Miranda repeated those words often in the next two months, for it was a chaotic time. Employees kept leaving; new employees had to be hired and trained. Rationing had begun, affecting both the store's suppliers and the store's customers. Space had to be found and designated for air raid shelters. Blackout curtains had to be ordered for the offices. There were endless meetings, and arguments over the smallest details. Because of wartime regulations, there was twice as much paperwork. Every day, or

419

so it seemed, there was another crisis.

New York was filled with young servicemen on their way overseas, and many of them came to Wade's. Miranda instituted a discount for military personnel. She organized war bond drives for the store's employees, starting them off with a contribution of five thousand dollars. In the spring she announced that the store would match all contributions raised by the various departments.

Late that spring, Miranda, Peter, and Daphne drove to Groton for Andrew's graduation. Miranda cried throughout the ceremony; Peter snapped pictures with his Brownie; Daphne gazed at the trees, in search of birds.

After the ceremony, after all the good-byes had been said, Miranda handed Andrew a set of car keys. "There's a convertible waiting for you in New York. A gift from your father and me."

He smiled, though his clear blue eyes clouded. "It's swell, Mom. It's really swell . . . but I wish you hadn't."

"You deserve it, darling. We're so proud of you."

"That's not what I meant."

Miranda was certain she knew precisely what he meant. She glanced away, taking his arm. "Come, let's see if your father needs some help with the packing. Come along, Daphne."

"Are we leaving?"

"As soon as we get Andrew's things into the car."

They walked to Peter's dark-blue Cadillac. He was hunched over the trunk, arranging suitcases and books and tennis rackets. The trunk would not close. He cursed, impatiently rearranging everything. On his third try he got the trunk closed and locked. "We're all set," he called.

They climbed into the car. Andrew and Daphne shared the back seat. She was sixty now, a radiant sixty. Weekly visits to the beauty shop had maintained the rich chestnut color of her hair. Her skin was as smooth and unlined as a child's. Her topaz eyes still seemed to shine from within. She had gained twenty pounds since Jonah's death, but the extra weight merely enhanced her figure. Dressed in yellow from head to toe, she looked lovely. Free to take care of her birds, to eat whatever she wanted, to shop all day, she was a happy woman.

Miranda, sitting in the front seat next to Peter, was far from happy. Her eyes went to the rear-view mirror. She studied Andrew's reflection, heard the jingle of car keys in his hand. He won't need a car, she thought to herself, if he plans to enlist. "I understand the Dempseys invited you to spend July at the Cape. Bill Dempsey's a very nice boy."

"I always work at the store in July, Mom."

"It's not a law. We can make other arrangements. Wouldn't you rather spend the month swimming and sailing? Think of all the pretty girls at the summer dances."

"No, I think I ought to stay in New York."

Peter's eyes darted to the rearview mirror. "Why?"

"I just think I should, Dad."

"No one in their right mind wants to spend July in New York. You must have a reason."

"We don't have to talk about it now."

"Now is as good a time as any. Spit it out, Andrew."

"Well, I'm going to spend the summer at home, and then—"

"And then you're going to Yale."

"No, Dad, I'm going to enlist."

"Over my dead body," said Peter, his hands tightening on the wheel. "You're going to Yale. Period, end of discussion."

Andrew shook his coppery head. "I don't see it that way, Dad."

"I didn't ask how you saw it. Your mother and I agree that you have to finish your education . . . You won't change the course of the war by enlisting, you know. You won't change a damn thing . . . Your responsibility now is to get an education. After that—well, whatever you do after that will be up to you."

"I'm sorry, Dad, but I have to do what I think is right." He turned his head. "Can you understand, Mom?"

Miranda had listened closely to the exchange, her heart sinking like a stone. "I don't understand why you're in such a rush," she replied. "The war isn't going to end overnight. They never do. They go on and on . . . You'd be of more use to the Army if you had some education behind you. Some seasoning." She swiveled around and gazed into his eyes. "The Army needs officers just as much as it needs enlisted men. If you had a year or two of college—"

"No, Mom. I'm sorry, but I'm not going to wait."

Miranda heard the quiet certainty in his voice. She recognized the determined lift of his chin. "You've made up your mind, then?"

He nodded. "Jim and I decided to sign up together."

"Sign up?" said Peter. "You're not talking about a golf tournament. War is serious business."

"I know, Dad."

"It's not like the movies."

"I know."

"How *could* you know? You're so young, Andrew."

"Dad, I just want to do my part. You and Mom raised me to do what was right. And when a guy's country is attacked . . . Heck, you know what I mean. I'm not trying to be a hero or anything. I'm not trying to be John Wayne."

"John Wayne! He'll be sitting nice and cozy in Hollywood while you're risking your life. John Wayne indeed! The only war he ever fought was in the movies."

"Such a handsome man," said Daphne.

Andrew laughed. His grandmother had always been a great curiosity to him, for she had never really seemed to be of this world. She was nothing like his friends' grandmothers. She asked no questions, offered no advice; most of the time she barely noticed him. Since Jonah's death she had been more generous with gifts, cash especially, but her affections were still limited to vague smiles and feathery pats on the shoulder. She was a stranger to him, a pleasant, beautiful, puzzling stranger. "Do you understand why I want to enlist, Gran?"

422

"Well, one's duty . . . Jonah's mother, your great-grandmother, felt strongly that we all must do our duty."

"Aha!" crowed Andrew with a disarming smile. "See—"

"I don't give a damn about great-grandmothers," replied Peter. "Stupid, silly old ladies—" Miranda poked him. Scowling, he bent his head over the wheel. "We're talking about *war*."

They talked about it all the way home, though Andrew's position remained the same. Miranda said very little, for she knew the argument had been lost before it began. Despite her fears, she was proud of Andrew. In many respects he had had a privileged childhood, but he had not come out of it with any exalted notions, with any inclination to find the easy way out. Like millions of other young men, poor and rich and in between, he wanted to serve his country. Like millions of other women—wives and sweethearts and mothers—she would hide her fears and let him go.

But letting go was not easy. All during the summer she had the feeling that every moment was the last, that every moment had to count. She was storing up memories, mental snapshots to be treasured the way old family albums were treasured.

It was no easier for Peter. He wanted to keep Andrew at his side in the time that was left; he, too, was storing up memories. But Miranda insisted that this was Andrew's time to enjoy himself, and grudgingly Peter was forced to agree. Together, they sent Andrew off to summer parties in Southampton, to sailing weekends on Long Island Sound. They watched him prepare for dates with Alison Russell and Margery Lockwood and all the other girls of his acquaintance. They slipped him extra money, and made sure he got the best tables at the Stork Club and El Morocco. There were no curfews. "Let him dance till dawn," said Peter. "There won't be any nightclubs overseas."

Andrew and his childhood friend Jim Selkirk enlisted

in the Army and were sent to Fort Dix for basic training. When their training was completed, they had five days at home before shipping out. On their last night in the city, the Dexters and the Selkirks hosted a joint farewell party. Young people thronged the house in Murray Hill. The rugs were rolled back; a rented piano hugged the wall; the buffet was laden with food. There was champagne and beer and Coca-Cola. There was an enormous cake decorated with flags and chocolate soldiers. It was a happy, noisy night.

"A great party," declared Natalie, sipping her third Scotch of the evening, "but I feel so *old*."

"Me, too," agreed Miranda. She gazed around the crowded room. "I watched most of these kids grow up. I can remember when an ice cream cone was the way to all their hearts. The strange thing is it doesn't seem that long ago."

"A lifetime ago."

"I found my first gray hair today."

"Just today? I'm a year ahead of you."

Tom laughed. "Why am I wasting my time with two old geezers? I should be talking to that blonde in the red dress."

"Never mind the blonde," said Natalie. "You have to stay here and be sympathetic."

Miranda shrugged. "Men never understand."

"Age is a state of mind, my dears," said Tom. "Look at me. I'm older than both of you and I'm happy as a clam. Look at Lily. Why, she's the belle of the ball."

They followed his gaze to where Lily stood. She wore a clinging dress of royal-blue satin, trimmed at the shoulder with tiny crystal beads. Her high-heeled shoes matched her dress. A glossy curtain of fair hair obscured the birthmark on the side of her face. There were several men around her, including Jim Selkirk's father.

"Lily's an exception," said Miranda. "She just gets more gorgeous as time passes."

"Do you suppose those guys know she used to be the

424

maid?" asked Natalie.

"Look at them. Do you suppose they'd care?" Miranda's eyes slid past Lily's admirers to the far corner of the room. Peter stood there alone, a large Scotch in his hand, a woeful expression on his face. Her eyes moved to the other side of the room, to Andrew. He was deep in conversation with Polly Craig, one of the young women he had been escorting around town. She studied his handsome profile and then quickly glanced away. "How will I ever be able to say good-bye?" she murmured.

Tom put his arm around her. "It'll be all right, Miranda."

She looked again at Andrew. "Tomorrow . . . It's so soon."

It was a clear, sunny morning when Andrew's troop ship pulled out of the harbor. The large crowd on the dock waved and shouted and blew kisses, straining for a last glimpse of the sons and husbands who were going to war. The dock was a sea of flags. Somewhere, music was playing.

"Well, he's off," said Peter, turning away. "At least he won't be going anywhere near the Pacific. We can be grateful for that."

"Yes."

"He seemed relaxed about everything. Did you notice?"

"Yes. A lot more relaxed than we must have seemed to him."

They found a taxi. Peter held the door open. "Do you feel like working today?"

"Not much, but where else would I go?"

"Right." He gave Wade's address to the driver and settled back in his seat. He was drained, all his energies spent. For the first time in many years he could look at Miranda without anger. Wade & Company was where he worked; it was a job, nothing more nor less. If he had been eclipsed by Miranda's success, it no longer mat-

425

tered.

He lighted a cigarette, exhaling a cloud of smoke. "The last war was supposed to *be* the last war."

"There'll always be wars, Peter," she said, drying her eyes.

"Between countries . . . And between men and women." He sighed. "A few years ago I was quite certain you were going to ask for a divorce. Was that my imagination?"

"No."

"What happened, then?"

Pain gripped Miranda's heart. "I changed my mind," she quietly replied.

"Oh? Well, if you still want a divorce, it's yours. But you'll have to go to Reno."

It's too late, she thought to herself. Too late. *I knew Sally long ago, when we were very young.* "I don't really see any point. Do you?"

Peter shook his head. "I've never let marriage interfere with my life. You should know that . . . But there was a time when I suspected you had a boyfriend. A little something on the side?"

"That's ridiculous."

"Is it? I was hardly a model husband. And you're a damned attractive woman."

Miranda looked at him. "Was that a compliment? It's been years since you paid me a compliment."

He dragged on his cigarette. "A lot of the time I hated you."

"I remember times when I hated you too. It hasn't been a marriage made in heaven, has it?"

"It's been a war, and I'm tired of wars. We probably can't be friends, Miranda, but we needn't be enemies. How about a truce?"

"I'd be delighted. I never wanted us to be enemies."

"It wasn't your fault."

"Don't let me off the hook so easily, Peter. I'm willing to share the blame."

426

Their taxi snaked into the crush of Fifth Avenue traffic. Peter stared out the window, watching a young sailor board a doubledecker bus. "I was thinking this morning what a wonderful job you did with Andrew."

We did. If I'm willing to share blame, you have to be willing to share credit. You were a great father."

"Yes. My one accomplishment in life."

Miranda smiled. "Now you're being dramatic."

"Perhaps."

"I'll tell you something, Peter: there's more good in you than you know. If you'd only let it come out."

"People don't change."

"You seem changed right now."

"That's because the chip on my shoulder is suddenly too heavy to carry around. I'm not as young as I used to be." He stuffed his cigarette into the ashtray and sat back. "But don't misunderstand; I'm still a bastard."

"Then I'm glad we have a truce. I'll settle for that." Fifteen years, she thought. Fifteen years of sniping at each other, of petty arguments and harsh words. Yes, she would happily settle for a truce.

Wade's came into view. "I expect we'll do well with the January sales," said Peter.

"Better than last year."

"There's always Wade's, isn't there? Come hell or high water, come the end of the world, there's always Wade and Company."

"Count your blessings," said Miranda, taking his hand.

And in the early years of the war, Wade's was indeed a blessing to them. For ten hours a day it provided distraction from their worries; it was a place to go, a place to be useful.

They immersed themselves in the war effort. They sponsored competitions amongst the departments to raise money for war bonds. They sponsored clothing drives and scrap drives. They set up collection areas for packages going to servicemen overseas. They saw to it that rationing was strictly observed. When morale flagged, they

427

sponsored company bowling teams, complete with uniforms and trophies. Peter became an air raid warden; Miranda gave time and money to the Red Cross.

At night, they settled in the study and listened to BBC broadcasts on the shortwave. They tacked a huge map to the wall, marking the progress of the war with pins. It was a sad progress. By 1943 Hitler's forces were occupying Poland, the Balkans, Holland, Belgium, Norway, Denmark, and Greece. Mussolini's forces were battling the Allies in Italy and North Africa. France had long since fallen to the collaborationist government at Vichy. England was under siege. And somewhere in the middle of this horror was Andrew.

They looked forward to Andrew's letters, though sometimes weeks passed without word, and sometimes letters came in bunches. Peter and Miranda knew he was in Italy, but that was all they knew, for military censors blacked out all references to specific locations. They both wrote to Andrew at least twice a week. They wrote to his friends as well, childhood friends who were also serving in Europe or in the Pacific Chip Lockwood was the first to die; not yet nineteen years old, he died at Guadalcanal in the winter of 1943. Peter and Miranda joined the boy's grieving family at the memorial service. Three weeks later they attended another memorial service, that one for Harvey Vaughn's eldest son, who had been killed at Anzio.

The stench of death hung over the world. Despite all the romantic movies, the songs, the flags, the reality of war was still the reality of death. Young men were dying in numbers and ways too terrible to comprehend. The lucky ones would return, but many of them would return crippled or blind or sick in heart and soul. "Don't ever lose hope," wrote Andrew. "We're getting the job done." At what price? wondered Miranda. At what appalling price?

It was a long, dismal winter, but in April the sun came back and the entire city seemed to burst into bloom. Trees grew new coats of green; flowers sprouted in window boxes. Terraces and fire escapes were covered with planters of all sizes and shapes—urban victory gardens that somehow survived the pigeons and the bus fumes and the soot.

Miranda, having failed with cherry tomatoes and radishes, now had a thriving herb garden. "Chives, parsley, and mint," she explained to Tom one early evening in May. "I'm thinking of adding sweet basil."

"Fascinating. You have hidden talents."

"Laugh if you want, but it's a nice feeling to plant something and watch it grow."

Tom stretched out on the couch opposite Miranda's desk. "I know all about it," he said. "Natalie's growing something she insists will turn into carrots. And the twins—well, God only knows what *they're* growing. Some sort of brown stuff."

Miranda smiled. "Let's finish this report so you can go home to your family projects."

"It's finished. I recommended we close two of the hosiery counters. Since there are no silk stockings to be had anywhere, we're just wasting space. I'd rather put in more cosmetics. There are no shortages of cosmetics."

"Done," said Miranda.

"The shoe department is a different problem. We can't close it, but shipments are coming in very slowly, if at all. The stockroom is practically empty."

"Ruth Weitz has just ordered a line of shoes with cloth uppers. They're not bad-looking."

"They're not good-looking, either . . . But with leather in such short supply, I guess it's worth trying."

Miranda made a notation on her big yellow pad. "See if Annie can dream up an interesting display. Oh, and talk to advertising. Maybe they can help."

Tom sat up. He brushed his hair off his forehead, sandy hair streaked with gray. "Do we have to collect ration coupons for these cloth shoes or what?"

"Ruth is trying to get a clarification."

"Well, we can be grateful the weather is warm. No one's going to slog through the snow in a cloth shoe." He looked at his watch. "Are we through for tonight, boss lady?"

"All through."

Tom stood and straightened his tie. "Come on, I'll walk you home."

"Don't be silly; it's out of your way. I'm used to walking home by myself. I enjoy it." She looked forward to it. In the dark and quiet of night, she shut out Wade's and the war and all her fears. She let her mind wander back to Daniel. She let herself remember. At such moments, she could hear his voice, feel his touch. She felt close to him, at least in memory. "Don't worry about me," she said now, taking her purse and gloves from a desk drawer. "I'll be fine."

"But will you be safe?" Tom laughed. "With all these young sailors around—"

"Young sailors! That's very flattering." She rose and walked with Tom to the door. Her secretary had gone home two hours ago. All the other offices on the floor were dark. At the end of the corridor she saw Malcolm Gill pushing a broom back and forth. A cigarette dangled from his mouth. "Look at that," she said. "First he sweeps and then he drops ashes all over the place."

"He's a real thorn in your side, isn't he?"

"That little office of his is *still* a mess."

"Why don't you fire him and be done with it?"

"Oh, Tom, you know why: I don't want him spreading stories about Jonah or any of the others. As long as he has a job here he'll keep his mouth shut . . . I suppose he's still peddling his dirty pictures?"

"Yep." Tom rang for the elevator. "By all accounts, business isn't what it used to be. But I don't think money is his main interest. I think it gives him a feeling of power."

The elevator door opened and Miranda stepped inside. "Maybe."

"Let's forget about Malcolm Gill . . . What do you hear from Andrew?"

430

"His letters are always cheerful. And very optimistic. He's always telling us not to lose hope. He's proud of his unit. Proud of himself, I think, and that's good."

"Send him my love."

"I will. I'm going to write to him tonight. I have my whole evening planned," said Miranda as they left the elevator. "A nice quiet walk home. A drink. Dinner. Listen to the radio for a while. Write to Andrew. And then off to bed. God, I'm tired! It'll be a pleasure to crawl into bed."

Addy was waiting at the door when Miranda arrived home. "Mr. Dexter would like to see you upstairs. He's with Mrs. Wade in her sitting room."

"All right . . . You look pale. Is something wrong?"

"I'm fine, Mrs. Dexter."

"Good," said Miranda, starting toward the staircase. "There's flu going around."

"No, I'm okay."

The house seemed very silent as Miranda walked up the stairs. It was a little past eight o'clock, but it seemed much later. No radios were playing; no one was moving about. When she reached the third floor, she heard the chirp of a bird, but no voices.

She knocked once at Daphne's door and went inside. A second ornate brass cage had been added to the room, this one for a pair of lovebirds which had been named Sweetie and Pie. Daphne stood near their cage. Peter stood several feet away. He was ashen. "You're home," he said, his voice flat.

"Yes. What's the matter? You look awful."

"There was . . . a telegram."

Miranda frowned. "A telegram? Is anything . . ." She froze, and suddenly all the color drained from her face. Her hand flew to her throat. "A telegram?" she murmured.

"Andrew . . ." Peter's voice broke. Tears misted his eyes. "Andrew's been killed in action."

"It's a lie! You're lying!"

431

Peter shook his head slowly from side to side. "I called a friend of mine in the War Department. He confirmed the telegram . . . Andrew was killed at Salerno."

"Andrew's *alive*."

"No, Miranda." Peter went to her and held out the telegram. "Read it."

"No. I won't. I *won't*."

"Then I'll read it. 'We regret to inform you—' "

Miranda slapped the telegram away. "It's a lie . . . A lie." But she knew it was not a lie. She sank into a chair, fighting off the blackness that threatened to engulf her. She glanced quickly at Peter. "Dear God, it can't be true."

Daphne put a glass of whiskey into Miranda's hand. She pulled up a chair and sat beside her. "It's all so terribly sad. Young people shouldn't die. Old people . . . Well, it's quite all right for old people."

Miranda swallowed the whiskey. She was shaking; she set the glass down. Again she looked at Peter. "Andrew's dead."

"Yes."

"When—when did it happen?"

"Two days ago."

"Two days." Miranda stared blindly into space. What had she been doing two days ago? What had she been doing on the day her son died? "My son," she said, and it was as if the words had been torn from her throat.

Chapter Twenty-five

A flag draped Andrew's bronze casket. Miranda stared at the flag until the stripes blurred and the stars seemed to shatter into pieces. Every few moments she lifted her veil, dabbing at her red, swollen eyes. Peter sat next to her, his eyes hidden behind dark glasses. Daphne sat at the end of the pew. She was still, her head bowed.

". . . Andrew Wade did not die in vain," continued the reverend Dr. Wisdom. "His was a soldier's death, ennobled by courage and love of country. Generations yet to come will bless Andrew, and the millions of other young men who gave their lives in the cause of freedom. Surely these young men will dwell in the house of the Lord forever. Surely they will know God, who is to all things and all people the Resurrection and the Light."

Peter and Tom helped a sobbing Miranda from the church. Limousines were waiting to take family and close friends to the cemetery. No one spoke during the drive there. Peter opened a small flask of brandy and drank. Miranda plucked at the edges of her handkerchief. Daphne gazed straight ahead, a frown creasing her brow.

It was a beautiful spring morning. The air was fragrant with flowers and the scent of newly turned earth. Reverend Wisdom offered prayers. An Army bugler played Taps. A military honor guard carefully folded the flag and presented it to Miranda. She swayed, but once more she fought off the blackness. "Andrew," she murmured, placing

433

a single red rose on his sun-struck casket. "My son."

No one spoke during the ride home. A cold buffet lunch had been prepared, but the food was scarcely touched. Andrew's young friends, their voices muted, stood in somber groups of two's and three's. The Russells and the Selkirks stayed close together, lost in thoughts of their own sons. Daphne glided about the room, looking a little lost herself. Tom and Natalie and Lily hovered at Miranda's side. Peter had disappeared.

"Where is he?" asked Tom.

Miranda shrugged. "I don't know. He went out."

"Out?"

"I guess he needed to be alone for a while."

"You need something to eat," said Lily. "I'll fix you a plate."

"No, I'm not hungry." Miranda sipped her drink. "This is all I want right now," she said, staring into her glass. "Dutch courage."

"You have courage to spare, kiddo."

"Have I?"

The guests left shortly after one. Daphne went upstairs to see her birds. Miranda went to her own room and closed the door. She sat wearily at the edge of the bed, but a moment later she stood and went to the closet, rummaging through a back shelf until she found a taped cardboard box. With shaking hands, she opened the flaps and removed a toy carousel, the carousel she had given to Andrew on his first birthday. She turned the key. Tears filled her eyes as the music began.

Miranda remained in her room throughout the day, throughout the long night. She ignored the condolence letters stacked on her desk. She refused phone calls, refused the meals Addy brought. She sat in a chair by the window and watched the carousel spinning around.

Miranda spent the next week at home. She reread all of Andrew's letters. She packed his things and sent them to the Salvation Army. She wrote thank-you notes, and a large check to the USO. She did little chores—repotting

434

her herb garden, cleaning out the closet, tidying her desk—unnecessary chores that helped pass the time. She still refused phone calls; visitors were turned away. She slept, though only with the aid of a late-night whiskey.

Peter stayed away all that week. When he finally appeared he said nothing about where he had been. Nor did Miranda ask. She saw his ravaged face, his bloodshot eyes; she understood how he felt.

"You can stop staring at me," he snapped. "And if you're expecting an apology—"

"I'm not."

"Good."

"Addy is bringing a dinner tray and a pot of hot coffee."

He took off his jacket, loosened his tie. "I happen to be sober. Sober as a judge, that's me."

"I didn't say you weren't."

"No, you didn't *say*. You *never* say. You just bore in with those big cow eyes of yours. Well, for your information, you don't look so wonderful yourself. As a matter of fact, you look terrible. Terrible!"

"I know . . . I thought we didn't have to be enemies anymore. Have you changed your mind?"

Peter glanced up. He shook his head. "No. No, I meant it. I'm just so damned tired." He threw himself into a chair, stretching out his legs. "Why did he have to die?"

"Don't look for answers, Peter. I've tried, and there aren't any . . . I've tried to think what Andrew would want of us now. I read all his letters again."

" 'Don't ever lose hope' "; he wrote that in every letter."

"Yes. He believed it. That's why I think he'd want us to remember him with pride, not tears."

"Can you do that?"

"I *am* proud of him, you know."

"And does that ease the pain?"

Miranda's eyes skidded away. "Nothing eases the pain. Except . . ."

"Except?"

"Well, perhaps it's best to keep busy."

435

Miranda returned to work the following week. She was thinner, still pale, but she was rested and that helped, for she returned to find her desk laden with messages and memos and sales reports. There were new ads to approve, budget figures to analyze. There were amended delivery schedules, estimates for the new light fixtures, and scores of government forms. There were more condolence letters, and those she put to one side.

It was a daunting accumulation, though not unwelcome. Work repaired her frayed spirit, soothed her grieving heart. The pain of Andrew's death was no less, but the passage of time brought a gradual acceptance. She began to feel stronger, better able to cope. When asked, she replied that work had saved her. She had lost her son, and she had lost the man she loved, but as Peter had once said, there was always Wade & Company. By the new year of 1944 she knew that the store—its distractions and demands—had held her together.

War still raged in Europe and the Pacific. Miranda remained active in bond drives and the Red Cross and the USO. She continued to follow the progress of the war, dying a little with every Allied setback, cheering every victory. Late at night, in the darkness of her bedroom, she prayed.

On the home front, rationing was strict and shortages were a fact of life. Newspapers and magazines were filled with recipes for meatless meals. To save gasoline, taxis permitted group rides. Shoes, like tires, were often mended but never discarded, for they could not be replaced. Silk stockings were a thing of the past and the supply of rayon stockings was small. Broken windows stayed broken, for it took months to get plate glass. Cars took much longer to repair, and at the height of the war, many of them came with wooden bumpers

But despite these wartime inconveniences, business was booming. The economy was booming. There were jobs for everybody; there was money in everybody's pockets. Wade

& Company was busier than it had been before the Depression. The aisles were always crowded and merchandise rarely lingered on the shelves. Miranda watched profits soar. She watched her own back account grow fat. She would have traded it all for an end to the war.

Although there now seemed to be no doubt of the Allies' eventual victory, casualties continued to mount. The month-long battle at St. Lo in June of 1944 took a terrible toll. That same month, the Normandy Invasion began. Jim Selkirk was killed at Normandy, as was Mrs. Sheen's youngest son, as were so many others on all sides. Hitler's armies launched their last major counteroffensive at the Bulge in December of 1944. After a month of fierce fighting in Allied territory, they were repulsed. After five years of war, of misery and death, Hitler was beaten.

President Roosevelt did not live to witness the formal surrender. The nation wept when the President's death was announced, but a month later there were tears of joy when the new President, Harry Truman, announced the unconditional surrender of Germany.

Miranda threw her arms around Peter when she heard the announcement. He went off alone to get drunk. She joined Tom and Natalie and the twins for a celebration.

V-E Day was celebrated all across the country, in towns and cities and tiny rural villages. In New York huge crowds thronged the streets, shouting and cheering. Strangers embraced strangers, tears streaming down their faces. Children sat atop their parents' shoulders, waving flags and tossing confetti. Church bells rang out, the glad sound a message of hope to a war-weary people.

There was another celebration three months later, a celebration more joyous than the first, for it marked the unconditional surrender of Japan. General MacArthur, accepting the surrender aboard the battleship *Missouri,* offered the hope "that peace be now restored to the world, and that God will preserve it always."

When the celebrations ended there were sober truths to

be faced, for much of the world lay in ruins. Cities had been bombed into rubble. Once fertile land had been blackened and scarred. Refugee camps were filled with people who had lost everything. Orphanages teemed with children — scared, sad-eyed children who had lost everything that mattered most.

Perhaps the worst truth was the revelation of Hitler's death camps. Ten million men, women, and children had been exterminated by the Nazis, six million of them Jews. A stunned world learned of Hitler's Final Solution, of the grotesque plan that had sought nothing less than the elimination of the Jewish people. In newsreels and news magazines, a stunned world saw pictures of the survivors — skeletal figures who had been starved and beaten and tortured, who had watched loved ones marched into Nazi gas chambers. It was considered a testimony to the human spirit that there had been any survivors at all, but to Miranda it was also a testimony to the evil lurking in the human heart. It was incomprehensible to her that such things could have happened. It was a nightmare, but to Natalie it was real.

"Whatever family my father had in Germany is gone now," she said one brisk autumn day. "He had cousins, and an old uncle. The uncle was the last to die. But not before they pulled out his gold tooth."

"Dear God!"

"It's a wonderful world, kiddo."

They were in Natalie's new showroom on Seventh Avenue, a handsome room with deep, ivory carpeting, wide mirrors, and cushioned booths for the buyers who came to view her designs. The models' dressing room was off to the right. At the rear of the huge loft were workrooms and stockrooms and a very busy shipping department.

"When I look at all this," replied Miranda, "I think it *is* a wonderful world. Thank heavens your father came to America."

"Yes, but let me tell you something: given the right circumstances, anything can happen anywhere, including

America. Jews aren't exactly beloved in America, either. Remember Jonah and his quotas? And *he* was part Jewish."

"There are no quotas now, Natalie."

"Not at Wade's. But at law firms, brokerage houses, universities . . ." She laughed suddenly. "Okay, okay, I'll get off my soapbox. In case you haven't noticed, I've been on edge lately. An old grouch."

"I noticed."

"It's all the money I sunk into this place. I hope I didn't make a mistake."

"Of course you didn't. You needed the space."

"I guess so. Come on, Miranda, let's sit down and relax. Your private fashion show begins in ten minutes."

"Where's Lily?"

"Oh, she's around here somewhere. The place is so damn big, we're still getting lost."

They settled in one of the booths. A showroom assistant brought coffee and pastry.

"I won't be doing any ordering, you know. I don't like to step on my buyers' toes."

"I know, but I wanted you to have a preview. I really believe it's my best work. It better be! It has to pay a lot of bills."

"Stop worrying, Natalie. You'll do fine."

"And how will you do?" She sat back, holding a slim gold lighter to her cigarette. "What's in the future for Miranda Wade Dexter?"

"Well, there's the store."

Natalie shook her dark head. "Boring. All work and no play, etcetera, etcetera."

"I think about traveling, but I don't know where I'd go. I've had a passport sitting in a drawer for ten years. I keep having it renewed." Miranda shrugged. "Don't ask me why. I certainly won't be going to Europe." She took one of Natalie's cigarettes. "I suppose I won't be going anywhere."

"Do you ever think about Daniel?"

Miranda exhaled a thin stream of smoke. "He's safe. That's all that matters."

"Safe?"

"The war. He survived the war. He's home in Ireland, safe and sound."

"How do you know, Miranda?"

"Oh, I kept in touch with the Fiddler Brewery. The one in Milwaukee. I told them I was his American cousin . . . So he can have a life now. He has his Sally, and the little girl . . . He and Sally will probably have children of their own . . . End of story."

"Then I go back to my original question. What's in your future? What are you going to do with yourself?"

"Who knows? My life is always taking strange twists and turns. Anyway, I have a responsibility to Wade's. The store has to come first."

"And what about you?"

"It's the life I chose, Natalie. Or *stole*. All those years ago in that hospital in Cornith, I made a decision."

"Would you make the same decision again? Knowing what you know now?"

"I don't think about things like that, Natalie. Not anymore." Miranda took a sip of coffee. "It's my turn to ask a question," she said. "Are there ever going to be any high fashion designs by Natasha Starr?"

"High fashion, maybe. Natasha Starr, no . . . It was a long time coming, but I'm proud to be a Jew. And if I ever do a high fashion line, I'll do it under my own name. Natalie Stern," she said, tracing her signature in the air. "And if anybody doesn't like it, that's tough!"

"What do you think I should name her?" asked Daphne, gazing at the beautiful white bird perched on her hand. "I've been wracking my brain."

Miranda smiled. She glanced at the new cage, the third and latest addition to Daphne's sitting room. "How do you get her to stay so still?"

"Oh, I have a way with birds. But I must think of a name."

"She's very pretty, isn't she? So snowy white."

Daphne blinked. "Why, that's perfect, Miranda. I'll call her Snow White. You know—like the fairy tale. The one with the dwarfs?"

"It's a fine name."

Daphne lifted the bird to the cage and put it inside. "Now we can have a nice talk, Miranda."

"Well, I wanted to talk to you about the new cook. I've narrowed the applicants down to two. There isn't much difference between them, but I thought you'd like to make the final choice."

"I?" Daphne looked startled. "I've never had anything to do with the servants. It was Jonah, you see."

"The woman will be living here, in your house. Isn't there anything you'd like to ask?"

"I'm sure you'll make the right choice, Miranda. But do remind her about my bridge club. Tea sandwiches and little cakes every Tuesday and Thursday afternoon. We're all especially fond of cream cakes. Perhaps you ought to mention that."

Miranda rose and walked across the room. "I've been thinking about taking a trip, Daphne."

"Really? How nice."

"You wouldn't mind, then? Peter's out most of the time; you'd be alone."

"Oh, not alone. Addy is always around. And there's Cook . . . Will it be a long trip?"

"I don't know. I don't even know if there'll *be* a trip. It's just something I'm thinking about. I feel kind of restless. It might help to get away. But I don't know where."

"You must choose the place that will make you happiest."

Miranda shook her head. "I don't know where that is. Which is why I'll probably end up staying home. As usual."

"If you learned to play bridge . . ."

"No, I'm not good at games."

"But games are fun."

A smile brushed Miranda's lips. "I'm not good at fun either." She turned, peering into the lovebirds' cage. Sweetie was preening her feathers; Pie was hopping about, snatching up stray seeds. She watched for a moment, and then turned away. "I'm going to have a bath before dinner," she said, walking to the door.

"Have you thought about visiting your family?"

"My family?"

"In Ireland. Ireland might be just the place for a trip."

Miranda's hand tightened on the doorknob. "No, not anymore. We—we haven't kept in touch . . . Time passes." She glanced over her shoulder at Daphne. "I'm getting old."

"Oh, no, I wouldn't say that. When you're *my* age . . . You know, it's rather an odd thing: when I look into the mirror I still see a girl of sixteen. Of course it's my imagination. Why, I'm almost *ancient*. But you have years and years and years."

Miranda frowned, for all at once she saw the years stretching ahead—lonely, empty years. There was a sick feeling in her stomach. She pulled the door open.

"Mocha cream," called Daphne.

"What?"

"Perhaps you ought to tell the new cook that mocha cream is my favorite. The cream cakes?"

"Yes. Yes, I'll see to it. Is there anything else?"

Daphne arranged herself on the chaise. "You really do worry too much, Miranda. It's bad for the complexion."

In the months that followed, Miranda's worries centered around herself. She would soon be forty, and this milestone birthday led her to examine the past, to question the future. A bleak future, or so it seemed to her. She saw nothing ahead but work; she saw herself as a dour, dried up old woman simply marking time.

There was a sameness to her days now, for Wade's was no longer a challenge. The store was running smoothly, and despite postwar inflation, profits were rising. Charge accounts had tripled. Frank North's clever, stylish ads kept hordes of new customers streaming through the doors. She felt she had accomplished all her goals. She was still busy—in some ways busier than ever—but she took scant pleasure in the daily round of meetings and reports. At times it was hard for her to concentrate. Her attention wandered; her thoughts skipped between past and present. She wondered where all the years had gone.

Now, on a freezing January morning in 1947, Miranda shifted her-briefcase to her other hand and opened her office door. An instant later she jumped back, startled by the chorus of voices shouting "Surprise!"

She saw the birthday cake, the table decorated with crepe paper streamers, balloons, and a huge gold cutout of the number 40. Beribboned gifts were heaped at one end of the table; at the other end were pitchers of orange juice and champagne. The executive staff was gathered in the room. Natalie and Lily were there also, the unofficial bartenders.

"I don't know what to say," laughed Miranda. "I really *am* surprised."

Peter took her coat and briefcase. Natalie gave her a glass of champagne. "Happy birthday, kiddo," she said. "This is the big one."

"The one I had planned to forget."

"Well, look at it this way: either we get older or we die."

"You're so comforting." Miranda glanced around the office, shaking her head. "It's lovely. Whose idea was it?"

"I thought you should have a party," replied Peter.

She looked at him. Years ago they had agreed to a truce, and from that had come something like friendship. They were not close. They still led separate lives; they still argued. But they had stopped hurting each other. "How did you manage all these decorations? You must have been here at dawn."

"I had help: Malcolm Gill."

"Oh? For how much?"

"He wouldn't take a penny . . . But he pinched a bottle of champagne."

"Only one?"

"It was all he could carry in his shirt."

"Drink up," said Natalie. "You have to cut the cake and open the presents. And I have to get to work."

443

"Woman's work is never done," said Peter.

Miranda kissed his cheek. "It was sweet of you to remember my birthday. Maybe forty won't be too terrible after all."

He moved away. "Ladies and gentlemen," he said, his gaze scanning the small group. "A toast. To Miranda, the guiding light of Wade and Company."

There was applause. Everybody gathered around her then; Harvey called for a speech.

She had been startled by Peter's toast. She was touched, for he had spoken the words without a trace of rancor. "A very short speech," she said, looking at the faces turned in her direction. "But from my heart, thank you. Thank you very much."

Tom lighted the candles on the cake. "You have to make a wish. Make it a good one!"

Miranda bent over the cake. She closed her eyes for a moment, and in that moment she saw Daniel. She wished she were with him in his wee village. *When the moon is shining and the waves are crashing and the gulls are dancing.* She drew a breath and blew out all the candles.

"That means your wish will come true," said Annie Wolfe.

But Miranda smiled, for she knew better. She picked up the knife and cut into the cake. "Come and get it everybody. First come, first served."

After the cake, she opened the presents. There were joke presents: a set of false teeth, a jar of wrinkle cream, a bottle of hair dye, a hot water bottle. And there were serious presents: a beaded cashmere evening sweater, a silk lounging robe, a crystal decanter, gold earrings from Natalie, a diamond brooch from Peter. Lily's gift was a slender charm bracelet with a tiny gold dustpan and brush.

"Do you remember when you used to pester me about the housework, Miranda? She always wanted to help," explained Lily to the others. "She was always in my hair."

"I wanted something to keep me busy," explained Miranda. "If you'd let me help with the housework, I might never have come to work here at Wade's."

"Then I did you a favor."

Miranda touched the locket that bulged slightly beneath her dress; Daniel's locket. "I'm not so sure," she murmured.

The party ended when the store opened for business. Natalie started to leave, but she stopped suddenly and retraced her steps to Miranda's desk. "What did you wish?" she asked.

"Don't tell me you believe in birthday wishes."

"I just want to know."

"It's supposed to be a secret."

"Are you going to aggravate me so early in the morning? I have a whole day of aggravation facing me. I have—"

"All right, all right," said Miranda, holding up her hand. "Not that it matters, but I wished for Daniel. I was standing there, blowing out the candles, and all I wanted to do was find Daniel and . . ."

"And?"

Miranda sighed. "And steal him away from his wife. I wished I could turn the clock back and start over. Silly, isn't it? But I can't get him out of my mind. I've tried; God knows I've tried. I just can't stop remembering."

"What about the store?"

"What about it? I've given twenty years of my life to Wade's. When I think this is all there'll be for the *next* twenty . . . Why are we having this stupid conversation?"

Natalie was quiet. She seemed to be debating with herself. "Because," she replied after several moments, "I have a piece of information for you. Daniel and Sally are divorcing."

Miranda's jaw dropped. She gaped at Natalie. *"What?"*

"We had a Christmas card from Daniel. He enclosed a short note, a very short note. He said he and Sally had tried to make a go of things, but it was no good. He also said you were still the woman of his dreams."

"You've known all this for a month and you kept it from me? How could you, Natalie?"

"Daniel asked me not to say anything unless your cir-

445

cumstances had changed. I thought it over and I realized he was right. There's no point in raising hopes if everything's going to turn out the same way. You lost him once and it broke your heart. There's no point in going through that again."

"No point!" cried Miranda, her eyes flashing. "Since when are you making my decisions for me? It was bad enough not to tell me about Daniel's note, but now —"

"Now I'm telling you the truth, so get off your high horse. You lost Daniel because you put the store ahead of everything else. I'm not saying that was wrong; I know you had responsibilities. I'm saying you made a choice and it cost you plenty. Okay, that's in the past. I think you'd make a different choice today, and today is what counts . . . It's a second chance, kiddo. Don't muff it."

Miranda's anger subsided, quelled by the words "second chance." Is it true? she wondered. After all this time, could it be true? "Did Daniel really say I was the woman of his dreams?"

"A direct quote. So what are you going to do about it?"

"I have to go to him. I . . ." Miranda's heart was pounding. She felt lightheaded, as if she were floating somewhere in the clouds. "I think I'm going to faint."

The worried look left Natalie's eyes. She laughed. "No, you're not. You're going to Ireland and live happily ever after." She poured the last of the champagne into their glasses. "Let's drink to it!"

In a small, cluttered basement office, Malcolm Gill was also drinking the last of the champagne. He tilted the bottle back and poured the last drops into his mouth. A moment later he tossed the bottle away and wiped his mouth on his sleeve. He belched.

Champagne was all right, but he preferred whiskey, rye whiskey. It was a man's drink, he thought, and like the heroes of his fantasies, he started every day with a shot of rye. This morning he had had a double shot — a bracer against the cold and the early hour. The champagne had been an unexpected bonus; Malcolm Gill took his opportunities wherever he found them.

He was a scavenger, and his office was crowded with thirty years of odds and ends. There were two headless, armless mannequins, several wooden file cabinets, scraps of grimy carpet, the remains of a display case, and an old window sash. There were mildewed packing crates, coils of twine, a broken staple gun, and a carton of rubber stamps. There were filthy mops, piles of dustcloths, and three or four empty soap boxes. In a corner of the office was a cracked mirror from one of the dressing rooms. Opposite it was a very large, sooty teddy bear from a long-ago window display. The shelves were filled with telephone directories dating back to the 1930's.

A current telephone directory sat atop his desk, which was littered end to end with requisition forms and work sheets and memo pads. Chewed-up pencils were strewn about. The ashtray overflowed with cigarette butts. Propped against the telephone was his lunch: a cheese-and-pickle sandwich in a brown paper sack.

Now, Malcolm Gill leaned back in his chair and looked at the big clock on the wall. It was a little before ten. It was quiet, for his office was at the rear of the store. There was no one about; he knew there would be no work for him today. He opened the newspaper and turned to the comics. After a few moments he put the paper down and rubbed his eyes. He was drowsy from rye and champagne, from the quiet and the steam heat. He stuck a cigarette between his lips; he lit a match. He looked at the clock again.

His old leather swivel chair scraped the bare floor as he rose. He threw his cigarette into the ashtray and stumbled off to his favorite napping place — a cushioned bench in the alcove at the top of the stairs.

He had not noticed the cigarette teetering at the edge of the ashtray, nor had he heard the soft rustle when the cigarette fell. It burned a ragged hole in the newspaper, a ragged black circle that was quickly ringed by flame. There was a crackling as the flame spread to other papers, feeding

447

on them, gathering strength. A shower of sparks exploded from the telephone directory; now the whole desk was engulfed in flames, in angry swirls of red and orange racing toward the discarded packing crates. Thick smoke filled the air and still the flames roared ahead, leaping at the filthy mops, at the bundled dustcloths and carpet squares, at the wooden file cabinets with their cache of whiskey bottles. Here the blaze flared into a huge fireball that burst through the wall and raced up the stairs.

Malcolm Gill, dozing on the bench in the alcove, had only enough time to lift his head before the flames consumed him.

The fire followed a natural line from the back stairs to the rear of the main floor. The first golden curls of flame raced unobserved through a darkened corridor, devouring trash bins and rows of neatly stacked cartons. Once out of the corridor, the flames sped along the carved baseboards. Within seconds, the rear wall was a solid sheet of flame.

People were screaming. Footsteps pounded toward the exits but not fast enough, for fiery sparks were bursting over the mahogany display cases, pinwheeling through the air to fall upon silk-clad mannequins, upon racks of scarves and gloves and blouses. The aisles were smoky columns of flame. The walls seemed to be crumbling, and the beautiful carved ceiling was a scorching, shimmering blaze of red.

Terrified screams grew louder as customers and employees found themselves trapped by the fire, by the debris. Great chunks of wood and plaster were crashing down. Glass countertops were shattering. Flames leapt higher and higher. Clouds of smoke blackened the air. Near the front of the store, two sprinklers emitted thin streams of rusty water. The other sprinklers, though open, were bone dry.

The lights flickered out just as the first fire engine came to a screeching halt in front of the store. The firemen wasted no time, for three floors were already in flames.

Miranda, in her office on the sixth floor, had heard only muffled cries, muffled sounds she had not been able to identify. She had tried to call downstairs, but the telephones had not been working. Now, as the fire engine arrived on the scene, she jumped to her feet and ran to Tom's office.

He, too, was on his feet. He looked tense, anxious. "We have a fire."

"Yes, I know. We have to get everybody out."

They ran to the hall, which had started to fill with confused employees.

"I heard a fire engine," said one.

"What's going on?" asked another.

"The lights have been flickering. I thought—"

"Hold it," said Miranda. "Listen to me carefully . . . There seems to be a fire downstairs . . . Quiet!" she called over the sound of nervous voices. "You must listen to me! We can't have any panic. There's no reason to panic. We'd better not try to use the elevators, but there are the front and back stairs. We'll all get out safely if we just don't panic."

"That's right," said Tom. "I suggest we break up into two groups. One group will use the front stairs, and the other group the back stairs . . . Women will go first," he added, motioning Miranda's secretary, and his own, to the exit. Several other women followed. He nodded. "Fine. Harvey, you take a group down the back way."

Miranda watched them leave. "Peter," she said. "Where's Peter?"

"Maybe he wasn't in his office," replied Tom. "No, I'm sure he was. He had the personnel budget to finish."

"Well, let's see."

They turned toward Peter's office, but they froze when they heard the shouts of "Fire!" They spun around to see Harvey and his group staggering out of the back exit.

"We can't get down that way," said Harvey. "The fire's coming up the stairs."

"The front way, then," said Miranda. "Hurry!" She

449

glanced at Tom. "You'd better go, too. I'll get Peter."

"We'll get him together. Come on."

They dashed to Peter's office. The door was open, but he was no where in sight. "Peter?" she called. "Peter!"

He emerged from the bathroom. "What the hell—"

"There's a fire," said Tom. "We have to get out of here."

"Christ!"

The three of them ran into the hall. They could hardly see, for the air was thick with smoke. They heard the sound of the fire on the stairs, a sound like the roar of cannon. In the next instant they heard a thunderous crash as the staircase collapsed.

They were coughing; their eyes were burning. Trapped in the sooty blackness, they had lost all sense of direction.

"This way," insisted Tom, gasping for breath. "It's this way."

But they were not really certain. They bumped into each other, into the walls. Peter ran his hand along the wall, searching for the elevator button. "If the back stairs are gone . . . so are the front stairs . . . We'll . . . We'll have to try the elevator."

"No," said Miranda, but a fit of coughing kept her from saying anything more.

"It's the only . . . way out. Stay low." Peter found the button and leaned his weight on it. Tom tried to pull him off; he shoved Tom aside. "I tell you . . . it's the only way."

There was a strange clanking. The elevator door opened. Miranda screamed as flames leapt from the car and covered Peter. He took a step, just one. With an agonized shriek, he dropped to the floor.

"Peter." Miranda was on her knees now, beating at the flames that enveloped him. "*Peter.*"

She was still screaming his name when Tom dragged her away.

He dragged her back to her office and closed the door. The smoke was thick here also, but light streamed through the window. "Come on, Miranda," he said. "We need air."

"But Peter—"

"There's nothing we can do for him now." Tom heard her sobs as he threw open the window. He saw crowds of people behind police barricades. He saw ambulances and rescue trucks and fire engines. The avenue had been closed to traffic; the sidewalk was a welter of fire hoses, oxygen equipment, stretchers, and rope. He saw a fireman spreading salt on the pavement, for the water from the hoses had turned to ice. He grabbed Miranda and pushed her head out the window. "Breathe . . . Come on, deep breaths."

The cold air seemed to choke her. She coughed. "Can't . . . can't we go back for Peter?"

"I'm sorry."

Tears splashed her blackened face. "Oh, God. Oh, God, this is *horrible.*"

But Tom was not listening. He leaned out over the ledge. "Up here," he shouted. "We're up here . . . Up here."

There was a commotion on the sidewalk as they were spotted. People started screaming and pointing. The firemen rushed to move a ladder into place.

"We'll be all right," said Tom. "They'll get us out."

Miranda gazed out at the last gasps of smoke coming from below. There was a sudden loud hissing sound; she turned to see the office door burst into flames. *"Tom,"* she cried.

"I know. It'll be all right. Don't worry. They'll get us out."

Miranda, watching the firemen struggle with the ladder, shook her head. "They can't get the ladder braced," she said. "It's sliding on the marble. And with the ice . . . Tom, the whole front of the building is covered with ice. What are we going to do?"

"They'll get us out, Miranda. They know what to do."

The firemen abandoned the ladder. In a flash, they had moved an immense round tarpaulin beneath the window.

"We'll have to jump," said Tom.

"Oh, no. No, I can't."

Tom glanced over his shoulder at the approaching

flames. "There's no choice. Take off your shoes."

"My shoes?"

He bent, pulling at the high heels and tossing them away. "Now get up on the ledge."

"I *can't*, Tom." *This isn't happening,* she thought. *It's not. It's some terrible nightmare. I'll wake up soon and then . . . Dear God, let this be a nightmare.*

"Miranda!" Tom was shaking her. The smoke was thicker now; the flames were almost at the desk. "You have to get hold of yourself, Miranda. There's no time."

"Don't make me do this. I can't."

"I'll help you up." He lifted her onto the windowsill. "Get out there . . . Go on, Miranda. You can do it."

She saw the flames racing up the walls, across the ceiling. A fiery beam crashed down on her desk and it, too, burst into flames. *God help us,* she thought, inching her way onto the ledge.

Shouts rose from the street, but she dared not look down. She took a tiny step. The ledge was slippery with ice; she fell to her knees. She was sweating, her heart pounding. Her eyes darted wildly about.

"Jump," screamed Tom.

"I can't."

"For Christ sakes, do you want to burn to death? We'll *both* burn to death. *Jump.*"

There was a fierce hammering in her ears. Points of blackness began to dance before her eyes. She swallowed. She took a breath, and then another. She closed her eyes and jumped.

She was screaming. Her hands were clawing desperately at the air. She felt her heart in her throat, felt a sudden piercing cold. Only one thought passed through her mind: *I'm going to die.*

There was a loud thump as her body plunged into the tarpaulin. Her dress was torn. Her face was mottled with soot and tears and perspiration. Blisters had begun to form on her burned hands. But she was alive.

"Are you all right, miss?" asked one of the firemen surrounding her. "The ambulance is waiting to take you to the hospital."

"I'm . . ." She coughed, for she could feel the soot and smoke at the back of her throat. "Yes, I'm all right."

They bundled her in a blanket and got her to her feet. Her legs felt rubbery, but after a moment she knew nothing was broken.

"I'm Dr. Robbins," said a slender, bespectacled young man. "Let me help you to the ambulance. The hospital is only —"

"No. No hospital."

"You need —"

"No."

She turned. The firemen were once again moving the tarpaulin into position. She looked up to see Tom hurtling through the air. "Dear God," she murmured. She staggered away to the curb and was sick.

Chapter Twenty-six

The crowds had dispersed, for the show was over. The fire engines had gone; only one rescue truck remained. Tom sat beside Miranda in the back of the truck. A doctor had salved and bandaged her hands, but she had refused to go to the hospital. She had refused everything—coffee, blankets, sedatives, consolation. She just sat there, staring at the charred shell of Wade & Company.

She had been there when the roof fell in, when most of the interior structure collapsed through to the basement. She had watched the tremendous explosion of sparks shooting fifty feet in the air. She had watched the final crash, heard the final, shuddering sigh that shook the avenue. Rescue workers were still sifting through the rubble, but it would be days before the toll was known. The bodies of Peter and Malcolm Gill had been burned to ashes. Heartsick, she wondered if others had met the same fate.

"Let me take you home now, Miranda," said Tom.

"No, the fire marshal may have questions," she replied, her voice like the rustling of dry leaves. "There may be something I can do."

"There's *nothing* you can do now. It's finished."

Finished. She stared at the blackened marble and limestone. The big display windows had blown out and she could see the gaping void beyond. Only hours ago,

Peter had offered a toast to the guiding light of Wade & Company, but Wade & Company no longer existed. The store that had been entrusted to her was gone. She felt empty, as if the gaping void were within herself. "Four generations of Wades," she said. "I've undone four generations."

"This certainly isn't your fault, Miranda."

"What happened to the sprinklers? Why didn't they work?"

"I don't know. There was an inspection in October. Peter . . . Peter always handled those things. I hate saying it at a time like this, but he occasionally took shortcuts."

"Shortcuts?"

"He had to deal with a lot of inspectors," explained Tom. "There were the fire guys, the safety guys, the elevator guys. And not all of them were honest. Sometimes it's just easier to slip a few bucks—"

"I don't want to hear anymore."

"Let me take you home. What do you say?"

Miranda turned her head and looked at Tom. "I haven't even thanked you for saving my life. You were very brave."

"*Scared* is more like it. I was trying to save my own skin."

"You could have left me there."

"Believe me, the thought crossed my mind . . . I'm sorry about Peter."

"Yes, so am I. He was right, you know. He never had any luck." She looked down at her bandaged hands. Her eyes were dry. She had no tears left. "He was never really happy."

"And you?"

"Oh, I've had my moments. Maybe that's all we get: moments. Her eyes returned to the charred shell of Wade & Company. "When did the fire department say we'd have a report?"

"By the end of the week."

"I'd like you to set up some meetings for next week,

then."

"Meetings?"

"We'll use my study at home. I want to see the store's attorney, the insurance agents, Hank Nelson, and Claude."

"What's the hurry? I know there are decisions to be made. There are loose ends. But there isn't anything that can't wait a while."

Again she stared into the black, gaping void. "Set up the meetings, Tom."

Hundreds of people had been treated for smoke inhalation, cuts, and bruises. A dozen people had been hospitalized. Miraculously, only four people had died: Peter, Malcolm Gill, and two clerks who had been killed during the stampede to the exits.

The fire department had traced the failure of the sprinkler system to a faulty switch in the main valve, a twenty-cent part that had caused a million dollars worth of damage and three of the four deaths. No blame was attributed to the management of Wade & Company. The final report stated that "management took all reasonable precautions and met all provisions of the New York City fire code."

The report eased Miranda's mind, but nothing eased the sense of loss. She could not help feeling she had betrayed a trust; in her worst moments, she felt she had betrayed the last twenty years of her life, for all those years of work and devotion had ended in ashes.

And in death, she thought to herself as Porter Harrington read the terms of Peter's will. She was the sole beneficiary of his estate, and to her fell the task of sorting and packing his things. She sent clothing and furniture and books to the Salvation Army. She gave his jewelry to Tom. There were hundreds of photographs — mostly of Andrew — and these she kept for herself. Now another room in the Wade house stood empty. Now the silence deepened, broken only by the chirping of Daphne's birds.

It was a happy sound, sharp contrast to Miranda's mood. She was irritable, impatient. At night she paced her room, unable to sleep. During the day, she locked herself in the study, filling notepads with figures she alone understood. Anyone watching her would have seen the anger simmering just beneath the surface. It was an anger born of conflict, for she had made her decision, and once again she had put Wade & Company ahead of Daniel.

She gazed around the study, her eyes lingering briefly on each of the three men seated there. Tom looked troubled, Hank and Claude merely confused. "There's a lot to talk about," she said, "so we might as well get started. Letters went out this morning asking the executive staff to remain in Wade's employ. I've rented office space. Telephones will be installed tomorrow . . . We'll have everything we need for the transition period."

"Transition to what?" asked Claude.

"To the new Wade's," replied Miranda. "We're going to rebuild."

"Rebuild! But Tom's been taking bids on the site. The Jastrow brothers offered two million. Do you mean to say you're turning down two million dollars?"

"That's right. Let the Jastrow brothers build their department store somewhere else. Wade's was there first and Wade's will *stay* there. We have the insurance settlement, Claude. I'm prepared to sink every penny of it into the new Wade and Company. If that's not enough, I'll put my own money in. And if that's still not enough, I'll take out a loan. One way or another, there is going to be a new store. But with the same old staff, I hope . . . Can I count on you?"

"Sure," said Claude. "I came to Wade's fresh out of college. That was almost thirty years ago. Why not play out the string?"

"What about you, Hank?"

"Full salary during this transition?"

457

"Full salary."

"Then I'm in."

Miranda nodded. "I'm glad, because I have a project for you. Peter left me fifty thousand dollars, give or take. I want to use it to set up some kind of employees' fund. Obviously our salesclerks and secretaries aren't going to wait for us to reopen. Neither are our buyers. They'll all be asked to come back, but they'll need jobs in the meantime. And that may not be easy, not with all the exservicemen competing for jobs. What I have in mind is a fund, a *loan* fund, so people won't be tempted to take advantage. If any of our old employees run into hard times, they can apply to the fund. Can you handle that?"

"We have duplicate records at the warehouse. The tax records. If I can track everybody down, I can handle it."

"Fine." Miranda glanced at her notes. She shook a cigarette out of Tom's pack and lit it. "Claude, your job will be to write a comprehensive budget. Start-up costs are what I'm interested in. Everything included, from advertising to wrapping paper."

"I hope you're not in a hurry."

"I'll pretend I didn't hear that," replied Miranda with a faint smile. She made a small checkmark on her pad and turned the page. "Now we come to Tom, our new vice president. He's going to begin interviewing architects."

"You have the easy job, buddy boy."

"Not so easy, Hank. Architects tend to have minds of their own, but any architect *we* hire is going to be on a short leash. Miranda has very specific ideas."

Claude laughed. "That's a surprise."

"I just want Wade's to look like Wade's," said Miranda. "But there has to be a modern feeling about it. Our customers have to *know* it's a new store. They have to know it's safe."

Tom sat back. "See what I mean? Not so easy."

Miranda opened her desk drawer. She removed two sets of keys, giving them to Hank and Claude. "I've taken a year's lease on the office space. I expect that's all we'll need."

"You don't honestly expect to reopen in a year, do you?"

"Yes, that's my plan. It can be done, Claude. We're all going to work hard and get it done. Harvey — and Jeff, if he stays on — will use a buying service until we're ready to hire a full staff. Hank will do the hiring, of course. We'll have our ads prepared, and displays. We'll have our budgets in place. We'll be all right . . . A year is longer than you think."

"I hope so, for all our sakes."

Miranda stubbed out her cigarette. "Let's just take everything one step at a time. We've come through a Depression, a war, and a fire. We'll come through this."

"Well, if you look at it that way —"

"I do."

Tom saw that Miranda was losing patience. He snapped his notebook shut and stood up. "We've had enough talk," he said. "I recommend a good night's sleep, because we all go back to work in the morning."

There was a shuffling of feet, a scraping of chairs. "I'll need some clerical help," said Claude.

"If you can convince me on the way downstairs," replied Tom, "it's yours. Come on, Hank. I'm sure you'll want to put your two cents in."

They left the study. Miranda looked over her notes, and then replaced them in a desk drawer. She rested her head in her hands. She was tired; she wished she could go to sleep and wake up a year from now, wake up to find Wade & Company restored and thriving.

"You need a drink," said Tom, walking back into the study.

"I need something."

"Are we finished here? Shall we rescue my wife from Daphne?"

Miranda smiled. "Poor Natalie," she said, rising. "I forgot all about her."

They went to the hall. They heard Daphne's light,

459

silky voice drifting out of the living room. She was talking about Pie, one of her lovebirds.

"Here we are," said Tom, as they entered the living room. "You must have wondered what happened to us."

"Oh, business . . ." said Daphne. "Business is always . . ."

"It certainly is," agreed Natalie with a relieved smile. "Are we off to dinner?"

Tom shrugged. "We have to decide where."

"*Any*where," said Natalie. "That little French place. The one near the park."

Miranda poured a sherry for herself, and a Scotch for Tom. "The food's very good. Won't you join us, Daphne?"

"Oh, I couldn't. Cook is fixing me a tray. I do enjoy television."

"Daphne has a new television set," explained Miranda.

"Yes." Daphne smiled. "I can't imagine how they do it, can you? Getting the picture into the little box?" She rose, gliding to the door. "Of course my mother had stereopticon slides. I suppose that's the answer."

Natalie shook her head. "The answer?" she said when Daphne had gone.

"Don't even try to figure it out."

"I won't. But while we're on the subject, I've been trying to figure out what *you're* up to, Miranda. Tom won't tell me a thing. What's the big secret?"

"I don't think you'll approve."

"If it concerns a trip to Ireland—"

"It doesn't." Miranda sat down and sipped her sherry. "It concerns Wade's. I've decided to rebuild."

"Rebuild! Why the hell would you want to do that? Oh, Miranda, you have all the money you'll ever need. You're *free*, for gosh sakes. For the first time in twenty years, you're free. Why start it up all over again?"

"It has nothing to do with money."

"Then *why?*"

460

"I've been asking myself the same question."

"And?"

Miranda's eyes swept across the living room. Draperies had been replaced over the years, and chairs had been recovered, but the look of the room had not changed. The house had not changed; it was as it had been the day she arrived in New York. She had come seeking refuge, and in a way she had found it within these walls.

"I'm waiting," said Natalie.

"It's hard to explain. Twenty years ago I stole something — another woman's life. I'm not sorry. Even with all that's happened, I'm not sorry. But I guess I always felt I had to give something back." Miranda glanced down, her long lashes casting dark, wispy shadows on her cheeks. "I can't leave Wade's in ashes," she said quietly. "I just can't. Wade's is all that's left."

"What about Daniel?"

"We make choices, Natalie. You said so yourself."

"We don't always make the *right* choices."

"We do the best we can."

Natalie slammed her glass on the table. "But you have a second chance with Daniel. Are you just going to throw it away?"

There was a brief silence. Miranda touched the locket beneath her dress. "I'm going to rebuild Wade & Company," she replied. And no one is going to stop me."

An architect was hired. The crumbling, blackened shell of Wade & Company was torn down, and the site cleared. Miranda was at the site almost every day. She had her own sets of blueprints and specifications. She was interested in even the smallest details, and she was not shy about asking questions. After a while she gained the respect of the construction crew, for she learned to speak their language, to be one of them. Clomping around in boots and a hard hat, she was not afraid to explore dark, narrow passageways, to climb out on girders, to ride an open elevator platform six stories

461

above the ground. She turned up everywhere, màrking each day's progress in the notebook she always carried.

When Miranda was not at the site, she was at the rented office space on Madison Avenue. She had rented an entire floor, a suite of offices complete with desks, file cabinets, typewriters, adding machines, and intercoms. There were a couple of secretaries and several clerks. Except for Harvey Vaughn, who had decided to retire, the executive staff was intact.

Jeff Woodrow was the new merchandise manager. A reserved man, he had waited patiently for this promotion. In his quiet way, he was determined to succeed. Now he sat down across from Miranda and placed a thick file folder on her desk. "I believe I have everything under control," he said. "There's no need to worry."

"Perhaps not, but I want you to hire some help. It's too much work for one person. Something is bound to go wrong."

"I've tried to anticipate."

"Look, Jeff, we're in a difficult situation. An impossible situation, I sometimes think. We don't have a staff of buyers to concentrate on individual departments. And I don t know how much faith we can put in the buying service we've hired. Which means every single order is going to have to be checked and checked again. Why, the paperwork alone is too much for one person."

"It's under control, Miranda."

"So far. But two-thirds of our orders haven't even been placed yet. There's going to be a deluge. It will . . . She paused, sighing. "It's no reflection on you, Jeff. Think back: Harvey had you and a whole staff of buyers and he was *still* swamped with work . . . You simply can't do it by yourself. I won't take the chance. I won't let Wade's reopen with empty shelves."

"I'm on schedule."

"Everyone else is screaming for more help, you know."

"I'm not."

Miranda sat back and clasped her hands together. "I

462

realize you're anxious to put your own stamp on Wade and Company, but you can't do it all at once. I'm telling you to hire some help. If you don't choose a staff, I'll choose one for you. Is that clear?"

"Yes, it's clear."

There was silence as Miranda waited for him to continue.

"I'll make the calls this afternoon," he said at last.

"That's what I wanted to hear."

Jeff glanced down at the file folder. "Would you like to go over these orders now?"

"Leave the file. I'll look at it later."

"Was there anything else?"

Miranda shook her head. "I hope we understand each other, Jeff. Damn it all, we're supposed to be on the same side."

"There won't be any other problems," he replied, rising. "You have my word."

Tom entered the office as Jeff left. Miranda motioned him to a chair. "You don't look happy," he said.

"I'm not. I'm beginning to think we made a mistake with Jeff. He was always cautious, but now he's not even willing to delegate some of his work."

"He's trying to prove himself, Miranda. You have to have a little patience."

"Patience! We're six months away from reopening. *Six months*. There's no time for hand-holding. This is business, not nursery school."

Tom frowned. "First of all, take it easy. Take a breath and calm down. You're going to make yourself sick if you keep—"

"Spare me the lecture."

"No, I won't. People are starting to call you the dragon lady, and I can see why. Everybody's doing the best they can. You know that. Everything's going very well, when you consider the circumstances."

"Jeff still doesn't have a staff," said Miranda.

"Okay, I'll admit Jeff's been difficult. But he worked in

Harvey's shadow a long time and now he's trying to prove he can do the job. I can remember when you would have understood that. Not so long ago, you would have tried to help. It *doesn't* help to have you looking over his shoulder every minute."

"He's never been comfortable working for a woman. Why did he decide to stay?"

"Because Wade's pays better than most stores. Because Wade's promotes from within. Because Wade's *used* to be a nice place to work. Take your choice."

Miranda left her desk and wandered over to the window. She plucked a dead leaf from her ivy plant, holding it up to the clear autumn sunlight. "So I'm the dragon lady, am I?"

"The one and only."

"It's all this work."

"Your heart isn't in your work; that's the problem, Miranda. You're an angry woman."

Because I don't want to be here, she thought to herself. *Because I want to be in Ireland. In a wee village, Carley by name.* "I'm sorry it shows."

"Would you like some advice?"

"No." She turned away from the window. "No, I wouldn't. It's a waste of time."

"And we mustn't waste time."

"That's right." She went back to her desk, riffling through a stack of files. "The cosmetics department is all set. Here are the confirmations . . . These are for hosiery, gloves, handbags . . . Well, you can look at them when you have a chance."

"What's this?"

"Jeff's file on lingerie and sleepwear. Check it, will you?"

"Sure." Tom glanced up as Miranda took her coat and purse out of the closet. "Where are you going?"

"To the warehouse. Annie's using part of the third floor to work on her window displays. She needs wide open spaces."

"Give my regards to the Bronx."

"I'll do that." She buttoned her coat and drew on her gloves. "I should be back by five or so. Keep everybody here; we're going to have a meeting."

"Oh, come on, Miranda. It's Saturday. People want to go home."

"Keep everybody here . . . Orders from the dragon lady."

Typewriters were clattering in the outer office; telephones were ringing. Miranda saw heads duck as she passed by. Sighing, she quickened her pace to the hall. She punched the elevator button, then punched it again. "You took long enough," she said when the operator slid the door open.

"Hey, lady, I got other floors."

"Don't tell me your sad stories, and I won't tell you mine. Deal?"

"Jeez, lady, I just work here."

Miranda found her handkerchief and pressed it to her face. "Sorry," she murmured. "I'm sorry."

It was a beautiful October afternoon. Puffy white clouds tumbled across the sky to uncover wide patches of blue. A quiet breeze stirred the trees, shaking the last leaves of the season from their boughs. The sunlight was pale gold, the color of wine.

Miranda did not pause to savor the day. She plunged into the crowd of shoppers and strollers, pointing herself in the direction of the subway. Her arm was jostled and someone stepped on her foot, but she never broke stride. At the corner, she looked at the changing traffic light, started across the street, then turned and hurried back to the curb.

"Oh, I'm terribly sorry," said the man who bumped into her. She looked around. Her hand flew to her throat, for standing there was someone she had not seen for more than twenty years. It was Gardner Logan, an old man now, an elegant, white-haired old man in a cashmere coat.

465

"I'm afraid I'm not used to the crowds in the big city," he said with a smile.

"It's — it's quite all right." She felt his eyes on her. She wanted to run, but she was trapped by the crush of cars and people. "Quite all right," she said again.

"You must pardon me for staring. For a moment I thought I knew you." Gardner Logan continued to stare. He saw a lovely, stylishly dressed woman with glossy black hair, porcelain skin, and extraordinary gray eyes. There was something about the eyes, something familiar. Where had he seen those eyes before? He shrugged. "Memory. The years play havoc with memory."

Miranda was praying for the light to change; when it did, she darted across the street and around a corner. She was running. Her heart was thudding. She turned another corner, and another, looking over her shoulder as if she were being pursued. *I've lost him,* she thought, and her steps slowed. She leaned against a building, trying to catch her breath. After a while she straightened up and looked around to see where she was.

She had reached Third Avenue when she glimpsed her reflection in a plate-glass window. Suddenly she started to laugh. She laughed until tears rolled down her cheeks. She fumbled for her handkerchief and dried her eyes, but an instant later there were more tears, tears she could not stop.

She never appeared at the warehouse. Instead she walked aimlessly about the city; crying, laughing, wondering if she were having a nervous breakdown.

Chapter Twenty-seven

Wade & Company reopened on a soft, sunny April day in 1948. The gleaming display windows were filled with spring dresses, with roses and tulips and masses of lilacs. Strung across the main entrance was a huge ribbon which Miranda cut with silver shears. The moment was recorded by photographers from all the daily newspapers, cheered by curious spectators and invited guests. After the ribbon-cutting, Miranda led everyone inside.

The new Wade's was a sleeker, more modern version of the old. The crystal light fixtures had been duplicated, but not the ornate, carved moldings. The mahogany and glass display cases had been duplicated, but they were slimmer, gently curved at the sides. The marble floor was brighter, shimmering with tiny golden flecks. The floor-walkers who had once worn black suits and white carnations in their lapel, now wore blue suits and red carnations. Saleswomen had been asked to wear cheerful colors, salesmen to wear cheerful ties.

The whole store had a bright, cheerful look. The spring-garden theme of the windows had been continued on the main floor. Annie Wolfe and her crew had arrived at dawn to arrange almost a thousand flowers — some of them real, some of them paper, some of them silk. The effect was breathtaking. Articles in the next day's newspapers would describe an "exquisite springtime fantasy," a "Garden of Eden risen from the ashes."

467

Three hours into the opening, Miranda acknowledged that the new store was a success. All the floors, all the departments, were thronged with customers. The new beauty salon was already booked weeks ahead. The new soup and sandwich bar was running out of food. The new toy shop was swarming with young mothers and wide-eyed toddlers.

"This is the department that worries me," said Miranda now, gazing at the sea of dolls and trucks and puppets and games. "I'm just not sure."

"Why not?" asked Natalie. "The kids look happy."

"We can't really compete with stores like Macy's and Gimbels. The big ones. We can't compete on price, or selection . . . It's a gamble."

"Every gamble you've ever taken has paid off in pure gold. I wouldn't mind having a piece of this action."

Miranda smiled. "You saw the crowds in the Natalie Inc. departments. You'll do fine."

"I damn well better. I had my people on overtime filling your orders. And an exclusive line, no less! Other stores are starting to complain."

"That's too bad for other stores. We have an agreement."

"I know we do. I wasn't trying to wriggle out . . . What's with you, Miranda? You can't even take a joke anymore."

"Sorry. My nerves aren't what they used to be."

"So I hear." Natalie's eyes narrowed on her old friend. "I've kept my mouth shut because I understood why you had to rebuild the store. Okay, now it's rebuilt. You have a smash hit. Your conscience is clear . . . So when are you going to do something just for *you*?"

Miranda shrugged. "I don't know. This isn't over yet. It'll be a year or so before we can be certain all the kinks are out. And we need to be certain."

"A year or so? My God! It just goes on and on. No wonder Daniel wouldn't . . ." The pained look in Miranda's eyes silenced Natalie. "That was below the belt," she said with a quick shake of her head. "You know me and my big mouth."

"Forget it." Miranda's gaze moved across the crowded aisles. "I see the twins have made their purchases. It was nice of you to keep them out of school this morning."

"I figured it was a special occasion. Besides, Tom was pretty excited about today. He wanted the kids to be here . . . Whoa . . ." Natalie laughed as the twins came running over. "Slow down. Nobody's chasing you."

Miranda smiled at them. They were handsome children, obviously brother and sister, though not identical. Jenny had curly dark hair, dark eyes and delicate features. She was taller than David, who had his father's sandy hair and his mother's hazel eyes. David was the instigator of their most devilish pranks, Jenny his willing accomplice. They were each other's best friend. In a few months they would be twelve. "What do you two think of the new toy department?"

"It's great," they chorused.

"What did you buy?"

"An ant farm," said David.

"A ballerina doll," said Jenny. "That's what *I'm* going to be — a ballerina."

Natalie straightened the bow on her daughter's dress. "Last month you were going to be a nurse. I can hardly wait to hear what you come up with next month."

"Don't you want to know what *I'm* going to be?" asked David. "A policeman! Bang, bang, bang," he cried, shooting imaginary guns at imaginary bad guys.

"Okay, Dick Tracy, that's enough . . . I'd better get them out of here, Miranda. We're having lunch at the Automat. Why don't you come along?"

"Another time."

"I know; you're going to stay here and start counting the money. There should be lots of it."

A tired smile flickered about Miranda's mouth. "Peter used to say everything I touched turned to money."

"Lucky you. Lucky Wade and Company."

469

The timing of Wade's reopening was lucky indeed, for it coincided with a great surge in the economy. The last years of the 1940's saw stable prices and rising employment. Shortages ended. Business flourished. It was a sound, healthy prosperity.

This prosperity marked the new decade of the fifties. There was a construction boom as young couples took advantage of expanded credit and GI loans to build the houses of their dreams. There were longer, wider highways, for the suburbs had been born. There were longer, wider cars glittering with chrome. There were shiny new barbecue grills and electric refrigerators and pop-up toasters. There was television, a wonderful new toy.

For retail stores, it was a time of fat profits. At Wade & Company, profits regularly exceeded expectations. The store was a solid success; the "kinks" had long ago been worked out, the problems solved. In 1950, Miranda was confident enough to plan a real vacation. She had talked to travel agents, read dozens of brochures, renewed her passport yet again. But the outbreak of the Korean War had changed her mind and her plans. Concerned about new personnel shortages, about the possibility of new government regulations, she had canceled her trip.

In fact, the war had little effect on Wade & Company. There was no rationing, and when Army Reservists on the staff were called up, they were easily replaced. There was nothing to keep Miranda from a vacation, nothing but Miranda herself. In her jittery state, her thoughts often returned to a small hospital in Cornith, to the decision she had made there. She had stolen an identity, and all the dreams that went with it. She had stolen a life. Had she been punished enough or was there more? Perhaps it was her punishment to stay here and live the life she had stolen.

Now, on a rainy September day in 1952, she walked into Schrafft's and went directly to Lily's table. "Sorry I'm late."

"Don't worry about it."

"There was a last-minute crisis at the store."

Lily nodded. She stared at Miranda, at the dark patches beneath her eyes, at the tense line of her mouth, at the tightly clasped hands. "What are you doing to yourself? You look worse every time I see you."

"That's our Lily. You never did mince words." The waitress came. Miranda ordered a martini, very dry. "I'm just tired," she said when the waitress left. "Can't a person be tired?"

"Not all the time. Aren't you sleeping?"

"Bad dreams." And they always start the same way, she thought to herself: a train speeding along a track. Snow. The hospital . . . "Where's Natalie? Isn't she coming?"

"She's with the buyer from the Lovely Lady chain. She said she'd stop by if she could."

"Lovely Lady. Twenty-two shops, right?"

"Never mind Lovely Lady. What about you, Miranda? You ought to be planning a nice, long trip for yourself."

"What's the use? Something always happens. And I know why. It's because I'm *supposed* to be here. I'm supposed to be looking after business. That's my fate."

"Who says so?"

The waitress brought Miranda's drink. "Ready to order?"

"In a few minutes." She took a swallow of her martini, glancing around the restaurant over the rim of the glass. All the tables were filled, mostly by women with stacks of packages beside them on the floor. The scrubbed, pretty Irish waitresses were in constant motion, bringing menus and cocktails and food, clearing dishes away. "The service here is excellent. Have you ever noticed?"

"It's fine. You're not."

"Fine? Of course I am. My nerves may be a little shaky. I told you I've been having bad dreams . . . Everybody goes through difficult periods, Lily. They pass."

"What if they don't?"

471

Miranda took another swallow of her drink. She shrugged. "Well, there's always gin."

"Not funny."

"I know. But fussing at me doesn't help anything. I'm doing the best I can. So let's talk about something else. Let's talk about you."

Lily held out her hand. A small but perfect diamond sparkled on her finger. "I'm engaged."

"Engaged!" Miranda stared at the ring and a smile spread across her face. "Congratulations, Lily. It's wonderful! Just wonderful! And aren't you the sly one, keeping a secret like that."

"Sam asked me three nights ago. Last night I said yes . . . I'm no kid anymore; I wanted to be sure."

"It's the best news I've heard in years. Who is he? Tell me about him."

"His name is Sam Roth. He's a jewelry buyer at Saks. My age, but he has an ex-wife and two grown sons."

"I'm so happy for you. When's the big day?"

"We haven't set a date yet. Probably around Thanksgiving. It'll be an honest-to-God Thanksgiving for me. I never thought I'd get married . . . There's one catch; Sam doesn't want me to work, so I'm quitting."

"Just like that?"

"Just like that," replied Lily. "Sam has a few dollars, and I'll still be collecting my share of Natalie Inc. profits. We won't starve."

"Are you ready to be a lady of leisure?"

"I've been ready for a long time." Lily fastened her calm, beautiful blue eyes on Miranda. "I wanted to say thanks. Everything good that's happened to me is because of you, or through you."

"Nonsense."

"No, I mean it. It's through you I invested in Natalie Inc. That changed my whole life. And there wouldn't have been a Natalie Inc. without your backing."

"I'll expect my medal by the end of the week."

"You can laugh if you want, but it's true. You've done

472

good things for everybody but yourself." Lily paused. She propped her elbow on the table, her chin on her hand. "I'm not sure if I should say this, but I'll say it anyhow . . . You don't have to go on paying, you know. Whatever you did in the past, you've made up for it."

Miranda frowned. "What are you talking about?"

"See, from the very beginning I figured it was Miranda Wade who died in that train wreck. I figured you were the friend. And now—"

"What?"

"You heard me. I grew up in Yorkville. It was full of Germans, but whoever wasn't German was Irish. The first minute I saw you I knew there was no Irish in you. And then you didn't seem to remember much about Donald Wade. When I mentioned Mr. Donald, you never knew what to say. It was strange, 'cause you were always trying to get a conversation started with me. You were always jabbering."

"But I . . . I don't understand. If you *knew,* why didn't you tell the Wades?"

"It wasn't my place. I was just the housemaid."

"Dear God, you and your *place.*"

"Maybe it was more than that. I never had any use for squealers."

Miranda touched her napkin to her damp brow. "I should have explained to you—"

"No, you didn't owe me an explanation. You loved Andrew; I could see that."

"Yes." Tears welled in Miranda's eyes. She brushed them away. "He was my son."

"I don't want to rake up the past," continued Lily. "I just thought maybe I could get you to see things clearly. Whatever you did, you paid for it. Now you ought to do something for yourself." She smiled. "Okay, I said my piece."

"Yes, you said your piece." Miranda picked up the menu. "We'd better order lunch."

* * *

It was two o'clock when Miranda arrived back at her office — fifteen minutes before the start of the executive meeting. On her desk were the afternoon newspapers and an advance copy of *Vogue*. She sat down, reaching first for the newspapers. She checked the store's ads, glanced at the women's pages. A few moments later she picked up the copy of *Vogue*. Wade's ad was near the front. She studied it briefly, and then leafed through the pages, studying the elegant clothes, the models' makeup. She pulled out her big yellow pad and scribbled some notes for the cosmetics department.

Miranda was about to put the magazine aside when an article caught her eye: "On Women: Four Very Eligible Bachelors." There were photographs of the four men, but one of the photographs jumped off the page. "Daniel," she murmured. She stared at his face, the handsome face she knew so well. The article described him as a "brewery tycoon" with holdings in England, Ireland, Canada, and the United States.

Her hands were trembling. She put the magazine down, picked it up again. Toward the end of the interviews, the men had been asked to define the perfect woman. Daniel's response was terse: "The woman I see in my dreams has big gray eyes and hair as black as night. She's too serious by far, but when she laughs, the world lights up. I'm thinking I knew her once, in another life."

In another life. Miranda bowed her head over the desk, pondering his cryptic remark. Had he been joking? Had he spoken in anger? In despair? She ripped the article from the newspaper, folded it, and slipped it into her pocket.

"Miranda?" Tom poked his head through the door. "We're ready, if you are."

"What? Oh, yes. Yes, I'm coming." She left her desk, returning a second later for her notes. "I hope it's not going to be a long meeting, Tom. I have a lot of work."

"I'll try to keep things moving."

They walked through the side door to the conference

474

room. "Good afternoon," said Miranda, taking her place at the head of the table. "Let's get started. Frank?"

Frank North stood, passing around the final layouts for the Christmas catalogue. "We have time problems. The printer wants everything by Friday, so I'll have to know now if anybody wants changes."

The catalogue was discussed and approved. The Christmas Shop was discussed, and the toy department. It was decided that Wade's would have a Santa Claus this year.

They moved on to other subjects — to the budget and the new pension plan and the repainting of the warehouse. Miranda paid little attention. She was fidgety; she could not concentrate, could not hold on to a thought for more than a moment. Several times she pressed her handkerchief to her brow. She kept lighting cigarettes, only to let them burn out in the ashtray.

Tom, watching her, decided to bring the meeting to a close. He gathered his notes together and glanced at his watch. "I think we've covered everything."

"Excuse me," said Jeff Woodrow, "but I've been working on a proposal."

"Proposal? For what?"

"For a branch store. The time is right; I'm convinced of that. Young families are moving to the suburbs. Long Island, Connecticut — it's a golden opportunity for us. Suburban husbands commute to work in the city, but suburban wives stay home. Why not make shopping convenient for them? And there's another angle: commercial real estate is still relatively cheap in the suburbs. If we moved quickly, we could get a bargain price."

No one had ever heard Jeff speak at such length; no one had ever heard him propose an idea. A good idea at that, thought Tom. A *great* idea. He looked at Miranda. "What do you think?"

She glanced across the table at Jeff. "I assume you've researched this project?"

"It's all here," he replied, holding up a thick binder.

"Yes, I see . . . Congratulations, Jeff. It's a fine idea. Of course it would be a very complicated project . . . It would be like rebuilding Wade's a second time." Miranda pressed her fingers to her throbbing temples. Rebuilding Wade's a second time. More architects, she thought to herself. More contractors and designers and inspectors. More meetings, endless meetings. More memos. More budgets. More worries. *Rebuilding Wade's a second time.* "I can't," she murmured. She pushed her chair back and stood up. "No, I can't do it anymore."

"Miranda—"

"No." She saw all the startled faces, saw Tom rising from his chair. She turned toward the door. "No," she said. "I can't."

"What's wrong?" asked Tom, following her out. "What can't you do?"

"If you want to build a branch store, go ahead. But I . . . I . . . No, I can't."

"Can't *what*, Miranda?"

"But don't you see? I'm not Miranda. I can't be Miranda anymore. It's over, Tom. Just leave me alone. Everybody leave me alone."

"I don't understand."

She shook off his hand. "It's over," she said. *"Over."*

"Where are you going?" he called. He sighed, for the only reply was the sound of Miranda's footsteps running through the corridor.

She ran all the way home. Daphne was out. The new housemaid, Alice, was vacuuming the stairs. "Oh, it's you, Mrs. Dexter," she said, switching off the machine. "And you're soaking wet! Did you forget your—"

"Let me pass, Alice."

"Yes, ma'am." She bent and unplugged the cord. "I'll bring you a cup of tea. Nice hot tea."

"That's all right; don't bother."

"You ought to get out of those wet things, Mrs. Dexter. You'll catch your death."

476

She stepped over the vacuum cleaner hose and rushed upstairs. She rushed to her room and closed the door, leaning against it. After a moment she sank into a chair. She pulled the magazine article from her pocket. It was soggy with rain, but carefully she unfolded the page and stretched it across her lap. *In another life.* The words sprang at her; she stared at them until they blurred. "Daniel," she cried.

She looked up, her gaze drawn to the large mirror above the vanity table. She stared at her reflection. A smile started at the corners of her mouth, growing wider moment by moment. She took a breath. "Hello, Jenny," she said. "Welcome back."

She felt as if the weight of the world had been lifted from her shoulders. Tears came again to her eyes, but they were tears of relief, for she felt wonderful. Almost before she knew it, she was racing around the room collecting the suitcases she had never used, digging out her passport and her checkbook.

Her mind was focused now; her thoughts were crystal clear. Tom could look after the store. He could look in on Daphne, too. Later tonight she would call him and everything would be settled. It would have to be, for tomorrow she was going to Ireland. "Not in another life," she declared with a laugh. "In *this* life!"

She was well rested, for she had slept during the Pan American flight to London, during the train ride to Liverpool, and during the ferry ride that had brought her, at last, to Dublin. Now, sitting in the backseat of an ancient taxicab, she turned her head to the window and smiled. It was twilight. The soft Irish rain had come and gone; the air was as misty as a wedding veil. "Are we very far from Carley?" she asked.

"Not far. Twenty minutes, I'd say."

"Do you think you could go faster?"

"Aye, I could, but me poor old taxi couldn't. Not on these old bog roads."

Miranda laughed. "These roads weren't really meant for cars, were they?"

"Sheep," replied the driver. " 'Twas a sheep crossing in oldern times. There's no sheep anymore. The place to see sheep is Roscommon. In me own opinion, you understand. The opinion of John Francis Clark!"

Miranda sat back. They had been driving for an hour, and in that time she had learned that John Francis Clark had many opinions on many subjects: the weather, soccer, the troubles in the north, the best way to plant summer roses. His friendly chatter kept her calm, kept her from bolting through the door and *running* to Carley. She said very little, for she knew that an occasional "yes," or "umm," or "oh?" was all the encouragement he needed. If the Irish were great ones for dreams, they were also great ones for talk.

She closed her eyes and thought about Daniel. She had sent him the briefest of cables: "Arriving Carley late Friday afternoon. Bringing all my love. Miranda." Less than an hour after sending the cable, she had boarded the plane for London. Had he tried to reach her? Had he tried to stop her? She conceded that years stood between them, that she and Daniel were different people now, but all these thoughts she pushed from her mind. She loved him; she had always loved him. She prayed it was not too late.

"Excuse me, Mr. Clark," she said, interrupting his monologue, "but are we almost there?"

"The next turn in the road."

"Thank you."

The mists were lifting. She leaned forward, straining for a glimpse of the village. She saw narrow cliffs sloping gently toward the sea; in the distance she saw beautiful old cottages weathered by time and salt air. Her heart began to thump, for one of the cottages was Daniel's.

The taxicab chugged along, following the curve of the road. After another hundred yards or so, it slowed to a coughing, wheezing halt. "And here's the moon coming

478

out to greet you," said John Francis Clark. "Aye, and a grand Carley moon it is."

"I hope it's a good omen."

"There's none but good in Carley."

"Is this where I get out?"

"Well, 'tis one way. From here, you'd have to walk down the steps. The other way—"

"Oh no," interrupted Miranda, smiling. "I don't mind the walk." She had left her luggage at a small Dublin hotel. She had only her purse, and this she tucked under her arm as she stepped from the taxi. "Thank you. I'm in a hurry, you see."

"Would you be wanting me to wait?"

"I . . . No, I don't think so. I'll telephone if I need a ride back." She pressed a large bill into his hand. "You've been very kind. Thank you again."

" 'Twas my pleasure . . . Mind your step on the path."

She waved and turned away. The path was slippery with wet leaves; just beyond was a set of stairs that had been carved out of the rocky cliff. She looked at the stairs, at the patches of moss curled in the corners. With a shrug, she started down.

The view was spectacular, a great canvas of sky and sea. The jagged coastline was silvery with moonlight. Little fishing boats were beached near the mouth of a cove, their nets fluttering in the salty breeze.

She reached the bottom of the stairs. Her high heels sank into the gritty sand; she took them off. She started walking. She stopped suddenly, for in the shadowy light she saw the figure of a man—a tall man with copper hair. "Daniel," she cried, running now. *"Daniel."*

From out of nowhere came two large dogs, handsome red setters. They bounded toward her, planting sandy paws on her shoulders. She fell, laughing as they licked her face.

"Alfie!" called Daniel. "Cornelius!" At the sound of his voice, the dogs bounded away.

Slipping and sliding, she got to her feet. She started

running again. She ran into Daniel's waiting arms. "You're here," she murmured through her tears. "Oh, thank God, thank God."

"Is it really you, Miranda?"

"It's Jenny. Jenny Porter. And I've come for the man of my dreams . . . It's not too late for us, is it?" she asked, anxiously searching his face. "Tell me it's not too late."

"I love you, lass. Never more than now. Never more than here."

"Our kingdom by the sea."

They gazed into each other's eyes. They touched. They kissed, their bodies pressing together as the waves drew the sand from beneath their feet. "I do love you, Daniel," she said when she was able to speak. "So very much . . . I love Ireland and Carley . . . I even promise to love your dogs. Are they yours?"

"Ours. They're our chaperones."

"Married people don't need chaperones."

He smiled, tangling his fingers in her hair. "And would that be a proposal?"

"From Jenny to Daniel."

"Then I accept."

Daniel swept her up into his arms, carrying her to his cottage. "We're going home, lass," he murmured. "Home."

She smiled. She lifted her head from his shoulder and looked back. The moon was shining. The waves were crashing on the shore. And somewhere on the craggy rocks, the gulls were dancing a jig.